THE GIRL IN THE LAKE

ALSO BY LAUREN OLIVER

Broken Things

What Happened to Lucy Vale

Replica Series

Vanishing Girls

Panic

The Delirium Trilogy

Before I Fall

THE GIRL IN THE LAKE

A NOVEL

LAUREN OLIVER

THOMAS & MERCER

This is a work of fiction. Names, characters, organizations, places, events, and incidents are either products of the author's imagination or are used fictitiously. Otherwise, any resemblance to actual persons, living or dead, is purely coincidental.

Published by Thomas & Mercer, Seattle
www.apub.com

EU product safety contact:
Amazon Media EU S. à r.l.
38, avenue John F. Kennedy, L-1855 Luxembourg
amazonpublishing-gpsr@amazon.com

ISBN-13: 9781662533716 (paperback)
ISBN-13: 9781662533709 (digital)

Cover design by Jarrod Taylor
Cover image: © Vintervit / Getty; © NARUDON ATSAWALARPSAK / Shutterstock

Printed in the United States of America

To Lauren O'Connor: my twin sister in a past life, and my dear friend and champion in this one

Past-life memory claims have been researched by academics from diverse backgrounds and fields (anthropology, psychiatry, psychology) in almost every country and culture. In America, the psychiatrist Ian Stevenson (MD) from the Division of Perceptual Studies at the University of Virginia devoted more than fifty years to scientific investigation of past-life memories, known as Cases of the Reincarnation Type (CORT). In all, more than two thousand such cases were recorded.

These cases reveal underlying patterns in the claims of past-life experiences. On average, children begin making statements about a past life when they are thirty-five months. Twenty percent of such children claim to recall the interval between two lives. Almost 75 percent describe the mode of death. More than 35 percent display phobias related to the circumstances of an unnatural death.

Other common features among the children studied are: philias, or skills unlearned but somehow acquired; birthmarks corresponding to some physical aspect of the alleged previous personality's death; memories of the places where they allegedly lived in a previous lifetime; their own name or the names of people they knew in a past life; as well as statements especially concerned with the later years of the previous personality's lifetime.

Many of these cases have been independently verified by researchers. Common methods for investigation in these cases include: interviews with the subject, their parents, firsthand witnesses, and the alleged previous personality's relatives and close friends; documentation and photographic analysis, as well as the consideration of medical and legal records pertinent to the claims.

At present, this phenomenon remains unexplained.

THEN

They were lying side by side on beach towels flung out over the grass. The trees cut the sunlight into shifting patterns that skated across their bare skin, August dark, freckled with mosquito bites. Their hair, still damp from their swim, was tangled in long ropes on the grass. The wind lifted gooseflesh on their arms. Summer was ending. Soon it would be time to go home.

Becca rolled onto an elbow. Her eyes were the same color as the sky—Technicolor blue—and full of the same drifting clouds.

"Kate, will you promise me something?"

Kate had been drifting—lulled by the rhythm of splashing and happy shouts from the lake, the periodic bark of the counselors' voices across the water, and the distant sound of a motorboat. Becca's voice, like an anchor, drew her away from the edge of sleep.

"Promise we'll always be best friends," Becca said. "No matter what happens. Swear it."

"I promise," Kate said.

"But do you swear? Like for real real? Cross your heart, hope to die, on your own grave, all of that?"

"Of course." Kate reached out, laughing, and hooked Becca's pinkie in hers. "I swear it. Happy now?"

Becca looked at her thoughtfully. After a minute, she settled down on her back again, squinting up at the sky, keeping Kate's pinkie locked in hers.

"You shouldn't laugh about this stuff," she said. She gave Kate's finger a squeeze so hard, it hurt. "Forever is a long time."

ONE

There was something wrong with the trees on the East Coast. There were too many of them. They crowded out the sky. They seemed to be running down to the lake in some desperate suicide pact to drown with their own reflections.

As a kid, Kate Willis had loved summers in Massachusetts. She'd loved the thick heat, which lay heavy on the afternoons like a damp beach towel. She'd loved the green swells of shaggy hillsides, the narrow thread of footpaths through the trees, the urgent chorus of tree frogs in the evening, the moths that battered the screen door after dark.

Now the woods seemed to her claustrophobic. The roads whiplashing between them—dizzying, disorienting, like the long tail of an undulating snake. Sheffield, Massachusetts, which she'd remembered fondly from camp hiking trips to Bartholomew's Cobble nature preserve, looked as if it had been struck by paralysis, frozen somewhere in the deep past, like a deer standing before headlights. Her cell phone service wavered, sputtered, and cut out.

She found herself wishing for the smooth, democratizing landscape of Virginia: its highways and superstores, fast-food franchises and parking lots, the reassuring big-box buildings, the tidy rows of modern town houses, the stately brick mansions on their mantles of green. In Virginia—at least in the Martha Jefferson neighborhood of Charlottesville, where she'd lived for fifteen years, ever since she'd landed a position in the University of Virginia's Psychology Department—the trees knew their place. Moored at tidy intervals around the neighborhood, or pinioned in decorative postures on even-keeled lawns, the trees were as harmless, as meek, as inoffensive as any houseplant.

They did not seem, somehow, to be alive in the same way as the trees in Massachusetts.

Kate slowed when she came upon the waste station just south of Great Barrington, scanning the trees for a narrow gap that marked the entrance to Camp Sauquamet. The sign was still there. Faded by years of exposure and overgrown with weeds, but visible, in part because of the "For Sale" sign shouting in red just in front of it. She felt a flutter in her chest—a vestigial imprint of the excitement she used to feel with her nose pressed to the bus window and a logjam of other campers at her back, when the driveway was at last within sight.

Just as quickly, the good feeling was snuffed out, replaced by something like dread. Quickly, she sped up.

She managed to seize hold of a cell phone signal just as she was navigating through an accelerated slurry of houses and shops dribbling out of the town center, where she and her friends had once gone for weekend field trips. It looked very little like the place she remembered. Fashionable art galleries had replaced run-down head shops; the quaint brick buildings had the spruced-up sheen of gentrification; a group of twentysomething weekenders—pale, tattooed, and looking slightly out of place among the greenery—stood in line outside of a new gastropub, as if they'd been cut and pasted into position from Brooklyn.

Her phone buzzed an aggregate of new text messages from Steve.

Where do we keep Moshi's heartworm medication?

Forget it. I found it.

Bo DOES need surgery, by the way. But the doctor says the growth isn't cancerous.

I thought we'd wait until you got back from Massachusetts.

How is Massachusetts, by the way? Are you enjoying your trip down memory lane?

Kate called up Steve's number through Bluetooth. He was still first, just as he was still listed as her emergency contact on every legal and medical form.

"You realize you text me more now than when we were married?" Kate said when he picked up. She could hear Steve banging around the cabinets for something. Moshi was keening in the background. Steve had probably promised treats.

"When we were married, you gave the dogs their medication," Steve said easily. "I didn't need to text you." She imagined him in his new condo in downtown Charlottesville, feet slotted into those dumb shower sandals she hated so much, wearing his faded U of V sweatpants and an ironic T-shirt. Then: "How's the walk down memory lane? Did you make it back to Camp Sasquatch?"

"Camp Sauquamet," she corrected him. "Not Sasquatch. Sasquatch is a cryptid."

"Ghosts and legends. Hard to keep them straight." A beat of silence tipped them momentarily toward the edge of a question—something about Kate, about camp, about whether Kate could bring herself to visit. Something about Becca, and that summer they all turned fourteen. But in the end, Steve veered toward safer conversational ground. "When do you meet the girl? Emily, right?"

"Emily's the mother. And we meet in"—Kate checked the time—"exactly fifty-two minutes." Kate had been referred to the Haskell family by Dr. Rushkin, chair of the University of Virginia's Division of Perceptual Studies. DOPS was one of the only serious academic facilities in the country devoted to the investigation of extraordinary cognitive and perceptual phenomena: near-death experiences, altered states of consciousness, anomalous psychic interactions between human beings and their environment, and children who claimed to recall past lives. It wasn't the first time Dr. Rushkin had tapped Kate to conduct a psychological review of this kind. In addition to chairing the psychology department and conducting research through her own dedicated lab, Kate was called in periodically to consult on DOPS cases that involved children. Six years earlier, Kate had flown to Sweden to investigate the mysterious episodes of refugee children who'd fallen into coma-like sleeps for years at a time. And only the previous year, Kate had published a book about a boy whose family had claimed he was possessed by demons.

But Kate had made the decision to investigate the story of six-year-old Henley Haskell, who claimed to be experiencing traumatic memories from a previous lifetime, on her own. It was summertime, the university was largely vacant, and Dr. Rushkin couldn't get a budget approved for her trip. Nonetheless, Kate had decided to spend a few days in Massachusetts conducting interviews. It had been a long time since she'd been to that part of the world; her own therapist had recommended the trip, suggesting that Kate might find it healing.

Besides, Kate was curious—and skeptical. She was eager to sit with this child persuaded that she had lived, and died, before. DOPS had a simple framework for assessing the validity of past-life claims. The information the child recalled of a previous life had to be consistent, persistent, and independently verifiable; also impossible, or extremely unlikely, to have been acquired by any other means. Even though DOPS was staffed with researchers devoted to studying phenomenology that made most serious academics laugh—or cringe—they were insistent that their research meet standards of scientific rigor. Their hypotheses—that there was scientific evidence for reincarnation, ditto for the existence of life after death—were considered fringe by any standard. They insisted that the research itself be bulletproof.

That was where Kate, who could and would happily blow holes through any theory that carried even a whiff of the supernatural, came in. And so far, the handful of cases that DOPS had referred to her had, in Kate's opinion, turned up absolutely no proof of the spooky or the supernatural—only scam artists, psychological abusers, and extraordinary environmental dysfunction, with commensurately extraordinary psychological forms of coping.

"Just promise me you'll keep an open mind," Steve said. Steve was a social anthropologist and one of the faculty members at DOPS. During their marriage, she and Steve had spent hours debating reports from people around the globe who'd supposedly been reincarnated or survived physical death with a memory intact of their passage through the light. He'd called her narrow-minded. A materialist. Even brainwashed by the mainstream. She'd accused him of being a mystic, overly credulous, and even antiscientific.

"Open minds are overrated," Kate said. "They wind up full of all sorts of junk."

Once upon a time, Kate had been a believer. In ghosts and legends. In hands that could reach back through the veil of death and snatch you from a bicycle or a boat.

But she'd been a girl then. Little more than a child herself.

She knew now: There was no story scarier than what people could do to each other.

~

Stockbridge looked unchanged—at least from a distance. But as Kate followed Route 7 onto Main Street, she noticed a Pilates studio and a juice bar, tastefully concealed inside of what looked like a log cabin. Stockbridge, too, had been altered by the rising numbers of urban hipsters in the area, driven out to the sticks by soaring real estate prices, or by Covid, or both.

A woman wheeled clothing racks of shapeless tunics onto the sidewalk in front of her store. A small pack of young teenagers were walking, huddled over their iPhones, giggling about something. Kate wondered where they came from, whether they lived here year round. She remembered that on Sundays, the oldest campers had been loosed into various towns to poke around, wander the streets, and buy junk that they would regret later. She and her best friends, all girls who'd bunked together since their first summer at the age of eight, had cherished that privilege and the freedom that came with it. There had been four of them in her set: Becca McGuire, Lennie

Anderson, Mariana Edwards, and Kate. The counselors had called them the "Bunk-Twelve Four," or the "Cat Pack." They'd been inseparable.

Until, suddenly, one of them was gone.

With thirty minutes to kill before she was due at the Haskells', Kate spotted a coffee shop and pulled over. When she stepped out of the car, the smell of the Berkshires hit her like a physical force, ricocheting her back to camp mornings when she rose at the sound of a bugle horn, shuddered out the door with her bunkmates, and flip-flopped down the damp slope to the communal showers, where the wood was always spongy with old moisture, and moss grew in the corners. God, she had loved it there. She had loved even the things she pretended to hate, like the chore wheel, and clipping towels to dry on the laundry lines, where spiders would weave webs between them overnight. She had loved the clatter of the mess hall and bouncing her voice across the lake as they marched in unison on competition days, singing made-up team lyrics to familiar music.

Where had that child gone? Where had that feeling gone? She had dropped it, as if down a well, along with all her memories of that final summer.

She had left it somewhere no one would ever find it.

She had left it next to Becca.

Inside, the coffee shop looked exactly as she would have expected: cozy, ad hoc, with a mishmash of wobbly tables and a long counter displaying oversize baked goods. The walls were wood, and papered with hundreds of flyers advertising local sites, businesses, cars for sale, theatrical performances, and farmers markets.

She ordered a coffee—large, hot, and splashed with actual cream, the way she liked it—and spent some time idling in the corner, scanning the various brochures and advertisements, looking at offers for dog walkers and brochures for ropes courses and local arts festivals. She even noticed a glossy brochure for Emily Haskell's pottery studio, Wheel of Fortune, showing off photos of kids with clay-slicked hands grinning from behind the wheels. There was no better place to get a sense of a community than on the walls of a coffee shop, Kate felt. This one seemed happy, and busy, and self-consumed. A proper bubble, but in the best way, and a welcome antidote to her iPhone news feed.

She was about to turn away when she spotted a face she recognized, and froze. Peeking out from beneath a flyer promoting dog-sitting services by *responsible and caring 16-year-old Brenna Hobbes* was the xeroxed photograph of a wide-eyed woman with the face of an overgrown child, a halo of light hair, and a sweet, unselfconscious smile.

Ms. Mariana's Music Studio. Music Lessons for Kids grades K-12. West Stockbridge, MA.

It was Mariana Edwards. Little Mari. The sweetest, and most innocent, of all of them. Twenty-six years older and no longer wearing glasses, but unmistakably the same—alive, here, teaching music only spitting distance from where they'd spent their summers.

Kate felt a strange bit of static behind her eyes, staring at Mari's picture, as if she'd just touched something electric. She wondered how and when Mariana had moved to the area; she seemed to remember that Mariana had grown up in North Carolina. Maybe South Carolina. Definitely somewhere in the South. She'd been a regular churchgoer, and the only camper, as far as Kate knew, who'd made use of the on-site prayer room.

She let sixteen-year-old Brenna's flyer fall back into place, obscuring Mariana's smile. She took her coffee and went out into the sunshine and the fresh air, which carried the scent of pines.

It was time to meet with the Haskells and see about the girl supposedly reborn from the dead.

TWO

The Haskells lived ten minutes outside of Stockbridge. There were about twenty houses on the street, each with a sweep of acreage and a long coiling driveway that whipped into the trees.

House #44 was painted white and clearly well loved. Kate noted a tire swing, and also an enormous plastic jungle gym and a trampoline she would have killed for as a child. The garden was neat and well tended. The lawn, too. No immediate signs of neglect or disarray, the kind that might inspire a young girl to begin inventing stories for attention.

But Kate also knew that looks could be deceiving. She'd once worked with a boy whose parents, both marketing executives, kept a beautiful home in Alexandria. The boy had developed a problematic attachment to an imaginary friend, to whom he was so loyal, and so psychically bound that he refused to participate in normal classroom activities if his friend expressed a distaste for them, which was often. He wouldn't join any teams unless his friend could play, too. He wouldn't eat unless his friend had a seat at the table. Kate had discovered eventually that his parents interacted with their child only rarely, leaving him instead locked up for hours in a basement playroom while they entertained guests or worked alone at their computers. The physical environment was only one indication of the psychic realities of a household.

Still—from the outside, at least—the Haskells' home looked happy.

Climbing out of the car, Kate took a moment to simply admire the sun yawning lazily across the slope of lawn. Invisible birds twittered her arrival. Two deer moved on stalky legs through the dappled shade of the trees.

"Isn't it beautiful up here?"

Kate turned around, surprised by the voice. Emily Haskell had emerged on the front porch: tall, willowy, as lithe as a ballet dancer, with brown skin and eyes that looked almost yellow in the sun. Her hair was loosely knotted and secured by a colorful headband. She was wearing paint-splattered jeans, a tunic, and clogs. An appropriate outfit for a Berkshires-based pottery instructor. Kate wondered whether the fat porcelain frog squatting on the front stairs with a "Welcome" sign was one of her pieces.

"I used to make fun of my sister for settling down here," Emily continued as Kate came up the stairs into the shade. Kate knew, from the brief that DOPS had given her, that Emily Haskell had moved to the Berkshires while her twin sister was dying of cancer. After her sister's death, Emily had chosen to remain. "I called her 'the country mouse.' I was 'the city mouse'—big apartment, big job, big social life. For almost twenty years, I was always hustling up that ladder. She used to beg me to slow down." Emily gave a little laugh, as if recalling the details of a compelling dream that now, on awakening, seemed ridiculous. "She was right. She was always right. I did better in school, but she was the smarter one." Then, reaching out a hand: "You must be Dr. Willis."

"Kate's fine," Kate said, shaking Emily's hand, somewhat surprised by the warm welcome. She had expected Emily to be anxious—closed off, wary, or outright defensive. Most parents were, at first meeting. They knew or suspected that Kate would find blame in the way they'd parented their child. The way they'd permitted, or coddled, or punished, or withdrawn. They often treated her like some kind of foreign incursion in a well-choreographed military operation, an intruder with an agenda and the weapons to do harm to their well-loved illusions of care and competence.

And there was some truth to that. Children absorbed and disgorged their parents' dysfunctions like sponges.

But Emily seemed perfectly at ease, even happy to see her.

"I thought we could talk a bit out here before you meet Henley," she explained, indicating a wicker chair where Kate could have a seat. "She's inside with her iPad. It's a special weekend treat . . . I'm very strict about screen time."

Kate smiled. There was, after all, a hint of anxiety in Emily's voice. A desire to please.

"Does she know that I'm coming?" Kate asked.

Emily nodded.

"Does she understand why?"

"I think so." Emily opened her hands, a helpless gesture. "I told her that you were a friend and a very smart person. I said that you were interested in learning about her 'other life.'"

"'Her other life,'" Kate repeated. A highly suggestive turn of phrase. "Is that what you call it?"

"That's what *she* calls it," Emily corrected her. "I don't know what to call it. At first, I assumed she was just imagining things . . ."

"But not anymore?"

"No," Emily said firmly. "No, not anymore."

Kate absorbed that. "Do you remember ever speaking to Henley about reincarnation?" When Emily shook her head, she said, "What about the afterlife? Heaven?"

"I'm not religious. Spiritual, sure—there has to be *something* out there bigger than we are—but I quit organized religion when I was still a teenager." Emily smiled a little self-consciously. "Henley's never even been to church."

"What about your sister's death?" Kate asked. "Have you ever spoken to Henley about it?"

Emily hesitated. "Not explicitly," she said. "I tell stories about Aunt Lily. There are pictures of her in the house. But she doesn't know the details. Only that Aunt Lily died before she was born."

"And do you think she understands what that means?"

"She understands," Emily said. Something shifted in her eyes—a cloud, darkening her expression. "Henley has nightmares . . ."

An alarm was tripped in Kate's head. "About dying?" she said. The average six-year-old would just be capable of understanding that death was both permanent and irreversible. But recurring nightmares were unusual for the age group.

Emily nodded. "About suffocating," she said, looking down at her hands.

For a moment, both women let the weight of this statement settle between them. Then, abruptly, Emily stood up. She moved over to the porch railing, leaning out over the lawn like a passenger on the deck of a ship, scouting for distant land. Without turning around, she said, "You don't believe in souls, do you?"

Caught off guard by the question, Kate took a second to answer. "What do you mean?"

Emily made an impatient gesture. "Souls. Essence. Something that lives beyond the body—beyond the brain, even. Something that might live on or even be . . . *shared.* Inside of people, and between them."

Kate couldn't help but wonder whether she was thinking of her daughter or her twin sister. "I think," she said carefully, "that the soul counts as a core belief for many people. And core beliefs themselves are very powerful. I think that they often can . . . manifest in ways that we have yet to explain or fully reconcile."

"So you don't believe," Emily said, but without hostility.

"My beliefs aren't relevant," Kate said. "They're only beliefs. They aren't necessarily in touch with reality. My job is to make sure I understand the difference."

Emily shot her a look over one shoulder, as if she suspected Kate of taking the easy way out. "When my sister died," she said, "I knew it. I *felt* it. We could always feel each other's pain, ever since we were little. If Lily got so much as a splinter, my finger would begin to throb. Whenever I had migraines, even in college, she would get nauseous."

Her hands tightened on the railing. "The day it happened, I was two states away and in the middle of a deposition, and suddenly all the breath went out of my body. I could feel my heart crack open in two. I *knew*."

"I'm sorry," Kate said, hating the words even as they came out of her mouth. She sounded like a Hallmark card. "That must have been devastating."

"It was like losing half of myself," Emily said simply. She turned back to face Kate again. "How do you understand *that*?"

Kate didn't have an answer. She could tell that Emily wasn't really looking for one.

Emily sighed. "When Dr. Rushkin first suggested that we speak to you, I thought you worked for him."

"I'm a colleague at the university," Kate said carefully. "I consult on special cases, where children are involved. Dr. Rushkin is very busy—"

"And he doesn't want to waste his time with scams and delusions. I get it." She ran a fingernail over the railing where the paint was chipping. Kate was struck by how beautiful she looked with the sun sliding off her shoulders. Beautiful, and unhappy. "I read about you. I looked up your work after we spoke on the phone. I read about the case you investigated in Minnesota—the little boy who claimed he had memories of being a fighter pilot in World War I. That was a scam, wasn't it?"

Again, Kate chose her words carefully. "It was," she acknowledged. "But by the time I spoke with Nathan—the boy—he truly believed the story himself. His parents had been feeding him information since he was a baby."

"Why?" Emily asked. "Why would anybody do that to a child?"

Kate peered at her. Either Emily was extremely naive, or she was doing an excellent job of pretending. "Nathan was the family's meal ticket," she said. "They published a book about him. They put his story all over YouTube."

Emily's expression shifted, hardening slightly. "Is that what you think? You think I've been feeding Henley stories?"

"I don't think anything," Kate said. "I haven't even spoken to Henley yet. I don't have any of the facts."

"The *facts*." Emily said the word disdainfully. Abruptly, she crossed to the front door and vanished inside. She returned a moment later, holding a sheaf of papers inside a manila folder.

"This is for you. Look through it. Then you can decide on the *facts*."

Inside the folder, Kate saw pages of handwritten and typed notes, each neatly dated, going back three years—along with a child's colorful drawings, presumably Henley's.

"I started taking notes a few years ago of Henley's memories," Emily said. "Her nightmares, too. I asked her to draw or paint all the places she remembered from . . . *before*."

Kate sifted quickly through the artwork—some pages warped by old watercolors, others punctured by colored pencils driven ferociously into the paper. There were only three subjects, seemingly repeated, each time with a steadier hand that signified the girl was getting older. One was a yellow house framed by tall trees—Henley had even drawn a tree house in the branches—and bordered by bright flower beds. The second was a steepled church with what appeared to be a wheelbarrow or an enormous bicycle in the yard. Something with wheels, definitely.

Emily saw her puzzling over it. "That's a cannon," she said, leaning a little closer. "I didn't even know Henley knew the word."

The third was a big expanse of blue, scribbled ferociously across the page, crowned with large semicircles that appeared to be growing straight out of the water.

"What's this?" Kate asked Emily.

"A graveyard," Emily said. "Henley says she remembers there was a graveyard on the lake."

For a second, Kate's heart stilled, as if she'd plunged headfirst into icy water. A sudden image of the ruins on Fair Isle shuttered in her mind—the tombstones, bleary from long years of exposure, leaping out of the green. She saw the mausoleum with its stone angel, her wings folded, eyes blank and staring, holding up a broken finger to the sky. The Gray Lady. She imagined for a second one of the spirits of those nameless dead clawing out of the grave to take hold of Henley's paintbrush.

But just as quickly, she shrugged off the fantasy. Lake Sauquamet was less than fifteen miles away. No doubt its legends were familiar to everyone around here.

"There's a graveyard on Fair Isle, in the middle of Sauquamet Lake. Have you ever taken Henley swimming there?"

Emily frowned. "Sauquamet Lake . . . that's the one off Route 22, right? Near that old camp . . . ?" When Kate nodded, Emily shook her head firmly. "I've heard the lake is dangerous. People have drowned. The South Beach is off-limits, you know, ever since the county stepped in to manage it."

The South Beach, Kate assumed, was the stretch of pebble and sand that once belonged exclusively to Camp Sauquamet. Still, the fact that Emily had heard the rumors about the lake meant that in all likelihood, Henley had, too. Maybe that was why she'd drawn a graveyard on the water. It might be her way of literalizing her fears. Kids did that all the time. They imagined angry monsters under the bed, dangers lurking in the closet, waiting to devour them, as a way of processing the undercurrents of tension in the home. They externalized their loneliness and neglect in the form of imaginary caretakers, friends who would never abandon them. They gave physical shape to whatever troubled them to help make sense of it.

But if that was what Henley was doing, Kate had to wonder: What was she *really* afraid of?

She put the folder in her briefcase and stood up.

"I'd like to meet her now," she said. She wouldn't have sworn to it, but she thought that, for a second, Emily was the one who looked afraid.

~

Inside, the house was pretty, quaint, and doused by heavy slabs of sunlight coming in through the open windows. Kate's mind immediately began to rove, seizing on select details, clicking them into an ever-growing impression of Emily's parenting style. The jumble of shoes near the front door, a mass of children's sneakers and floral rain boots, hastily shoved into a wicker bin. *Attentive, but not obsessive.* Framed artwork interspersed with family photos, showing Henley at different ages: sticking her hand through a chain-link fence to pet a woolly lamb; holding up fingers covered in paint and grinning toothily at the camera. *Proud, but not overly concerned with appearances.* There was a piano in the corner and an obese cat lolling happily in the sun, barely bothering to assess the stranger in the room. Ceramic vases, overflowing with wildflowers from the garden, gave the living room a natural feeling.

"Are all of these yours?" Kate asked, gesturing to one of the pieces.

"Mostly," Emily said. "This one's Henley's." She picked up a misshapen bowl, splotchy with colorful glazes, and smiled. "I teach a class every Sunday for parents and kids. It's been a hit. We had to open a waitlist last fall." She selected another item from the shelf—a delicate fluted vase, tastefully neutral. "And this was my sister's."

"Your sister was a potter, too?"

Emily nodded. "We learned together as children. My mother was a painter. Well, still is, I guess, although arthritis has slowed her down some. That's hers." She indicated a pretty oil painting of a city landscape covered in snow, hanging next to a photograph of a bundled-up Henley posing next to a snowman in front of the house. "Lily and I both applied to art school. I transferred to Columbia after my first year and started in prelaw. I thought I was being practical." She shrugged. "It was Lily's dream to have her own studio."

In the kitchen, open shelves displayed more ceramics: cups and plates and bowls, all stained prettily or painted minutely with leaves and cherries. Kate noticed glass jars filled with beans, rice, cereal, and pasta; a bowl of fresh eggs on the table; butter softening in a dish on the table. The refrigerator was covered in more of Henley's artwork.

These drawings felt different, less compulsive, freer. One was a big blue dinosaur; one a wash of colors, jubilant and messy, running off the page.

Kate found herself thinking of her home in Virginia, of its white walls and bland, tasteful furniture, and the slightly anodyne smell of the air conditioner humming a comfortable seventy-one degrees into the house at all times. It was lucky she and Steve had never had kids. This house—Emily's house—felt like the kind of home that every child deserved.

So what, she wondered, had gone wrong?

"Go ahead and grab some coffee, if you'd like." Emily indicated a French press on the counter. "It might take me a minute to drag Henley off her iPad."

While Emily disappeared up the stairs, Kate laid out some drawing paper and the markers she'd brought with her. It was easier for children to get comfortable and open up when they were engaged in play. Dimly, she could hear Emily's muffled voice and a child's piped response. A minute later, there were footsteps on the stairs again, and Emily reappeared, with Henley trailing shyly behind her.

The girl was the spitting image of her mother, except for her eyes. Henley's eyes were light blue, vivid, and startling against the rest of her coloring.

The second she saw Kate, she froze.

"Henley, this is the friend we spoke about, Dr. Willis," Emily said. Then, correcting herself, "Sorry. *Kate*."

Kate doubled over, hands on knees, so she would appear less threatening. "Hi, Henley," she said. "It's nice to meet you."

Henley said nothing. She just stood there, mute and staring.

Kate tried again to engage her. "I really like your earrings." Henley had on a mismatched pair of stick-on earrings—one a shoe, the other an apple. "I'm wearing earrings, too." She angled her head so that her studs—a pair of raw emeralds that Steve had bought her for their wedding gift—were visible. But Henley displayed no interest. Her eyes stayed locked on Kate's.

"Come on, Henley. Dr. Willis drove a long way to see you. Can you say hi?" Emily tried to nudge her daughter closer, but Henley pivoted and ducked behind her legs.

Kate pulled out a seat at the kitchen table, trying to draw Henley's attention to the art supplies she'd laid out there. "Your mother told me that you love to draw," she said cheerfully. "I thought we could color together for a while."

Still nothing. Henley's body was rigid, and her lips thinned into a small tense line.

Emily sighed. "I'm sorry," she said. "Henley's not usually so shy . . ."

At last, Henley mumbled something.

Emily turned to her. "What's that, honey?"

"I said I'm *not* shy." She raised her voice, this time with insistence. "I don't want to color with her."

"Henley." Emily's tone was stern. "You're being very rude. Dr. Willis brought you all those pretty markers . . ."

"That's okay," Kate interjected, seeing Henley physically recoil. Clearly, Henley felt threatened. Kate kept her voice light. "We can do something else together. Do you like puzzles?"

"Henley loves puzzles," Emily answered for her daughter. "Don't you, string bean?"

"No." This time Henley's voice was an explosion. She was still hiding behind her mother, using Emily as a human shield. "I don't want to play with her. She's bad."

Emily and Kate exchanged a bewildered glance. Emily contorted, trying to get an arm around her daughter, but Henley kept shuffling behind her.

"Henley, please. Dr. Willis is a friend—"

"She's *not*!" Henley's voice crested toward a shriek. "She's mean! She's a liar!" Henley wrenched away from her mother's grip, turned, and darted up the stairs again, leaving Emily and Kate in startled silence.

"I'm so sorry," Emily said. She looked mortified. "I don't understand. She seemed so excited to meet you this morning . . ."

Kate wondered why she felt shaken. It was the girl's eyes. They were so pale, almost electric, as if she were lit up by foreign energy from within. "She doesn't know me," she pointed out. "And you *did* say that I was a doctor." She'd once seen a child cower in the corner when she tried to engage him in play. It took most of the session for him to admit that he was afraid Kate was going to cut into his brain. Who knew where he'd gotten the idea.

But Emily still looked troubled. "Usually, she's very friendly with strangers . . ." She gestured helplessly. "What do you think? Should I go talk to her?"

"She probably needs some time to calm down." There was no point in trying to force Henley to engage. It would only make her hysterical. The best thing to do was give her space and reapproach her later.

Kate packed up her art supplies and let Emily escort her back to the door. The whole time, she was half listening for sounds of distress from upstairs—crying, shouting, evidence of a tantrum working its way out of Henley's nervous system. But there was nothing but heavy silence, inscrutable and somewhat unnerving. She had the sudden idea that Henley was listening back, keenly attuned to Kate's footsteps as they tracked to the door.

Not distressed. Alert. Watchful.

"I'm sorry." Emily apologized for at least the fourth time as they exited onto the porch. "Really, she never behaves that way. It was almost like a fit or something."

"Kids have their moods," Kate said. "Hopefully she'll be ready to talk soon. In the meantime"—she lifted her briefcase, full now of the notes and drawings Emily had compiled—"I have my homework."

She half meant it as a joke. But Emily only nodded. Kate could tell she was still unsettled by her daughter's explosion in the kitchen. As Kate headed for her car, Emily just stood there, looking puzzled.

"It's funny," Emily said. "It was almost as if . . ." She trailed off, letting the thought remain unfinished.

"As if what?" Kate said.

For a second Emily stood there on the porch, twisting up her mouth, as if sucking on the words before speaking them. "It was almost as if she *recognized* you."

Before Kate could respond, Emily whirled around and disappeared inside the house.

THREE

It was almost as if she recognized you.

On the short drive back to town, Emily's final words looped again through Kate's mind, tangling with secondary impressions of a woman haunted by loss. It was like this, when she first encountered people: like they were made of long threads, a ravel of fears and tragedies and secrets, that needed only to be teased and pulled apart, sorted and categorized. It had driven Steve crazy, the way she could never quite turn off her diagnostic training, her tendency to tease behaviors into clinical categories that could be labeled and subsequently treated. He'd accused her of deterministic thinking, of approaching humans as if they were machines. But the human mind *was* a machine—a vast neural processor of inputs and outputs, stimuli and response.

And there was no such thing as the soul.

She wondered whether Emily would turn out to be something of a fabulist—someone who invented, exaggerated, fictionalized her own importance—possibly using her daughter as a proxy. She hadn't gotten that impression—for one thing, Emily's personal Instagram was private, and she'd turned up only a single image of Henley on the Wheel of Fortune's website—but it was possible, even so, that Emily was compelled to derive meaning where there wasn't any. It was a relatively standard response to an experienced loss of control, say, after a personal tragedy, such as an unexpected death. It was easy to imagine how Henley's stories and babblings about her other family might have quickly grown in significance in Emily's mind, weaving into an imagined narrative of a past life.

Of course, there was always the possibility that something even darker was at play. In her time as a clinician, Kate had encountered a handful of parents, all of them mothers, who were subsequently diagnosed as suffering from factitious disorder imposed on another. The disorder, formerly known as Munchausen syndrome, was originally named for the fictional hero of a 1785 novel characterized as an extravagant liar. Traditionally, mothers with factitious disorder imposed on another tortured their children with unnecessary medical procedures, often going to extreme lengths to convince their families, and the medical establishment, that their children were suffering from grave physical diseases in order to garner sympathy and attention. But Kate had been toying with the idea that there might be purely psychological expressions of the same dynamic: parents who, for example, convinced their children that they were under the control of demons, malevolent spirits, or poltergeists.

Or a mother who persuaded her six-year-old daughter that she'd once lived, and died, before.

Free, unexpectedly, of her afternoon obligations, Kate's mind began running down Route 7, back to the old Camp Sauquamet. She had promised her own therapist that she would make a visit to the site. *For closure,* she'd said. But when she tried to point the car in that direction, she found instead that the wheel kept turning her elsewhere—up Church Street, which ran past the cemetery where Norman Rockwell was buried; then onto a dead-end loop called Sergeant Street, where a discreet pawnshop tucked away between cafés and historic buildings displayed a dusty clutter of musical instruments in the window.

Instantly, she thought again of Mariana. She could go see Mariana. As soon as she made the decision, she felt silly for not thinking of it immediately. She'd spent six years bunking with Mari, exchanging handwritten letters over the course of the school year, and eventually emails, through the glacial dial-up AOL connection in her basement.

They'd gossiped, giggled, and consoled one another; Kate remembered how Mariana had sat with her for hours, stroking her back, after Kate had gotten the news that her dog, Buster, had been hit by a car one July. Later that night, Mari had slipped a prayer for Buster under Kate's pillow, a Bible verse that Kate still recalled all these years later.

The Lord is close to the brokenhearted, and saves those who are crushed in spirit.

But Kate had run from those bonds, and from her memories of their shared summers, all because of what had happened to Becca.

She got the address of Mari's music school from Google. It was a short drive, only a few minutes outside of town. It was only when Kate slowed down to squint for #84 among the mailboxes nestled along the side of the road that she realized Mari's music school must be located in her home.

Driving up to the modest Colonial, she began to feel apprehensive. It had been twenty-six years since she'd spoken to Mari; she had no idea what Mariana remembered or how she felt about what had happened their final summer. Maybe Mariana even blamed her for not standing up to Becca more forcefully—or even for the stupid, fateful choices they'd made that night, when they'd all rowed out to the island on the lake.

Or maybe Mariana still believed that the Gray Lady had made them do it.

The painted sign tucked next to the driveway, cheerfully pointing the way to the "Music School," made her feel only a little better. As she cut around the back via a flagstone path somewhat inelegantly painted with musical instruments, she could hear someone—presumably a student—blowing flatulently into a horn. A tuba, maybe. Or a bassoon? Kate could never tell the difference. She remembered that Mari had been a clarinet player but had kept her instrument tucked beneath her bunk bed all summer, bringing it out to practice whenever Becca wasn't around. Becca liked to make fun of her playing; she used to call it Mari's boyfriend, and joke that Mari was practicing how to give a *blow job*.

Becca could be like that. Mean. Especially that last summer.

Through the sliding glass doors, Kate could see into a cheerful basement room scattered with music stands and a litter of musical instruments. She spotted a baby grand piano in one corner and a full drum kit in another. Between them, a boy who couldn't have been more than nine was straining into a tuba—it was definitely a tuba—nearly his size. The woman watching him, her back to the door, could only be Mariana. She still had the same halo of blond curls, just shorter, and lightened by gray.

Kate hadn't anticipated that she might be in the middle of a lesson, and was debating turning around, when the boy broke off from his ferocious blowing, opened his eyes, and spotted her. A moment later, Mariana turned around, and Kate felt an absurd instinct to duck. Instead she stood there, locking eyes with Mariana, wincing an awkward smile.

Mariana took a step closer to the doors, then two. Confusion worked its way across her face. Kate's stomach hardened into a weight. She felt idiotic. Mariana didn't recognize her.

Then, all at once, Mari's expression cleared, locked into some kind of recognition. She let out a belt of a laugh—fast, startled, amazed—and then quickly covered her mouth. That gesture, the way she ducked her smile behind her hand, cut all the years between them clean away, made thirteen-year-old Mari surface in the adult so clearly that Kate half expected to hear a counselor's whistle, summoning them to their next activity.

Mari slid open the doors. "Kate?"

Kate's arms suddenly felt like deadweights. "Hi, Mari," she said. And then, with a little shrug, "Surprise."

Mari laughed again. She took two steps outside and enfolded Kate in a tight hug. The top of her head just grazed Kate's breastbone. Her hair smelled clean, like mint. Kate was surprised to feel the sudden pressure of tears behind her eyes.

"I can't believe it. I thought I was hallucinating or something. It's been—what?—twenty-five years?"

"Twenty-six," Kate said.

"What are you *doing* here? How did you find me? You look amazing, by the way. I love your hair. Is it colored?" Mari still ping-ponged gleefully between topics when she was excited.

Kate couldn't help but smile. "You haven't changed," she said.

Mari gave a self-conscious laugh. "Except for the grays and the wrinkles," she said. In the music studio, the child with the tuba gave a doleful, pointed toot. Mari startled, as if she'd already forgotten about him.

"Please, please, come in. I'm just finishing up with Oliver. Then we can sit and catch up." She was already piloting Kate inside by the wrist. "It's a light day for me. About half of my usuals are on family vacations. I really can't believe you're here. I thought you lived in Maryland."

"Virginia," Kate corrected her, as Mari steered her into a chair. She watched as Mari turned her attention back to the boy, Oliver, coaching him through a series of breath-work exercises until he managed to sound a single, sustained note into the mouth of the instrument. By then, Oliver's father had arrived to collect him, and Oliver was red faced, a little sweaty, and flush with pride.

Afterward, Mari brought Kate upstairs. Kate noticed a clutter of religious objects on the shelves—Buddhist sculptures, Hindu prayer candles, a framed print of the Kabbalah Tree of Life—and reflected that Mari's religious fervor must have fractured into an expansive, if disorganized, spirituality. The small kitchen asserted dozens of self-help blandishments on kitchen towels, mugs, and even refrigerator magnets. One in particular caught Kate's attention. *It's never too late to start over.* She only wished that were true.

"I've read all your books," Mariana said without preamble, as she siphoned coffee into an ancient drip machine. "I follow you on Instagram, too. I just heard that interview you did on NPR—the one about that poor boy in Texas. Is it really a federal case now?"

"Wire fraud," Kate said vaguely. She always felt embarrassed talking about her books, especially because she knew the human cost of the stories she'd exposed as delusions, or deliberate scams. "The boy's parents collected over a hundred thousand dollars in donations online."

Mari shook her head admiringly. "Lennie and I used to talk about you all the time, you know. You were always so smart . . ."

"You still talk to Lennie?" For a second, Kate felt a pang of jealousy. Like she was back at camp, and it was her day to be excluded from the group. She quickly reminded herself that she'd chosen to distance herself.

"I did, until last year." Mari glanced at her sideways, as if sizing her up for something, then returned her attention to the coffeepot. "She died in February."

"Lennie died?" Kate was stunned. She remembered Lennie as the athlete, the healthiest of all of them. A former gymnast turned star soccer player, with a big mouth and a lot of swagger. It seemed impossible that she could have died so young. It seemed impossible that she could have died, period.

"Cervical cancer," Mari said. "It was all over Facebook."

Kate was ashamed to admit out loud that she hadn't followed either of them. Dimly, she thought she remembered ignoring a Facebook invitation to connect from Lennie. That must have been—what?—seven, eight years ago.

"She fought so hard for years," Mari continued. "You know how Lennie was."

Kate said nothing. She wasn't sure she did know Lennie, or this music teacher in front of her cheerfully brewing coffee, seemingly untroubled by the past that united them.

"I'm so happy to see you, Kate. Really." Mari came to the table and took a seat across from Kate while the coffee brewed. "What brought you back?"

Back. Not *here*, not *to the area*. Back. As if Kate had come home again.

"I'm consulting with a family in the area," she said, which was basically true. When Mari raised her eyebrows, she added, "A six-year-old girl. Her mother believes she has memories of a past life."

Mari nodded, as if that made perfect sense. "I've read about cases like that. Like that woman who could remember being an Egyptian princess . . . what was her name again?"

"Dorothy Eady," Kate said, instantly annoyed. Dorothy Eady was one of the most well-known historical cases of supposed reincarnation, and often used as definitive proof by its proponents. As a child, Dorothy had become obsessed with ancient Egypt, seemingly overnight. She'd persuaded her parents that she had memories that dated from that time. Most mysteriously, as an adult she'd actually led a team of archaeologists to concealed rooms within an ancient temple, insisting that she'd lived there millennia earlier, and thus could recall its footprint perfectly.

"That's right. And all those cases in India . . ." Mariana was obviously a believer. Kate wondered what had happened to her Christian faith. As a girl, Mari had never been far away from her Bible. She'd regularly fiddled with her gold cross when she was anxious, and prayed on her knees every morning, despite the fact that the other campers made fun of her for it. At the same time, she'd been the most affected by the stories about the Gray Lady, seemingly convinced that her wandering ghost really was haunting the lake.

She'd been the one who insisted: Going to the graveyard on Fair Isle was a terrible idea.

Of course, they hadn't listened. They'd never listened to Mari.

It was Becca who always chose.

"What about you?" Kate said. "When did you move here?" She stopped herself from blurting *And why?*

"It was kind of a fluke, really. I went to college in Massachusetts. The music conservatory at Berklee. I swore I'd run right away from the winters as soon as I graduated. But then, of course, I met a man. Well, he was really a boy, then. We were both juniors in college when we got together." Mari smiled ruefully. "After graduation, we moved into his mother's house in Hillsdale, just across the border. But of course, you remember Hillsdale. That was the last time I saw you . . ."

Kate looked at her, shaking her head. The name didn't even ring a bell.

"*Hillsdale.* New *York*," Mari repeated. Then, when Kate just stared at her blankly, she clicked a little. "Don't you remember Becca's memorial service? We all went over to her grandparents' house afterward. So sad. That pretty yellow house, with all those cute flower beds. My eyes were swollen for days afterward . . . so much crying . . ."

Just like that, a memory surfaced: a raw September day, and the uncomfortable itch of the tights her mother had insisted she wear. Kate's mother had been too sick to travel, so it was Kate's father who'd driven them up from Virginia to attend the service. She remembered that even then, even after everything that had happened, Kate was hoping that Cameron Dunbar would be there as well. She remembered scanning the yard for him, and spotting instead the camp nurse, Mrs. Berger, and head counselor Jenny Lin, smoking cigarettes by the old tree house, shivering in the gusts of wind that cascaded leaves across the yard, foreign looking in black dresses and lipstick. She'd gone room to room, searching for him among the crowd of mourners, hoping for—what? A sudden confession, a private gesture, a stolen romantic moment that would prove that their fantasized connection had been real. Kate saw now that she'd been deluded. Deluded, and grieving. Cameron had been eighteen—four years older, one of the counselors—and half the girls at camp had been in love with him. But she remembered the hollow disappointment in her chest when she realized he hadn't come.

The memory troubled her now. She'd been young, and stupid, and fixating on the wrong things.

But there was something else, too. Something about the recollection of that yellow house . . .

" . . . 'Course, the marriage fell apart soon enough." Mari was still talking, bounding on through her history. "I was twenty-two when we got married. I had no idea what I was doing. Alex—that's our son—was only eighteen months when we divorced. But we wanted to raise him together, so I had to stay local—"

"Does Becca's family still live in the area?" Kate blurted.

Mari looked startled. But she recovered quickly enough. "Oh, I have no idea," she said. She stood up to pour out the coffee into mugs. "Why? Are you thinking of visiting them, too?"

"Maybe," Kate said. Actually, until Mari had mentioned that yellow house, it was the last thing she would have considered. She didn't remember Becca's grandparents well—only that Becca had called them "the old pair," as in *the old pair sent me a package* or *the old pair want me to call*—and she didn't recall, now, the exact circumstances that had led Becca to live with them. She knew Becca's mother struggled with drug addiction.

"It's just so terrible, what happened to that family," Mari said as she returned to the table. "Those poor people. Can you imagine? I think about Becca sometimes, you know. All those years lost. All that potential. It's just tragic, what happened to her."

Kate felt a touch of energy in her spine, a stiffening, as if she'd just become aware of danger. She searched Mari's face for some obscurity, some clouded meaning, and found nothing.

"What . . . *happened* to her," she repeated, testing out the words carefully, scanning Mari's face to see how they landed.

Mari nodded. "Just awful. And to think, they never even found her body. All those divers. All that time spent dredging the lake. All for nothing."

Kate stared at her. Mari, seemingly oblivious, was carefully leveling sugar into her coffee.

"You think . . ." She stopped and took a deep breath. "You think Becca drowned."

Mari looked up. She blinked. "Well, of course she drowned," she said. "We found her canoe. Don't you remember?"

Kate closed her eyes. She saw the empty canoe, skimming out across the lake in the moonlight. "Yeah," she said. "Yeah. I remember the canoe."

"And Becca had been drinking. Remember, she got that bottle of—what was it?—Fireball? And she wanted all of us to drink?" Mari shook her head. "We should never have made that trip out to Fair Isle. I knew it was a bad idea."

"So you don't remember what happened there?" Kate felt suddenly lightheaded. She had never spoken to anyone, even Steve, about what had happened that night. She had relived it only in her nightmares, in the dreams where Becca came to her, skin purpled by death, hair entangled with algae, to accuse her. *Why did you leave me alone? What did you do to me?* "I mean, you don't remember what happened on the island?"

"I remember we scared ourselves silly," Mari said. "All those stories about that ghost—what did we call her?—the Gray Lady. Of course, I do think there was something wrong with that place. Energetically, I mean. Have you ever done Reiki? I have a friend in town who practices—if you have time, you might think about popping by—"

"And that's it? That's everything?" Kate couldn't believe it. She found herself growing angry at Mari, sitting here talking about Reiki and the Gray Lady in the same breath, as if what happened the night that Becca died was all just some unfortunate glitch in the energetic field. She was either an extraordinary actress, or she'd truly forgotten the truth: finding the mausoleum; Becca taunting each of them to go inside; the way that Lennie had lashed out. She'd forgotten all about their plan for teaching Becca a lesson.

She'd forgotten, too, what they had done to Becca afterward. What she, Mari, had insisted they do.

"What do you mean?" Mari must have heard the edge in Kate's tone. Now she appeared slightly wounded. "What else is there to remember? It was an accident."

It was an accident. Kate had told herself the same thing many times. She had even believed it in her head.

But was it? On some level, they had *wanted* Becca dead.

Suddenly the room felt airless. She'd had too much coffee. Her thoughts were skating around like deranged flies.

Kate stood up. "I should go."

Mari no longer wore glasses. Still, her eyes seemed to redouble in surprise. "But . . . you just got here."

"I forgot I have a call," Kate lied. "I'm sorry."

"Will you come back?" Mari stood up, too, and seized Kate's wrists, searching her face for a promise. "How long are you here? Can we have dinner? We could look through old photos—I still have all our camp yearbooks. And I'd love for you to meet Alex. He'll be a senior this fall, can you believe it?"

Kate gently disentangled herself. "I'll let you know," she said. She had no intention of returning—it had been a mistake. There was no shared past between them—at least, not the same shared past. Kate wondered, briefly, if she was the one who'd imagined everything. Still, Mari was looking at her so hopefully, she heard herself saying, "I promise I'll try."

Mari trailed Kate to the door as they exchanged numbers. Kate thought about how Becca had always called Mari their puppy. So eager to please. Always wagging her tail, begging for a treat, following them everywhere. There was some truth to it.

At the door, Mari gave her a hug. "Please come back," she said. "It's so good to see you. Really. I used to wonder—" She broke off, then tried again. "Well, we were such good friends. You guys were like my family. And then you disappeared, and you wouldn't answer any of Lennie's messages, and I started to wonder . . ." Again, she trailed off, looking puzzled.

"Wonder what?" Kate said.

"I started to wonder if we'd done something wrong."

Kate didn't begin to breathe normally again until she was back at her car. The insects were threshing the heat into sound, texturizing the air with their endless song. She stood there for a minute, thinking about what Mari had said. *I started to wonder if we'd done something wrong.*

How was it possible that she didn't remember? And if Mari could forget, why couldn't she?

She heard the faint notes of a clarinet from inside the house, warbling through a melody that seemed somehow familiar. It took her a second to place it. A camp song. A song they'd adapted a million different ways, lacing the lyrics with personalized details, names, and even complaints.

She got in the car and punched on the radio, drowning out the sound.

Fucking Mari.

FOUR

Kate's Airbnb was located in one of the converted outbuildings of what had once been a functional farm. Only traces of the property's original purpose remained: in the main farmhouse itself, and the row of chicken coops behind it; in the picturesque red barn across the street. An older woman—presumably the owner—waved with a garden spade as Kate bumped her roller bag to the cottage door. There were flowers everywhere—running in terraced waves down the slope of the backyard, coiling up trellises, massed around the side of the main house.

It was as pretty a place as any to work.

Inside, it was bright, cozy, and somewhat eclectic. A shabby jute rug ran up to a potbellied stove. Porcelain cows marched in a proud row across one kitchen shelf. A pair of battered wooden oars, mounted on the wall above an old-fashioned standing television, reminded Kate keenly, sharply, of the camp boathouse: the smell of moss and wet corners, the feeling of standing, shivering in her bathing suit, on the spongy ground, contemplating the canoes stacked to the ceiling like the knobs of a spine. A sagging bookshelf displayed water-warped copies of decades-old bestsellers, pulpy romances, and, mysteriously, a five-year-old SAT prep book. All left here by generations of guests, undoubtedly.

As she scanned the titles, her attention snagged on the title of a slender paperback, wedged between two battered volumes of a YA trilogy that had been popular when she was a teenager: *The Gray Lady, and Other Massachusetts Legends*, by an author named

Martin Sheehy. She wriggled the book off the shelf, surprised—even shocked—to discover that the Gray Lady had not simply been an invention of Camp Sauquamet. The Gray Lady was almost embedded in camp lore, like the fact that the mess hall was decorated with a moose head that always made eye contact, no matter where you stood in the room, or the fact that saying the camp motto backward brought rain. She'd been told ever since her first summer that a terrible spirit haunted the lake, prowling for new souls to pull down to their watery grave.

She thought back to that final summer, when the legend of the Gray Lady had begun, slowly, to consume them, to poison their sleep and curdle their dreams. She remembered that moment in the woods with Becca, stilled by a sudden dread, and the conviction that someone was out there.

Haunted. They'd been haunted, that summer.

Before she could read any further, her cell phone rang. It was George Turner, a graduate student and one of Kate's advisees. She tossed the book onto the nightstand and picked up the phone.

"You're supposed to be on vacation," Kate said.

"You never take vacation," George fired back. George used they/them pronouns and favored androgynous clothing, but they had the sweet, chirruping voice of a bird, even when they were scolding. "Speaking of . . . did you talk to the subject yet?"

"Her name is Henley," Kate said. "And I tried. She wouldn't talk to me."

"First impression?"

"Not sure yet. Too early to say. And remember, I'm not diagnosing her." Kate was always encouraging the graduate students who worked at her lab to avoid jumping to conclusions too early. They were doctors first, and clinicians second. But above all, they were scientists. Rather than study the cosmos, or the workings of quantum probability fields, they studied the liminal space where the brain became the mind, and the mind became personality, or its many disordered facets. “What about that Tulpa research? Did you gather it?”

“Already in your inbox,” George said. George was researching Tulpamancy, a phenomenon rooted in the Tibetan concept of Tulpa, or the practice of creating an external body, an agent, with the mind. Modern usage of the word referred to the practice of giving psychic birth to another personality, who would then cohabitate the mind and body of the individual. The psychological phenomenon was both connected to and distinct from dissociative identity disorder, formerly known as multiple personality disorder. Kate had followed the progress of George’s dissertation for the past year, but was now interested in knowing more about their field of research. Tulpamancers were disparagingly known as people who willed an imaginary friend into existence; the community might, she thought, shed some light on Henley’s claims of a remembered past self.

As if George knew what Kate was thinking, they immediately threw cold water on the idea. “I’m not sure the profile fits. Real *plurals*”—another more technical term for Tulpamancers—“change behavioral patterns, even speech patterns, depending on which personality is in control. In that way, they’re just like people with DID. Someone else, a second personality, literally takes the wheel.”

“But the core personality can report details about the others, right?” Kate said. This was one of the features that distinguished pluralism from dissociative disorders as a whole, and had provoked the most controversy about how “real” it was as a psychic phenomenon. People suffering from severe dissociation often lost time. They had no knowledge of the other existent personas that controlled their behavior during those periods, and might ferociously deny that they were operating with multiple identities. “In other words, if Henley does have some kind of invented other self, she would be able to talk about it.”

“But not as a *historical* self,” George pointed out. “If Henley is a plural, then all of her identities would be alive to her in the present.

And you would expect to see behavioral shifts that go along with the change in persona-control."

Kate wondered whether that might explain Henley's sudden tantrum in the kitchen. She would have to know more about this "past self" and its personality features before she knew whether to count it as evidence of pluralism, dissociation, or something else—some kind of external influence, a story that had been encouraged by her mother or another influential figure in her life.

After she'd hung up with George, Kate brought her computer and a stack of research out onto the patio, where she could watch the late afternoon lengthen and soften into evening. She briefly reviewed the materials about the Haskells that Dr. Rushkin had sent over from DOPS. At the age of thirty-six, Emily Haskell had used a sperm donor to get pregnant. Henley had been born a year later. When Henley had first inquired about her "other grandparents" at the age of three, Emily had assumed that she wanted to know why she had only a single set, unlike her other friends. Emily had prepared an answer about the donation, and about Emily's desire to have a child on her own, but Henley had only grown frustrated. She was asking about her *other grandparents*. The ones she lived with *before* she became Emily's baby. Back when she lived with Nana, Poppa, Sammie, and Noodle.

Within a year, Henley would refer to this period as the time before she died. It was uncommon for children of that age to speak about death, or even comprehend it. Typically, the concept began to emerge between the ages of five and seven. She wondered whether the family had suffered a loss at that time—maybe one of Henley's relatives, or even a family pet, had passed away—that might help explain her sudden preoccupation. She made a note to herself to inquire.

Next, she turned her attention to the folder that Emily Haskell had given her. She spread out all of Henley's drawings of the yellow house. All told, there were about a dozen of them, each dated by her mother. She stared at them for a while: the tree house sloppily listing in the branches to the left of the house; the loopy flowers running up to the door. Why had Henley painted the same scene, over and over again, for three years? What did it mean to her?

A niggling suspicion, a ridiculous thought, seized hold of her imagination. She thought of what Mari had said. *Don't you remember Becca's memorial service? That pretty yellow house, with all those cute flower beds.* Was it possible that Henley was drawing *Becca's* old house? Immediately, she dismissed the idea. A coincidence, likely. There must be millions of houses like it in the country.

She pulled open her laptop and started a file for Henley. Opening a blank Word document, she wrote her first notes.

Dissociative disorder

Pluralism—invented self?

Mom's fantasy life—?

She stopped. She had nothing more to say—no proof, no observations, nothing but speculation. She stared at the yellow house until she was dizzy, until the colored lines began to change shape, swirling her down toward a memory she didn't want to face. Then, abruptly, she swept the pictures back into a stack.

Next, she scanned the drawings Henley had made of the church. She found herself wondering how many revolutionary-era churches there were across the country, and then immediately felt stupid. These were nothing but drawings, expressions of a child's fantasy life. Henley's happened to be repetitive, fixed. That was all.

But it was with a sense of dread that she extracted the final drawings, the ones of the graveyard on the water, from the folder.

There were dozens of them—some scrawled in crayon and dating from when Henley was a toddler; some, more recent, were warped with watercolor paint. She sifted through them carefully, scanning for details she hadn't noticed before. In some paintings, the headstones were interspersed with trees, branches raised to the sky as if haggling with it. They might, she thought, be depictions of Fair Isle, the island in the middle of Lake Sauquamet that had formed the basis of the legends of the Gray Lady. It was hard to say. If so, Henley must have heard about the lake, even if she'd never been there herself. It was reasonable to imagine that kids were still telling stories of the people that had gone missing there, weaving the tragedies into a fable, as they had when she was a camper.

She landed on one of Henley's most recent watercolors—dated from earlier this year, according to a note her mother had added—and froze.

Between the trees, hovering above the headstones in a splotchy bit of shadow, was a woman.

Henley had used pen to color her enormous black eyes, which appeared to be swallowing her face. Her hair was a frenetic tangle of dark ink. Her mouth was open in a grin. She was clearly there, and yet barely visible, disappearing into the tree branches, concealed beneath a layer of gray paint that Henley had added to the scene.

Kate's heart seized up in her chest. The thought appeared from nowhere: *She knows.*

With a noise of frustration, she jammed all the artwork together into the folder.

She'd been back for less than a day, and already, the past was tugging at her, drawing her back toward superstition and magical thinking. Drawing her back to the lake, where it had all begun.

She stood up, suddenly restless. It was just before six o'clock. The sun wouldn't set for another hour and a half. She thought of the promise she'd made to her therapist. *For closure.*

Suddenly determined, she grabbed her keys and headed for the door. Might as well get it over with now. No more delaying.

After twenty-six years, it was time to bury the dead.

~

It had been two decades since Camp Sauquamet had closed its doors, its reputation permanently damaged by the scandal that had engulfed the camp in the aftermath of Becca's disappearance and the discovery that, among other things, many of the counselors had a history of delinquent behavior themselves. Kate knew that the longtime owner, Hannah Bartosz, had tried to rally community support for the camp, in the face of legal challenges and widespread accusations of negligence. But she had caved, ultimately, to public pressure.

As far as she knew, the property had cycled in and out of the hands of various buyers since then. Emily Haskell had indicated that the land now belonged to the county. She'd heard from a gas station attendant in nearby Great Barrington that new developers were sniffing around, hoping to raze the place, to put up lakefront homes that would attract weekend buyers from the city.

Kate angled the car past several "No Trespassing" signs onto the gravel service road now tufted with weeds. The trees closed in around her, knotting their arms, shouldering out all but patchy sunlight. Then, abruptly, the woods released her, gutting her out again into the sun. A slope of overgrown hillside ran down to the lake, glowing almost russet in the late afternoon sun. Weed-choked trails ran between the cluster of administrative buildings and down toward the cabins.

Kate parked and got out, surveying the scene—so vastly different from the place she remembered. So forlorn. So quiet, most of all. Still, someone had been here recently. The arts and crafts center was a mess, but the padlock on the door was new, and the cabins, also padlocked, were in good shape. Someone had been keeping them up—patching the roofs, replacing the screens in the windows. A few of them even had new trim. Seeing large swaths of mowed grass carved into the slope where they used to play kickball and capture the flag, she thought for the first time in years of Ferdinand, the old maintenance director, whom the girls had always badgered for the gum he kept in his pocket. She wondered what had happened to him. Maybe he was dead by now. Maybe not—back then, everyone who wasn't a camper had seemed impossibly old. Hard to imagine that all of them, Ferdinand and the counselors, Mrs. Berger, who both doled out calamine lotion and Band-Aids at the infirmary and taught the campers archery, had gone on to other lives. They'd all seemed to exist only inside the bubble of summertime, rising up fully formed to greet the buses as they lumbered down the dirt road to the drop-off area, then dispersing again in late August without a ripple.

Kate picked through a litter of empty beer cans and alcohol bottles in the overgrown grass to reach the lake. She was amused, and half relieved, to find the "Friendship Wall" still intact next to the boathouse. A low wall of slab concrete that had been poured that final summer, it was patterned with handprints and initials. Kate remembered the day she'd seen the counselors gather to place their hands in the wet concrete. She paused for a moment, searching the wall for Cameron Dunbar's handprint—a habit that had become reflexive that last summer, when she'd often paused to fit her palm inside the larger impression of his hand, imagining that it might carry some magic, bring them closer together in real life.

Today, all she felt was the cold touch of cement.

She continued onto the docks, where she had once sat among her friends, her knees brown and scabbed and bare, watching the counselors show off on water skis. The cleats were wearing an undercoat of green algae. A single rowboat was overturned on the stubbly pebble beach. The lifeguard chair had keeled over in the bushes, like someone drunk.

Across the water, about half a mile in the distance, Fair Isle sat tight lipped behind a tight thicket of trees. That was what they'd called it—Fair Isle. She doubted it really had a name. Once, about a decade ago, she'd tried to google it, to see whether any of the rumors were true. On aerial maps, it was visible only as a splotch of green marring the almost-perfect circle of blue. But for the locals, it was Fair Isle—a rough two acres of red cedar and pitch pine, home to an abandoned graveyard, and the remnants of a large stone structure whose original purpose was a continued source of local debate. Some people had claimed it was the ruins of an old mansion, built by a wealthy trapper in the early 1800s to house his daughter, who went crazy after the death of her young children. Others said that it had been a summer place for an industrialist looking to escape the threat of tuberculosis. She'd heard, as a kid, that the site had once housed a sanitarium, or a home for troubled girls. Others said the ruins weren't evidence of a larger structure at all—just proof of a folly once built on the site, perhaps to give shelter to passing rowing parties.

But that didn't explain the graveyard.

Kate stood there, looking out over the water, waiting for something—a feeling, an instinct, even dread. Long, spindly shadows tipped from the overhanging woods onto the surface, reaching for something in the water. But they quickly ran out into sky-colored water, whitened by the early afternoon sun.

"You're not supposed to be here."

Kate turned at the voice behind her. A man about Kate's age was loping down the hill toward the docks, wiping his hands on an oil rag. She noticed the paint-splattered jeans, the forearms roped with muscle, and the work boots, and sized him up for a landscaper: the same person responsible, she assumed, for the recently mowed kickball field that she'd spotted on the way down.

"Sorry," Kate said, without meaning it. "I just wanted to see the lake." It was true. The cabins, the kickball field, the mess hall—all of them were skeined with memories, phantom impressions of a childhood lost. But Lake Sauquamet was their gravitational center. It pulled every memory back toward that last summer, toward that terrible night. She added, "I used to go to camp here."

"County property," he said apologetically. A fan of blond hair showed under his baseball hat, and he had the weathered complexion of someone who'd spent long hours in the sun. But as he got closer, Kate saw that his smile was dazzling. "I'm supposed to run off any trespassers with a pitchfork. Kids come around here, use this place like a garbage dump." He gestured ruefully at the blackened remains of a campfire on the beach, ringed with a litter of bottles and vape cartridges. "I'm Matt, by the way. Matt Bishop."

She almost introduced herself as Dr. Willis. Force of habit. "Kate Willis," she said. "Are you the one who hung all the padlocks?"

He tipped his head. "Doing my civic duty. You should have seen this place six months back. We found squatters in two of the cabins. Runaways. God knows how long they'd been living here."

At one point, Kate had fantasized about doing something similar. She and Becca had imagined all the places they could hide when the summer came to an end, had talked for hours about how they might survive the fall and winter, scavenging supplies from local farms, fishing trout from the lake. Never mind that neither one of them had ever gone fishing. "Someone told me the land is up for sale . . . ?"

"Oh, sure. There are a few developers at the table. It's not the first time. But the deal's not closed." He shook his head. "If you ask me, it's a shame to clutter up this side of the lake with houses. But there's plenty of people who'll pay for the view, even if—"

He broke off abruptly, as if remembering that Kate was a stranger.

"Even if what?" she prompted him.

Kate could see a war of indecision playing out behind his eyes. "People say it's not safe to swim," he said cautiously. Suddenly, he laughed. He had a great laugh, deep and clear, like a bell. "It's local rumor. Old-time stories." Then, sheepishly: "Some people think the lake is cursed."

"Really?" Kate played the role of the interloper, the wandering tourist from Virginia, and feigned surprise. "Cursed?"

"See that island over there? There's a woman buried in those trees. They call her the Gray Lady. People say she walks around at night, calling for someone to join her. I know some people around here who'll swear they've seen her late at night wandering in the trees, or even standing right here on this dock."

"People will swear to a lot of things," Kate said. "Especially late at night."

Matt made a face that said, *True*. "We've had some bad luck around here. That's probably what started it. Boats turning over for no reason. Kids getting lost in the woods. Someone drowned a while ago . . ."

Kate's whole body tensed. She held her breath, waiting for the man to mention the camper, *Becca*, the poor fourteen-year-old beauty whose body had never been found.

"A local guy. Twenty-seven years old, just married. Worked as an English teacher over in Pittsfield. I knew his dad a bit. It just broke him up."

Kate exhaled. "I hadn't heard about that," Kate said. Of course, she knew about the lake's many tragedies. Lake Sauquamet's dangers had been the backbone of the stories they'd told at camp about the Gray Lady. But she had never known details. The rumors of drowned teenagers and vanished hikers had simply been interwoven with the mythology itself—justification for, and elemental to, the legend.

"It was two, three years ago now. Really gutted everybody. That's when we started talking about getting cameras, maybe fencing the whole place off . . ." He shook his head. "It's these kids, come out to party and wind up thinking it's a good idea to go swimming. The town tried putting up signs, but of course that won't stop anyone, especially after a six-pack."

"No," Kate said. "No, signs never do stop anyone." Then, impulsively: "What about Fair Isle? Do people ever go out there to party?" She knew the counselors had used the island for bonfires and wondered whether the tradition continued.

"Town put a stop to that. They fenced the whole site off about five years ago. You can't see from here, but they got ruins out there that go back a hundred, a hundred and fifty years. The whole island counts as a historical site. That mostly took care of the foot traffic."

She felt suddenly, unexpectedly relieved. She could have laughed; there was no one here. There was nothing to see but sunlight, and old trees, tipsy with green, leaning their heads over the water. Maybe, she thought, she would come back with her bathing suit. She would bring a book. She would sit in the shade and read, or swim out to Fair Isle and back, when Matt Bishop wasn't here to stop her. Why not?

Becca was gone. Lennie, too. And Mari believed that Becca's death had been an accident. In a way, it was as if that night on Fair Isle had never even happened. There was nothing to be afraid of anymore.

Closure.

Kate said her goodbye to the handsome Matt Bishop. She felt his eyes on her all the way up the hill. By the time she turned out of the old Camp Sauquamet, it was seven o'clock. She stopped in town for a burger, texted with Dr. Rushkin, and confirmed with Emily Haskell that she would come again the following morning to interview Henley—with more success, hopefully. She drove back to the Airbnb with the windows down, enjoying the warm, syrupy smell of the pines, feeling lighter than she had in many years.

But that night, for the first time in a long time, she dreamed of Becca.

THEN

"You're mooning again." Becca surfaced, throwing an arm up toward the ladder.

It was afternoon, a few hours after lunch. Free swim. Kate was sitting on the floating platform that Lennie had nicknamed "Seal Beach," her legs submerged to her shins in the cold water. The sun rebounded maniacally off the lake stirred by a hundred splashing campers.

Becca hauled herself out of the water, her hair slickened like a seal's fur against her skull, and settled in next to Kate. Her skin was cold.

"I'm not mooning," Kate said, feeling suddenly self-conscious, childish, in her rainbow-colored one-piece. Becca was wearing a bikini that showed off the long slope of her stomach, and the B cups that had materialized over the school year. Kate hunched her shoulders toward her ears, caving her flat chest in even farther. "What does that word mean, anyway?"

"It means you look like this." Becca widened her eyes grotesquely with her fingers. Kate couldn't help but laugh. "It means you look like you've got moons for eyeballs."

Kate watched a cluster of younger campers, who'd been clinging to the raft like an aggregation of barnacles, scatter quietly away toward the shore.

"He's going to catch you staring at him all the time," Becca said. "He's going to figure out you're obsessed with him."

"I'm not obsessed with him," Kate said quickly. She couldn't help it; her gaze kept pivoting back to Cameron in the lifeguard chair, drawn to the lick of sun bouncing off his whistle, to the geometry of his arms, to the long,

tan fingers, which she loved to watch skim over his guitar strings. Cameron had been a new counselor the year before, and Kate had barely noticed him. But that summer, he began to bloom through her thoughts, opening her up to sudden fantasies of kissing. Sometimes, whenever he caught her eye across the campfire circle, she imagined that it was just the two of them alone, that he was singing just for her. The idea that he would catch her staring, that he would know how she felt, thrilled and nauseated her at the same time.

"He's old, you know," Becca said.

"He's only eighteen."

Becca shrugged. "He has old-man nipples."

Kate nudged her with a shoulder. "He does not."

"Swear to God. Cross my heart. He has major saggy old-man nipples. But if that's what you're into . . ."

Kate toed a bit of water at her, and Becca shrieked. For a second, Cameron's gaze swept across the water and latched onto them. Kate froze. Becca noticed and barked a laugh.

"You loooove him," she said, drawing the word into a taunt.

"Be quiet. He can hear you," Kate said. Her whole body was burning, electric with embarrassment. She was too afraid to check and see whether Cameron was still looking at them. A little lower, she said, "And I don't . . . love him. I just think he's cute, that's all."

"Oh, come on. You're obsessed. You want to lick his teeth and tweak his old-man nipples—"

"You're an actual pervert, do you know that?"

Becca batted her eyelashes, as if Kate had meant it as a compliment. "I'm not the one dreaming about sucking on those hairy little lollipops—"

"I said keep your voice down—"

"Gray Lady's got you beat.*" Lennie and Mari surfaced suddenly next to the raft, seizing hold of Kate's ankles and giving her a hard yank. A second later, Kate went into the lake, shouting. She came up spitting water, pretending to be annoyed.*

"Seriously, guys? Are we really still playing this game?" Secretly, Kate was relieved that Lennie and Mari had interrupted. Being alone with Becca

had felt different recently. Like there was some kind of invisible charge that ran beneath Becca's words, something electric and unpredictable that might hurt.

"Of course we're still playing," Lennie said, stroking for the ladder. "And technically, I'm trouncing your asses."

This, the dunking, was part of a game they'd learned from the older campers back when they were little—a ritual act, like touching the oars mounted on the boathouse for good luck or starting every dinner with a rowdy rendition of a camp song. Even the counselors played sometimes. The goal was to surprise another swimmer, or even someone sunning unsuspecting on the dock, and drag them underwater for a point. They called it playing Gray Lady. It had taken Kate half a summer to agree to play. She'd been terrified of the game, terrified of swimming out into a roil of campers and feeling the icy slick of a hand around her ankle. She'd screamed the first time anyone had managed to dunk her, inhaling big drafts of water that left a mossy taste in her throat. Even now, there were times when she became suddenly aware of the darkness of the lake, of its depth, of all the things swimming around and underneath her that she couldn't see. Mostly, she tried not to think about it.

"So what were you guys talking about?" Even when Mari wrestled off her goggles, deep red gouges around her eyes made the impression of glasses.

"Nothing," Kate said quickly, shooting a warning glance at Becca. "Becca was just talking shit."

"Big surprise," Lennie said. She was standing now, bouncing water out of one ear and then another. "So who do we hate this week?"

"No one," Kate said. She was still thinking about Cameron, about the freckles on his nose, about the way he gnawed on his fingernails when he was listening. The way he hunched around, looking apologetic, like a stray who'd wandered into camp by accident.

"That's a first," Lennie said. She peered closely at Kate, and then Becca, as if she could read a secret between them.

Fortunately, Becca's attention had drifted. Now she was gnawing on a thumbnail, staring out in the direction of Fair Isle.

"Do you guys think she's really out there?" she asked abruptly.

"Who?" Mari asked.

"Who do you think? The Gray Lady."

Lennie rolled her eyes. "Here she goes again."

"If you're so sure there's nothing out there, then how come you won't go check it out?" Becca shaded her eyes with a hand.

"I won't go," Lennie said with a heavy sigh, "because it's crazy."

"We're not allowed to go to Fair Isle, Becca," Mari pointed out. "It's off-limits."

"That's only so the counselors can keep the island all to themselves. They go out there all the time," Becca insisted.

Mari looked shocked. "They do not."

"They do. They have bonfires out there. Cameron told me. Besides, I've seen the lights."

Kate stared at Becca. "Cameron told you that?"

Becca smirked. "He's public property, Kate. You're not the only one who gets to talk to him."

Kate looked away. She felt a squirming discomfort in her stomach. It was that look on Becca's face—like she was holding on to a secret, clutching it like a weapon she intended to use.

"But what about the curse?" Mari piped up meekly. She scooted up the ladder a bit, as if suddenly afraid of what might be underneath her.

"There's no curse, Mari," Lennie said with a heavy sigh. "That's just a story."

"But Ferdinand told me—"

"Ferdinand's a liar," Lennie said impatiently. "And a drunk, by the way. He reeks of alcohol. Haven't you noticed?"

"Maybe that'll help cover up the smell of cow shit." Becca said it casually, but Kate felt a pain. She felt sorry for Ferdinand, a local landscaper who'd been tending to the grounds for as long as the camp had been open. His fingers were crooked with arthritis, and his hands badly liver spotted. But still he kept working, raking mulch into the flower beds, tracking his wheelbarrow back and forth in the hot sun, pulling weeds on his knees in the dirt. He seemed like he must be a hundred years old.

"People have died." Mari's voice was quiet, but insistent. "They go out there looking for the Gray Lady. And if they find her, they're dead by morning."

Lennie was losing patience. "If that's true, then all of the counselors should be in the dirt. Becca's right. They do go out there at night. I've seen the lights."

"Maybe they just haven't seen her yet," Mari said stubbornly. "Maybe they've just gotten lucky."

Lennie shook her head, muttering something under her breath.

"So why not us?" Becca's eyes came alive, sparking with concealed laughter. She raised an eyebrow, cocked her head like she always did when she was about to talk them into something. "I don't know about you guys, but I'm feeling pretty lucky. Aren't you?"

FIVE

Kate was up before dawn. She'd been an early riser ever since she'd quit drinking, about six months before her divorce from Steve. Before then, the bottle of red wine she slugged through every night to carry her through her final hours of work had been a source of constant tension in her marriage.

But it was only after Kate got sober that their marriage, already strained and frayed and stretched to the limit, had simply unraveled. There was no big denouement—no tears, even. They'd barely spoken about it at all. By then, their lives had already separated. They'd both spent years retreating from each other and down into their own ways of coping. In retrospect, Kate wasn't sure they'd ever known how to connect. Not really.

For both of them, work had always come first.

She spent the morning digging through the University of Virginia's medical archives for relevant cases involving severe dissociation. There was the case of a fifty-five-year-old woman who reported seven different personalities, including a seven-year-old child and a heterosexual man—known to her only because the personality shifts had been reported to her by others, and had subsequently been measured and observed in clinical trials. A thirty-year-old woman with concurrent borderline personality disorder and a history of substance abuse claimed the power of clairvoyance and premonitory dreams, as well as a second male self that occasionally took over, often with self-destructive and violent results. The university had conducted a medical study of a forty-year-old man who, in the grips of a dissociative fugue, had walked out of his job as a successful actuary and away from his wife and children and been discovered three years later, homeless in San Francisco, with no memory whatsoever of who he was.

But in all these cases, the dissociated self was an unknown or poorly understood "other," a separate psychological being that took control, usually without the patients' awareness. Henley, on the other hand, had assimilated details about her past self into the narrative of her identity, into the history of who she was. She wasn't two people. She had been one person; now she was another.

The research George had assembled about Tulpamancy was slightly more ambiguous. Tulpamancers participated in the creation of a separate identity, essentially willing a companion personality into existence; the term *tulpa* itself referred in the original Tibetan to a physical being, a thought-form made manifest in the real world. This reminded Kate not of Henley but of the Gray Lady—the times when she'd been sure she saw the silhouette of a woman, watching them from the trees; the moments when she could have sworn she saw a leering face, grinning up at them from the murky water. She wondered briefly about that night on Fair Isle, when they'd gone looking for the Gray Lady's grave and stumbled upon the creepy handmade altar in the woods. And then afterward . . .

What? Kate had never been sure what they'd actually seen in those woods. For years, she'd assumed it had been a kind of group hallucination, like the waves of hysteria that occasionally afflicted whole groups of teenagers with mysterious symptomology—tics, spasms, fits of sudden laughter. Now she allowed herself to imagine, just for a minute, that they'd somehow willed the Gray Lady into existence. That all their stories, all the time they spent speculating about who she was and how she'd died, had somehow given birth to her spirit in the real world.

But that wasn't science *or* psychology. That was myth.

At just before eight o'clock, she packed up her briefcase and headed over to the Haskells'. When she arrived, Henley was sitting with Emily at the kitchen table, bent over a piece of paper, a handful of stubby crayons fanned out in front of her. When Kate saw the yellow house once again taking shape on the page, she felt an almost physical revulsion, and had to force herself to step closer.

"Sorry about the mess." Emily was bustling around the kitchen, shunting the breakfast dishes into the dishwasher, her hair coiled inside a towel. "It's a little chaotic this morning. One of my instructors called out sick, so I need to drop Henley at camp and get over to the studio by ten. Have you already had some coffee?"

Kate waved away the offer. She took a seat next to Henley. Henley didn't look up. She just kept carefully drawing the windows into the facade. Six on the ground floor, seven upstairs.

"Mom says I have to talk to you," Henley said after a minute.

Kate pulled out her phone. Emily indicated with a nod that it was okay for her to begin recording. "Is there some reason you don't want to talk to me?"

A small furrow darkened the space between Henley's eyebrows when she scowled. "I don't like you. You're not my friend."

"True," Kate said. "We don't know each other. But maybe we can *become* friends." She picked up a green crayon and began studying it, as if it fascinated her. Henley tensed. Her eyes ticked up to Kate's face. After a beat, she lunged for the crayon.

"That's mine," she said. "I need it for the grass."

Kate relinquished the crayon. At least Henley had made eye contact, if only for a second.

"You're a good drawer," Kate said. She was, actually. She had an eye for detail that most kids lacked at her age. The eaves on the roof, for example. She had drawn them with large, overlapping squares.

"I know," Henley said.

Emily cut in with a warning: *"Henley."*

Henley shot her mother an injured look. "Thank you," she mumbled, again without looking at Kate. But she seemed to relax a bit. Her grip on the crayon loosened. She sat up a bit taller, giving Kate a better view of her work.

"That's a pretty house," Kate said. "Can you tell me who lives in it?"

Henley began to fill in the roof, carefully moving the black crayon back and forth between the lines. "This was my house before."

"Before what?"

"Before I became a baby in Mommy's stomach." Henley said it casually, as if it was the most obvious thing in the world.

"And can you tell me about before?" Kate said. "Did you live with another mommy?"

Henley hesitated. Her crayon slowed on the paper. "Mommy didn't live with us," she said finally. "She only came to visit. I lived here with Nana and Poppa, and Sammie and Noodle."

"Noodle? Was that your dog?"

Henley gave her a brief scornful look. "Noodle was a *baby*," she said. "*Sammie* was a dog."

"What else can you tell me about your life before?" Kate asked. Henley was obviously attached to the idea that she'd been alive before, living with a different family in a different place. If she suspected that Kate was trying to invalidate or dismantle the fantasy, she might decompensate—get hysterical, or shut down completely. It was important to explore Henley's fantasy world on her terms and figure out how deep it went, where it intersected with things she might have heard or seen and where it dissolved into imagination. "Do you remember where your house was? Do you remember what town you lived in?"

Henley's face furrowed with concentration. She thought about it. "It was in a hill," she said after a minute.

"You mean *on* a hill," Emily cut in.

"No. It was *in* a hill," Henley insisted. She redoubled her coloring now, leaning on her crayon until it flaked smears of color. Kate flashed to what Mari had told her about the location of Becca's memorial. *Hillsdale,* she'd said. *Hillsdale, New York.* Kate pushed away the thought. Henley was just fantasizing. Inventing details, a mishmash of fairy-tale imagery and personal narrative.

"Which one was your room?" Kate asked her. "Can you point to it?"

She was expecting Henley to select one of the second-story windows. But she just shook her head. "You can't see my room from here," she said. "It was in the back. And it wasn't just my room; I shared with Noodle and Sammie."

Her answer was surprising. Kate would have expected that Henley's imagination would stretch no further than the facade she was always coloring.

"And what about here, in this house?" she asked. "Is your room in the front or in the back?"

Henley wriggled a bit in her seat. She looked to her mother uncertainly.

"Neither," Emily answered for her. "Henley's bedroom is next to mine. Her window overlooks the side of the house."

That might explain it, Kate thought. Side, back—it was the same thing, really. Henley couldn't see her bedroom window from the front of the house. It made sense that she would graft the fact into her imaginary life.

"Can you tell me more about your Nana and Poppa?" Kate said. "Do you remember their names?"

Henley gave her the same scornful look. "Nana and Poppa *are* their names," she said.

"All right, then. And what did they call you?" Henley stopped coloring. "Do you remember *your* name?"

Henley squirmed a little, as if the question had dislodged some discomfort. Then, abruptly, she let her crayon drop and pivoted on her chair to face Kate. "Can I show you my room?"

"Of course," Kate said. With her attention suddenly released from the page, Henley seemed lighter, happier, less encumbered, as if she'd freed herself from some gravitational pull. Henley slid off her chair and bounded at once for the stairs.

For the next hour, Kate sat on the floor of Henley's pink-and-yellow bedroom, a happy explosion of toys and books, stuffies and stickers, while Henley declared and presented various possessions. Kate felt as if she were on the receiving line for a whimsical ball, attended by dinosaurs and dolls, plush turtles and smart toys. Henley was lively and engaged, spinning from her bookshelves to the plastic bins under her bed and barely pausing in a monologue that landed on every object within sight.

"This is the mommy T. rex . . . You can tell she's the mommy because this T. rex is smaller, and that means he's the baby . . . And this is Phoebe. She used to have a backpack . . . Mom, have you seen Phoebe's backpack? The yellow backpack . . . she needs it for school . . . Oh, and this is Lambie. I've had Lambie since I was just a little baby . . ."

All in all, Henley seemed like a happy child. Confident, unselfconscious, properly attached to her mother and her small domain.

But Kate noticed a small dream catcher hanging above Henley's bed, dangling right above her pillow. She asked about it. Henley's smile quickly faded.

"That's for catching bad dreams," she said. She was carefully lining up her plastic dinosaurs on the rug, smallest to biggest. "But it doesn't work."

"Do you have a lot of bad dreams?" Kate asked.

Henley nodded.

"Do you want to talk about it?"

Henley shook her head. "I want to keep playing."

Kate decided to let it drop. Henley wasn't her patient. She wasn't here to treat her, or even to diagnose her. She was here to assess whether Henley and her mother truly believed that Henley could recall another lifetime. So far, the answer was yes.

Where that belief came from—what constellation of influences or fantasies had given birth to it, and to what extent it was damaging the little girl—was undoubtedly a question for Henley's therapist.

Henley quickly recovered from the momentary darkening of her mood. She turned away from the dinosaurs and plopped down in front of her dollhouse, a massive plastic mansion whose rooms were now the receiving end of an enormous quantity of creative detritus, from errant stickers and small plastic bears to mismatched dolls and even poor Phoebe's missing backpack. Henley quickly began to shuffle objects from room to room, situate dolls in different chairs, and rattle off another breathless stream of information.

"This is where Mr. Bear lives with Kitty. They're having a party today. That's why they're both dressed up in tutus . . ."

While a now-dressed Emily lingered in the doorway, watching, Kate scooted closer to Henley, momentarily marveling at the mysterious logic that housed a half-dressed Barbie doll, a plastic kitten, and an old stuffed bear in the same place. It was one of the reasons why she loved working with children.

"You can be Kitty, if you want. I'll be Mr. Bear . . ."

As Henley worked—either to tidy the house or further deconstruct it, depending on your point of view—Kate noticed that one room, a bedroom, had been defaced with strips of gaffing tape and a scrawl of black crayon. It looked as if Henley had tried to cover up a closet door, to scratch it out or tape it closed.

"What happened here?" Kate asked. When she lifted a hand to indicate the closet, Henley grabbed her wrist.

"Don't touch it," she said. "It's locked."

"How come?"

Henley looked troubled. "That's where we keep the Lady. She's a bad person. So we had to lock her up."

Kate felt a tickle on the back of her neck, as if a phantom hand had brushed against it.

"What Lady?" she asked, keeping her voice neutral.

Henley didn't answer. Studiously, she rearranged Mr. Bear on his armchair in the dining room, retrieved Kitty, and tucked her nicely into bed.

"Henley." Kate tried again. "Who's locked up inside the closet?"

When Henley looked at Kate, her eyes seemed to be the color of sky, big enough to fall inside and drown. She leaned forward, hugging her stomach, as if to keep in an explosive secret.

"My name was Becca," she whispered. "*You* remember." Then she sprang to her feet and ran out.

THEN

Kate. Kate. Wake up."

Becca's voice summoned Kate up from a dream—something about swimming. For a second, she was trapped in heavy reeds, drowning somewhere in the dark.

"Don't make me lick you."

Then she was awake, and Becca was leaning over her with a flashlight.

"What time is it?" The cabin was dark except for the sweep of several flashlights, which snagged on the other girls in their bunks. Britney and Christiana were still asleep, open mouthed on their pillows. Mariana was sitting up, yawning, fumbling for her glasses. Kate picked out Lennie in quick flashes: already dressed, toenails vivid in a cone of light as she shoved her feet into a pair of battered flip-flops.

"It's time for revenge." Becca held her flashlight to her chin so that shadows leaped up her face, deforming it into eerie hollows. She grinned. "Come on. Get up."

Kate's head was thick, as if a clutter of dreams were now battle-ramming behind her eyes, trying to get out. Of all the girls in Cabin Twelve, she was the heaviest sleeper. Frequently last to the mess hall in the morning, she was known for sneaking naps between activities—curling up in the boat shed, dozing off on the dock when she was supposed to be learning how to kayak.

Becca, on the other hand, was practically an insomniac. As a kid, she had suffered from night terrors. Kate was the only camper undisturbed by Becca's frequent thrashing above or below her—they'd alternated top and bottom bunk their first year, hoping it might help. Later on, Becca had begun sleepwalking. The summer after seventh grade, she had wandered down to the lake and wound up submerged to her waist before she woke up. The counselors had proposed tying her arm to the headrest to keep her in bed, or installing a lock on the cabin door so at least she wouldn't wander off into the woods, where coyotes howled about their kills at night.

But that summer, now fourteen years old and no longer a child, Becca had lit on a new solution: If she couldn't sleep, then neither would her best friends.

And there was no saying no to Becca. Not that summer. Not when she proposed a middle-of-the-day dance party, or wanted to compete to see who could do the biggest belly flop from the docks. Not when she wanted to sneak into the kitchen and stuff their pockets with chocolate chip cookies.

Not when she'd decided on middle-of-the-night revenge, either.

So Kate rolled out of her bunk and took the backpack that Becca held out to her. She could hear the faint rattle of purloined cans of whipped cream when she swung it over her shoulder. Now if they were caught, she would look like the thief.

Becca carried nothing but a flashlight and a smile.

Outside, it was muggy, still soupy-hot and full of fireflies. As usual, a rampage of insects was swarming the screen door, hurling themselves against the exterior light, hell-bent on self-immolation.

Idiots, *Kate thought.*

"This is stupid." Lennie's mass of black curls was coiled into a scrunchie, and her flip-flops made a whapping punctuation with every step. "If you really want to teach Natalie a lesson, I don't see how whipped cream is gonna help."

"I *don't want to teach Natalie a lesson.* We *want to teach her a lesson. One for all, remember?"*

It was too dark to make out Lennie's expression clearly, but Kate knew she was rolling her eyes. "I wasn't the one who called her a head case and started this whole thing in the first place."

"I call it like I see it," Becca said simply.

It was true. Kate had always envied that as much as she resented it. The first thing Becca had ever said to Kate was, What's wrong with your legs? *At the time, they were eight years old. Kate was wearing braces to correct a problem in her gait that rolled her weight onto her insoles and bowed her knees together to touch. She remembered the way her face had caught fire under Becca's gaze. She'd had a panicked desire to run.*

But Becca had just stood there, looking curiously at her. Are you crippled or something?

No, *Kate had said.* I'm not crippled.

Okay, good. *Becca had reached out and seized her hand.* Let's go look for candy.

It was like that with Becca. One second, she could knife you with a word or even a look; the next second, she would slip her hand in yours and pull you away toward some insane adventure. It was dizzying and awful and addictive.

Earlier in the summer, Becca had started feuding with the girls of Cabin Eight. In previous summers, they'd all been friendly, even though they were frequently pitted against one another on race days or during games of capture the flag. But in early July, one of the Cabin Eight girls had sprained her ankle during a game of kickball and accused Becca of deliberately shoving her. Two days later, Becca had found a dead frog in her shower caddy. Kate had tried to argue that it was a coincidence—Becca had left her shower caddy on the front porch overnight—but Becca insisted it was proof of deliberate retaliation. That weekend, Becca and a reluctant Kate had conspired to torpedo Cabin Eight's synchronized dance performance at the weekly talent show by replacing their chosen CD with a collection of meditation chants. Since then, the feud had escalated into an all-out war, a back-and-forth of cruel rumors, cold shoulders, and petty pranks.

"I'm just saying, whipped cream isn't gross. It's delicious."

"It's gross when it's all over your underwear."

Lennie and Becca were still arguing when they came within sight of the lake. Becca stopped, seizing hold of Kate's arm, letting out a short gasp.

"The moon," she said.

"What about it?" The moon was huge, centered almost perfectly above the black fringe of trees, casting an ivory reflection over the water.

"It's full," Becca said breathlessly. "That means the Gray Lady walks tonight."

Lennie snorted. But Mari lifted a hand to the cross around her neck. Her big glasses bounced back the moonlight, giving her a wide-eyed look.

"You haven't really seen her, have you, Becca?" Mariana asked. She was the youngest of the four—she'd turned thirteen only in June—and the sweetest.

"Kate saw her, too," Becca said. She turned to Kate, temporarily dazzling her with the flashlight. "Didn't you?"

Kate hesitated. She thought back to June, when the counselors had taken the campers on a night walk through the woods. They'd walked in silence down a narrow path carpeted in pine needles, hemmed in on all sides by the trees, supposedly listening for screech owls. Kate had been the very last in line, dropping behind even the counselor, Erica, when she needed to lace her shoes. She'd felt the darkness on her like a weight, the press of something about to happen.

Becca had been standing next to her when it happened—a sudden chill, the electric lift of sensation on the back of her neck. Someone was watching them.

Becca had felt it at the same time.

"Did you hear that?" Becca had seized Kate's arm, hauling her back to her feet. Kate suspected at the time that Becca was trying to scare her.

Then she'd heard it—a snap, a rustle, as if something had stirred in the trees.

"It's her," Becca had whispered breathlessly. "It's the Gray Lady."

Kate couldn't explain it, then or afterward—the sudden invasion of fear, the way her breath froze in her throat, the certainty that someone was there with them, waiting in the dark. She couldn't explain the silhouette that had seemed to materialize in the shadows—a face, horrible, grinning at them—

"Didn't you?" Becca prompted.

Kate took a deep breath. She hated disappointing Becca. But Mariana was agitating her necklace. She looked frightened.

"There's no such thing as ghosts," she said.

Becca looked at her pityingly. "You don't really believe that, do you?" she said.

SIX

Hillsdale, New York, was an old farming town, newly popular with weekenders and New York City expats. Kate could see their influence in the signs pointing the way to a new microbrewery, and in the disheveled fashion of the young people sipping lattes outside a café.

Slowing at the town's only stoplight, she saw a white church edge into view across the road, a long white spire with its finger in the wind. She squeezed her eyes shut and opened them again. There, on the lawn, was an old bronze cannon on wheels, right next to some kind of historical plaque.

She told herself it didn't mean anything. Emily was the one who'd suggested that the wheeled shape on the grass in Henley's drawings was a cannon. For all they knew, it was a wheelbarrow, or a misshapen rocking chair, or a poorly imagined cow. Besides, Hillsdale was only forty minutes from Henley's house. Out of the way, sure, but close to many of the area's prettiest hiking trails and a bike path popular with tourists. She might have driven by the church any number of times.

Still, as Kate navigated past it, she felt a crushing pressure on her chest. Henley's final words—*you remember*—still echoed in her mind. Henley had looked so strange when she said it—triumphant, almost, and subtly altered, as if a stranger had taken temporary hold of her face.

And those eyes . . . Becca's eyes had been blue like that, too. Electric, stormy, prone to sudden surges of anger.

It hadn't taken her long to find the location of Becca McGuire's grandparents' house. She'd pulled Ruth and Eddie's names from a fifteen-year-old announcement of Ruth's memorial service at St. Paul's Episcopal Church. Online records indicated that Eddie McGuire had moved down to Florida sometime in the past decade. Still, their old address was listed as a contact.

33 Green Farms Road.

She didn't know what she was hoping to find, only that she had to see it. Pulling up to the house—still painted a sallow yellow, with heavy black trim—she felt her hands slickening on the steering wheel. Her breath was painful in her chest, as if it was catching on something.

The tree house, where she had seen Mrs. Berger and Jenny Lin smoking cigarettes on the day of the service, was gone. But the flower beds bracketing the front path were the same. She sat there, gripping the steering wheel, torn between the idea that it was all a coincidence—that she was imagining significance, connections to her history, that might help absolve her of guilt—and the idea that it was all an elaborate, and very sick, practical joke. She couldn't shake the idea that she'd been somehow lured here, back to Stockbridge, back to camp, back to Becca McGuire and the night she'd died.

Kate had a sudden memory of the evening she'd spent, years ago, getting drunk with Evan Waller. The controversial head of Psychology at Columbia, Waller was popularly known as the "Pope's therapist"; he specialized in investigating cases of supposed demonic possession to rule out possible psychological causes before the Catholic church would approve an exorcism. She had seen him at a conference a few years earlier, and they had stayed up late after the day's sessions, drinking more than they should have.

Ninety-five percent of the time, he had told her, *it's just trauma. Trauma, personality disorders, psychosomatic symptoms. Ninety-five percent of the time, what these people need is medication.*

What about the other five percent? she'd asked. *What do they need?*

He had looked down, squinting into his glass, as if he might find an answer there.

A priest, he'd answered simply.

At the time, she'd thought that he was the one who had lost his mind.

Suddenly, the door of #33 opened, and a man came out onto the front porch. He raised a hand to his eyes, squinting down to the street, where Kate's car was idling. She realized, with a jolt, that she'd been parked for ten minutes.

Feeling suddenly exposed, she put the car in drive and wheeled a U-turn. She lifted a hand in what she hoped was a reassuring wave as she started back down the street. But the man stayed where he was, watching her.

Coincidence or not, she didn't like where this was heading.

It was time, she thought, to get the truth from Henley's mother.

~

The Wheel of Fortune pottery studio was housed in a converted grain shed, stranded in the middle of a grassy parking lot as if it had been deposited there by a hurricane. Inside, it was bright, airy, and surprisingly spacious, despite the high racks of metal shelving that displayed a litter of half-finished ceramics. Half a dozen students were bent over their wheels, working their hands in enormous lumps of clay as Emily paced between them, making gentle corrections to their fingers. Kate saw an older man punch down a lopsided bowl into a shapeless ball, and then winnow it again into form between his hands. The transformation took only seconds—from form to mass, and then to form again—giving the impression of the clay as a live thing, blooming and decaying under his touch.

Emily looked surprised, but not displeased, to see her.

"Don't tell me you came for a lesson," she said, smiling. "Our wheels are booked up through the afternoon."

Emily's warm greeting annoyed Kate. Her thoughts were ricocheting between objects, like insects responding to the promise of distant lanterns. "Is there somewhere we can talk?" She added pointedly, "In *private*?"

That snuffed the smile off Emily's face. "In my office," she said. She gave Kate a searching look. "Is everything okay?"

Kate just shook her head. Emily, disconcerted, made a quick apology to the class, and shuffled Kate off through the canyons of shelving and through a small door marked "Private." Inside, studio brochures, calendars, and bills were neatly sorted into stacks. The window opened onto a view of the gigantic kiln in the back.

Kate made no move to sit, even after Emily indicated a chair next to her desk. "How do you know about Becca McGuire?" she blurted out, even before Emily had settled into her seat. She scrutinized Emily's reaction, searching her face for recognition, guilt, or surprise.

Emily only looked confused. "Becca who?"

"Becca McGuire. She lived in Hillsdale until she disappeared from Camp Sauquamet. She was fourteen."

Still, Emily showed no reaction but bewilderment. "Hillsdale . . . that's in New York, isn't it?"

"It's forty minutes from here," Kate said. "It's right next to the Catamount ski resort."

Emily shrugged. "I don't ski," she said with a little smile. "You'd be surprised how small life gets in a place with so much space. I hardly ever cross the border, honestly. And I don't know Becca McGuire. Why?"

Kate dodged the question. She wasn't convinced that Emily was as oblivious as she seemed. "What year did you say you moved up here again?"

Emily rolled her eyes to the ceiling. "Let's see . . . my sister died twelve years ago this fall . . . I sold my apartment about six months later . . ." Emily shrugged. "Just over a decade, I think. Why?"

If Emily was telling the truth, she had arrived in the area at least fifteen years after Becca had vanished—swallowed up by the lake, presumed dead. Still, Emily might have heard about Becca's disappearance from her twin sister. Kate wondered, too, whether there had been recent news coverage of the cold case, whether Emily might have seen stories about Becca and the circumstances of her death without registering them consciously; she would have to check. In all these years, she had never googled Becca McGuire's case. She had no idea what strangers had dredged up about the twenty-six-year-old incident, how they'd construed what happened, and what stories people were telling online. For all she knew, other campers had written or blogged about it. Emily had insisted that Henley wasn't allowed to use the internet unsupervised, but Kate knew that didn't mean much. If Henley had even one friend with an older sibling or cousin, she might very well have access to a laptop and all the horror stories that the internet could invent.

She wondered what it had to say about the Gray Lady, and the tragic drowning of the fourteen-year-old Becca McGuire.

Now Emily was scrutinizing her. "I don't understand. What's so special about Becca McGuire?"

Kate looked away, letting her gaze settle on the window. The kiln outside was the wood-firing kind, made of brick, with a vaulted entryway large enough for a full-grown adult to pass through. It reminded Kate, uncomfortably, of the mysterious mausoleum on Fair Isle.

What's so special about Becca McGuire? There were so many ways she could have answered that question. *Becca was a leader. Becca could talk us into anything. Becca was electric. Compulsive. Beautiful. Cruel.*

Instead she said, "The summer Becca was fourteen, she snuck out of her bunk and took a canoe out to the graveyard on Fair Isle, in the middle of Lake Sauquamet. The same one I mentioned earlier."

Emily nodded. "I looked it up after you left."

"Becca was drinking. She'd somehow gotten her hands on a bottle of Fireball. No one knows how." Kate remembered Becca tilting the bottle toward her, saying *Go on. Drink. Don't be a bitch about it.* "She must have capsized. The lake is cold, and very deep in places. But near the island, there are lots of big rocks under the surface. The police think she may have hit her head when she went under." Kate heard her own voice as if from a distance, piped into someone else's words, as flat as newsprint.

Emily was still watching her, as if she suspected there was more to the story. "That's awful," she said. "I knew that there had been drownings, but . . ." She shook her head, as if to dislodge the idea of them. "I still don't understand why you think there's a connection."

"Because Henley has been drawing Becca's house for three years." As soon as Kate said the words out loud, she was aware of how crazy they sounded.

Emily was obviously stunned. "You can't be serious. You think that Henley—" She stopped, and took a breath. "You think that Henley is remembering this girl's life? You think that she remembers being Becca?"

"No. I don't," Kate said flatly. There was no point concealing the truth. "I don't actually believe in so-called 'past-life memories.' In all my time working in the psychiatric field, in all my research, I've never found a single compelling instance of recovered memories that couldn't be explained by normal psychological or behavioral mechanisms."

"But what about that boy in India?" Emily protested. "The boy who identified his old village, down to the details of his family—"

"India is a perfect example. In that country, claims about past lives proliferate. At the same time, reincarnation is broadly accepted by the culture. If past lives were real, why would they be *more* real in a country that believes in them?"

"Maybe more children speak up. Maybe more parents are inclined to listen." Emily's eyes flashed, and for a second, Kate detected the old attorney, prepared to argue the case.

"Maybe. Or maybe the cultural beliefs work on those children, and those parents, and incline them to look for meaning where there is none."

"You're the one who just said that Henley has been painting pictures of an actual, physical place," Emily said. "You're the one who thinks she's drawing from details of Becca McGuire's life."

"She is," Kate said. "But that doesn't mean she's *remembering* those details. So the question is—how does she know? Why does she think she used to be Becca McGuire? And how did she learn so many details of her life?"

For a moment, Emily fell silent. She stood up from her chair, suddenly agitated, pacing around the small space as if looking for an exit.

"I told you yesterday that I didn't understand Henley's reaction in the kitchen. I told you that she's normally very friendly with strangers," Emily said at last.

Kate was surprised by the apparent change of topic. She observed the way that Emily fretted with the items on her desk, avoiding eye contact as she shuffled papers together, realigned the pens fanned out in a cup.

"I told her she'd been very rude," Emily continued. "I explained you drove a long way to meet with her." Finally, Emily looked up. "She told me it wasn't the first time."

Kate didn't follow. "*What* wasn't the first time?"

"That you'd met." Now Emily held her gaze—firm, almost accusatory. Her eyes were so bright, they looked almost yellow, like a cat's. "She told me that you were there that night."

Kate felt her palms growing sticky, charged with static that touched her whole body through her spine. "What night?"

Emily sighed. "The night you all went to the graveyard," she said simply. She looked almost apologetic. "The night that she never came back."

THEN

I've got a surprise for you."

Becca slipped her arms around Kate from behind. She smelled like sunscreen, vanilla, and the lake. Kate had been sitting on the hill, half-heartedly practicing guitar, mostly hoping that Cameron might walk by and try to speak to her.

"You missed swim," Kate said, twisting around to look at Becca standing over her. With the sun almost directly behind her shoulders, Becca was no more than a dark outline.

"Stomachache. I went to the infirmary. You want your surprise, or not?" Becca was holding something behind her back. Kate wondered if this was her attempt to apologize for a fight they'd had that morning. It was small, stupid—they'd been arguing about the lyrics to a pop song—but Becca had called Kate a dumbass, and suggested that she might get checked for brain cancer. Kate wasn't sure whether the comment was a deliberate reference to her mother or not. But Kate hadn't spoken to her for the rest of the morning. She'd taken her breakfast tray to the end of the table and eaten in silence next to a sheepish-looking Cheryl, while Becca picked sausage off Mari's tray, and laughed extra loud at Lennie's jokes. She was relieved that Becca hadn't showed for lunch, but by free swim, she felt Becca's absence keenly, almost physically, like a phantom limb.

She could never stay angry at Becca for long.

Now she caved. "All right, let's see it."

"Close your eyes," Becca instructed in a singsong. Kate obeyed, and felt the whip of fabric across her face. When she opened her eyes, she saw a pair of red boxers in her lap.

Kate's thinking turned to sludge. She felt a rush of blood to her cheeks. "What are these?"

"Surprise!" Becca said, and burst into a peal of laughter.

Kate balled up the boxers immediately, stuffing them under one thigh, as if someone might see them over her shoulder. "Where did you get these?"

Becca plopped down next to her in the grass. "Where do you think?" She nudged Kate with an elbow. "Are you going to say thank you, or what?"

"You have to put them back." Kate felt as if the boxers were burning, smoldering under her bare thigh, sending up invisible smoke signals that would draw Cameron's attention.

"Why? He'll never notice they're missing. He has, like, twenty pairs. Trust me."

"You can't just go through other people's stuff," Kate said. "You can't just steal things."

"Clearly, I can. Security around this place pretty much sucks." Becca waited for Kate to smile at her joke. Then she rolled her eyes. "Come on, Kate. I thought it would be funny. I mean, this is what you want, right? To get in Cameron's pants?"

"You're insane." Kate felt a twin urge to laugh and to cry. What if Cameron found out Kate had his boxers? What would he think? "You're actually certifiable. Someone should lock you up."

"I'm not the one who's in love with a creep." Becca rolled onto her feet again and blew Kate a kiss. "You love me, by the way."

"Not always," Kate said.

Becca was already distancing herself up the hill. She lifted an arm to wave. "You're going to miss me when I'm gone," she shouted.

Kate didn't answer. At the time, she didn't think much of it at all.

SEVEN

The closest library was in West Stockbridge, a sweet brick building tucked among a sweep of elms. Kate felt her mood lift as soon as she spotted it. She'd always loved libraries. Libraries were places of order, of systems and knowledge, where facts were bound tidily inside of hardcovers, and history was indexed and preserved for consultation. When she was a child, her mother had been a volunteer at their local library in Richmond. Kate remembered a big room striped with columns of light, the susurration of quietly turned pages, the *shush* of the librarians' shoes on the carpet, and all those proud books parading spine-straight on endless shelves. She'd been so proud of getting her own library card; it was the first time she'd ever seen her own name printed, and her mother had even bought her a little wallet of her own so she could keep it safe.

That was before her mother got sick, and her life slowly ebbed into an interminable series of tests and treatments, drugs and radiation, hospital stays and, eventually, hospice.

In college, Kate had retreated to the UVA library to escape the dorm—where someone was always playing music so loudly it reverberated through the walls, or banging into her room to ask for a hair curler, or mascara, or an extra cigarette—and later, in graduate school, as an excuse to get away from her live-in boyfriend, Lars, who spent most of the day in his boxers, smoking weed, playing video games, and conspicuously avoiding his dissertation. She had always felt safe among all those books, marooned inside of an academic silence; a place where nothing was ever lost.

Inside, the West Stockbridge library was small and cheerful with the passage of parents and their small children—no doubt looking for as much distraction in the final stretch of summer as possible. Kate found a table by the window and opened her laptop.

Then, for the first time ever, she googled Becca McGuire's name.

She was shocked by the explosion of results. Very quickly, she saw that Becca's case had become linked in the annals of the internet to an area dubbed the "Berkshires Triangle," supposedly a stretch of land that encompassed both Lake Sauquamet and the state park just to its north known for mysterious disappearances and tragic events. Becca's name was one of a handful in a list of victims of the supposed triangle.

But Becca's case had attracted, by far, the most online conversation. It wasn't surprising. Becca had been young, and beautiful, and supposedly safe at camp; and more importantly, her body had never been recovered. In the months after Becca McGuire vanished from sleepaway camp in the middle of the night, the county newspaper, *The Berkshires Gazette*, had published twelve front-page articles about the search for her. Kate had forgotten that the police had been inclined, at least initially, to treat Becca as a runaway. She remembered little about the final days at camp—a stranglehold of dread and guilt and panic, a frantic mobilization to send the campers home early; the phone in administration shrilling constantly; police cars; strangers by the lake—and had felt nothing but relief when she left, disappearing back into the comfort of her home, and the ritual rhythms of her mother's illness, as if she'd surfaced from a bad dream.

Now she read about the organized search parties. Interviews with people who claimed to have spotted Becca. She made notes of everyone important or even superficially connected to the investigation of Becca's disappearance—from the county police detective, George Lyons, in charge of the case to Jenny Lin, who had spotted an empty canoe floating in the lake to Becca's next-door neighbors, who had provided an unflattering portrait of the fourteen-year-old, and not-so-subtly insinuated that she might simply have run off. Early reporting of the case hinted at the possibility that Becca might have snuck away with an older boyfriend, using epithets like "rebellious" and "overly friendly" to describe her. Several articles reported, incorrectly, that she was a foster child. Another one featured an interview with her eighth-grade teacher, who pointed out that Becca had been very popular, even with high school boys, and had once been busted at a school dance for having alcohol in a mouthwash container. A therapist who'd seen Becca only briefly—a Marcy Liebowitz—came forward to state that Becca had a history of self-harm. Kate thought of the day that Becca had touched her skin with a hot lighter, to mark her, and the look on Becca's face when she had turned it on her own skin. Peaceful, almost ecstatic.

Kate wondered what treatment she might have recommended for Becca, if she'd been in charge of her care. Nowadays, Becca might have been diagnosed with oppositional defiance disorder. Possibly, she would have qualified as a borderline personality. She wondered how much of her life, and her career, had been influenced by those early experiences with Becca, and her attempt to make sense of her troubled childhood friend. To make sure that for the rest of her life, she could parcel people into patterns, into circuitry that could be disrupted or rerouted. That could be fixed.

According to the official story, one of Becca's bunkmates had woken up in the middle of the night, only to discover that her bed was empty. Fearing that Becca was sleepwalking again, she had alerted several other girls to join her in a search. They'd taken flashlights and set out to scour the camp for her. They never thought of waking one of the counselors, and certainly not of alerting the camp director, Harriet Rowlings; the previous summer, Harriet had attempted to restrain Becca to her bunk every night.

Besides, they were fourteen years old. The oldest campers.

They thought they could handle it on their own.

Half an hour after setting out, one of the girls had noticed that the door to the boathouse was open, and one of the canoes was missing. At that point, Becca's friends assumed that she had made good on her promise to venture to the graveyard on Fair Isle before summer's end. They decided to go back to sleep.

It wasn't until dawn, when Becca still hadn't come back, that they woke up Harriet Rowlings. Harriet immediately telephoned the police, and roused the counselors for another search. It was Jenny Lin who spotted Becca's canoe drifting on the lake, empty of everything but a single oar and one of Becca's earrings. The prevailing theory was that Becca had snuck out of her bunk to visit Fair Isle, trying to verify the legend for herself. Something had gone wrong on the way there or back; and she had drowned in the dark water.

It was a good story. Convincing. Plausible. Everyone knew that Becca was a sleepwalker, and that she really had bucked against Harriet's suggestion to tie her down at night. Everyone knew, too, that Becca was obsessed with Fair Isle and the legend of the Gray Lady. She'd begged for a day trip out to the island. She'd threatened, only half jokingly, to try and swim there herself. She liked to spook the younger campers with stories about the old graveyard, and the curse that befell anyone who dared to stand beneath the stone angel at midnight. And Becca was headstrong, especially that last summer—often in trouble for being up after curfew, penalized for smoking cigarettes behind the boathouse, busted trying to shoplift beer from a convenience store on a Sunday outing to Great Barrington. Several times that summer, Harriet had threatened to send Becca home early. But she'd always begged and apologized and sniffled her way out of trouble. Kate suspected that Harriet knew all about Becca's mother, and simply felt sorry for her.

Kate continued reading, clicking away from the newspaper articles about Becca's disappearance and tunneling down into websites and Reddit threads still devoted to the mystery. Over the years, all sorts of fantastical theories and explanations had been bred online to explain the circumstances of Becca's disappearance. Online detectives had managed to unearth Becca's mother's record of arrests and court-ordered rehabilitation stays, and hypothesized that Becca had staged her own death, and run away to escape a chaotic childhood. They pointed to the fact that Becca's canoe had been found floating right-side up; surely, if she had capsized, the boat would have been turned over in the water. Other people speculated that a serial killer had been active in the area around the time that Becca McGuire slipped out of her bunk in the middle of the night and was never again seen alive. Still others suggested that the testimony of Becca's friends—minors who had never, thankfully, been named by the press—was suspicious.

> *My money's on Becca's "friends"*
> *They let her walk out in the middle of the night and claim they have no idea where she went??*
> *They DID know where she went. She went to Fair Isle, to look for the Gray Lady's grave.*
> *Oh, sure. Blame the dead girl.*
> *Convenient story, no? Did police for sure rule out their involvement?*
> *Not sure. But my guess is those girls were hiding something.*

Kate read the words over and over, until they tunneled her into a dark space in her memory. Until they drew her back to Fair Isle, wrapped with fog that looked among the branches like so many funeral shrouds.

Back and back, until she was standing again at the mausoleum, watching the mouth of its stone door widen into darkness.

She saw Becca's face, leaping into her flashlight.

Who's first?

She slammed her computer shut so abruptly that a librarian startled and gave her an injured look.

"Closing's in half an hour," he said.

She was surprised to realize that she'd been reading for almost two hours. She stood up, lightheaded, feeling suddenly exposed, violated, as if the guts of her childhood had been bled all over the internet. It wasn't a stretch to believe that Henley might have been exposed, might have absorbed the stories, and allowed them to affect her. The legend of the Gray Lady had only multiplied in the years since Becca's death, breeding new stories that crawled across the corners of chat rooms and message boards.

But even if Henley had heard about Becca's death—even if, in the intervening years since Becca went missing on the lake, the story had become layered into the legend of the Gray Lady, as was likely the case—she still didn't understand how Henley could possibly know that she, Kate, had been there that night. She didn't understand, either, how Henley could have known where Becca had lived, a biographical detail Kate hadn't seen referenced online.

Nonetheless, she imagined the house itself might have achieved some notoriety. Even if Emily Haskell claimed ignorance of the case, small-town mysteries did have a way of lingering and even growing more potent over time. And some of the other details that Henley had reported—of having a puppy named Sammie and sharing a room with a baby mysteriously nicknamed Noodle—Kate felt sure were simple inventions. Becca, she knew, had been an only child. It was one of the reasons, she suspected, that Becca had both struggled in her friendships and relied on them so desperately, why she'd demanded so many proofs of loyalty and love. She'd been testing her friends, probing their connection for weak spots, half terrified and half insistent that it would someday fall apart. Kate, the psychologist, understood this now. At the time, she had only the increasingly desperate sensation that nothing she did would ever be enough, that Becca would never stop demanding that she, Mari, and Lennie prove their friendship over and over.

Kate was sure there had never been another baby in Becca's household. She was almost positive, too, that Becca had never had a dog. She remembered that Becca had been extremely unsympathetic after Buster was run over by a car. She'd been impatient with Kate's grief, and at one point had even accused her of leveraging the bad news for sympathy and attention. *It's a* dog, she'd said. *Can't you just get another one?* And yet, a week later on one of their trips to town,

Becca had surprised Kate with a stuffed dog that she'd purchased from a CVS display. And for the rest of the summer, she'd insisted they keep a water bowl in the cabin, so that the little stuffed dog wouldn't get thirsty.

That was Becca: mercurial and imaginative, sometimes cruel, loyal and punitive, mesmerizing.

Before leaving the library, Kate found a number listed for an Eddie McGuire in Florida. She remembered that Becca's grandmother had died; she estimated that Eddie must be in his eighties. She doubted that he would be inclined to talk to a relative stranger about his long-dead granddaughter, but she dialed his number anyway as soon as she was in the parking lot, before she had time to second-guess the decision.

She was surprised when a woman answered the phone. Quickly, she reached for her notes in her car and found Becca's grandmother's name scrawled in one of the margins.

"Is this Ruth McGuire?" Kate asked.

The woman on the other end wheezed a laugh. "Ruth's gone," she said. "Passed away a good ten years ago. This is Tammy McGuire."

Kate shuffled furiously through her notes before it occurred to her—"Becca's mother?"

The sigh that came through the phone sounded like the rattle of wind through autumn leaves. "Yeah, that's right," she said. "I'm Becca's mother." Tammy's voice was edged with suspicion. "What's this about?"

Kate hesitated. It hadn't even occurred to her to try and reach out to Becca's mother. She knew little about Tammy—just that she'd been in and out of Becca's life intermittently until directly after her disappearance, when she'd suddenly presented in front of television cameras as a heartbroken mother to announce her multimillion-dollar lawsuit against the camp for negligence. Skeptics said she'd leveraged the tragedy for personal gain. If the rumors online were credible, the settlement Tammy had received from the camp didn't represent the end of her relationship with the legal system. Two years later, she'd been arrested for a third DUI and charged with possession.

But Kate knew drunks—she'd been one—and the woman at the other end of the line sounded sober. Maybe she'd changed.

"My name's Kate Willis. I'm a psychologist. I used to go to camp with Becca. We were . . . very close." The words almost strangled her on the way up. "We actually met once, at Becca's memorial."

"I barely remember it," Tammy said matter-of-factly. "I was all kinds of messed up back then. Still boozing."

So she was sober. Kate's confidence lifted a bit. Maybe Becca's death had changed her. That, or going to prison. So she plowed on. "I was hoping you could confirm a few details about Becca's early life."

In response, Kate heard the snick of a lighter, and then a long exhale, as Tammy pulled on a cigarette. "You doing one of those docuseries? 'Cause I already told another guy that we don't have nothing to say about what happened. We settled out and Becca's still gone. What's done is done."

"There's no documentary," Kate said.

"So what? You writing a book or something?"

"No book. This is more of a . . . personal project." She realized, as she said it, that it was true. No matter what Henley was ultimately experiencing, it had led her back to Becca, her memories of that night, and all the questions she had buried with them. "Becca and I used to write each other letters," she blurted. This was true; it had been long enough ago that email was in its infancy. "I've been sorting through them again. I found references to things I don't remember, parts of her life I must have forgotten. It sounds silly, but I was hoping you could help me fill in the gaps." The sun was beaming off her car, lighting her face on fire. She felt guilty about lying—felt guilty, too, for tossing those letters out when she was in high school, after she'd found them bundled in a shoebox underneath her bed. She remembered that she could hardly stand to look at Becca's loopy handwriting, the hearts bubbled in the margins. But she couldn't exactly tell Tammy the real reason she was calling.

"I can try," Tammy said. She sounded uncertain. "Truth is, Becca and I weren't close when she was little. I only had her until she was five.

After that, she went down to New York to be with my parents. I stayed up in Maine for a few years, going in and out of rehab. I could only come around to the house to visit when I was clean and sober."

Kate felt a pull of sympathy for her. Of all the burdens to carry, that must have been one of the heaviest: Tammy had not been a mother to her child when she was alive. Now she would never have the chance to apologize.

"Becca was an only child, wasn't she?" Kate asked.

That earned another wheezy laugh. "Oh yeah. Yeah, she was my one and only. I was pretty dumb, but I wasn't *that* dumb."

"And she never had a dog, did she?"

"She wrote about that in her letters, huh?" Tammy sighed. "Nah. Becca was always begging for a dog." Kate found herself relaxing. Clearly, Henley couldn't be remembering true details of Becca's early life; she was mixing up reported facts with her own fabrications. "But she was allergic. She was all kinds of allergic when she was a kid. Couldn't eat peanuts. Couldn't stand pollen. She had pretty bad asthma when she was little."

"Really?" Kate was momentarily stunned. She didn't remember Becca using an inhaler. Only that she'd often complained of headaches. She said it was her blue eyes, and claimed they made her more sensitive to light.

"Well, she was embarrassed about it. You remember how Becca was. Proud as hell. She didn't want anyone thinking she was weak."

Yes, that was it. Becca always had to be in charge. She always had to be in control. Kate couldn't remember that Becca had ever showed any vulnerability, even when they were little. The summer that they met, Kate had been viciously homesick, and spent the first few nights crying into her pillow, desperately regretting her decision, wishing she could tap her heels together and rematerialize in her familiar room, with her father cooking breakfast downstairs and her mother's blow-dryer sounding in the bathroom.

Becca couldn't understand why Kate was crying.

There's no point in snotting all over your pillow, she'd said, standing on her bunk to peer at Kate curiously. *You're not going home. So deal with it.*

That was how Becca was: brave, imperious, and pitiless. That was how she'd appeared to Kate, anyway.

"Becca begged and begged for a dog. She wouldn't quit asking. Finally, my dad got her one of those big stuffed animals—cost an arm and a leg, I couldn't believe it when he told me—just to shut her up."

Kate felt a funny itch at the base of her spine—a twinge, almost of fear. "Right," she said. "I remember she told me about that. What did she name it again? Sam? Samson? Sammie?"

"*Sammie.* That sounds right." Tammy rasped a laugh into the phone. "Oh man. She loved that thing. Dragged it around with her for years."

Even though she was standing in the sun, Kate felt her fingers go numb. It was as if someone had tipped ice water down her back. "What about Noodle?" she blurted out.

There was a short pause. "Noodle . . ." Tammy repeated thoughtfully. Kate felt a momentary relief—clearly, the name didn't mean anything to her. But then Tammy inhaled sharply. "Oh, you mean *Spaghetti.* Becca had a doll named Spaghetti. Or maybe Spaghetti was her stuffed cat? Hard to remember, now. My dad always spoiled her." Turning away from the phone, Tammy's voice grew partially muffled. "Hey dad, do you remember what Becca used to call that doll of hers? The one with the funny hair?"

Kate heard the creak of a male voice in the background. Then Tammy turned into the phone again, triumphant. "He doesn't remember. But I'm pretty sure it was Spaghetti . . ."

Kate felt the ground seesaw beneath her feet. The world seemed to flip, do a cartwheel, land her in the middle of an unfamiliar place. The trees, the daggers of sunlight between them—none of it looked right, none of it made sense.

"I'm sorry, Tammy." She had to get off the phone. She had to think. "I'm getting another call . . ."

"Oh, well. Happy to help. Feels good to talk with someone who knew her. She was a funny kid." Tammy sighed. For a beat, she was silent, and Kate fought against the urge to just hang up. Then Tammy said, "What did you say your name was again? Kate-something?"

"Kate Willis." For a second, Kate wildly regretted giving her full name. If Tammy somehow discovered that she'd been in Becca's bunk . . . that she was one of the girls who'd told police that Becca had paddled out to the island that night . . .

Then what? Tammy couldn't possibly know that Kate, Mari, and Lennie had actually been with her that night. She couldn't possibly know what they'd seen, what they'd done out there. She couldn't possibly know they'd lied. No one knew. Not even Steve.

No one . . . except for Henley.

"I'll ask Dad if he remembers you. Some days he's pretty out to lunch. But when he's sharp, you'd be surprised at how much he's got locked up in that attic of his."

"Don't worry about it," Kate said quickly. "I'm sure it's painful for him. Besides, I only knew her for a little while."

Tammy grunted. "Hey, listen. You weren't there the summer that Becca—the summer it happened, were you?"

"No." The lie was out of her mouth before she had consciously decided on it. "No, I wasn't there."

After she hung up, she sat in her car for a minute, letting the heat prick up sweat under her arms and neck, watching the trees across the road, shifting in the light wind. In the pattern of shadows, she saw faces form and dissolve. She ran a hand over the bald square of skin on her shoulder where Becca had once touched her with a hot lighter—a scar, she'd said, to mark their bond forever.

She'd been too afraid to say no. Too afraid to cry when the hot metal bit into her skin.

It wasn't the Gray Lady's hand she'd felt around her throat, pulling her down into the darkness. It was Becca's.

She should have known. Becca would never die so easy.

EIGHT

For the first time in a long time, Kate wanted a drink. On the drive back to the Airbnb, every bar and liquor store seemed to jump out at her, like a deer startling before headlights. She wished now that she hadn't quit A.A., that she could still ring up the woman who'd been her temporary sponsor, back before Kate decided the program wasn't for her.

All that God talk. Turning over the will to a higher power.

Kate didn't believe in stuff like that.

Still. She wished now that she had someone to talk to. For the first time in decades, she found herself missing Lennie. Lennie always had her head on her shoulders. Even as a kid, she'd been immovable, and the most inclined to stand up to Becca when she was in one of her cruel moods.

She white-knuckled the drive. Getting drunk wouldn't change what Emily had told her, what she truly believed about Henley, or what Henley herself believed. She would wake up hungover, and full of the same doubts.

The idea skittered into her awareness—was it possible, was it even remotely hypothetically possible that Henley was telling the truth?

As soon as she had the thought, she quickly shooed it back into darkness. She knew what Dr. Rushkin would say, of course. He would point to all the cases that the researchers at DOPS had assembled, indicating that reincarnation was a viable theory. He would point her to the work of

Ian Stevenson, the department's founder, on reincarnation specifically. He would flood her inbox with scholarly articles, proof of biographical facts recalled in detail that could not be known by any other means, proof of birthmarks that eerily corresponded to injuries sustained in another lifetime.

She'd seen it all before. To her, it was proof of only one thing: that humans could, and would, make meaning out of every coincidence.

She wondered now if she wasn't making the same mistake.

Steve FaceTimed her as she was pulling up beside the cottage. She leaped on the phone, as if it were a lifesaving device hurled out to her in the middle of the ocean.

"Check it out," Steve said without preamble. He was on-screen only for an instant before he angled his phone to a pan bubbling oil on the stove. "I'm making doughnuts."

"Doughnuts for dinner?" Kate said.

"It's every divorcé's right." Steve was back, grinning, before his face creased up with concern. "What's the matter? You look like you swallowed a mosquito."

"Thanks," Kate said sarcastically. She flipped on the cottage lights and was startled, almost alarmed, by the emptiness of the room. It was her dogs, she realized. She missed her dogs.

"I'm serious," Steve said. "Is everything okay?"

"I'm not sure," Kate answered honestly. She hesitated, debating whether to tell Steve the truth. Undoubtedly, the news would immediately make its way back to the rest of the team at DOPS. But she had to tell *someone*. "The six-year-old, Henley Haskell? She thinks she was *Becca McGuire* in a previous life."

"Becca . . . ?" Steve shook his head, confused.

"Becca McGuire. My old camp friend?"

Now his mouth fell open. "The one who drowned?"

"Right." Kate turned her face away from the camera; Steve could usually tell when she was lying.

"You're joking." Steve looked stricken. "Have you told Dr. Rushkin?"

"Not yet. I still haven't figured out how Henley knows so much about Becca. But it's a famous case around here, even today. Apparently, Massachusetts has its own Bermuda Triangle of sorts. And Camp Sauquamet is smack dab in the middle of it."

Steve only grunted. "So Henley *does* know a lot about Becca," he said. "You've verified that her memories are accurate?"

Kate hesitated again. She knew where Steve was going. "Some of them," she admitted, thinking back to her conversation with Tammy McGuire about Becca's beloved toys. It was hard to believe that the information would have found its way online, and from there to Henley.

"Is it possible that Henley is simply reporting the truth?" Steve said.

"Anything's possible," Kate said, although she didn't really believe it. "What's *likely* is that she heard about Becca from someone—or somewhere."

"So you think it's a hoax?"

"Not a hoax, exactly." So far, the Haskells hadn't sought any publicity. On the other hand, Becca's disappearance was a high-profile case, at least locally, which improved the likelihood that the Haskells might be planning to leverage Henley's claims for attention. "Have you heard of source amnesia?"

"Remind me. I forgot."

Kate rolled her eyes at the joke. "With cases of source amnesia, patients can recall informational content, but not *situational* context. In other words, they can know things, but they can't recall *how* they know them. So they might, for example, confuse a news report they saw on TV about a car crash with an actual memory from their own life; they'll start describing how they witnessed a ten-car pileup. They'll really believe it."

Steve squinted at her. "So you think—what?—that Henley has some form of source amnesia?"

"Well, we all have it to some extent. But I was using it as an *example*. There are conditions—underlying conditions, or psychological states—that cause people to confuse received information for their own memories. That's especially true of children."

Steve sighed. Kate could tell he was skeptical. "Maybe," he said. "Not everything can be explained by logic," he said.

"And *no* explanation is good without it," Kate responded.

Steve only shook his head and told her to be careful.

Of what, he didn't say.

She felt a little better, a little saner, after she'd eaten and showered. She reminded herself who she was now: a respected psychologist, a well-liked professor, an expert in exposing the delusions that kept people tethered to an imaginative past, or an invented present. She sat down with her computer to answer emails, but was instead drawn to the Facebook icon on her desktop. She rarely used social media—she found it too anxiety provoking to monitor what people were saying about her research—but impulsively, she opened Facebook and searched for Lennie's name in her messages. She turned up a decade-old request to connect, along with a message: Hey, girl! Been too long. Let's talk?

Kate felt a squeeze of guilt. She clicked over to Lennie's Facebook page, which was still active, and now served as a memorial wall dedicated to loving messages from her friends and family. She saw photos of Lennie crossing the finish line at the Boston Marathon, arms up, legs roped with muscle, sweaty and exhilarated and, Kate had no doubt, in record time. There were photos of Lennie with her nieces, and singing in a church choir, and sorting through bins at the annual church drive, waving cheerfully from a long line of volunteering congregants. It was funny. Kate didn't remember that Lennie had been religious. But apparently, Lennie had found Jesus, and Mari had found Reiki.

What had she, Kate, found in all these years? Liars. Damaged children. Parents who manipulated, deceived, and abused. Adults who saw demons inside of their children's tantrums, or invented stories of psychic abilities to leverage their kids to YouTube fame. The family at the heart of the case she'd consulted on most recently, this time in association with the FBI, had spent years staging seeming acts of supernatural violence in their house—doors that rattled on their own; symbols that appeared on the walls, written in blood—all for the benefit of the cameras. And yet their youngest child wasn't in on the joke; he grew up fearing that he was at the mercy of unseen forces that wanted to do him harm. He'd gone practically mute with terror by the time that authorities were alerted. The boy was drastically underweight and had developed all sorts of ritual habits to try and protect himself, including picking at his own skin to "clean" it.

It was like Kate had once said to Becca: *There's no such thing as ghosts.*

Only people, and the darkness that haunted them.

Kate shut down her computer, feeling troubled again, still trying to ignore the inner voice whispering to her of a nice cocktail and a long, dreamless sleep. Henley's drawings were still shut away in a desk drawer, where she had put them. Kate retrieved the remaining notes that Emily had compiled and brought them into bed—imagining, as she did, Steve lecturing her about creating separate spaces for work and relaxation—and propped herself up on her pillows.

Some of Emily's notes were brief, only a sentence or two.

> June 22, 2021
>
> Henley told me today that I'm much prettier than her "old mother." She said her old mother never wore dresses.

~

> November 9, 2022
>
> Henley saw a girl at the playground today wearing a bright-purple jacket. She got very excited. She told me that before she was my baby, she had a jacket just like that.

Some entries were more elaborate and had the reflective tone of a private journal.

~

March 11, 2021

Henley had a nightmare again. She woke up sobbing in the middle of the night, screaming that she couldn't breathe. She was so hysterical, she really was having trouble breathing. I tried to speak to her about bad dreams, to try and help her understand that it wasn't real, but that only made things worse. I don't understand. During the day she seems happy. She loves day care. She's made lots of friends. But the nightmares are getting worse, and they're always the same. She's alone somewhere, trapped, and she can't breathe, and she can't escape. Recently, she won't even let me close the door when I take her in to use the potty. She's afraid of getting trapped. She told me that had happened to her once. I have no idea what she means.

~

March 13, 2023

We heard today that the Richardsons had to put their dog, Budgie, to sleep. Henley was very sad. She remembers Budgie from when we dog-sat him two summers ago, which surprised me. Of course, they got very close in those ten days. She was so gentle with him, and he with her. She insisted we move the dog bed to her room, and she spent hours on the floor, petting his long fur.

I told her that Budgie went peacefully, that he didn't feel any pain. She got very agitated. She told me she didn't believe me. She said that *dying hurts.*

~

Kate underlined the words *dying hurts* without intending to. She wondered whether it was true.

After she turned out the lights, she lay awake for a long time, listening to the gasp of wind through the trees, and the distant hysteria of coyotes. She seemed to imagine that she heard, too, the echo of Becca's voice.

Let me out. Let me out, or I swear to God, you'll regret it!

She recalled the whip-slap of leaves as she, Lennie, and Mari had fled through the woods, distancing themselves from her voice. How long had they left Becca alone? Twenty minutes? Thirty? Long enough to feel regret scratch up their spines—Becca would surely punish them later.

Long enough to scare themselves half to death.

Long enough to come face-to-face with the Gray Lady.

She set the notes aside, then got up to turn on the bathroom light, leaving the door cracked a bit, so that a ring of illumination touched the objects around it.

She didn't feel like sleeping in the dark. Not tonight.

Not when she could still hear Becca, screaming from the past.

THEN

On bonfire nights, the counselors rang the old bell, and the campers went spilling out of the mess hall and down the hill, jostling onto the narrow path that carved through the trees and over to the firepit. It was a race, a competition to get a good seat—not too close to the blaze, but not too far, either. The oldest campers laid claim to the logs ringed around the pit—a benefit of age and patience that was universally understood, and rigorously enforced, without ever being made explicit. The younger campers sat cross-legged in the grass, or crowded in around the circle, leaning on their friends.

Sometimes a counselor brought down the bongo drums and a guitar, to lead the campers in round after round of camp song. Sometimes, the campers took turns roasting s'mores over the pit, scavenging for sticks to skewer their marshmallows and elbowing for space by the fire. Sometimes, they swapped ghost stories: of an escaped convict from a long-ago-dismantled insane asylum still prowling the woods; of the ghost of a drowned girl who would appear to cars on the roads late at night, begging for a ride back to the graveyard.

But every year, Harriet Rowlings told the story of Fair Isle, and the legend of the Gray Lady's curse.

"A hundred and fifty years ago," it began. "Fair Isle had no name, and nothing on it but sycamore trees and screech owls."

Kate and Becca pressed their thighs together, a wordless communication of excitement, like squeezing hands. Becca's eyes picked up the sparks from the fire, her face alive in the reflected glow. Next to them, Mari was worrying her necklace, teasing the cross on its chain. Lennie picked idly at a scab on her knee, her hair pinioned underneath a bandanna.

"The trouble started with a young woman," Harriet said.

Cameron said, "It usually does," and everyone laughed. Kate examined him from across the circle. He had a large chin, but excellent hands that were usually in motion—drumming his thighs, or seeking to unravel the cuff of his jeans.

He looked up, caught her staring, and winked. She looked away quickly.

"This was just after the civil war. Katherine Gray had lost her father and two brothers. Her mother had died early. So she was an orphan—all alone in the world."

The wind poked sparks out of the flames, coaxing plumes of smoke down toward the lake.

"Fortunately, she had plenty of marriage proposals. This woman was known to be loyal, and kindhearted. And they say she was so beautiful, she stopped traffic whenever she left the house."

"You mean horse traffic," Lennie said. That got another laugh. "It was a hundred and fifty years ago, right?"

Harriet barely lost a beat. "That's right. She brought horse traffic to an absolute stop. All of the men in their carriages would stop and stare. Some of them even fell at her feet, begging her to marry them. But Katherine Gray had a problem. See, she didn't love any of these men. And she was secretly engaged already."

Becca and Kate exchanged a smile. Last summer, it had been Mary Gray; Harriet never told the story exactly the same way twice. It didn't matter. This was the place she was happiest: here, by the fire, with the flames leaning toward the lake and the ash drifting like upward-falling snow toward a sky freckled with stars; knee to knee, thigh to thigh, hand to hand with her best friend. Legs bare, feet dirty, wrist looped with bracelets they'd already swapped and sworn to wear all summer.

"Katherine Gray had fallen in love with a soldier during the war. The man was wealthy, the son of a timber baron, and the woods they'd cleared for roads now stretch from here to California." Harriet's face looked in the firelight as if it, too, had been carved from wood, ridged and creviced from years of sunlight, grooved with the impression of old laughter. But she was beautiful, in a way. "He promised Katherine they'd settle down right here in Massachusetts just as soon as he was done with traveling. He even gave her a ring, which she wore on a necklace every day. What he didn't tell her was this: He was already married."

"Cheater!" all the older campers chorused together. That was part of the story, too.

"That's right. He was a cheater, and a liar. And poor Katherine Gray loved him like the moon loves the sun. And who knows? Maybe he loved her, too, at least at the beginning. But soon Katherine learned she was pregnant, and her boyfriend decided to act.

"What they needed, he told her, was a home—a beautiful home, where they could live after they were married. When he purchased an island in the center of Sauquamet Lake, he promised to build her a mansion, and a private dock so that they could boat back and forth. Katherine wasn't sure she wanted to live on the island. She'd never learned how to swim. But she was so overjoyed that she would, at last, get to marry her love, she agreed to move there to be with him.

"Trees went down. The mansion went up. Soon moving day came, and Katherine packed up all her belongings and set out in her fiancé's boat across the lake.

"If Katherine had been paying attention, she might have wondered why he had left space for a graveyard. She might have wondered about the wood, which was stacked up for twenty winters. She might have wondered why her fiancé came with only a single trunk, and a vague story about returning for the rest of his belongings soon.

"But she didn't wonder. She wasn't paying attention. She was about to have a baby. And she was in love."

Kate snuck a glance at Cameron, trying to read the expression on his face. She wondered if he'd ever been in love. She wondered if he could ever be in love with her.

"For one week, Katherine stayed with her love on the island. It was the happiest week of her life. At the end of seven days, Katherine's fiancé surprised her with a beautiful wedding gown. He told her that he was returning to shore to find a priest, and that they would be married tomorrow, right on that island. So he kissed her goodbye, and set out in the rowboat across the lake.

"Katherine put on her dress and waited."

Even though the fire was hot, clawing greedily around the firepit, Kate felt a comfortable shiver in her spine. This was the part she liked best.

"All the next day, she waited for her lover to return. And the next day. And the day after that. She waited in that wedding dress as the days turned into weeks, as the summer faded into autumn, and her dress grew soiled with dirt and ash from the fires she raked up every morning . . ."

"What about the baby?" one of the younger campers asked. She had big moon eyes and pigtails, and she scuffled her feet anxiously in the dirt.

Harriet had evidently forgotten about the baby. "Stillborn," she said, and the pigtailed camper made a circle with her mouth. "Buried somewhere on the island—while still Katherine waited for her vanished lover. She waited until the lake froze over in wintertime, and finally she set off, calling for her lover in the woods and listening for the sound of his return.

"And they say that ever since then, the Gray Lady has haunted the island. In the wintertime, she crosses over the frozen lake to roam these woods, where you can still hear her calling her lover's name. In the summertime, she paces endlessly along the shore of Fair Isle. And if you get too close . . ."

Harriet paused, eyeing the campers triumphantly. Kate held her breath. The fire cracked, sending a plume of embers into the dark.

"Well, if you get too close, they say she'll pull you down into the depths of the lake, where she'll keep you forever prisoner, forever doomed to roam the island as a spirit."

There was a long moment of silence, except for the groaning of the wood where it came apart in flame. Kate thought of Katherine Gray, wearing a wedding dress ruined by time, waiting interminably for relief that would never come. She thought of the woods, with their press of darkness, and strange shadows that lunged at you when you weren't paying attention. She thought of the mysterious island, with its ruin of stone structures, where a mansion might once have been laid as a prison.

"What about the graveyard?" Becca blurted out. "If she was all alone, who buried her?"

"Oh! Thank you, Becca. I forgot that part of the story." Harriet had moved as if to stand up; now she settled down again. Kate was glad. She wasn't ready for the walk back to the cabins in the dark. Not yet. "As I said, years went by. And no one knew about the house built on the island in the middle of the lake. But as the decades passed, this area got built up—with new towns, new roads, and new resorts in the mountains. At some point, the locals became curious about the mansion they'd spotted in the trees. Sometimes they even saw smoke coming from the chimney. But they never saw anyone coming or going from the dock. There was no boat to bring anyone back to shore. So one day, they held a meeting, and decided to investigate.

"By then, it had been a long time since they'd seen smoke from a chimney. When they arrived at the island, they found the house unlocked. Inside, the rooms were encased in spiderwebs, so thick they looked almost like a covering of snow. In the dining room, the table was still set for two people.

"And upstairs? They found Katherine Gray, by now little more than a skeleton, still wearing her wedding dress, still sitting by the window, looking out onto the lake, and watching."

That was it. The story was over. The campers stirred. Giggles went around like a wind. Harriet stood up with several of the other counselors. The circle began to fracture, breaking apart into knots of separate conversation. Harriet clapped her hands, trying to restore order. They would follow Jenny Lin, beaming a flashlight up at the sky like a beacon to orient them, back to the cabins.

"Two by two," she reminded everyone. On the wood trails, they must always go two by two.

Lennie, Mari, Becca, and Kate hung back, waiting for the counselors to shunt the fluid body of younger campers into a line.

"She should've just gotten a new boyfriend." Lennie stood up, smacking dirt from the seat of her jeans.

"I hate that story. It's awful," Mari said. "But it's not really true, is it?"

"No way," Lennie said. "No one's that dumb."

"Well, someone lived out there. There are people buried on that island for sure," Becca said.

"Exactly. People. Plural." Lennie yawned. "If she lived all alone out there, then what are all the graves for?"

"I don't know," Becca said. She flashed a smile. "But don't you want to find out?"

Kate didn't think she was serious. It was summertime. They had another four weeks together, time that laid like a slab over everything that frightened or worried her. And she wasn't scared of the Gray Lady. She didn't believe in the Gray Lady. Not really.

Not when she had her friends beside her, arguing good-naturedly, and Becca's hand to hold as they traced their way home in the dark.

NINE

Kate spent a sleepless night, consumed with paranoid thoughts of blackmail, or some form of psychological revenge in which she, Kate, was the primary target. Her anxieties kept weaving in and out of shallow dreams in which Becca appeared to her, wearing the long flowing robes of the Gray Lady, her skin chewed up by insects and her long hair snarled with dirt.

In the morning, she was back at Mari's house. Mari answered the door with her hair still wet from the shower, and one of their old camp yearbooks braced against her chest. She turned it over carefully, with both hands, as if reluctant to release it.

"You'll take good care of it?" she asked. "There's a great picture of Lennie in there."

"I promise," Kate said, easing it out of her hands.

"This one's from summer six," she told Kate. "I never got one that last summer. I'm not sure Harriet ever mailed them out. There was all that bad press . . . And Becca's parents were talking about a lawsuit, remember? I wouldn't be surprised if she just forgot."

Kate did know about the lawsuit; Tammy had even made an oblique reference to it in their call. But it had never occurred to her to wonder about the impact of Becca's death on Harriet Rowlings, the longtime camp director. She'd assumed, vaguely, that it must have contributed to the decision to shut down camp operations only a few years later. She'd received the news by mail, in one of the old camp newsletters—the final one, as it turned out—that had been distributed throughout the year to all camp alums and donors. She remembered feeling sick, and then ashamed, and stuffing the newsletter to the very bottom of the trash, as if it were proof of something.

To her, Harriet and the camp had been synonymous; one couldn't exist without the other. Now Kate wondered what had happened to her, how she'd recovered after the collapse of her life's work.

Mari was, blessedly, hurrying to get ready for her first lesson ("Third grader, guitar. I'm barely any better than he is. You used to play guitar, didn't you? You signed up to do sessions with that counselor we all went so crazy over—Cameron, wasn't it?"). Kate left with a promise to return the yearbook as soon as possible, after neatly deflecting another invitation for dinner. She didn't know why seeing Mari gave her an airless, suffocated feeling, like the constant pressure of her cheerfulness was driving all the oxygen from her lungs.

The closest Salvation Army was forty-five minutes away. Kate spent a good hour selecting an assortment of items to present to Henley alongside the yearbook: an old puzzle, undoubtedly missing some of its pieces; several books, including a vintage copy of *Goodnight Moon*; a stuffed panda bear; even an old Slinky. She wanted to see whether Henley would respond differently to the camp yearbook than she would to the other objects. This would help her ascertain, too, how susceptible Henley was to the power of suggestion. She couldn't explain, yet, how Henley knew so much about Becca's former life.

All she knew was that *someone* had told Henley a story, until Henley began confusing it for her own.

But the experiment was a failure, at least from Kate's point of view. Henley showed only limited interest in the items Kate unpacked in her living room. But as soon as Kate removed the camp yearbook from her bag, she stiffened, as if run through with a current.

"You found it," she said in a voice full of awe. She reached out gently and began stroking the cover, the way Kate had observed her do with the cat, currently draped over the back of the couch. Then, suddenly, she launched to her feet. "Mommy! Mommy! Look!"

Emily emerged from the kitchen, where she had been prepping Henley's lunch, with a dish towel in her hands. "What's that, honeybug?" Emily said.

Henley faltered. She seemed uncertain. She looked down, still stroking the cover, perhaps trying to work out its story for herself.

"Can we look at the pictures together?" Kate suggested. Henley nodded silently, returning to sit next to Kate on the couch. Her mood had changed in a moment. Now she seemed grave.

Perhaps sensing the shift, Emily took a seat on the chair in the corner, folding her dish towel in her lap. Kate felt a strange sense of unreality as Henley opened the yearbook, as if she were seeing the scene from outside, as if they were all actors on a theater stage. The late morning sun fell in great slabs through the living room windows. The pages whispered as Henley turned through them, one by one, pausing on certain photographs to point.

"I liked to go here." She had a finger on a picture of the administrative cabin, where the girls had fetched their mail, along with the care packages that arrived periodically from their families. "But I didn't like the woods. It was dark." Now she indicated a picture of three campers grinning at the entrance to the south trail, which they had walked to reach the firepit. It had, in fact, been dark along the trail, even during the day; the overhang of pine crowded out the sunlight, keeping it always in an artificial cool that had reminded Kate uncomfortably of church. Emily tipped forward in her chair, spellbound. Kate felt a growing nausea. She knew they would soon reach a picture of Becca on the dock, standing in a tight cluster of her best friends. She had seen it earlier and felt a hard pull in her chest, as if someone had knocked the wind from her lungs. Becca had been so beautiful.

And so, so young.

She had the urge to reach out and slam the yearbook closed. To backpedal all the way back to Virginia. To forget the Haskells even existed, to close the door on them, like she'd closed the door on her memories of that summer.

Instead, she waited. Page by page, the tension gathered. She could feel it like an overhanging presence in the room. Like something waiting to fall.

"Look closely," she said. She sounded calmer than she felt. "Tell me if you see anyone familiar."

Henley's little forehead furrowed in concentration. Spotting a photograph of Ferdinand, the longtime maintenance director, she gave a reflexive kick of her feet.

"This man was mean to me," she said. "He got me in trouble."

Kate said nothing. She knew that Becca had disliked Ferdinand; she thought that Ferdinand might have busted her once with a pack of cigarettes that Becca had pilfered from his belongings. She found herself searching for her recollection of that day—she remembered standing behind the boathouse with Lennie and Becca, swapping the cigarette between them when they heard Ferdinand shout—and realized that on some level, she *did* believe that Henley had access to Becca's real memories.

Henley turned the page again. There it was: the photograph of Becca, waving, standing with Kate, Lennie, and Mari on the dock. They must have been going boating. They were all wearing life jackets over their swimsuits. But when Kate reached back for a memory of that day, she found nothing but air and dark space.

Henley's fingers groped for Becca's face on the page. "That's me," she said. Her fingers inched over to land on Kate's picture. "And that's you."

Emily brought her hands to her mouth. "Oh my God." Her eyes were bright; Kate wondered if she was going to cry.

Kate felt nothing. No fear, no surprise. Just a numbing cold that traveled through her blood and froze her thinking. "Henley—are you sure?"

Henley nodded somberly. Emily eased off her chair, coming to her knees beside her daughter. "Where? Can you show me?" When Henley pointed, Emily looked to Kate, as if for confirmation.

"That's Becca McGuire," Kate said. The name tasted awkward in her mouth, like a misplaced bone. "The one I told you about." She found herself thinking, savagely, that Emily might have rushed home to google Becca's picture, preparing Henley to identify her later. But that wouldn't explain how Henley knew about Becca's favorite toys, or to identify camp landmarks.

Emily kept staring at Becca's picture, her fingers webbed over her mouth, her eyes wide with horror. "You said—you said she drowned?" she asked in a hoarse whisper.

Before Kate could respond, Henley cut in. "I didn't drown." Henley lashed out with her feet again, this time catching the underside of the coffee table and sending a crack through the glass. At the same time, the kitchen fire alarm began wailing. The pungent smell of burning drifted into the living room on curls of smoke.

"Shit." Emily launched to her feet. Then: "Henley, you didn't hear that."

She ducked into the kitchen.

"I didn't drown," Henley repeated, when her mother was gone. She shoved the yearbook off her lap, sending it thudding to the floor, and hunched back against the couch with her arms folded. Sulky, now. Distancing herself from the damage to the coffee table, and the punishment she might receive.

Kate took a deep, steadying breath. She reminded herself that Henley wasn't Becca. That reincarnation was impossible. That restless spirits did not return to infect the living. Still, a strange feeling began to walk up the back of her neck. She realized she was searching for Becca on Henley's face, looking for signs of her. "Okay, then. Do you remember how you died?"

Henley twisted her fingers in her lap. She looked miserable. "Someone hurt me," she said. "I couldn't breathe."

Kate imagined she could hear the undertow of Becca's voice. Afraid, alone. Begging to be let out. "Henley, this is important," she said. "Do you remember who hurt you?"

Henley looked up at her sullenly. "*You* did," she said. All of Kate's training, all her education, her academic work, the years of distanced research and careful diagnoses, seemed to vanish. Kate fell back through a veil of years into her adolescent self. She was looking at Becca, looking at her in Henley's eyes. "You locked me in a dark place with the bad woman. The Gray Lady. And then she took me away."

THEN

It was Kate's favorite time of day: the hour before dinner, when the girls filtered in slowly from various activities, or came plodding into the cabin freshly showered, wrapped in voluminous towels that would slowly drape the wooden roof beams, letting off the exhalation of raspberry body wash and mint soap.

The windows were open to the evening, and spiders spun quietly in the corners. Her daily chores—to sweep the porch of grass shavings and clods of dirt, and collect laundry from the lines clipped behind the cabin—were done. The sky was full of vibrant clouds, tinged faintly pink, like long fingers of cotton candy.

Mari was sitting cross-legged on her bunk bed, practicing clarinet. Cheryl, the oldest girl in the cabin, was popping pimples by the light of the window. Poor Cheryl had suffered an explosion of acne since arriving, and went to bed with her face caked beneath astringents and cleansers and topical medications that made her skin peel off in heavy flakes, and seemed to inflame her acne even further.

She heard the pitch of voices nearing the cabin. A second later, Becca and Lennie banged through the door, laughing about something. Kate should have felt relieved—Lennie and Becca had been at each other's throats only that morning, and giving each other the silent treatment at lunch—but instead she felt a spike of jealousy, and even paranoia.

She wondered what was so funny.

"It smells like an armpit in here," Becca announced. Mari faltered a note. Kate tensed. It didn't, of course. It smelled like mowed grass and old wood, like dew and like the hair products that Mari painstakingly sleeked

over her curls after a shower. But the announcement was a warning sign, a signal of Becca's mood, which blew into the quiet of the late afternoon like a sluice of cold wind. Cheryl quickly scuttled away from the window, pocketing her handheld mirror, and ducking her head to conceal the bits of toilet paper clinging to the open sores on her face. Mari continued on gamely, eyes trained on the sheet music open in her lap.

Instinctively, Kate shucked her journal under her pillow.

A mistake. Becca turned to her, attracted by the sudden motion. "What's so secret?" she asked, sidling casually up to the bunk, looking mischievous. She let her fingers run along the headboard, then down toward Kate's pillow.

Kate thumped down a hand to keep it in place. "Don't," she said.

Becca rolled her eyes. "Let me guess. You're writing about Cameron."

Kate felt blood leap to her face. She had, in fact, been writing about Cameron. Earlier that afternoon, she'd intersected him on the trail that led out to the archery field. He'd been exiting the arts and crafts cabin with Rachel, one of the head counselors, when he spotted her.

"KW!" *he'd shouted. He always called her by her initials, to distinguish her from half a dozen other Kates.* "We missed you in group today."

We missed you in group today. *She'd been turning these words around and around in her head for hours, spinning them like a thread until their fabric was large enough to touch her whole body, until she felt warm and full. Ever since Becca had informed her that her crush on Cameron was so obvious that she might as well announce it over the loudspeakers, she'd been terrified to get close to him. She couldn't face the guitar lessons she'd signed up for so eagerly a few weeks earlier, when he would be sitting so close that their knees sometimes touched and he'd reach out to correct her finger placement on the strings. Other than Kate and Becca, only four other campers had signed up for afternoon guitar over water-skiing, sailing, or one of the other water sports.*

She couldn't get over the idea that she was wearing her feelings all over, inhabiting them like a second skin. She couldn't bear the idea that he might find out; she couldn't bear the idea that he wouldn't.

She was fourteen, and had been kissed only once—by Kyle Growsky, at an eighth grade dance, after they'd both taken a sip of the warm purloined beer that Kyle's friend Pete had managed to smuggle in under his bike seat. It had been sloppy and confused and extremely embarrassing, especially when he prodded hopefully at her nonexistent breasts under her dress, as if willing them to grow into his hand. Kyle Growsky, she'd decided then, was a nothing.

That summer, Kate believed she had fallen in love.

Becca wouldn't give it up. She pivoted toward the other girls—her audience—pretending to swoon and adopting a breathy high-pitched voice that sounded nothing like Kate's. "Dear Diary," she said, "today I found a piece of lint from Cameron's sweatshirt. It's so beautiful . . ."

"Stop it." Kate could feel her pulse beating through her neck, carrying a rush of heat so strong she felt dizzy.

"Maybe tomorrow I'll find some of his nose hair . . . or even some earwax . . ."

Kate balled her hands into fists, squeezing her fingernails into her palms until she felt bright starbursts of pain. She had been collecting little things of Cameron's—a guitar pick he'd misplaced during one of their lessons, a pen cap he'd been chewing during morning assembly and later discarded with his breakfast tray. She'd been sure that no one had seen her, that no one knew about the items she'd been stashing in a tampon box. But somehow, Becca knew. Becca knew everything. She noticed everything.

There was no escaping Becca.

"I said shut up." The pressure in Kate's head at last exploded into a shout. Mari broke off from her practice. Lennie just stared at Kate open mouthed. "Just shut the fuck up about Cameron."

Even Becca was taken aback. For a moment she stood there, frozen, staring at Kate as if she didn't recognize her. Kate thought she might even apologize.

But finally she just said, "Jesus. It was a joke. What crawled up your ass and died there?"

Mari mumbled something. She was always after the rest of them to stop using the Lord's name in vain. Becca rounded on her.

"What was that, Mari? I didn't hear you."

"Leave her alone, Becca," Lennie said warningly. Becca ignored her.

"Just go back to tongue-fucking your boyfriend," Becca said.

Instantly, Mari's eyes began to well up. She was so sensitive. "I'm practicing," she said. "For the talent show on Friday . . ."

"Please." Becca reached out and snatched the clarinet, ignoring Mari's protests. She held up the instrument with two fingers, as if it were a dead mouse. "Be honest. Do you get busy with this thing when the rest of us are sleeping?"

"No." Mari looked horrified. Kate felt a gut-wrench of sympathy for her. Mari didn't even use tampons. She didn't even like to talk about tampons.

"Becca." Lennie's voice was a warning. But Becca was gone—over the edge of her mood, down in the dark place that consumed her more and more.

"What? There's nothing wrong with it. If Mari wants to masturbate with a clarinet in her free time—"

"Stop it!" Mari launched to her feet. Her chest was heaving, her voice shrill, almost hysterical. "I do not—I never—just stop it!" She grabbed the clarinet from a smirking Becca and shoved past her, hurtling outside. The door banged shut against a long moment of silence.

Lennie turned to Becca coldly. "You," she said, "are a bitch." Then she shoved outside after Mari.

For a moment, Becca looked uncertain. Small, standing alone in the center of the room. Then she forced a laugh. "God, since when did everyone get so sensitive?" She turned to Kate, seeking an ally, trying to include her in the joke. "We used to be fun."

Kate felt lightheaded, dizzy with rage and something close to hatred. When she opened her fists, small, angry half moons scored her palms where she'd dug her nails into them.

"You'd better be careful," she said. "Or else—"

"Or else what?" Becca dropped the act. It was like a veil fell down—suddenly her eyes were sparking, her face an open taunt, full of nothing but contempt. "Or else what, Kate?"

The question hung there between them on a long rope of tension, swinging at some locked door in the back of Kate's mind.

What, Kate?

Or else what?

TEN

Steve feigned exasperation when Kate asked if he could handle the dogs for another week. Kate knew better than to buy it; both Bo and Moshi slept in Steve's bed, got Christmas and birthday presents from their "father," and were allowed to kiss his mouth.

But he got quiet when she told him about her reasons for staying in Massachusetts.

"Have you called Rushkin yet?" Steve's question was a reprimand. He knew that she hadn't, and he knew what Marc Rushkin would say: If Henley's memories were credible, and she showed no signs of psychopathy, Kate should pass the referral back to the Division of Perceptual Studies, for inclusion in one of their official studies.

"Not yet," Kate said. "I just want a little more time."

"Do you think that's a good idea?" He sounded skeptical. "You're pretty biased."

"Of course I'm biased," Kate snapped. "Henley believes she was my best friend in a past life. My *bias* is the whole point."

"Wait a second—you think this is about *you*?"

"Maybe," Kate said. She felt a little wild, a little out of control. "It's hardly a coincidence. Maybe someone *wanted* me to come back."

In the short silence that followed, Kate felt suddenly breathless, as if she'd taken an elbow in the chest.

"Let me get this straight," Steve said in a slow, quiet voice that made Kate's skin crawl. She hated when he spoke to her as if she were a child. "You think that someone has spent three years coaching Henley, all so that her mother would reach out to DOPS, in the hopes that somehow the case would get referred to you?"

It did sound crazy. But not as crazy as the possibility that Henley was simply telling the truth, and that Kate had been drawn back to the mystery of Becca's death by her reincarnated spirit. She said as much to Steve. "DOPS has referred cases to me before. I've written books about it. I've done interviews. Anyone could have guessed that Henley's story would wind up with me."

"So does that mean Emily's in on it, too? Is she part of this little conspiracy theory?"

"I don't know," she answered honestly. "She says she'd never heard of Becca's disappearance before I mentioned it. I don't think she's necessarily lying. But she might have been influenced by someone unconsciously—a friend, someone in her social group, someone with access to Henley."

"And do you have any idea who this Svengali might be?"

She thought of all the beaming children pictured on the flyer for Ms. Mari's music school. She thought of the piano in Emily Haskell's living room.

She thought of the only living person who could possibly know what they'd done to Becca on the night she'd died, and yet claimed to remember nothing.

"Yeah," she said. "Yeah, I've got an idea."

~

It took some convincing to get Mari to agree to meet at Camp Sauquamet, ostensibly to pay respects to both Becca and Lennie's memory. Kate felt bad about lying.

But returning to the site might put pressure on Mari's defenses, get her to admit to remembering more than she'd claimed. It might destabilize her, make her vulnerable to direct questioning.

"All that land belongs to the township," Mari had protested. "They've made it illegal to swim."

"Then we won't swim," Kate answered. She could hear in Mari's reedy sigh the echo of the old rule follower, the worrier, the girl who'd memorized the entire booklet of camp rules and used to cite them hysterically like a spell to ward off her friends' bad behavior.

But now, as then, she eventually caved.

"Maybe I'll pick up some flowers. Lennie was a gardener, you know. It's funny. I never would have thought she'd have the patience for it . . ."

Kate agreed: Flowers were a nice idea.

Mari was waiting by the old administration building, cupping her hands to peer in through the cobwebbed glass, when Kate wheeled her car into the old gravel parking lot. She'd been half anticipating a run-in with Matt Bishop, who'd warned her away from the property on her first visit. But she saw no sign of his truck. Only new swaths of mowed grass on the hill, paint cans outside the boathouse, and the suggestion of walking paths reemerging from the overgrowth of weeds. Obviously, he'd been busy these last few days.

Mari turned away from the window at the sound of Kate's car. She gave a vigorous wave, as if hailing Kate from across a crowded room, then bent to scoop up two paper-wrapped bouquets from the porch. She carried them down the hill in her arms, like a swaddled baby.

"Lennie loved hydrangeas," she said by way of a greeting. "She grew heaps of them in her garden. She sent me pictures every year. We could leave them on the dock." As always, Mari spoke a little breathlessly, as if chasing after her own thoughts before they bolted. "It's so strange being back here. I was just thinking of Mrs. B. I remember Becca trying to steal candy back from her contraband drawer. Do you remember that? She must have had ten Halloweens' worth of candy in there . . ."

"When was the last time you were here?" Kate asked.

"Not since the day they pushed us back onto those buses, and I spent the whole five hours back to New York City crying. My mom said my face looked like a balloon. She barely recognized me at the pickup." Mari shook her head. Her hair was loose, wild with curls that picked up the sunlight. "I couldn't bear to come back. Not after what happened. It's sad, what's happened to this place. Remember how pretty it was? All those flower beds by the mess hall . . . Ferdinand might have drawn them with a ruler."

They made their way slowly down to the lake. Every few feet, Mari stopped to point out something that had vanished, or simply to reminisce. "That's where they used to have the—what was it called?—Wishing Pole. Oh God. Remember when that stomach bug went around the younger campers? And we tried to use clothespins on our noses when we used the bathroom." And on and on. "Wasn't that where the counselors used to sneak off for cigarettes? I was so shocked when I found out. Do you remember when we tried to sneak into Cabin Eight with those cans of whipped cream? And Lennie drew a giant—you *know*—on the door."

Kate found it amusing that Mari still couldn't say the word *penis*. "I remember the raccoons swarming their bunk in the middle of the night," she said. "The counselors were freaking out. All the girls were screaming."

"*I* was screaming," Mari said. "I've never liked raccoons." She stopped, eyeing Cabin Eight suspiciously as if she half expected to see some at the door. "And you stole Natalie Horace's diary from her cabin. We passed it around for days."

Kate stopped. "*I* stole it?"

"Well, it was Becca's idea."

The memory startled out of nowhere: Becca and Kate, surrounded by their bunkmates, passing a sparkly pink journal around by flashlight. She felt a twinge of guilt. She'd forgotten that she and Becca had begun "collecting" things that summer—items purloined from other campers while they were at their activities, small things mostly, like scrunchies and bottles of body lotion. It was for the thrill of it, really, to see if they could get away with sneaking into other cabins undetected. But Kate had forgotten all about Natalie Horace's diary.

She wondered how it was possible for Mari to remember so many details of that summer twenty-six years ago, and yet claim to remember nothing about that night on Fair Isle. She had either blocked it out completely, or a kind of trauma response had warped her memory around the official story.

Either that, or she was lying.

The old dock, scabbed to a faded gray by years of sun, creaked under their footsteps. Mari set both flower bouquets down and stood for a moment, eyes closed, hands gripped in front of her. Kate wondered if she was praying. When she reached for the idea of God, she found nothing but dark space, physical forces that impelled the bodies of the universe into endless senseless rotations. The heat raised sweat on Kate's neck, and between her breasts. Clouds of gnats swarmed the surface of the water. Everything was motionless, stricken by the August sun.

"Poor Becca," Mari said after a while. She opened her eyes again. "She was so young."

It was the opening that Kate was looking for. "Do you ever feel guilty?" she asked, watching Mari's face for a reaction. Kate had lived for years with a belt of guilt that tightened relentlessly around her chest, a feeling almost indistinguishable from panic. Only drinking had helped. No. Not drinking. Being drunk. Blacking out. Forgetting. "I mean, about what we did?"

"Sneaking out to the island, you mean?" Mari said. "I used to. I used to feel horrible about it. I knew it was a bad idea. I know it sounds crazy, but I could feel that something terrible was going to happen. But I wasn't—I wasn't strong enough, you know? I didn't want you guys to be mad at me."

"But once we *got* to the island," Kate said a little more forcefully. "Don't you feel guilty that we never told anyone what *really* happened?"

Mari paused. She seemed to be working out the question, puzzling over it, letting it rearrange her expression. "You mean, about what we thought we saw?" She shrugged. "Who would have believed us? Even I don't understand it, after all these years. Do you?"

"You're talking about the Gray Lady," Kate said slowly. "You're talking about the moment we . . . saw her."

"It's impossible, isn't it?" Despite the heat, Mari crossed her arms, as if chilled by sudden wind. "We saw her. We all saw her. We couldn't just imagine her, could we?"

"Maybe," Kate said. "We were there looking for her, remember. We'd come for that reason—to see if the curse was true. And it was dark, and unfamiliar. We might have seen something else—an animal, or even a statue—and mistaken it . . ."

"But we didn't see an animal," Mari said. Now her eyes turned sharper, keener. "We saw the Gray Lady. She was there, in the woods, she was physically there. Don't you remember? She pointed at us."

Kate felt suddenly lightheaded. It was the heat, and the sun, glaring at them from the surface of the water. "The Gray Lady is a myth, an urban legend. She isn't real," Kate said. "We couldn't have seen her."

"But we did," Mari said. "We did, and we screamed, and then Becca took off running. By the time we got back to the canoes, she was gone." She said it forcefully, as if it was an argument repeated many times.

And maybe, in her head, it was.

Kate took a deep breath. "No, Mari. That isn't what happened. Becca wasn't with us when we saw the—when we saw whatever we saw."

"What do you mean?" Mari shook her head, frowning. "Of course she was. Otherwise, why would she run—"

"She *didn't* run, Mari. She didn't panic, or run back to the canoe, or start out across the lake on her own. That's not what happened."

"But I remember." Mari's voice pitched higher, closer to a whine. "I specifically remember you, me, and Lennie running through the woods. Becca wasn't with us. We heard her screaming . . ."

"That's because she was trapped. We'd barricaded her inside the old mausoleum. Don't you remember?" The words tasted like bits of metal, like shrapnel fired out in an explosion. "She tried to push you inside. You were crying, you were so scared to go in, and she tried to force you inside. She was laughing. And you just snapped. At the last second, you just *pushed* her—"

"No. No way. I would never—"

"—you pushed her, and we all slammed the door. It was like we all just . . . *decided*. We locked her up in that horrible place. Lennie said that would teach her."

Mari turned away, closing her eyes again. Kate saw her shoulders moving to repress a sob.

"Becca was banging, screaming for us to let her out. The whole time she was threatening to kill us . . ."

"I thought—I thought I dreamed it," Mari said finally, her voice thick with feeling. "I used to have dreams of finding Becca in that mausoleum, dressed as the Gray Lady . . ." She turned back to Kate, swiping her eyes with a wrist. "But I don't understand. If Becca was trapped inside the mausoleum when we saw the Gray Lady, how did she get out? How did she get back to the canoe? How did she *drown*?"

"She didn't." Kate said. She felt suddenly awful. Mari had been happy with her story. It was Kate who couldn't stand to live knowing the truth. "When we came back for her, she was dead."

Mari said nothing. She just stared.

The sun was blinding; the water burned with it. Kate wondered, vaguely, if she might faint.

"We were the ones who put her in the canoe, Mari," she said. "It was Lennie's idea, remember? She said we had to do it. It was the only way to break the curse. So we put her body in the canoe, and then we sank her in the lake."

THEN

They had agreed to leave at eleven o'clock: two hours after lights-out, and an hour after the counselors, too, should have been asleep in their cabins. Becca had planned their departure exactly for the night after the end-of-summer talent show; according to Becca, the counselors had their own end-of-summer tradition, and had stayed up drinking by the bonfire after the performance. They would be too tired, she insisted, to break curfew two nights in a row. Even Harriet had been sluggish that afternoon; Becca speculated that she, too, had joined in the festivities.

Harriet is pathetic, *Becca had said.* It's like she thinks she's still a teenager or something. Can you imagine dedicating your entire life to this stupid camp?

That was the kind of mood Becca was in as the hours funneled them fast toward evening. That was how she'd been acting for weeks—superior, and bored. Over it. Like camp was a place to be endured.

Or escaped.

The moon was almost full, pinned outside the window as if it had been hung there to leer at Kate in her bunk. She had worried about drifting off to sleep—both feared, and hoped, that she might wake up to discover her friends had gone without her—but instead she lay in paralyzed stillness, her heart battle-ramming her chest, locked in the slow ooze of minutes. Becca was alarmingly still in her bed. From the corner, she could hear their bunkmate Cheryl, lightly snoring through a nose always congested with allergies. She hated Cheryl in that moment—dumb Cheryl, who plodded around like a cow, looking helpless and hopeless, and would wake up in the morning with no idea of what they'd done.

Ten forty-five. Occasionally, she heard the piercing shriek of an owl from the woods, and the touch of the leaves in the wind. Otherwise it was still, deadly silent.

Like a grave, *she kept thinking. She kept picturing the body of the Gray Lady—awfully decayed inside a funeral shroud, with black beetles nesting in her open mouth.*

But that was impossible. If the Gray Lady was buried out on Fair Isle, she would be nothing but bones by now.

Bones. The creak of the branches outside reminded her of bones.

She squeezed her eyes shut and opened them again. It was so quiet. Deathly still. She felt a sudden overwhelming terror that Becca, Mari, and Lennie were no longer breathing, struck down already by the spirit of the Gray Lady; that she would find them all lying dead in their beds.

Ten fifty-five. Finally, she couldn't bear it anymore. She sat up and seized the flashlight she'd stored under her pillow, next to her sweatshirt and a granola bar—just in case. She'd been taught again and again never to venture out into the wilderness without provisions.

She turned on the flashlight and angled it across the room, to Lennie and Mari's bunk. Immediately, Lennie winced, lifting a hand to her eyes. Mari sat up with her hand around her necklace and whispered, "Is it time?" Then at last she heard Becca rustling in her sheets. A second later, Becca stood up, dodging the beam of light before reaching for Kate's flashlight and angling it to the floor.

"Are you trying to blind me?" she whispered. Kate felt a flood of relief so strong, she nearly laughed.

It was fine. Everything was okay.

They were just going to have an adventure.

The girls wriggled on their clothing in silence. Mari had packed a backpack, with water bottles, a compass, a flint, and a matchbook, as if they were setting out to go camping. All the girls had flashlights. Lennie kept turning hers toward the corner, where Cheryl was humped beneath her sheets, facing the wall, breathing heavily, until Becca told her to stop.

"I don't think she's really sleeping," Lennie whispered. "I think she's faking."

"So what?" Becca said.

"So if she tells someone . . ."

"If she tells someone, I'll gut her like a fish and hang her fat ass from the dock," Becca said, deliberately raising her voice a bit. Cheryl didn't stir. Becca glanced at Lennie, satisfied. "There. See? Now even if she is faking, she'll know what will happen if she rats."

They eased out the door, which barely whined on its hinges. Two days earlier, Becca had used suntan oil to grease the rusted hinges. The moon touched the slope of grass silver and buffed the surface of the lake to a dull sheen. They were halfway to the boathouse when Becca stopped suddenly.

"Wait. I almost forgot." She pivoted and jogged back up the hill, dissolving almost immediately into the darkness. They tracked her progress by the bounce of her flashlight beam until it vanished around the cabins.

Lennie, Mari, and Kate stood waiting for her. With Becca gone, all of Kate's fears came rushing back, as if suctioned into the vacuum. What if they couldn't get the boathouse open? What if Harriet heard them rowing across the lake? What if they couldn't find the grave?

What if they could?

Then Becca reappeared, breathless, holding up a small bottle in the light.

"Provisions," she said. "Who wants first sip?"

"You have alcohol?" Mari pitched over the word, as if her throat had tripped over something unexpected.

"Where did you get this?" Lennie grabbed the bottle away from Becca and angled her flashlight over the label. "Whisky? Seriously?"

"It has cinnamon in it," Becca said defensively, as if that explained it. She uncapped the bottle. "Try it. It's good."

"Where did you get that?" Lennie demanded again. Becca ignored her. She held the bottle out to the circle. No one took it.

"You're going to get us kicked out," Kate said, nudging away the whisky when Becca tried to pass it to her. "If Harriet catches us with that—"

"Then let's not get caught," Becca said. She took a performative swig, barely suppressing a cough, before she recapped the bottle and slid it into the pocket of her sweatshirt. "Come on. Let's go."

The boathouse was secured at night by a padlock with a rusty four-digit combination lock, set to Harriet's birthday. It was an open secret; the lock was meant, Kate suspected, mostly to keep out raccoons.

Kate held the flashlight while Lennie put in the combination. Afterward, Lennie slipped the lock in her backpack.

"So it doesn't get lost," she said when she caught Kate staring.

But later, Kate wondered if she had a plan even then. Or maybe not a plan—maybe a suspicion, an intuition, that the lock would come in handy.

Maneuvering the canoes was the hardest part. They were heavy, and slotted into gigantic canoe racks that groaned at the slightest pressure.

Lennie and Mari took the first canoe; Becca and Kate took the second. Becca kept letting her end of the canoe dip suddenly, as if she had dropped it, making Kate whip around in a panic. Becca made faces, stifling giggles. Kate wondered if she was already drunk. She felt annoyed at Becca, annoyed that she was treating the whole thing like a joke, when she'd been the one who insisted.

This was their final summer as campers. This might be their final summer together, ever.

They had one last chance to find out if the Gray Lady really did haunt Fair Isle, and if her supposed curse was real.

They nudged their canoes into the shallows, side by side. The metal hulls raking against the pebbles made an awful, hollow screeching sound, which Kate was sure would bring the counselors flying out of their bunks and down the hill. But no one came. They sloshed into the water, climbed aboard, and pushed off with their oars. It was always tricky, the first couple of strokes—striking bottom, then churning up a slosh of useless waves. But after a bit of thrashing, they broke free of the shallow water. The bottom dropped out of the lake, and left them coasting on a deep, dark surface—moving with barely a hiss, and the wet smack of their oars submerging. Kate kept her eye on the cabins as they receded, softening into the slope of darkness, and strained to see movement on the hill. Halfway to Fair Isle, Becca suddenly stood up, lurching the canoe in the water.

"What are you doing?" Kate whispered. For a second, as Becca stumbled toward her, she gripped her hands on the oar, and pictured sending Becca into the lake.

"Come on, drink." Becca was hiccupping laughter. She tried to force the bottle to Kate's lips. "Swear to God, you'll like it."

"You'll capsize us," Kate said. "Sit down." She gave Becca a push, thudding her backward. Once again, the canoe convulsed on the surface. Kate heard Lennie whisper something across the distance—a word of caution or alarm.

"Okay, all right, God." Becca knifed her oar hard into the water, sending up a spray that caught Kate in the chest and face. "You don't have to be such a bitch."

"I'm the bitch?" Kate felt her temper rising, like a hand throttling her throat from the inside out. "Are you serious?"

"What is your problem?" Becca shook her head. Kate couldn't see her face, but she could hear the disgust in Becca's voice. "You used to be fun."

"Yeah, well, that was before you turned psycho." The words were out of Kate's mouth before she could stop them.

Instantly there was a deadening quiet. Becca was perfectly still, frozen at the other end of the canoe, her face a dark hole, her eyes barely visible. Burning.

"Psycho, huh?" Abruptly, Becca seized hold of her oar, and shoved it deep into the water, stirring the boat into motion. "We'll see about that."

ELEVEN

After Mari had gone, Kate sat for a long time in the car, waiting for the insufficient air conditioning to blow away the bad feeling. Mari had left in tears—still in denial, and furious at Kate.

She had accused Kate of being sick, of trying to confuse her.

You hated Becca, Mari had said out of nowhere, practically spitting the words. *Maybe* you're *the one who killed her.*

Kate had merely let her vent. It was projection. Transference. But the accusation stayed with her, touched some bit of unease in her mind.

Had she hated Becca?

Sometimes. A little.

Hadn't they all hated Becca, just a little bit?

"What do you want from me?" Kate said out loud. She saw a flash of movement in the rearview mirror and spun around, heart ramming in her chest. But there was nothing there; just a swallow, swooping low over the field and coming to perch on the roof of Cabin Ten.

She was losing it.

She put her car in drive. She felt better as soon as the trees spat her out onto the main road. Saner. The engine of her brain slowly started grinding again.

She was persuaded now that Mari really had blocked out what happened on Fair Isle, twisting the memory to fit the alibi they'd created—which meant she *couldn't* have been the one who'd told Henley about Becca. Mari had insisted, anyway, that she knew the Haskells only incidentally—she'd once tuned Emily's piano, and her son, Alex, had babysat for Henley a handful of times when he was in high school. But Mari hadn't ever interacted with Henley directly.

So who else had known? Lennie, of course, but Lennie was dead. And besides, she'd spent her whole adult life in Atlanta. And Kate had kept her promise, and never told a soul.

That left Becca.

Becca, who'd been dead since they found her, who'd been lying for twenty-six years at the bottom of the lake, her sweatshirt pockets stuffed full of rocks.

What would it mean if Henley was right about the life she recalled? What would it mean if some remnant part of Becca—some mentalized idea of self, some sparse assemblage of memories—had persisted, intermingling with the developing identity of a stranger more than twenty years after her death? What would it mean about Henley, about Becca, about memory, about death? She thought then of her mother, who'd spent most of Kate's adolescence passing like flotsam between hospital rooms, rotating through endless cycles of chemo and radiation, always either recuperating or getting sick again. By the time she died, her skin had been paper thin, the same unnatural white as the hospital walls, and so sensitive that even the touch of sheets was painful. She'd been a runner, once—she'd met Kate's dad on the night before her very first marathon—with muscled legs, a toothy smile, and a laugh that Kate could recall only fuzzily. If Kate reached back far enough, she could excavate a handful of memories of her mother before the first diagnosis. Driving with the windows down, belting along to the radio. Dancing with Kate's father in the living room one Christmas. Jogging next to Kate on her first bicycle, shouting encouragement.

She imagined, for a second, her mother's spirit loosed from her dying body, spinning around like so much tumbleweed before latching on to a new form: a child, younger than Kate, possibly by many decades, possibly born halfway across the world. The idea was intolerable, repellent. It would be a loss even greater than the first—a world where Kate's mother had been alive all this time, and even happy, but no longer Kate's mother, and no longer carrying her share of the grief.

She refused to believe it.

Maybe Lennie had stayed in touch with other camp friends. Maybe she'd confessed to somebody before her death. Kate couldn't imagine Lennie caving to guilt—she wasn't sentimental enough—but twenty-six years gave plenty of time for self-reflection, and so did a cancer diagnosis.

The idea reenergized her. This was a puzzle, that was all. The appearance of illogic was only because Kate didn't have all the pieces yet.

She dialed Emily's number as soon as she got a bar of service. Emily started talking even before Kate could greet her.

"Henley was all over that yearbook after you left," she said. "I had to practically wrestle it away so I could open up the studio. Memories were just pouring out of her. I tried to take notes . . ."

"I'll need to see those," Kate said.

"Now do you believe me?" Emily said. "Henley couldn't be inventing all of this."

"I agree," Kate said simply. "Henley knows things that only Becca could have known. But," she added, before Emily could cut in, "that doesn't mean Becca's the only one who knew them."

"I'm not following."

"Becca grew up one county over. She went to camp just down the road. Think of all the friends that Becca had. All her teachers, counselors, babysitters, people she might have confided in. Any number of them might have crossed paths with Henley."

"You think someone—what? Coached her? You think someone could have taught her all this, everything about Becca, without my even knowing?" Now Emily sounded offended.

"It wouldn't necessarily take much coaching," Kate said. "Children are very porous. Sometimes, they latch on to an idea with hardly any prompting. A single bad experience in the tub can trigger a lifelong fear of drains. A superstitious rhyme can provoke ritual behavior that lasts for years. And Henley isn't with you twenty-four seven. You must have help caring for her."

"But why? She's *my* child. Why would anyone. . . ?" Emily trailed off.

"I don't know," Kate said honestly.

Emily was silent for a bit. Then she sighed. "What do you need from me?"

"A list. I need the names of all the adults who have regular access to Henley. I need to know who was spending time with her when she first started reporting these memories."

"That was years ago . . ." Emily said uncertainly.

"Do the best you can. Babysitters, day-care staff, even doctors. You said Henley takes a pottery class with you at the studio. Does she study anything else? Dance? Music?"

"Henley only started taking dance this year," Emily said. "We haven't started her on piano yet."

Kate felt dimly disappointed. "Well, just do the best you can," Kate said.

Emily said nothing. Kate sensed that she was gathering another question in the silence.

"You told me that Becca drowned," Emily said. "But Henley says that someone hurt her. She says that she was murdered. What do you think it means?"

"I don't know," Kate answered honestly. It was a question Kate had never allowed herself to consider. Not once in twenty-six years.

Now, all at once, it roared into her consciousness. Her memory opened, and she fell back inside that night: sweeping her flashlight over the stone floor of the mausoleum only to snag on Becca's body, lying on her back, already draining color. Cold and still and marbled with blue, like a fallen statue. Eyes open, face locked in a grimace, as if she'd been scared to death.

She squeezed her eyes shut and opened them again, forcing back the image of Becca's face. Becca had been alive—shouting to be let out, swearing she would make them sorry—only half an hour earlier.

So what—or who—had killed her?

THEN

There was no beach on Fair Isle. The trees clawed all the way to the lake, pitching off the shore to drag their knuckles in the water. The girls unloaded when they heard the bottom of their canoes scraping rock, and sloshed the last few feet to shore.

Kate's jeans and sneakers were soaked, and she was cold. Camp looked impossibly far from here, the single light mounted outside of administration nothing but a distant wink. Mari's teeth were chattering. Fear, or cold, she couldn't say. Mari was always cold.

They angled their flashlights on the density of growth, looking for evidence of trails. They knew there must be some. Supposedly, the counselors sometimes snuck out to Fair Isle.

Finally, Lennie spotted graffiti on some of the trees close to the water. There were strange markings alongside the usual tags. A painted eye, a skeleton.

"There." Lennie tipped her flashlight toward a barely perceptible break in the trees, where the underbrush had been flattened, slicked with the passage of feet and canoes. "See that ribbon on the tree? It's a trail marker."

But still they didn't move. The water here was shin high, and thick with weeds that grew around fallen stumps and chunks of stone, loosed from the rest of the shore like a dribble of teeth. Even Becca appeared to hesitate. Kate wondered if, at last, she was regretting the idea to come.

But when she spoke, her voice was full of wonder.

"She's here," she said. Her voice was thickened, slurred a bit with the alcohol. Or maybe Kate was imagining things. "I can feel her. Can't you?"

Mari whimpered, grabbing hold of her cross. Kate wished now that she had something to hold. She reached for a prayer but couldn't find one. Just the words to "Baa, Baa, Black Sheep," leaping to her mind on a loop. Her mother had sung it to her when she was a baby. She thought of her mother, of the veins standing out in her hands. Corpse hands, *her mom called them. She wanted to run, screaming back to the bunk, back to her bed, back to last summer, when the Gray Lady had simply been a story, part of a game they played. The trees seemed to her almost deformed, gnarled and stumpy, like they were growing on poisoned ground.*

She felt it, just like Becca had said. There was something evil in this place.

"Well, are we doing this or what?" Lennie was the first to move. She fought her way up the slick of ground, bumping the canoe into the trees after her. "Mari, a little help?"

That broke the spell a bit. They maneuvered onto the bank, squelching water in their shoes, complaining about their ruined socks, and secured their canoes in the underbrush. There was, in fact, a trail leading deeper into the island—barely perceptible, but there—and faded ribbons tied at intervals around the tree trunks. Kate felt a little better, finding evidence of recent activity on the island as they inched cautiously down the trail: a crushed beer can here; a trampled cigarette pack there; someone's abandoned CD, half concealed in a rut of dirt.

Lennie brought her compass out. "The ruins are on the south side of the island," she said. "We should be heading that way."

"We should stay on the trail," Mari said. She kept one hand looped around Lennie's sweatshirt, as if she was afraid of losing her in the dark. "We'll get lost."

"We won't get lost with a compass," Lennie argued.

Sensing a fight, Kate cut in. "Mari's right. Let's see how far the trail takes us. We can strike out if we don't find anything."

Lennie merely shrugged. Becca took another sip from her bottle. "Are we having fun yet?" she said.

It felt like they moved at a crawl, at first; barely shuffling forward in a line, whipping their flashlights around to point in every direction, seizing on every branch that dipped in the wind, startling at every rustle. But soon the trees thinned out into bluestem grass and chokeberry bushes, and Lennie confirmed that the trail had turned south, toward the ruins. Here they found the blackened remains of a bonfire, and a filthy beach towel looped around a tree branch.

"I told you the counselors used this place to party," Becca said, striking out at a beer can with her foot. She missed, and pitched into laughter. She was definitely drunk.

From the bonfire site, they found multiple trails, all of them marked with ribbons, radiating off in different directions. They came across an abandoned bicycle, collapsed on its side; even a minifridge, mysteriously lying in the dirt. A little farther south and they saw the roof of the old mansion, or asylum, or whatever it had been, sloping out above the trees. Impossible to say what had been here, even when they approached. Only one portion of the building was still standing. The rest had collapsed into a rubble of stone. But it was big, far bigger than it had looked from a distance. They spent half an hour walking the perimeter, shining a light on the old stones, many of them now defaced with graffiti or carved up with old initials. Becca counted every bottle and beer can she found. There were dozens of them. But they found no graveyard.

"I don't get it," Lennie said. "She should be buried right next to the house."

"Maybe there is no graveyard," Mari said hopefully. "Maybe it's all just a story."

"Let's split up," Becca said. She rolled her eyes at Mari's immediate protest. "We'll each take one side of the house and look around. Just scream if you see the Gray Lady." She reached out suddenly and seized Mari by the waist. Mari screamed. "Perfect. Like that."

Reluctantly, they agreed to separate. They had only one compass between them. Lennie cautioned them to keep the ruins always in sight. She'd heard about hikers getting lost only a hundred feet from a trailhead, wandering for days before eventually starving to death. Kate imagined getting lost out here, in darkness that seemed so complete, so total, she couldn't imagine daylight standing up to it. She ventured off alone, turning every few feet to shine her light backward, making sure she could still make out the roof above the trees, trying to memorize features of the specific path she was taking. A huge pile of stones, possibly the remains of a wall; a tree fissured by lightning; someone's sweatshirt, now a moldering pile of cloth. Every so often, the girls shouted to one another, sending their voices ricocheting across the distance. Kate wondered how far they would carry, whether anyone at camp would hear them scream.

She doubted it.

It was Kate who found the graves. She nearly tripped over the first headstone. It listed suddenly out of the ground into her light. She nearly mistook it for another pile of rubble, but the shape was unmistakable. Crouching down, she could see the faintest etch of old letters on the granite. With a sense of dread, she aimed her flashlight beyond it. A stubble of headstones, each leaning at a crazy angle, led into a small clearing.

And there it was: an enormous stone vault, a mausoleum, looming toward the sky. Her throat caught, and her stomach felt suddenly alive with writhing things.

"Guys," she croaked out. Then, louder: "She's here! I found her!"

She didn't dare go any closer until her friends had gathered. Then they picked their way through the old graves, inching closer to the mausoleum and the stone angel weeping black above it.

"Who are all these people?" Lennie whispered, shining her light on the headstones one by one.

"Victims," Becca said.

Mari broke. "I want to go back," she said. "Please, Becca. Please, can we go back?"

Becca ignored her. She pocketed her bottle and, stretching out a hand, made a final lurch to the mausoleum. She seemed to be in a kind of trance as she ran her hand up and down the stone. "Remember," she said in a low voice, "if anything comes, shut your eyes. Anyone who sees her has to die."

"Let's go back," Mari pleaded again. Again, Becca ignored her. She found the rusted padlock, hanging from a coil of steel chain, and gave it a hard tug.

"It's stuck," she said.

"It's locked," Kate said, half to reassure herself. "We're not supposed to go in there."

"That's exactly where we're supposed to go. That's part of the challenge."

"The challenge?"

Becca barely glanced over her shoulder. "Ten seconds inside the Gray Lady's tomb. Cameron told me about it."

"No way," Mari said. "No way I'm going in there. You can't make me." She looked at Lennie, as if for reassurance. After a second, Lennie put her arm around Mari's shoulders.

"She can't make you," Lennie said. But her eyes found Kate's in the dark, and Kate knew what she was thinking. Becca had gotten them this far.

They had never been able to say no to Becca for long.

Now Becca was working on the chain. She gave it a hard tug. Kate felt a flood of relief when it held.

Becca tried again, this time pulling harder. The iron made a horrible clanking sound, and the old lock shuddered on its chain.

"A little help?" she said. Neither Kate nor Lennie moved.

"Leave it alone, Becca," Lennie said firmly. Kate wondered if she could feel it, too—the horrible pressure of the darkness, the faceless angel, deformed, molten from years of exposure, somehow watching them, listening, aware of their presence.

"I'm telling you, it isn't locked," Becca grunted. "It's all gummed up. If I could just—" But she broke off as, with another heave, the padlock popped off the door, and the chain thudded into the dirt.

For a moment, even Becca froze. They stood there in shocked silence, as the heavy metal door seemed to breathe open on its hinges, just a crack, as if something inside was exhaling relief.

"Don't," Mari whispered. But it was too late. Becca reached out and seized the handle. She pulled. With an awful groan, the door widened several inches, revealing a cavernous black that seemed to gobble up the beam of their flashlights into nothing.

Becca turned back toward her friends. She grinned.

"All right," she said. "Who's first?"

And her eyes landed on Mari, trembling.

TWELVE

Kate hated dead time. Hours that fell like a bludgeon, with no work to do, no phone calls to make, nothing to focus or fixate on. There was nothing she could do to ascertain where Henley might have received her information until she could look over Emily's list. In the summertime, emails even from the graduate students working at her lab turned sluggish—especially when she was traveling. And she was straight up avoiding the only recent message in her inbox, this one from Dr. Rushkin, and very brief.

Thoughts on Henley Haskell? She credible?

She drove back to the cottage with the windows down, trying to concentrate on the view along the way: swells of tawny farmland, billowing off into the distance; gullies that dropped off into sparkling streams, running parallel to the coil of road; the distant Catskills, edging into the sky. But she couldn't take pleasure in it. She saw the landscape as if through a veil of vanished teenagers, bodies mysteriously turned up, half consumed by animals. So many places to die alone, so many ghosts ranging through the woods, lingering on the roads.

Her mind kept pulling her back to the same question: What had happened to Becca in that mausoleum? At the time, they hadn't questioned it. They'd been convinced that Becca had fallen victim to the Gray Lady's curse. It was the only reason that Kate had gone along with the plan to sink her body in the lake. Mari insisted they *had* to do it.

Otherwise, they would die, too.

She remembered, all of a sudden, a song that Cameron had sung for the campers on bonfire nights. Something about an old covered bridge, a location in his Vermont hometown supposedly haunted by a woman who'd hung herself in the rafters. Out of nowhere, the chorus came back to her:

Annabel's tired of waiting so long.
Annabel's rope is sturdy and strong.
Annabel's neck fits the rope like a glove.
Annabel's life, for the loss of true love.

She wondered again what had happened to Cameron. Whether he'd moved back to Vermont. Whether he'd ever started that band he was always talking about. He was probably married. Or divorced.

There was heartbreak everywhere, these days.

She was surprised to find the door to her cottage open a crack. Kate was sure she had locked it. She entered warily, surprising a gray-haired woman in the corner who startled to her feet.

"Oh! I'm sorry. I thought you were gone for the day . . ." The woman had the face of a Christmas elf, creviced deeply with laugh lines. Kate recognized her host and instantly relaxed. "I'm Susan. You must be Kate."

They shook hands. Susan's fingers were calloused and knobbed with age, but strong. The hands of a gardener.

"Sorry for barging in on you," Susan said. "We've had some problems with the Wi-Fi in the main house today. I thought I would pop over and reboot it when you were out."

"Don't worry about it," Kate said. She liked Susan instinctively and was glad for the company, especially after losing the afternoon to a funnel of memory. "I love the cottage, by the way."

"It's cozy, isn't it?" Susan beamed. "First time in the Berkshires?"

"No," Kate admitted. "But it's been a long time."

"Well, you picked the perfect time of year." Unconsciously, Susan began neatening—brushing stray coffee grounds from the counter into her hand, stacking the magazines on the table. In fact, she seemed incapable of standing still. "I hope you're getting to spend plenty of time outside. Careful of all that Gray Lady stuff. Might scare you out of the woods."

Kate stared at her. For a wild second, she thought that Susan had somehow read Kate's thoughts on her face. Then Susan tipped her head toward the book still lying out on the coffee table, the one that Kate had found on the bookshelf. Instantly, she felt relieved.

"The author, Martin Sheehy, is a friend of mine. Kind of a kook, but a good writer. Lives right downtown, spends his retirement chasing down ghosts and ghouls and writing about it." Susan shivered performatively. "You're an author, too, aren't you?"

"I'm a psychologist," Kate said. "And yes, I've written several books. How did you . . . ?"

"Google, dear," said Susan. "I google all our guests before they arrive. Just in case. Most of our visitors are lovely people. Quiet, respectful. Like you. But once in a while . . ." She gave another dramatic shudder.

Finally, Kate managed to politely shunt Susan to the door, after fending off several offers of more towels, soap, and coffee creamer. After a quick shower, she forced herself to sit down and respond to Dr. Rushkin's email about the Haskells. Even though the university hadn't sponsored Kate's trip to Massachusetts, Dr. Rushkin had made it clear that he intended to include Henley Haskell in one of DOPS' official research studies, pending the results of Kate's investigation.

And Dr. Rushkin wasn't known for his patience.

She found herself reviewing all the biographical details that Henley had so far gotten correct about Becca. Anyone might have found out where Becca lived with a little digging. And it was possible that someone close to Becca—a teacher, a childhood friend—could have known about her favorite toys.

But what about all of the memories that Henley seemed to possess of Camp Sauquamet? How quickly she'd identified landmarks and trails that no longer existed?

What about her memories of the night they'd all gone to Fair Isle?

She sat there staring at her email inbox, unwilling, or unable, to write the truth.

Henley claimed to remember Becca's life. And Kate had so far turned up no convincing alternative to the theory that she really did.

Eventually, she decided on a short reply. Too soon to tell. Looking for the research you've collected on credible past-life claims. Can you send over the files?

She hit send before she could regret it.

Now, confronting an empty afternoon—all those hours of silence, of inactivity—Kate felt that old sense of panic, like a swarm of insects, rising beneath her skin. Not so long ago, she would have headed to the nearest bar, quickly thinning out the pressure with glass after glass of rosé. Maybe an Adderall or two, to keep her speech crisp. It occurred to her that she was all alone in Massachusetts. No one looking over her shoulder. No one to know if she got drunk in the afternoon, slept away all the time until the morning.

It occurred to her then that she could, after all this time, come clean to the police. Then Becca's remains might, at last, be recovered. She could be buried, possibly next to her grandmother. The police might even find an answer to the mystery of what had killed her so suddenly. Wasn't that, after all, what Kate's drinking had been about? Wasn't that why she had tunneled herself into ninety– to one hundred–hour work weeks, and sipped away her free time until the world slipped away into a fog? So she would never have time to remember? So she would never have to face what she'd done?

Kate imagined how simple it would be to confess. To let go of the lie, after all these years. It might almost be a relief.

But she knew that she wouldn't. She couldn't. Not yet. The mystery of what had happened that night—what they'd seen, and done, and sworn never to reveal—had been hers for twenty-six years. It had belonged to her, to Mariana, and to Lennie. Somehow, it had now entangled a six-year-old girl and her mother. And although Kate didn't believe in mysticism, in some higher mental order to the universe that shunted everything into its proper place, she couldn't shake the idea that she'd met Henley Haskell for a reason. That there was a pattern here, something she was meant to do, or see, or resolve.

Even if she did tell the truth, Kate knew that she could never explain it. Not why they'd followed Becca there. Not what they'd planned as her punishment.

Not what they'd seen in the woods.

How could Kate ever tell the truth about that? It would mean the end of her career, the end of her credibility. Possibly, the end of her sanity.

We saw the Gray Lady. She's real. She was there.

We saw her, and then she killed Becca.

Impulsively, she pulled up her browser and searched for Massachusetts' Gray Lady. She wasn't surprised to find reference to the legend in dozens of online articles with titles like, "Massachusetts' Most Haunted Places" and "Mysterious and Unexplained." These were the same rumors about Fair Isle, and its putative ghost, that her friends had swapped around the campfire, and whispered to one another late at night, after lights-out. One blogger suggested that Fair Isle had been used as a burial ground after the first spate of influenza deaths had touched the area in 1919. Another had dug up records of a nineteenth-century sanitarium that had existed somewhere in the region to treat "nervous disorders," and speculated that the graves on Fair Isle dated from their remnant population, or perhaps from patients who had died during God-knew-what kind of barbaric treatment.

One article in particular caught her attention, this one a blog post by the Berkshire historical society.

> *In the early 1900s, forty-two-year-old widower and heir to the Rhodes railway fortune, Andrew Faher, fell under*

> *the unfortunate influence of an early spiritualist named Marcy Dobbes. Very little is known about Dobbes, other than the fact that she claimed to be receiving messages from the angel Ezekiel, warning her that the destruction of the world was imminent. Over the next few years, she apparently convinced Andrew Faher that his four daughters had been "contaminated" by pernicious spirits, and needed to be segregated from society, disciplined of their attachment to worldly things, and resurrected as servants of light. A 1910 deed shows that Andrew Faher purchased a tract of land that included much of the lakeshore and rights to Fair Isle itself, and set to work constructing a makeshift prison for his daughters, including nineteen-year-old Liesl Faher, who was compelled to break off her engagement and look after her younger sisters in almost permanent isolation. One record indicates that she died in 1910, even before her father closed on the land in Massachusetts. However, there is also indication that Andrew Faher stripped his daughters of their legal names before permanently exiling them, giving them instead generic titles suggested by Marcy Dobbes during one of her channeling sessions, meant to cure his children of their sinful identities.*

As far as she knew, this was the only online reference that had bothered to give the Gray Lady a name, an identity, a place in actual history. In every other story, she was reduced to her modern horror-film incarnation: a grieving mother, in some cases, or a spurned fiancée out for bloody vengeance in others. But she couldn't find any additional references to Liesl Faher, or what might have happened to her and her sisters on that island in the middle of the lake.

Then there were the mysterious deaths and disappearances that had been attributed to the Gray Lady over the years, at least by conspiracy online. There were the accidents that happened on the water: a six-year-old who'd drowned after wandering away from his family's camper; a car full of teenagers that had crashed through the ice while doing doughnuts on the lake.

She turned up Becca's name, too, mentioned incidentally in a front-page article about a John Doe whose body had been found fifteen months before Becca had allegedly vanished from her bunk in the middle of the night. The boy's partially decomposing body had been discovered by local hikers. Two days later, the police had turned up his tent, sleeping bag, and backpack in a remote campsite in the state park, little used since park upgrades had rerouted most families to the areas with working barbecue pits and better access to service roads. They'd found no ID, no wallet, no credit cards—no identifying papers, not even a receipt to show where he might have purchased his equipment. Someone had either stripped the boy of his identification, or he had dumped it himself; given the quantity of supplies he'd been carrying with him, police suspected he might be a runaway. Kate clicked over to a police reconstruction of the boy's face, which had been issued to the press on the ten-year anniversary of his death. She spent a minute scrutinizing the image. He was probably seventeen or eighteen when he died, with prominent ears, a narrow forehead, and the glazed, slightly plastic state of all police reconstructions.

She perked up when she read that the boy's cause of death was undetermined. Other than the damage inflicted postmortem by scavenging animals, the boy's body showed no outward signs of trauma. His tox report had come back clean; his organs were healthy. One line in particular jumped out at her, a quote from one of the hikers who'd discovered his body, reflecting on the experience years later.

It was creepy. I still see him, lying there, totally blue, with his mouth open. Like he'd seen something awful, and dropped dead.

Kate thought of Becca, lying in that mausoleum, mouth open as if she'd been felled mid-scream.

An old voice filled her head, whispering to her about *the curse.*

She jumped when her phone rang, slamming her computer shut, as if the person on the other line might be able to see the direction of her thinking. It was Emily Haskell.

"I have your list," she said without preamble. "I went back through my phone to make sure I didn't miss anybody. I can email it to you, if you like."

Kate felt a spark of excitement. A list would be like a rope; she'd have something solid to hold on to, names to consider, a path out of the morass of memory and bad feeling.

"I'm not sure you'll find anything," Emily said, immediately deflating her. "Henley was so young when she first started talking about her old life. On most days, she was glued to me. But you should really talk to Henley's old preschool," she continued. "The woman who runs it may have ideas that I missed. She used to invite guests into the classroom all the time. I know they used to invite in local authors to read to the kids. I think one time they brought in a gymnastics coach. It was a really special place. Jenny's a wonderful woman, really fabulous with kids."

Kate felt a prickle on her spine. "Jenny?"

"The woman who runs the preschool," Emily said. "Jenny. Jenny Lin."

THIRTEEN

According to Emily Haskell, in the summertime Jenny Lin picked up shifts at an eighty-year-old restaurant called the Dell Inn. When Kate called for a reservation, she was informed by a flustered-sounding hostess that every table was booked up.

Kate was welcome, however, to a bar seat.

The Dell Inn was inauspiciously located across the street from a Sunoco. But the parking lot was packed, and the door unleashed laughing families back into the night.

Inside, it was clamorous with sound, all battered wood and boating paraphernalia and hunting trophies mounted on ancient walls. Kate had waited until eight o'clock to try her luck, and even though the restaurant was currently packed, she judged that the crowd would soon begin to dwindle. It was late for this area of early risers and comfortable retirees; most of the tables had already finished with their meals. Half a dozen waiters and waitresses slipped around the room, ferrying desserts and coffees and bills. But she didn't see Jenny.

The hostess was a girl with a moon-shaped face and multiple piercings. She couldn't have been more than eighteen.

"Is Jenny Lin working tonight?" Kate had to lean in to talk over the noise.

The girl pointed her toward the bar—a beautiful curved mahogany piece, lit up from below with embedded lights—and Kate slid her eyes from the bottles of alcohol and spotted Jenny. Her heart quickened as she made her way to the bar, trying to ignore all the luminous bottles, glowing cheerfully on their mirrored shelves.

She had been down that road too many times.

Kate took a seat and closed the cocktail menu before she could be tempted to look at it. Jenny's eyes seemed to glitch when they landed on Kate's face. Kate held her breath, wondering whether Jenny would recognize her.

But after a moment, Jenny simply peeled away from her conversation and gave Kate a friendly, impersonal smile.

"Something to drink?" she asked.

"Just seltzer," Kate said. She felt an old sense of awe, and a niggle of shame, being face-to-face with Jenny. Jenny had always struck her as being hopelessly sophisticated, with her long rope of dark hair and the piercings coiling all the way up one ear and her college major in art history. Jenny couldn't have been more than seven years older than her, but at the time that had been an unimaginable gulf, a stretch of years that mysteriously turned children into adults, living on their own, working jobs, spending money, having sex.

"You got it," Jenny said. Kate watched the way she moved behind the bar, with the same fluid command she had once used to direct the campers into groups before games of capture the flag. People didn't really change, no matter how many years elapsed, no matter where you put them down.

After all, here she was at forty years old, still chasing after Becca.

Kate requested a dinner menu and took her time ordering—an appetizer and an entrée, which she would enjoy as the restaurant emptied. Dimly, she had the sense of eyes on her, knew from experience what it meant: a man, probably alone and on the prowl, angling for the opportunity to speak to the only unaccompanied woman in the restaurant. Studiously ignoring him—whoever he was—she instead pulled out her iPad and tapped open the link that Dr. Rushkin had returned to her of all the case studies DOPS had conducted about children who claimed to remember past lives. She wasn't surprised that he had gotten back to her within an hour; Dr. Rushkin was a notorious workaholic, just like Kate.

The accompanying message was even briefer than her initial email. Just a Shakespeare quote: There are more things in heaven and earth, Horatio, than are dreamt of by your philosophy. Not very subtle.

She had just started to sort through the various files when the couple next to her stood up to leave. Within seconds, a man was sliding into the empty stool beside her.

"You again," he said. Kate was surprised to recognize the same man—Matt Bishop—she'd run into at Camp Sauquamet. Now he was wearing dark jeans and a blue polo shirt that complemented his eyes. He looked good. He smelled amazing. "Tell me the truth—are you following me?"

"Possibly," Kate said. "Or this is one of three restaurants in town."

"Coincidence, huh?" He wagged a finger at her. "I don't believe in coincidences."

He was flirting with her. Kate was sure he was flirting with her. Wasn't he? She could hear it in the teasing lilt of his voice, and the way his smile seemed to flicker on the edge of dangerous. She wondered what it would be like to go home with him.

She wondered what he had been drinking, whether his kisses would taste like whisky.

"Late night?" he said. For a confused second, Kate thought it was a proposition. Then he jerked his chin toward her iPad, still showing a graph that had been first among the files that Dr. Rushkin had sent her.

"Not yet," Kate said. "Depends on how long it takes me to do my homework."

Jenny Lin was back with Kate's salad. She cast an amused glance in Matt's direction, then winked at Kate. "Just let me know if this guy's bothering you, okay? I'll sic the cops on him." It felt like a joke between them, but Kate didn't entirely get it.

After Jenny pivoted away again, Matt stuck out his hand to Kate. "I'll leave you to it," he said. Kate felt a twinge of disappointment. But she noticed he squeezed her hand for a second longer than was necessary. "Hope to bump into you again."

"I thought you didn't believe in coincidences," Kate said.

"There's plenty of things I don't believe," Matt said, shooting her a grin. "But when there's a beautiful woman involved, I can be convinced."

Okay, yeah. He was definitely flirting.

She watched him go with some regret, then forced her attention back to her work files. She skimmed over the first graphs. Almost 75 percent of the two thousand children who'd been interviewed could recall detailed facts about their manner of death. Sixty percent could remember the names of friends and family. Fifteen percent had birthmarks that corresponded with violent features of their death, like gunshot wounds. And 20 percent of the two thousand children who'd been interviewed recalled their time between lives, in a psychic space that showed remarkable parallels between subjects.

By the time that Kate had made it through her main course, she was the only person at the bar, and the crowd had winnowed down to a few tables lingering over coffee and dessert. Jenny was busy wiping down the bar, and kept looking at Kate sideways.

Finally, she said, "I swear, you look familiar. Have you come in here before?"

It was the opening Kate was waiting for. "Kate Willis," she said. "I was one of your campers."

Jenny stopped, letting her mouth fall open. "Kate Willis," she repeated. Jenny came closer, letting her eyes travel over Kate's face, as if aligning it with the one she remembered. "Of course! You were friends with Becca. You're all grown-up."

"I guess we all are," Kate said, and Jenny gave a rueful laugh.

"Don't remind me," she said. She folded up her rag and tossed it aside, leaning forward on the bar. "So what are you doing here? You don't live in the area, do you?"

Kate shook her head. "I'm actually here to visit one of your old students. Do you remember the Haskells?"

"Henley? Of course. We had her in school just a few years ago. Lovely girl. I like her mother, too." Jenny looked puzzled. "How do you know the Haskells?"

"It's complicated," Kate said, purposely dodging the question. Henley wasn't her patient. Their interactions weren't privileged; still, she was a child, and Kate imagined that Emily wouldn't want the news to spread that her daughter was claiming to be the reincarnation of one of the area's most notorious missing teens. Fortunately, Jenny didn't press.

"Well, tell them both hello from me," Jenny said and began wiping down the bar. "Henley was one of my favorites."

Kate leaned forward. "I have to ask you kind of a funny question. Did Henley ever mention Becca to you when she was in your school?" She stopped herself from saying *or vice versa.*

"Becca?" Jenny stared at her. "Becca *McGuire*?"

Jenny seemed so stunned, Kate nearly retracted the question. But she pressed on. "She might not have used Becca's name," Kate said. "Maybe she mentioned Camp Sauquamet, or grandparents in Hillsdale . . . ?"

"Henley was three when she started preschool," Jenny said. "She was just learning her letters. If she mentioned anything, it was probably about wanting a snack."

Jenny straightened up. She scrutinized Kate the way she used to when she was trying to parcel out a lie. There had been plenty of them over the years. "I don't understand. What is this about?"

Kate hesitated. "Henley seems to know a lot of details of Becca McGuire's life. *And* her death."

Jenny frowned as if she suspected Kate of telling a bad joke. "Are you saying that Henley Haskell knows what happened to Becca?"

"I'm saying she *thinks* she does," Kate clarified.

Jenny picked up her rag again and began polishing the immaculate bar top—a reflexive habit, obviously. "Becca McGuire's famous around here," Jenny said. She evidently shared Kate's instinctive view, that Henley had simply absorbed the information, and integrated it into her developing sense of self. Of course, she didn't know about the details that Henley could recall—details about Camp Sauquamet, and the night that Becca and her friends took the canoes to Fair Isle. "You know they still haven't closed the case. Not officially. But before Matt got promoted, no one had cracked open the case files in years."

"Matt . . . ?"

Jenny glanced up at her, amused. "Matt Bishop. The guy you were just talking to?" She shook her head. "He's a lieutenant detective with the county police. He's working Becca's case again. You didn't know that?"

Kate was too stunned to answer. In her mind, she wheeled back to their interaction at Camp Sauquamet. She'd assumed he was a landscaper, someone hired to take care of the property, rescue it from dereliction. Now she remembered how he'd answered when she'd asked him directly about his presence there. *Doing my civic duty.*

Was it possible he'd been there investigating? Looking for a decades-old trail?

Kate realized, with a sense of horror, that her name must be all over the initial reports made about Becca's disappearance. Matt must have known who she was immediately.

Jenny didn't appear to register Kate's reaction. She simply went on, "I had to go in for an interview just six months ago, go over the whole story again." She sighed. "It was rough. I hadn't thought about Becca in years. I kind of forced myself not to think about her. Know what I mean?"

Kate did, very much. It had taken a PhD, and then an MD, plus a sea of alcohol to hold Becca back, to keep her still beneath the waters of Kate's mind. But she simply said, "What did you tell the police?"

"That I felt guilty." Jenny was wiping the same place on the counter, back and forth. "I knew someone was out on the lake that night. I got up to use the bathroom. I saw that someone had opened the boathouse."

Kate felt the touch of electricity in her spine. As far as she knew, Jenny hadn't mentioned the boathouse to the cops twenty-six years earlier. It hadn't been in any of the news accounts of the case, anyway.

"I didn't think much of it at the time," she said. "When I saw the three boats missing, I figured that some of the counselors had gone out to Fair Isle without me."

"So you *did* go out there to party," Kate said. Lennie had seen intermittent lights on the island, and Becca had claimed it was where the counselors went to drink and smoke cigarettes. But even after they'd found proof of old parties on the island, Kate couldn't believe that their *counselors* were responsible.

Jenny sighed. "Harriet didn't know. She busted us once, coming back, and she was furious. She forbade us from sneaking out again. I tried to persuade the others that we had to stop. I was head counselor, you know. Harriet said it was my responsibility." She made a fitful gesture. "I just thought they'd slipped out behind my back."

"So you didn't say anything to the cops about finding the missing boats," Kate said.

Jenny nodded. "Back then, I was worried about my *job*. I was in charge. Besides, I thought it was my job to protect them."

"Them?"

"There were nine or ten of us who used to boat out to Fair Isle. Riley Haddock, Lily Wright, Ben Mosley, and Cameron Dunbar went the most." Hearing the names touched off a series of memories: Lily, leading an improv class with a feather boa wrapped around her neck; tattooed Ben, bent over a younger camper's arts and crafts project, his hair stirred by the fan circulating the smell of glue; Riley Haddock, showing off on water skis while the eager campers waited on the docks for their turn. "Of course, they all swore up and down they hadn't left their bunks all night. But who *else* could it have been?"

Kate looked away. The old guilt gnawed at her stomach. "What did Harriet think?"

Jenny smiled ruefully. "Are you kidding? I was even more scared of telling Harriet than I was of talking to the cops. I knew she'd fire all of us if she thought we were still sneaking out at night. And we all *needed* that job. We loved that camp. Harriet saw the camp as a safe haven, a place where the counselors and campers could grow together. She pulled a lot of hires from the Valley Farm School. You've heard of it?" Kate shook her head. Jenny went on. "It's an alternative school outside of Pittsfield. Lots of kids who flunked out of regular high school, or got in trouble for drugs and alcohol. Lily, Ben, and Riley had all graduated together. Lily was stoned half the time. Ben gave out his Adderall. It was pretty wild that summer."

Kate absorbed this. She'd had no idea. The counselors had seemed to her to be a single entity, a physical reality of the camp, much like the lake and the cabins. She'd loved Lily, and complained about Riley and the way she barked her speech, as if every word was a command. But for the most part, she hadn't ever imagined the counselors as single individuals, with backstories, and secrets, and their own reasons for being at camp.

All except for Cameron. Cameron, she had wondered about, and obsessed over, and pursued in private moments. That last summer, she had kept careful track of all their conversations, parsing every bit of extra meaning from the smallest interactions, even the way he routinely called her by her initials, or pretended to tip his hat at her when they crossed paths.

"Do you guys keep in touch?" Kate asked.

"Who? Me and Harriet?" Jenny shrugged. "Just on Facebook. What happened to the camp really crushed her. She moved back to North Carolina a year or so after Sauquamet shut down."

"I meant you and the other counselors," Kate said.

Again, Jenny shrugged. "Some of us," she said. "Ben's in and out of jail. He's still using. Lily's doing well. She runs a yoga practice in Kingston. No one knows what happened to Cameron."

Kate perked up. "What do you mean?"

"Someone told me he moved over to Columbia County. That's on the New York side. Lily even thought she saw him once, at the Strawberry Festival over in Chatham. But . . . I've looked him up, you know, a few times. The only Cameron Dunbar I could find was some runaway from Dallas. It wasn't him," she added, off Kate's look. "Cameron grew up in Vermont. Besides, I checked the picture."

Kate felt a twinge of disappointment. She would have liked to know how Cameron was doing now, all these years later. It was stupid, really—a remnant of that very first crush, and the intensity of the feelings she'd nurtured, fed, and tended like a fire. He probably wouldn't remember her, or the time he'd touched her face after she'd been crying and told her she had pretty eyes.

"You said you went out to Fair Isle a lot that summer," Kate said. "Did you ever . . . see anything out there?"

Jenny raised an eyebrow. "What? Like a ghost?" She peeled away to the register and started punching at the screen. "No. No, we never saw the Gray Lady. We never got hexed or cursed or struck down where we stood. It was creepy as hell, though. Those ruins . . . something bad happened out there, that's for sure."

"What do you think happened that night?" Kate asked. "What do *you* think happened to Becca?"

Jenny sighed. For a second, she stood motionless by the register, her back turned. Finally she turned around, sliding Kate's bill across the bar. "Becca was . . . difficult. You remember. You guys were best friends, right?" Kate nodded.

"Something happened to her that summer. She'd always been a challenge—the sleepwalking, you know, and the tantrums—but as soon as she hit fourteen, it was a whole different ball game. Always provoking people, always defiant. Ferdinand caught her with cigarettes. Then Ferdinand caught her *stealing* cigarettes." Kate's mind flashed, briefly, to the time that Becca had brought her a pair of

Cameron's boxers. Those, too, had been stolen. "She tried to buy alcohol on a field trip. She was always flirting with Cameron."

Kate felt a curious twist in her stomach, as if she was still the fourteen-year-old with a crush. "Becca was flirting with Cameron?"

"She flirted with all the male counselors. But with Cameron it was bad. I caught her going through his stuff one day, when he was reffing a game of kickball. She cornered him alone in the boathouse, tried to get him to kiss her. At least, that's what Cameron says. Who knows. I had to caution him twice for being alone with her."

Kate thought of how ruthlessly Becca had teased her for the crush, how she'd called Cameron "old man," as in "old-man nipples," and insisted that Kate's obsession was visible on her face. Maybe she'd been right. But now Kate wondered whether she'd also been jealous.

"I figure that Becca saw Cameron and the others sneaking off to the island, and decided to follow them there," Jenny said. "Like I said, they all denied taking the boats out that night. But they would, after what happened, wouldn't they?"

For a second, Kate hovered again on the edge of confessing. It would bring relief to Jenny, but it would also open the door to gossip, and further complicate the question of what exactly Henley knew, and how.

By now, she was the only person left in the restaurant. Two servers were stacking chairs, while another made a ferocious attack on the floor with a broom. Kate signed her bill and stood up.

"One more thing," she said. "You mentioned that *three* canoes were missing from the boathouse. Are you absolutely sure it was three?"

Jenny nodded. "I counted. I was trying to figure how many of the counselors snuck off without telling me. Of course, in the morning, I realized that Becca had taken one of them."

Kate thanked her. They exchanged a brief and awkward hug over the bar.

Outside, the moon was shockingly large, ballooning low over the trees, a giant spotlight tacked to the dark. The wind had picked up, hissing the trees together in gossip. Kate stood there for a while, picking out the constellations from a sky freckled with stars. Cameron had taught them about constellations that last summer, dragging out the camp telescope and patiently shepherding them one by one to the eyepiece, teaching them to locate the Big Dipper and the Little Dipper, Orion's Belt, and even, one night, the tiny orange promise of a distant Mars. Becca had insisted on making up her own constellations, cracking the other girls up as she pointed out Orion's Package and the Giant's Ass Crack until Cameron reprimanded her sharply with a single, *"Becca."*

She wondered about Becca and Cameron. She wondered about Jenny's claims that Becca had been caught rifling through his belongings, looking for—what, exactly? Something private, something personal, something she could use against him later. Collateral, Becca called it.

She wondered about the time Cameron had touched her face and called her pretty. She wondered if he'd done the same to Becca.

More than anything else, she wondered about the fact that three canoes were missing from the boathouse the night they'd all rowed out to Fair Isle.

Kate and Becca had taken one canoe. Lennie and Mari had shared another.

So who, she wondered, had taken the third?

FOURTEEN

Kate slept badly, waking up in the middle of the night certain that someone outside the window was watching her. When she turned over in bed, she found Henley sitting beside her, and dimly understood that she was still in a dream. Henley was dressed like a doll in a high-collared wedding dress, holding a dead puppy in her lap, cooing to it like a baby. Later, Kate was at the lake. Lennie was waiting at the beach with a shovel, insistent that they bury the flowers they'd let rot in the sun. No one could know, Lennie said, that they'd forgotten to tend the gardens. But when they tried to dig a hole, they struck concrete; too late, Kate realized they'd been mistaken for grave robbers and were locked inside the old mausoleum.

Now, hours later, she still couldn't shake the muddle of past and present. Setting off for the Haskells' house, she nearly turned right to go to Hillsdale. The longer she stayed, the more memories returned to her, thickening like snow into the shape, the feeling, of being fourteen again, just straddling the cusp of adulthood.

She'd sent Mari a text and left a voicemail, but hadn't heard back. She resisted the urge to reach out again. Mari was likely reeling from their conversation; Kate wasn't sure, in the end, that she would believe or accept Kate's version of events. She had another sudden yearning for Lennie—clearheaded, forceful, pragmatic. Lennie always knew what to do. Lennie could always figure out a way to get them out of trouble.

It had been Lennie who'd given their statement to the police.

Coming up the Haskells' driveway, Kate startled half a dozen wild turkeys turning over pebbles in the grass. They scattered before her car wheels, vanishing into the trees like so many children peeling off for a game of hide-and-seek. Kate thought of the first summer she'd spent at camp, how she and Becca would wander into the woods, threshing the underbrush to look for fat mushrooms they could toe over with their sneakers, or searching for evidence of fairies.

She tried not to think about what she was about to do, what it meant about Henley's case and about her objectivity—which every day decayed further, like some radioactive isotope. She had decided the night before that there was, perhaps, a way to figure out what had really happened to Becca the night they were all on Fair Isle.

She could ask the girl who claimed to remember.

Henley was outside, clambering up her play set to one of two towering platforms, when Kate arrived. She stood for a second at the top, watching Kate emerge from her car. Then she sat down on the slide and pushed neatly to the ground. Immediately, she pivoted to the swings, glancing over her shoulder to make sure that Kate took the cue.

"Wanna see how high I can go?" she called out.

"Sure." Kate caught sight of Emily inside the house as she crossed over to Henley. She stood watching Henley pump her legs, arcing higher and higher until she was nearly parallel with the bar. Kate feared the momentum might carry her into a flip. But at the last second, Henley dug her sneakers abruptly into the scuff of dirt, bringing the swing to an abrupt halt.

"Sometimes I jump," Henley said. "But last time, I hurt my ankle."

"That was very impressive," Kate said. "Do you like to swing?"

Henley shrugged. "It's okay." She returned to the plastic ladder and began to climb.

"Did your mom tell you I was coming?" Kate asked. "Did she tell you that we were going to talk for a bit?"

"Yeah," Henley said doubtfully. "But I didn't think you'd come back."

"Why?" Kate asked.

Henley disappeared into a plastic tunnel that linked the two climbing platforms. "I thought you were mad at me." Her voice, distorted through the space, came out muffled.

"Why would I be mad at you?" Kate said.

Henley re-emerged at the slide and came down again, this time inch by inch, stopping herself with her hands. At the bottom she stopped, letting her feet dangle to the grass. "You were mad at me *before*," she said.

"Before?" Kate repeated, turning the word into a question.

"When I used to be Becca," Henley said. Suddenly, she stood up and darted off. Kate followed her at a trot, tracking Henley's yellow shirt as it flashed between the rhododendron bushes and rounded the corner of the house. Kate found her on the back patio, using a stick to scratch out patterns in the stone.

"Henley?" Kate took a seat next to Henley, on a cushioned chair still wet with morning dew. "Why did you think I was mad at you?"

"Because," Henley said, "you left me alone. You pushed me."

Kate closed her eyes. The memory startled out: Becca, standing in front of the open mausoleum, letting out a musk of cold air and the smell of rot. Mari was hysterical by then, shaking, practically incapable of speech. Lennie was shouting at Becca for breaking the lock. Kate was trying to get everyone to calm down. Becca had called all of them pathetic, said that she couldn't wait until summer was over, when she could go back to her real friends. Kate remembered feeling a charge of anger so hot, so intense, it was like lightning flashing inside her head.

But it was Mari who'd pushed her.

It was definitely Mari who'd pushed her inside.

Wasn't it?

"Henley, do you remember who was with you that night?" Kate asked.

Henley had scratched an entanglement of circles in the stone, all of them overlapping, collapsing in on one another. "You were," she said.

"Besides me."

Henley hesitated. "I don't remember their names," she said. Then: "They were in the book."

Kate's heartbeat picked up in her chest. "Could you show me?" she asked. "Could you point them out?"

Henley stood up, sighing, just as Emily slid open the back door.

"You're here," she said. "I thought I heard your car."

Henley was already trotting past her into the house. "I need to get my book," she said.

"What book?" Emily said, but her daughter had already vanished.

Henley's answer came rebounding back, distorted by distance. "My photo book."

Emily accepted this without comment. But Kate could see the worry on her face. In the brief moments of silence, she slid the door closed again and crossed the patio to sit with Kate. "I hope we're doing the right thing," she said, casting an anxious glance at the house. "Henley had another nightmare last night."

"Worse than usual?" Kate asked.

Emily rubbed her forehead. "No. Yes. The same. How do I tell?" She sighed. "I just wonder . . . can it be good for her to relive all of this stuff?"

Kate wished she had an answer. "That depends," she said.

"On what?"

Kate took a deep breath. Her whole world was tilting, falling into some kind of darkness she didn't understand, where children could come back from the dead, where memories could stretch back in time to land in forgotten spaces. "On whether she's telling the truth."

Emily looked at her sharply. For a second, she said nothing. Then: "So you believe her now? Finally? You believe that she might really be remembering . . . ?" She trailed off.

"I don't know," Kate answered. She felt a squeeze of hard guilt in her chest. She was supposed to have the answers. She was supposed to understand the *mechanisms*. She was supposed to know how to solve Henley like a puzzle, to reorder her psychic and emotional spaces into greater harmony.

But she didn't. Instead, she *needed* Henley. She was relying on her to answer twenty-six-year-old questions. She wasn't thinking about what Henley wanted, what was best for her.

She was only thinking of Becca. She was thinking about what Becca needed.

It was Becca, not Henley, who needed to tell the truth.

Before Emily could respond, Henley was back, sidling out the door with the camp yearbook cradled in her arms. She had grown attached to it already. Kate noted she had referred to the book as hers, and already dreaded taking it back from her.

They sat together at the outdoor table, watching Henley as she paged carefully through the yearbook, scrutinizing every photo. To anyone watching from a distance, it might have appeared to be a sweet, familial scene: a child engrossed in old pictures, enraptured by the evidence of people and places from her past.

"Now, look very closely," Kate said when they reached a photograph of all the girls from Cabin Twelve, crowded at the railing in front of the cabin, making goofy faces. "I want you to tell me who was with you on the night that you got hurt."

Henley sat for a moment, staring. Then she inched a finger along the page until it landed on Mari's face. "Her," she said. Then she looked up, confused. "I think she had a puppy."

Emily looked at Kate questioningly.

"Becca used to call Mari our puppy," she said. The words tasted bitter as she spoke them. Mariana had always hated that.

"Mariana," Emily repeated. "You mentioned her the other day."

Kate nodded. "She's local. I thought you and Henley might know her from her music school."

"She tuned our piano once," Emily said with a helpless shrug.

Henley was hopscotching uncertainly over the picture with her fingertips. Kate found herself hoping that she would get it wrong, that she would miss Lennie, that this would all prove to be a mistake. But then she pressed a thumb to Lennie's face.

"I don't like her," she said. "She's mean." Kate registered the change to present tense.

"That's Lennie," she said, and she thought she saw a momentary relaxation on Henley's face, the relief of recognition. "Was she there that night?"

Henley nodded. Kate could feel her heart scraping against her ribs as if desperate to escape. "Who else?" she said.

Henley twirled her hand over the page, taking her time, making a game of it. She dropped a finger on Kate's face.

"That's right," she said. "I was there."

"You pushed me," Henley said again. Kate didn't bother to correct her. She wasn't sure—she couldn't be positive—that Henley wasn't right.

"Do you see anyone else in the picture who was there with us that night?" Kate asked, and Henley shook her head. "Do you see anyone who was with us on the island?" She felt both relieved and vaguely disappointed; she wondered whether Jenny Lin might have mistaken the number of boats that were missing from the boathouse that night after all. "Are you *sure*?"

"Wait," Henley said when Kate reached out to shut the book. "I want to see more pictures."

Kate and Emily exchanged a glance.

"I thought you said no one else was there, sweet pea," Emily said.

"I said I didn't see her," Henley corrected her mother. She watched as Kate slowly flipped forward through the yearbook, her attention absorbed by the images of various campers posing in front of their bunks.

"There," she said abruptly, plugging a hand down on the page. "That's her."

"Which one, sweetie?" Emily asked.

But Kate didn't need to wait for Henley to answer. She leaned forward unconsciously, staring at the pretty dark-haired girl posing in front of Cabin Eight, surrounded by grinning bunkmates. She didn't need to consult the caption to recall her name: It was Natalie Horace, Becca's mortal enemy, the subject of so many of their pranks that summer. The girl who'd allegedly left a dead frog in Becca's shower caddy and told everyone that Becca's mom was a drug addict.

"Are you sure?" Kate asked. She no longer knew whether she was talking to Henley or to Becca. She no longer knew if she cared. "Are you sure that Natalie came with us?"

Henley looked up at Kate fearfully. Slowly, she nodded.

By now, Kate could feel her heartbeat in her throat. If Henley was right—if Natalie had followed them to the island—it would explain why Jenny Lin had found three canoes missing from the boathouse. And it would mean that there was someone else with them that night—someone who hated Becca, someone who might have even wanted her dead.

"Henley, I want you to think very carefully." Kate spoke extremely slowly, carefully, fighting the urge to take Henley by the shoulders, to shout her words down to Becca, or the part of her that was still buried in Henley's memories, alive. "Was Natalie the one who hurt you that night? Was she the one who took you away?"

Henley fidgeted. "I don't know." She looked up at Kate reproachfully through a fan of dark lashes. "I told you. It was the Gray Lady who did it." Then she pivoted in her chair toward her mother. "Can I go play now?"

"Of course," Emily said. "But only for a little while. Remember, we have your swim class today." Henley was already off, darting across the porch and vanishing around the house, probably back to her play set again. "We call it swim class," Emily added in a lower voice. "But we're just trying to get Henley to put her face in the water. She's still terrified of going in without her floaties. All the other kids her age are learning the crawl already . . ." She sounded tired. "So what now?"

Again, Kate didn't have an answer. She reached for her training, for diagnostic and therapeutic frameworks, but found nothing. "I'll have someone at the department review Henley's case files," Kate said. "Dr. Rushkin may want to interview Henley himself."

"*More* interviews?" Emily squeezed her knuckles tightly around her coffee mug.

"If Henley's memories are real—if they're verified—then she's important," Kate said.

"Henley's important because she's my daughter," Emily said sharply. She shook her head in disgust. "I thought that knowing the truth about her memories—finding a name, seeing the yearbook, revisiting her past . . . I thought it would help Henley. I thought it would bring Henley closure. But she spent hours last night staring at pictures, just fixated. I could barely tear her away for dinner. And she's still having nightmares . . ."

Kate looked down at her hands. She'd been picking at her cuticles again, leaving her fingernail beds bloody. Stress. Anxiety. Old habits. "Maybe Henley won't have closure until Becca does," she blurted. She was relieved, and a little embarrassed, once she'd said the words out loud. It was an idea that had been skating just outside the boundaries of her rational mind, teasing her for days.

Emily stared at her. "What do you mean?"

"The police never did find Becca's body," she said. "No one knows how she really died."

"What do you mean? I thought she drowned," Emily said.

Kate felt the old thrash of guilt in her stomach. "That's what the police assumed after they found the canoe. But no one knows for sure. No one knows what happened to Becca that night." This, at least, was true in the strictest sense.

"And you think Henley won't be able to . . . move on until Becca does?" Even though the sun was falling heavily across her, Emily shivered. "It sounds like a ghost story, doesn't it?"

"It's a theory," Kate said. "Look, no matter what, it's obvious that Henley identifies with Becca. She identifies with her death. Until she has words for what happened, until she can assign meaning to that trauma, she'll continue to replay it."

Emily looked at her sideways. "Even if she's somehow imagining everything?"

Kate nodded. "Especially then."

Emily looked away. She was quiet for a bit, rotating her mug between her palms, clearly warring with her thoughts. After a minute, she roused herself. "If the police never found Becca's body," she said slowly, "how will we ever find out what happened to her?"

This was it: the moment that Kate tipped over the precipice of her beliefs, of her credentials, of her own expertise, and dropped.

"Maybe Henley will tell us," she said simply. "Maybe she already has."

FIFTEEN

Natalie Horace, now Natalie Gersch, had three children, a large house, and a flourishing dental practice in Greenwich, Connecticut. Her Facebook profile picture could have been lifted from an advertisement: There she was, bracketed by towheaded children, beaming at the camera like someone trying to sell a new fitness campaign. Kate's profile picture, by contrast, was just a photo of Kate at a lectern, hair unruly, wearing an unflattering blazer she had picked up at Filene's Basement an hour before her keynote in front of the American Psychological Association. Ten minutes of checking Natalie's feed, and she already felt self-conscious—the lingering effects, she assumed, of many summers envying Natalie's adorable matching duffel bags, real Tiffany charm bracelet, and designer T-shirts from afar.

In general, Camp Sauquamet had done a good job of holding the real world at bay, pinioning the girls' economic realities and home situations on the far side of an invisible protection that equalized all the campers. But as the girls had grown older, small rifts had appeared in the psychic wall that had for years kept them all friendly. Everyone knew that Natalie's parents were extravagantly wealthy, a halo of privilege that seemed to extend, fairly or not, to all the girls in her bunk—but only that last summer had it seemed to matter. Ditto the rumors of Becca's mom's addiction, and even the stories of Kate's mother's illness, which began to contaminate the atmosphere, fissuring the camp unity like a fungal blight.

It made sense, from a developmental standpoint. The girls had been on the verge of high school, increasingly under pressure to self-define and differentiate. The camp's commitment to unity of spirit simply couldn't hold up under the unrelenting impact of adolescence, which battered them all with insecurities and demanded an answer in hierarchy. Throughout much of the last summer, Becca and Natalie had been battling for control, for influence, more than for anything else.

Now she wondered how far that tension had extended—and where it had ultimately led.

Scrolling through Natalie's pictures—filled with wholesome family shots of day hikes, ski houses, beautifully appointed dinner tables, and purebred Labs lolling on expensive carpets—she found it hard to imagine that Natalie might once have tailed the girls out to Fair Isle with the intention of doing harm to Becca. On the other hand, she wouldn't be the first charming socialite type to be holding on to a violent secret. Early in her career, when she was still doing routine clinical work, Kate had treated the twelve-year-old daughter of a prominent Virginia couple who'd reverted to bed-wetting in middle school, and had, seemingly out of nowhere, developed a whole manner of tics. Her mother—a tennis-skirt socialite with impeccable manners and speech faintly inflected with the South—had been ingratiating, concerned, and adoring. Over time, however, Kate had discovered that she'd badly abused her stepson, whose eventual sudden death was initially ruled accidental. The woman's daughter, however, intuited the truth: Her mother was a murderer.

She found herself wondering who Becca might have become had she lived long enough to grow up, and what pictures she might be posting to Facebook now, at the age of forty. Maybe she would have gotten her mansion on a California beach—Becca had dreamed of becoming a model, or an actress, and marrying rich. Or maybe she would have outgrown her early difficulties—her impulsivity, her volatility, and her emotional lability, all signs of attachment trauma—and gone on to live a regular life full of modesty and dignity, with a family and child of her own. She might have gone on to be a social worker, or even a therapist, as many kids from troubled backgrounds did once they themselves got help.

Maybe she would have gotten help.

It took Kate an hour to compose her Facebook message to Natalie. She agonized over whether or not Natalie would remember her—and if so, whether the sight of Kate's name would mean the message went straight to the trash. According to Mari, it had been Kate who'd actually stolen Natalie's diary from Cabin Eight; Natalie might remember it the same way. She didn't know whether to mention Becca. If Natalie really did have information about the night Becca died—if she'd actually been there—then there must be a reason she, like Kate, had never come forward. Seeing Becca's name might spook her. On the other hand, by keeping her message vague, Kate ran the risk that it would be ignored. Natalie might simply assume she was looking to reminisce, to reconnect with people she had known during childhood.

She wrote and deleted a dozen drafts. She paced circles around her Airbnb. She answered emails from the university. She washed her hands with lemon dish soap to keep from biting her nails.

Finally, she wrote a single line.

I need to talk to you about that night on Fair Isle.

She hit send.

She was relieved, but not surprised, to reach Marc Rushkin in his office during summer vacation. His wife, Rosemarie, liked to joke that her husband had been having an affair with the office ever since he'd been a young hire under Dr. Stevenson, in the earliest days of the department. But somehow, despite his fabled work ethic and commitment to DOPS's research, Dr. Rushkin had managed to build a whole life in a way that eluded Kate. He'd told her once that forty years studying and appreciating the mysteries of consciousness, and the evidence that our physical reality was just one impoverished dimension of human experience, was enough to put any to-do list in proper perspective.

Kate wished she found comfort in the idea of a life beyond the physical plane. But all she could picture was an immense dark space, a place of interminable waiting. A forever trap. She pictured Becca, her mind and memory slivered into fragments, alive mostly in Henley's fragmentary nightmares, replaying the endless, circular repetition of her death.

What kind of comfort was that? What perspective could it bring? To Kate, the comfort was in the order, the regular procession of tasks and to-dos, a causal and linear march through the days.

But toward what? Dr. Rushkin would say. *Where are you actually going?*

Kate had never had an answer for that.

"Well, Professor Willis, what's the verdict?" They'd switched over to Zoom. As usual, Kate found the sight of Dr. Rushkin comforting. He was the epitome of the absent-minded academic, frequently covered in crumbs and usually surrounded by towering mesas of books and peer journals. Sunlight through the office windows behind him lit up heavy cones of twirling dust motes. Kate could practically smell the university through the screen.

"I wish I could tell you," Kate said. "Has Steve filled you in?"

"He mentioned something about a personal connection." Dr. Rushkin peered at her intently. "Want to tell me about it?"

Kate reminded him about the details of the case—that the girl, Henley, reported intense and detailed memories of a previous lifetime; that these memories corresponded with the biographical details of a local girl who'd disappeared mysteriously some twenty-six years earlier.

"A local girl," Dr. Rushkin repeated. "How local?"

"Forty minutes away," Kate said. "But the case was well publicized through the area."

Dr. Rushkin grunted. "And is it possible that Henley picked up these details from an alternate source? The media, local gossip, a friend's parents?"

"She may have," Kate said. "But some of the details that she knows were never released to the media. Some of the things she knows, no one knows. No one but Becca."

Dr. Rushkin inched his reading glasses down his nose to peer at Kate over the rim. "And how do *you* know that?"

"Because Becca was my friend," Kate said. "We went to camp together. And I was there the night she—the night it happened."

Dr. Rushkin leaned back in his chair. He said nothing for a bit. He sat for a minute, twirling a pen in his fingers, as he did when he was thinking. "That's an extraordinary coincidence," he said. A smile twitched beneath his overgrown beard. "*If* you believe in that kind of thing."

Kate knew that of all the possibilities that Dr. Rushkin considered plausible—life after death, souls that incarnated over and over, psychic tethers that linked humans across time and distance—*coincidence*, strictly defined, was not one of them.

"I'm honestly not sure *what* to believe," she said. "I've spent time with Henley and her mother. I don't see any red flags. No attention seeking, no evidence of deception or even delusion. But I still can't accept—" She broke off. She had never told Dr. Rushkin directly that she didn't believe in the validity of any of DOPS's findings. She and Steve had had that fight in private.

But Dr. Rushkin smiled as if he knew what she was thinking. "It's mind blowing, isn't it? It's a completely different paradigm. For us, anyway. Plenty of cultures accept reincarnation as a fact."

Reincarnation. There it was—the word Kate had been avoiding, even in her head. Reincarnation implied that Becca's identity, her core essence, had been slotted into a new form, like water poured between vessels. But she'd known Becca when they were eight years old—only a year older than Henley was now—and she found no similarities in their personality. Where was Becca's edge, her stubbornness, her mischief? Where was her moodiness, her brooding, and, conversely, her dazzling moments of enthusiasm, when she could persuade anyone of anything, convince you that by jumping high enough, you could in fact scrape the sky with your knuckles? What did it mean for Becca to exist again, if there was nothing left but a shrapnel of her memories?

She said as much to Dr. Rushkin, and he laughed.

"Now you're asking questions better answered by religion," he said. "I'd be happy just getting mainstream science to admit that there's something going on with these phenomena. There's something real here that can't be explained by our current models."

Kate remembered again the long-ago evening she'd spent with psychiatrist Evan Waller, talking about exorcisms, and what he'd said about 5 percent of his cases: that what they needed was a priest.

"Look," Dr. Rushkin added, leaning forward again, "you're a psychologist. You know the impact of early environment on childhood development. You know how significant those first attachments can be. The real question is, who would Becca have been if she'd been raised from birth by a stable mother in a home where she was safe and cared for? Would she have been the Becca you knew? *That's* the question."

Kate imagined, for a second, some gigantic karmic spreadsheet of corrections, sending Becca back to experience a mother's love. It was a comforting thought, but absurdist. The universe didn't keep track of pain and suffering; it certainly didn't correct for it. Anyone with half a brain could see that.

The fact was, Becca wasn't back. Even if it turned out that Henley really had lived, once, as Becca—an extraordinary claim, an earth-shattering fact, if they could only prove it—she had also died as Becca, too.

Either way, Becca's story was over.

But not quite. Not all the way.

Not until they knew how she'd died, and why.

"So what should I do next?" Kate said.

"You've collected Henley's claims? You've observed her home environment? You've found no credible alternate explanation for what she remembers?" Dr. Rushkin peered at Kate closely. She nodded. He agitated a little in his chair, then—a visible sign of excitement. He had caught the tailwind of a new subject, a new proof for his team. "Then send over what you have. We'll reach out to the Haskells and take it from here."

Kate felt the wing tip of panic brush against her ribs. "Hang on," she said. "I'm not done. I'm barely getting started."

Dr. Rushkin startled. "You just said the girl's claims were credible . . ."

"Credible, yes," Kate said. "That doesn't mean they're true. There's still a chance that Henley has been influenced by someone in her orbit."

"Is that your clinical assessment?" Dr. Rushkin gave her another long look over his glasses.

"I'm not prepared to say," Kate said stiffly.

Dr. Rushkin sighed. "What's the goal here, Kate? What's your endgame?"

Time, Kate thought. She needed time. Time to make sense of Henley's memories, time to make sense of what had really happened to Becca. "Henley's still having nightmares. She's still phobic about water, and enclosed spaces—"

"That isn't uncommon in cases like this." Dr. Rushkin cut her off. "In fact, it's one of the principal features of valid past-life recall. Phobic behaviors emerge as the result of some trauma experienced in a previous lifetime. We've even linked birthmarks and physical anomalies to a person's previous identity—"

"So how do we fix it?" Kate said. She was getting angry for reasons she couldn't quite explain. "If Henley's tormented by these memories—"

"Is she tormented, Kate?" Dr. Rushkin asked. "Are these recollections really impairing her ability to live a healthy, full identity? Is she unable to function in her present life? Or are *you* tormented?"

Kate didn't answer.

"She's not your patient, Kate," Dr. Rushkin reminded her. "Your job isn't to cure her."

"When Henley's mother reached out to DOPS for help, you referred her to me," Kate said.

"Because you were convinced there must be a *psychiatric* explanation," Dr. Rushkin said. Kate heard in his tone a slight reproach. "But if Henley is telling the truth, then DOPS *will* help her. We have thousands of reports—verified reports—of similar cases from around the globe. We can give the Haskells a way to understand Henley's experience, to validate it, to normalize it."

"And what about Becca's experience?" The words were out of Kate's mouth before she could unthink them. "Who's validating that? Who's listening to what she has to say?"

For a long moment, Dr. Rushkin said nothing. Kate looked away from the screen, her face burning. She felt, uncomfortably, as if she were the one under assessment.

"This must be tough for you," Dr. Rushkin said. "The fact that you knew the previous personality . . . the fact that you actually befriended her . . ." He shook his head. "It must be very disconcerting."

"It's crazy," Kate spat out. "It's lunatic. I don't understand any of it."

"Maybe you don't have to," Dr. Rushkin said gently. "Maybe you can simply accept it, as one aspect of the Great Mystery."

Kate thought of Becca's body, lying still and blue on the cold stone slab of that mausoleum. She thought of Becca's bones, lying in a tumble at the bottom of that deep, dark lake.

"Mysteries are meant to be solved," she said shortly. "I'll let you know when I have the answer to this one."

She hung up. She sat for a moment, breathing hard, as if she'd been running somewhere. Slowly the room came back into focus. She became aware of the desk, and the sun lolling through the sliding doors, and her phone, chiming a new notification on her desk.

It was a message from Natalie. A phone number, and two words.

Call me.

THEN

They ran through the wet slap of branches, and the thickening of spruce massed along the beach, leapfrogging the ruins of old stone walls, their flashlights bouncing back strange visions: the blackened remains of a campfire; paint marks slashed across the trunk of a dead pine; the twin flare of animal eyes that caught their light before vanishing with a rustle. Lennie pitched and bounded ahead of them, shouting, "Come on, come on," breathless and exhilarated, distancing them from the ever quieting echo of Becca's voice. Kate felt her heartbeat exploding, trying to pump straight out of her chest and rocket into the night. She didn't want to think about what would happen next, about how Becca might repay them. She wanted to run. She wanted to keep running forever, to vanish deeper and deeper into the trees until they absorbed her, protected her from whatever might come next.

Mari let out a sharp cry and went down. Kate felt her drop. She turned around and saw Mari on her hands and knees in a sludge of mud.

"My ankle," she wailed. She was gasping and crying at the same time, her glasses misted, her hair plastered to a slick of sweat against her forehead. The first thing that Kate thought was how ugly she looked, like a mauled animal. She had a sudden urge to strike out and kick her, or to leave her in the mud and keep running.

Immediately she felt guilty. She started to crouch beside Mari, but Lennie jerked her hard by the elbow.

"Wait," she said. She angled her flashlight toward the cluster of leaves crowding the narrow trail they'd beaten through the woods, only a few inches from where Mari had collapsed. "Poison ivy. See?"

Mari screamed, scrabbling backward, backing up against a tree. "Did it touch me? Did it touch me?" She kept repeating hysterically. Kate felt the pitch of her voice in her teeth, and imagined that it might carry all the way across the lake.

"Calm down, Mari," she said, while Lennie said, "How the fuck am I supposed to know if it touched you? You're the one who fell."

They got Mari to her feet, eventually. She was still whimpering, sucking on her lower lip, all damp and snotty looking.

"Is Becca going to be mad?" she asked.

"Oh, she'll murder us," Lennie said flatly, and Mari wailed again.

Now that the adrenaline was ebbing, Kate felt a knot of bad feeling in her stomach. "She'll calm down," Kate said, mostly to convince herself. "It was just a joke."

"Yeah. It's not like we're going to leave her there forever," Lennie said, still in that strange, expressionless voice.

For a moment the idea hovered between them, the possibility, twisting in their imagination like a signal of smoke. They could leave Becca behind. They could shut her up for good.

Then they would be free.

They'd lost sight of the lake. The trees, grayed by their flashlights, sutured by strangleholds of climbing vines, narrowed silently into the darkness above them. Kate's flashlight fell on another stone wall, heaped up in the underbrush. Next to it, someone had spray-painted GO BACK *on the trunk of an old tree, collapsed by lightning, now exposing black guts to the sky.*

"Check it out." Lennie edged a little farther toward the wall, stepping carefully over fists of poison ivy, angling her flashlight at the rubble of old stone. "It looks like an eye, doesn't it?"

She was right. Someone—or something—had scratched an eye into several stones. Kate began to be aware of whispers in the trees, the faint rustling of movement above them, and felt a notch of fear.

"I don't like this place," Mari said. Her voice still sounded shrill, strangled. "I want to go back."

"What's that sound?" Lennie said, and they stood in tense silence, listening. Lennie was right: Along with the movement of leaves was a faint tinkling, like the hollow sound of laughter.

"We should turn around," Mari said insistently.

Lennie ignored her. "What is it?" She angled her light into the canopy, illuminating branches that ran like thick veins along the seam of sky. Then they saw it: high up in the branches of a sycamore, a strange collection of tin cans and trash and bird feathers, strung together with what looked like fishing wire, rotating slowly in the wind. Looking at it made Kate feel unaccountably nauseous; she had a growing nightmare sense that they'd stumbled across a forbidden place.

"What—what is that?" Mari whimpered.

"I don't know. It looks like a marker or something." Even Lennie sounded afraid.

"This is it," Kate said. She didn't know where the idea came from, only that, all of a sudden, she knew. "This is the place where she died."

"Where who died?" Mari said.

"The Gray Lady." Kate felt almost peaceful, like she was speaking from a dream. "This is where her heart broke. Right here, on this spot."

"Lennie, please—" Mari started to say.

But Lennie hushed her sharply. "Did you hear that?" she whispered. Suddenly fear invaded Kate again. She felt a creeping sense of cold, a numbness that froze her fingers on her flashlight, made her breath painful in her chest.

They all heard it: the crack of a twig underfoot, a rustle in the bushes.

Someone was there. Someone was watching them.

Mari started whimpering. Lennie swung her flashlight around wildly.

"Who is it?" she shouted. "Who's there?"

Kate could hardly bring herself to turn around. She knew what she would see—she knew what she would find the second she looked behind her. It seemed to take forever to move her feet, as if that small, half circle was a revolution of her entire world.

But finally she did. At the same second, Lennie's flashlight sweep landed right at the woman's feet, near the filthy hem of her white gown, and crept upward to her face—hideous, deformed, bloated with death, surrounded by long clumps of tangled hair.

The Gray Lady.

She lifted a trembling hand. She pointed at them.

Lennie cursed and dropped her flashlight. Mari screamed. Kate had never heard anyone scream like that. Then Mari was running, careening back through the woods, and Kate felt Lennie's hand close around her wrist. She could still see the Gray Lady, her shoulders barely touched by moonlight, standing there, watching.

"What are you doing?" Lennie was half dragging her. "What the fuck are you doing?" Kate knew she was partly directing her words to the specter, the horrible vision who'd raised a hand, marking them all.

She could barely make her legs work. She kept stumbling into Lennie, almost taking her down.

They were whiplashed by branches. Lost, careening, tripping over uneven ground, over broken stones that seemed to leap up under their feet. It was too late, anyway, to escape. The Gray Lady had already seen them.

We're cursed, *Kate thought.* We're all cursed.

One of them would have to die tonight.

SIXTEEN

Getting to Greenwich Point Park cost Kate two hours, and forty dollars in a nonresident day pass. She'd spent the drive from Massachusetts listening to *Returned*, a podcast Steve had recommended years earlier about children who claimed to remember past lives.

Steve was actually interviewed on the third episode, talking about the famous case of the Pollock twins, who'd developed eerie memories and preferences that mimicked those of their older sisters who'd died tragically before the twins' birth. Kate found his voice comforting, even if she didn't find the evidence itself compelling. She found it hard to believe that the Pollock girls' parents had never, as they insisted, kept any photos or memorabilia from their eldest daughters, insisting that the girls' existence be kept a secret from their youngest. She suspected there might be valid nonverbal mechanisms for the transfer of information between parents and their children, as there had seemed to be in several studies of identical twins that had intrigued her.

Still, she wondered whether there was any meaningful difference between accepting that minds could get somehow entangled in the present—absorbing information never verbally expressed—and the belief that they could be entangled through time.

But why only some minds? If these children really could recall previous identities—if the phenomenon was real—what made them special? Why did only some children remember?

And why did only some lives get to be recalled?

After two hours and four episodes, Kate was left feeling more conflicted than ever. Some of the cases were, in Kate's mind, obvious fabrications: wishful thinking at best; delusional fabulism at worst. One woman, for example, claimed to have rediscovered memories of countless previous identities—all of them conveniently famous, like Joan of Arc and Cleopatra—through work with a past-life regression "therapy," a form of guided hypnosis that had been debunked as a clinical tool over and over. Other cases were less clear cut, and one in particular captured her attention: a London-based child who had actually led police to the location of his old body, and correctly fingered the culprit who'd killed him.

She wondered if that was what Henley was doing—pointing her in the right direction. Pointing her, at last, to the truth.

Greenwich was beautiful, idyllic, in a manicured, ruthlessly curated kind of way, like a gigantic Instagram promotion about East Coast summers brought to life. The park lay along a promontory girded with pristine beach, overlooking the absurdist mansions dotting that portion of the coast. Most of the women were blond, all of them dressed almost identically in coral pinks and summer whites. Kate had the funny impression she'd entered a simulation filled with duplicate characters, all of them performing the same scripted and rote tasks: jogging in Lululemon workout gear, or unloading the same coolers from identical SUVs next to WASPy looking children who'd been cut and pasted into position. She found a parking spot, eventually, between a Range Rover and a Porsche, quickly tried to wrangle her hair into some semblance of a ponytail—ruefully aware of all the streaks of gray—and climbed out of the car.

Natalie was waiting on a bench near the public grills, overlooking the water, as she had promised to be. When Kate approached she sprang to her feet, and then quickly sat down again, as if remembering belatedly that she and Kate were practically strangers.

Still, she smiled. It was a shy smile, and unexpectedly self-conscious. Kate noticed that despite her tan, and the cascade of blond hair flowing impeccably down her shoulders, she looked very thin, and very tired.

"Thanks for meeting me here," Natalie said. "I hope you didn't hit traffic."

"It was easy," Kate said. Then: "Where are your boys?"

Natalie had explained to her on the phone that she was separated from her husband, and navigating a tricky divorce. It was her week to have the kids; but she thought, if Kate could come to Greenwich, that she could maneuver some time to speak alone.

"They're out on the water." Natalie gestured to a fleet of Sunfish, navigating courses on the water, sails puffed up like offended clouds. "They sail every day in the summer. It's a relief for them, you know? Especially now. Things have been . . . *difficult*. Especially for my youngest. He's very close to his father."

"I'm sorry," Kate said. The thought of her own divorce—painless, quick, almost incidental—flashed in her mind. She thought again of entangled lives, intimacies that wound deeper than words could express.

Perhaps Kate just didn't understand any of it.

Natalie looked down at her hands. "I'm sorry if I sounded so urgent on the phone. I think I was in shock. When I saw your message . . ." She trailed off, shaking her head. "How did you find out?"

Kate weighed the question carefully. She hadn't told Natalie, explicitly, that she knew that Natalie had followed them to Fair Isle. She still didn't know what Natalie's intention had been, and what she'd done once she got there.

"Someone told me," Kate said simply. Luckily, Natalie didn't ask who.

She only sighed. "You know, I think that I've been waiting all this time for you to write me. All these years, I've just been holding on to it . . ."

Kate felt that they were on the verge of something, standing together on the precipice of a black hole that had opened in their childhoods.

"Holding on to what, exactly?" she prompted gently.

For a second Natalie was silent, twisting a ring on her finger, over and over, as if debating whether she could bear to speak the words out loud. "That it was my fault," she said at last, in a whisper that barely rose above the wind. "That I'm the one who killed Becca."

THEN

They'd gotten lost trying to find their way back to the ruins. The footpath through the woods turned them out onto the wrong side of the island, where across the silver-tipped lake they saw the unfamiliar, rangy shores of the state park. Kate couldn't have said what time it was by then. The darkness, all-consuming, seemed to swallow up the minutes, distorting them into days. She had the sudden terror that they would never find their way off the island, that this was the Gray Lady's plan, and her strength: to trap them, turn them endlessly in circles, until they died of hunger and exhaustion.

But eventually they spotted the roof again, etched into the sky above the trees. Kate half expected to hear Becca's voice, still screaming about revenge, but it was silent in the old graveyard. Too silent, *Kate thought. She imagined Becca waiting for them, crouching in the shadows, ready to leap at them. The whole place felt alive, now, with bad intentions, with the same willful malevolence that had appeared to point a finger at them. She wished, more than anything, that they'd never come.*

"Becca?" Mari ventured as they drew close to the mausoleum. Lennie tugged at the lock on the door, as if to be sure that Becca hadn't gotten out. "Becca? Are you there?"

"She's there," Lennie said. "Where else would she be?" Then, lifting her voice to call to Becca, she added, "Are you ready to behave now?"

There was no answer. The hair on Kate's arms was standing up, and her heart was still ramming forcefully in her chest, as if she were still running.

"She's probably sulking," Lennie said. Still, she hesitated to unlock the doors. She gave them a rap with her fist. "Hello? Becca? Are you going to play nice?"

Again, there was nothing. Suddenly Mari started to shake.

"She's not there." Her voice cracked over the words; she seemed to be on the verge of hysteria. "She's gone. The Gray Lady took her."

"Will you stop that?" Lennie whirled on her. "There's no such thing as the Gray Lady. It's just a story."

"We saw *her. She was standing right in front of us. She's* real. *And now she's taken Becca—"*

Lennie reached out and seized Mari by the shoulders. "Stop. Just stop, okay? You're acting crazy."

"Open the doors," Mari said with a hollow laugh. "Open the doors, and you'll see."

"Just open the doors, Lennie," Kate echoed. She had a sudden overwhelming fear that Mari was right—that they would open the doors and find nothing but shadow and empty space. A question mark, where Becca had simply vanished.

Lennie spun open the lock, and removed it from the door handles. For a second they all stood there, waiting for something to happen. Waiting for Becca to stir, to come bursting out at them like a devil, clawing for their eyes.

Still, it was silent.

Finally Lennie reached out and wrenched open the doors. "Come on, Becca. Time to go."

Their flashlights tipped down the open throat of darkness inside the mausoleum. For a long second, Kate didn't see her, and her stomach leaped to her throat, thinking that Mari was right—Becca had disappeared, swallowed up by an old stone curse.

Then Lennie said, "Is that . . . ?" and she followed Kate's light where it dropped to the floor, settling around one of Becca's sneakers.

"Becca?" Kate thought, at first, that it still must be a joke, a prank. A way of getting back at them. Only Becca's feet were visible from where they were standing; the rest of her body arched sideways, out of sight. She took a

hesitating step forward, and then another, as if her flashlight were a cord, and she was feeling her way along it. "Becca, get up."

Slowly the light crept up her legs, and picked up her hands, flung open on the stone. Up her sweatshirt, to her neck. Suddenly Becca's face blinked into the glare of the flashlight—mottled, blue, deformed around a look of terror—and Kate knew.

"Becca!" She didn't remember moving, but suddenly she was on her knees next to Becca, reaching for her face, trying to remove the death from it. Becca's skin felt horrible, cold and waxy, like some kind of doll. "Becca. Becca, wake up."

"She's dead, Kate." It was Lennie who said it. The words fell in the empty space like a gavel. "She's not breathing."

"She can't be dead." Kate's skin was hot, inflamed with panic. She kept shaking Becca, thinking that at any second her eyes would come alive again, her skin would flood with color. Or maybe she wasn't thinking—just reacting, trying to undo it, trying to pull Becca back from wherever she'd slipped away. "She was fine when we left her."

"Look at her, Kate. Look at her face. She's dead." For the first time all night, Lennie's voice scraped toward a shout.

Kate realized, suddenly, that she'd been shouting at a dead body. She stumbled to her feet, chest heaving, wiping her palms on her jeans. In the careening arc of her flashlight, she pinned Lennie, looking sick, and Mari, standing still and silent and trembling in the door. They looked like strangers.

"It's the curse," Mari said in a whisper. "I told you the Gray Lady took Becca away."

"We have to get her back to camp." Kate felt numb. She couldn't think, couldn't make sense of it. Becca was dead. Becca couldn't *be dead. "We have to get her help."*

"What help, *Kate?" Lennie seized Kate by the shoulders. "Don't you get it? She's* dead. *Dead, dead, dead."*

Kate's stomach gave a violent twist, bringing acid to her throat as she wheeled away from Lennie. She still had a frantic sense that they should be doing something, working to unwind the past thirty minutes, raveling time back on its spool, back to the moment they'd locked Becca, alive, in the mausoleum. She wanted to scream at Lennie and Mari to do something, to fix it. But they were just standing there.

As if it was too late.

As if there was nothing in the world that could bring Becca back.

The night seemed to come alive around them, hooting with distant animal cries, the rustle of unseen creatures in the dark. Kate wanted to wake up, to break out of this nightmare, where Becca's body was lying at her feet, and the smell of decay seeped from the stones.

"We can't leave her here," Kate said, her voice cracking.

"Well, we can't bring her back to camp," Lennie said flatly. "They'll never believe us about what happened. Never."

"What do you mean?" Kate had a sense that Becca's body on the floor had dropped through the fabric of her life, cleaving it forever in two. "They won't think we killed her."

"Are you sure about that?" Lennie's voice oozed sarcasm. "And what are we supposed to tell them? That a ghost got her instead?"

Lennie was right. It was impossible. Becca had been alive when they'd left her only thirty minutes ago. And no one had touched the lock. She must have had some kind of fit, like an allergic reaction.

But looking at the strange color of her skin, Kate wasn't so sure. Her mind flashed to police sirens, to a prison cell the size of the mausoleum. She thought of her mother dying—always dying. This would kill her for real.

"What are we supposed to do?" Kate's voice cracked over the words. She felt as if she were falling, falling—tipping over the edge of reality, letting go, plunging into darkness.

There was a long silence. They stood above Becca's body, spellbound by panic. Then Mari spoke up in a whisper.

"We have to give her to the Gray Lady," she said. "Otherwise, she'll never leave us alone."

The idea fell between them like a shadow: the lake.

"It's not like we can help her, anyway," Lennie said slowly. She met Kate's eyes and then quickly looked away. Kate wanted to protest. She wanted to scream, to shatter them out of whatever nightmare this was. But already the idea was gathering force, like a tide drawing her out into the center of the lake, where Becca could rest in the dark water.

Still, for a long minute, no one moved. Then Mari came forward, moving as if in a trance. She crouched down. She gripped Becca by the ankles and pulled. Becca stirred fitfully on the floor. Kate felt again as if she might throw up. It was all wrong. It was impossible.

Mari looked up at her, her face huge and pale and blown up in the flashlight. Her eyes glittering.

"Help me move her," she said.

And they did.

SEVENTEEN

"I don't know when it started, the thing with me and Becca," Natalie said. Now that she had finally confessed, it was as if she couldn't stop speaking. "We'd never really clicked, I guess. We mostly just ignored each other. But that last summer . . ." She trailed off, shaking her head. "It was stupid stuff at first. She pushed me once when we were playing capture the flag. I stole one of her bathing suits off the line where it was drying. She told Jenny Lin that I'd offered to get her high on cough medicine. Jenny Lin told Harriet, and the camp went through all my stuff. They found three bottles of Sudafed in with all my underwear. I couldn't believe it."

"You think Becca stashed them there?" Kate said.

"Or got one of the girls in my bunk to do it for her. I didn't even know you *could* get high on Sudafed, honestly. But my parents didn't believe me. It turned out to be a whole big drama. They almost yanked me from camp, threatened to send me to rehab. My father was a recovering alcoholic," she added. "They were always on the lookout for warning signs."

"Did Becca know?" Kate asked.

"I think she must have," Natalie said. "I'd complained about it before, you know, how strict they were. And Becca always paid attention. She had a . . . skill for that, for knowing things that were supposed to be a secret."

It was true; Becca had been an almost preternatural gossip. Collecting secrets had been her hobby, very nearly an obsession. She'd joked about becoming a private investigator someday, or maybe a spy for the CIA.

"Remember those two girls who got caught sharing a bed? And we had to do a whole camp meeting about boundaries?" Natalie's question sparked a faint memory of sitting cross-legged in the theater, yawning with boredom, while several of the counselors acted out a cringeworthy piece about personal space and inappropriate touching. "Becca was the one who ratted on them to Harriet. But she tried to blackmail them first."

"Blackmail them?" Kate repeated. "What do you mean?"

"She wanted money," Natalie said. Then, seeing Kate's face, she added, "Oh, nothing crazy. Twenty dollars or something. Spending money for when we took our Sunday trips to town, probably. But still."

"But still," Kate echoed. Becca had always referred to secrets as collateral, as in, *want to hear some collateral?* or *I've got some new collateral.* Kate had thought of it as one of her linguistic quirks, like the fact that she always mixed up *conscious* and *conscience*, or peppered her speech with curse words. It had never occurred to her that Becca had chosen the word deliberately, and that she meant it literally, as a means of demanding obedience, keeping control of the other girls.

"If they wouldn't pay, she wanted more secrets," Natalie went on. "Things that other campers were embarrassed about. Rumors, bad habits, hidden contraband. She was looking for new targets. When my diary went missing, I knew Becca had stolen it. I *knew* it. But she swore up and down she didn't have it, and Harriet believed her. She was a good liar."

"Yeah," Kate said. "Yeah, she was." Kate recalled the nights they'd snuck down Natalie's diary from where they'd hidden it in the rafters and read passages aloud by flashlight. At the time, it hadn't seemed like a big deal. The stolen journal was an inside joke, a shared bond. It wasn't like it contained anything outrageous—just average insecurities, fleeting crushes, daily frustrations. Just emotions, laid bare on the page.

Now she knew that that was even worse. Natalie had been insecure about her weight back then, so Becca had started making pig noises whenever they passed Natalie's table in the mess hall. Kate squirmed with discomfort now, remembering how Natalie's face had darkened like a storm cloud, distended with pain and embarrassment, and how she'd simply laughed.

"I wanted Becca to pay," Natalie said. "People let her get away with whatever she wanted, because everyone felt sorry for her, you know? Because she didn't really have parents. I never got away with anything. I had to be Miss Perfect."

Kate didn't bother pointing out that in her recollection, Natalie had gotten away with plenty. Natalie had retaliated by spreading a rumor that Becca's mom was a prostitute, and that Becca's grandparents were trying to give her up for adoption. When Becca got a pimple just above her lip, Natalie had claimed that it was a cold sore, that Becca had mouth herpes from giving blow jobs after school. All of this had occurred in an undertow of whispers, rumors, and accusations that had largely escaped the counselors' attention.

"How did you know that we were planning to go to Fair Isle?" Kate asked.

"Cheryl Hayes told me," Natalie said.

Kate stared at her. "Cheryl?" She hadn't thought about Cheryl in years. She was the kind of girl who'd slipped through gaps in attention, even then. An afterthought, really. An unremarkable feature of their bunk, like the cubbies where the girls stashed their belongings.

"She hated you guys," Natalie said. The wisp of a smile, like a passing curl of smoke, tugged at her lips. "You ignored her. She always felt left out. And Becca called her Stromboli."

Kate winced. It was true that Becca had made fun of her complexion, which had turned riotous with acne. But she was shocked to find out that Cheryl hadn't liked them. She'd been a bunkmate. For better or worse, she'd been one of theirs.

"The whole thing was her idea," Natalie said. "She told me that Becca had a plan to sneak out to the island. She knew that you were looking for the Gray Lady. At first, I thought I would just get you guys busted. That I would wait until you snuck into the boathouse, and then wake up Harriet, claiming I'd heard a noise. I figured you'd all get kicked out of camp."

"So what changed?" Kate asked.

"It was Skit Night. The August Skit Night. You remember," she said. "All the bunks got seven minutes onstage. We thought it would be funny to write a skit where the Gray Lady returned from her grave to prove she had the most camp spirit. But at the last minute, we cut it. We were too short on time. Then someone—I don't remember who—said it was a shame that all the props would go to waste. And suddenly, it just hit me.

"We had a wig. We'd found one in the prop boxes behind the auditorium. It was old and ratty and smelled like feet, but it was perfect. And Lily Wright had bleached a maxi dress white for us"—Lily Wright had taught all the campers drama, and sewn costumes for some of the camp productions—"Then cut it up with scissors, so it would look all old and ragged. In the dark, it would look just like a wedding dress.

"I knew that you were planning to hunt for the Gray Lady's grave—Cheryl had told me that—and I thought it would be funny to sneak up on you." She shrugged helplessly. "It was stupid. It was just a dumb prank, like when you guys put whipped cream all over our bunk. I just wanted to scare you. But somehow, Becca found out."

Natalie rushed on, slightly breathless now, "I think Cheryl must have told her. You know, ratting me out so that Becca would be grateful. She was the only one who knew. I thought Becca was going to kill me." Natalie stared down at her hands. "But she didn't. She thought it was a great idea."

Kate felt as if she were grasping at the edge of a thicket, trying to get purchase in a wilderness of old stories and dark memories. "I'm confused," she said. "Becca found out you were planning to follow us to Fair Isle, and she *wanted* you to go through with it?"

Natalie nodded. She looked up at Kate. Something flashed in her eyes. Pity, Kate thought. "She wanted to scare you," she said simply.

Kate felt a sudden flush of anger. Fucking Becca. She thought about that time on the night walk when she'd stopped to tie her shoelaces and Becca had fallen behind to wait with her. She remembered the way that Becca had tensed, like an animal, and the viselike clamp of her grip as she'd pulled Kate to her feet. *Someone's here.* Her whisper had been half terror, half excitement, as if she'd been expecting it. *Someone's watching us.*

It was power, Kate realized. The Gray Lady, her mythology, the idea of the curse—all of it had given Becca power over her friends, power to control their moods and attention, power to frighten and bully them. Kate wondered why the legend of the Gray Lady had consumed so much of Becca's attention. Maybe she'd understood, on some deep level, what it was to be abandoned, to be separated by a small but meaningful distance from the world where happy people went on, oblivious, with their lives.

"If you hated Becca so much, why did you go along with her plan?" Kate asked.

Natalie shrugged. "I didn't always hate her," she said. "Summer four and five, we were actually friends."

"You thought it would make her like you again," Kate said.

"I thought at least it would make her stop torturing me," Natalie said. "You have to understand, I was . . . scared of Becca. She could . . . do things to people. Control them. Know what I mean?"

Kate thought of Becca holding a hot silver lighter to her shoulder blade, making her swear that they would be friends forever. She remembered biting down a shout as the metal made contact, blinking fast to keep back her tears.

At the same time, Becca had protected her, made her feel invincible; Kate remembered one time when they were eleven, Becca had given a boy named Theo Bates a bloody nose after he told Kate she looked like a horse. Kate had been on the verge of tears. But Becca had just balled her hand into a fist and clocked him. *And you look like you're bleeding,* she'd said flatly. After that, Theo had ducked his head and veered off in another direction whenever he saw Kate coming.

Power. Becca had wielded it, and gifted it, and taken it away when she wanted to.

"Yeah," she said. "Yeah, I do know."

"On the night you guys snuck out, Cheryl pretended to fall asleep, and waited until she heard you leave the bunk. Then she snuck over and scratched on the screen door. That was our sign."

"After that, it was easy. The boathouse was already open. I'd stashed the wig and dress in a plastic bag not far from the docks. You were already halfway to the island by the time I got that damn wig on. And afterward, I followed you."

"What happened when you got out to the island?" Kate could feel her pulse rising in her neck. It was here—the answer to the mystery, the truth about what happened to Becca. Here, on a park bench, watching sailboats dip and sway over the sound.

"You were gone," Natalie said. "I hid my canoe. I was so worried you would see it. It took me twenty minutes to find the ruins, and all those creepy headstones. But you weren't there. I didn't know what to do. Then I heard a scream." She looked down at her hands.

"From the mausoleum?" Kate prompted her. Becca must have been frantic. Alone, with the spirit of the Gray Lady, the vengeful ghost of a woman who marked trespassers for their graves, and her friends vanished on the other side of those iron doors.

Natalie looked at her, confused. "From the woods," she said. "I followed the sound, until I could hear you guys talking."

Kate's excitement, her certainty, collapsed in an instant. "What do you mean?" she said. "When did you kill Becca?"

"I didn't kill her," Natalie said. "But it was my fault she died. If I hadn't followed you—if I hadn't gone through with the prank—you wouldn't have turned on Becca. You wouldn't have sent her back in a canoe alone." She shook her head. "When I found you guys in the woods—when you saw me standing there . . . I'll never forget how you looked. Terrified, just terrified. For a long time, I wondered . . ." She trailed off.

"Wondered what?"

"Whether *you'd* killed Becca," she said. "All three of you. To get back at her, you know, for scaring you so much."

A deep hollow of disappointment opened in Kate's chest. She felt suddenly exhausted. "We didn't know that it was a prank," she said. "We thought we'd really seen the Gray Lady." She didn't know whether she wanted to laugh or cry. "Besides, Becca wasn't with us in the woods."

Natalie stared. "What do you mean, she wasn't with you?"

Kate took a deep breath. "Becca was locked up inside the mausoleum. We'd left her there."

"In the mausoleum . . . ?" Confusion opened Natalie's face, converting it into a question. "I don't understand."

"We'd locked her inside, to teach her a lesson," Kate said. She was too tired to lie; besides, there was no point. The mystery of Becca's death kept receding, like a coastline driven farther and farther away by a current. "You didn't hear her? She wasn't shouting? She wasn't calling to be let out?"

"Becca?" Natalie shook her head. "No. There wasn't anyone in the graveyard. I didn't hear anything, until someone screamed in the woods."

Kate's mind was working frantically over the facts, trying to slot Natalie's story into a timeline. She'd looked for them at the graveyard when she'd heard a scream from the woods; that might have been Mari, when she went down over a tree root and thought she'd twisted an ankle.

"I don't understand," Natalie said. "If Becca was locked up, when did she take her canoe back to shore? When did she drown?"

Kate took a deep breath. "She didn't," she said. "Becca was dead when we went back to get her."

Natalie's hands seized in her lap—a reflexive spasm of shock. "Dead?"

Kate couldn't believe she was telling the truth to Natalie, of all people, after all these years of keeping the secret. She'd come for Natalie's confession, not the other way around. But suddenly the desire to speak broke open in her chest, spilled up into her voice before she could stop it. "We opened the door to let her out and found her lying there. Eyes open. She looked terrified. Mari tried to wake her up, but it was obviously too late. We didn't know what to do. It was our fault. We'd left her in there alone."

"You thought she'd been—what?—scared to death?" Natalie said.

"We weren't thinking," Kate said. "We panicked. We'd seen the Gray Lady in the woods . . . at least, we thought we had . . ."

"The curse," Natalie said. "You thought that Becca was the victim." When Kate nodded, she dropped her head, covering her mouth with a hand, as if she could feed the words back inside. They sat in silence for a long minute. Kate could see the sailboats on the water turning around, winging back to shore like a fleet of white-winged birds.

"Oh God," Natalie whispered finally. "It was supposed to be a joke." Then: "Why didn't you tell anyone?"

"We were too scared. We thought for sure that we would be blamed. Lennie said we might even get arrested. It was her idea to sink Becca in the lake," Kate added. "Honestly, I think we were all in shock. We'd only left her alone for twenty, thirty minutes. We'd run away when she started screaming . . ."

"She wasn't screaming when I got there," Natalie said. "It was silent in the graveyard. I remember. I'd never been so creeped out in my life. That horrible stone angel, with the black around her eyes . . ." She shivered. "There's something wrong with that place."

Kate knew exactly what she meant. She'd felt sick with fear the moment they all stepped foot on Fair Isle, as if they were trespassing somewhere dangerous. She'd imagined strange movement in the shadows, and the whisper of voices every time the trees touched together in the wind. And the ruins . . . huge, incomprehensible, pulled into a senseless rubble by the centuries. The graveyard was small—other than the mausoleum and a stone folly, there were fewer than a dozen headstones, rubbed naked by rain and wind—but its *feeling*, the absorptive impression of death, lingered everywhere.

"It doesn't make any sense," Kate said out loud, without meaning to. She wondered when and why Becca had stopped shouting to be let out. Maybe she'd heard her friends' voices growing distant, and decided to save her energy. Maybe she'd been busy looking for a way out.

Or maybe, just maybe, she was already dead—collapsed in that window of time between the moment Lennie padlocked the door and Natalie arrived, looking for them.

Natalie worked her lower lip with her teeth, thinking. "When you reached out to me," she said slowly, "it was because you thought I'd . . . hurt her. That's why you came to see me. Isn't it?"

"Becca was alone for maybe twenty minutes before you followed us to the island," Kate said. "Somehow, she wound up dead. Can you think of any explanation?"

"Besides the Gray Lady, you mean?" Natalie's smile was fleeting and pained. She shook her head. "It's been a long time since medical school. Unless it was death by cavity, I'm the wrong person to ask. Maybe she had some sort of attack?"

"Maybe." Kate considered it. "But what kind of attack?"

Natalie opened her hands. Helpless. "I've got no idea. A heart condition, maybe. Something sudden. Maybe she was scared to death. If Becca believed that the Gray Lady was coming for her . . . if she really got worked up . . ."

Kate remembered that Becca's mom had said that Becca suffered from asthma. She wondered if, after all, the explanation was that simple. Still, it seemed incredible that she would die so quickly. She was breathing fine the whole night; she'd had enough air in her lungs to yell that she was going to murder them all, that they were dead to her, only minutes earlier.

There was nothing left to say. Kate and Natalie hugged, possibly for the first time ever. Kate could feel Natalie's spine through her clothing. She was too thin.

"I'm sorry," Natalie whispered, before she let Kate go. "I'm so sorry. It was so stupid."

"It wasn't your fault," Kate said.

"It wasn't yours, either."

Kate winced a smile. "Maybe," she said. "But tell that to Becca."

EIGHTEEN

On the way back to Massachusetts, she felt the urge to try Mariana again, to reveal to her that it had been Natalie Horace, Natalie Horace in a costume, trying to scare them, all along. They might even laugh about it. It was a relief, an absurd but inevitable conclusion to the summer-long feud.

Except.

Except that it didn't change the fact that Becca had died, possibly only minutes after they'd left her.

At a rest stop, she picked up her phone and thumbed over to the number for her old college roommate, Courtney. They'd bonded over a shared love of pop music that made Kate cringe to think about and had remained close all these years. Courtney and her husband were both oncologists at Johns Hopkins. She wasn't exactly an expert in sudden deaths—her form of morbidity was of the decidedly incremental kind—but Kate suspected she might know someone who could help. Courtney was one of those rare people who never forgot a name; she'd always seemed to collect friends like lint.

When the call went through, there was a moment of silence. Then Kate heard a clatter and a giggle.

"Aiden," she said. Aiden was Courtney's five-year-old, and Kate's godson. "Aiden, is that you?"

"I'm playing with trucks," he announced.

"With trucks, huh? What kind of trucks?"

"There's a fire truck," he said. "And . . . another truck. Mr. Kitty is driving."

Kate heard Courtney's voice in the background, rising from among a clatter of plates. "Aiden, did you take my phone again?"

"It's Auntie Kate," Aiden said, unruffled. "I'm telling her about my trucks."

A second later, Courtney had taken the phone, sounding breathless. "Sorry about that," she said. "Mark's traveling this week, so I've got Aiden all to myself. Swear to God, I don't know how single parents do it . . . anyway, you good? You enjoying your break?"

Courtney romanticized academia, always imagining that it meant summers filled with lazy mornings and lounging poolside. She had never understood why Kate cluttered up her schedule with consultation and a frenetic pace of writing, reviewing, and publishing new articles and, increasingly, books. She didn't understand Kate's drive to disentangle the psychic layers of the human brain, which she viewed as simply the product of either healthy or flawed wiring, like the human personality was just an image playing out on a screen, a result of the technological architecture that transmuted electrical signals into pixels. She had always seen psychology as a whole as a "soft science," and Steve's work as nothing short of paranormal. Still, Courtney and Steve had always gotten along; their philosophies and beliefs were so far apart, they had never even been in conflict.

Kate wondered what Courtney would say if she knew that now, for the first time in her life, Kate had begun to wonder whether Steve, and the DOPS team more generally, had been onto something.

"Something like that," Kate said. "I'm actually in Massachusetts. Well, I'm about to be." She was almost at the end of the Taconic, which meant she was about forty minutes out from Great Barrington.

"Beautiful place. For about three months out of the year, at least," Courtney said. "First time there?"

Kate almost laughed. Courtney had been her first best friend after Becca. From the beginning, they had been inseparable, spending hours in their dorm listening to CDs, or drinking purloined beers and talking about boys. Courtney knew about Kate's mom, how she'd finally died just before Kate's junior year, and how Kate had shuffled through the rest of high school like someone in a dream, slipping through the fissures between friend groups and social divisions, retreating into books written about the human mind, like a phantom alive only in their pages. But Kate had never told Courtney about Camp Sauquamet, or about Becca. She had vowed to put all of that behind her.

Now she simply said, "I actually went to camp here for years." And she left it at that.

"Oh, really? You never told me that." Courtney sounded a little stern. She prided herself on being Kate's oldest friend, had for years needled Steve about knowing Kate better. "So what's up?"

"Do you know anyone who specializes in respiratory diseases?" Kate asked. "Childhood asthma, specifically."

"Not off the top of my head. But I'm sure I could find someone." Courtney was obviously herding Aiden out the door; Kate could hear his plaintive voice in the background, railing against the need for sunscreen. "Why?"

"It's a work thing," Kate said. She was hoping that Courtney wouldn't ask any more questions. Courtney knew, at least, that psychology often intersected with biology—more often, it seemed, than anyone had suspected twenty years ago. Gut bacteria caused inflammation of the brain, and inflammation of the brain caused interruptions and malfunctions in any number of brain systems, and those, in turn, could lead to auditory and visual hallucinations, or disrupted impulse control: manifestations of an underlying illness that would previously be considered purely psychological.

"Sure. I can put you in touch with someone," Courtney said. "I'll get you on an email chain."

"You're the best," Kate said.

"I know," Courtney replied. She made a fat kissing noise and hung up.

~

Back at the rental, Kate spotted Susan aiming a hose at a crowd of violently-colored azalea bushes. She waved, then hustled inside before Susan could draw her into conversation, grateful for the cool, slightly clinical embrace of the air conditioner.

Right away, she searched online for Cheryl Hayes. It was easy enough to find her. Cheryl had grown up, it seemed, to be a prominent children's book editor. She had a beautiful Instagram account, filled with careful images of books set against interesting backgrounds, and more than three thousand followers. Kate double-checked that Emily Haskell wasn't one of them before sending Cheryl a message. It felt like a formality. Even if Cheryl had crossed paths with the Haskells—plenty of New Yorkers kept a second home in the Berkshires—it seemed unlikely that their contact would have been more than incidental. More and more, Kate was coming around to the idea that Henley's knowledge about Becca's life—and her death—couldn't, in fact, be explained.

More and more, Kate felt that it was Becca, not Henley, who'd called her back to Massachusetts.

Her browser tabs were still open to several articles about local mysteries attributed to the "Berkshires Triangle," and more specifically to the legend of the Gray Lady. Unsure of what to do next, Kate returned to them. Most of the mysterious deaths reported in the area over the past forty years had nothing in common with Becca's. A car full of teenagers had dropped through the ice one winter; a college student had been raped and strangled, her body dumped near the entrance to the state park, and her boyfriend was later convicted.

But she kept circling back to the case of the Twin Falls John Doe, located by hikers only fifteen months before that night on Fair Isle. The police had determined that the boy had died of exposure, but to Kate, that didn't make any sense. A tent, sleeping bag, and change of clothes had been located not fifty yards from where his body had been found. There was evidence at the campsite of a firepit, along with fire-starting equipment, a camper stove, and plenty of food. The boy had obviously had some experience of the outdoors. So why was he dressed in a T-shirt in thirty-degree weather? What had happened to his jacket? And why hadn't he gone back to the camp to get warm? Even if he'd gotten confused, somehow—lost or turned around in the cold—it made little sense. He'd been less than half a mile in any direction from either the lake, where he could have oriented himself, or a nest of parking lots and service roads that brought hundreds of daily visitors into the park at peak season, and even at that time of the year would have been patrolled by volunteers.

She read the quote given to the county paper by one of the hikers who'd found him. *I still see him, lying there, totally blue, with his mouth open. Like he'd seen something awful, and dropped dead.* Now it was the description of the John Doe's coloration that jumped out at her. Totally blue.

Becca, too, had been blue when they found her—skin marbled, lips purplish, like someone who'd been pulled from the frozen lake. It was the reason they'd known, as soon as the light fell on her, that she was dead. Now, for the first time, it occurred to Kate that it was strange that Becca had been so blue. She knew a little about lividity—the way that blood pooled after death to the lowest regions of the body, depending on its position, leaving the skin a bluish color—but a quick return of search results revealed that even after an hour, the change to her complexion should hardly have been noticeable.

The sudden drum of water against the sliding doors surprised her. She looked up to see Susan, now casting her hose at the rhododendron bushes edging the patio, waving at her cheerfully. Suddenly inspired, Kate grabbed her bag and headed outside.

Susan's face was red from the heat. She cut the water as Kate approached.

"I swear, I'm thinking 'bout taking off my clothes and watering myself down," she said. "They say we got two days of ninety-plus ahead of us. The AC doing okay for you?"

"The AC is fine," Kate said. "Listen, you mentioned you knew the author who wrote that book about the Gray Lady legends . . . ?"

"Martin Sheehy. He's written lots of books. He's our local history buff. He's head of the historical society, down on Route 203—although why they store all that spooky stuff around in there, I don't know. Martin says the legends are part of our history. I say history should stick to the *facts*."

"All that spooky stuff . . . ?" Kate shook her head.

"All that junk that gets printed about the Gray Lady striking people dead or vanishing hikers. Anytime somebody gets lost around here, someone'll start squawking about the 'curse.'"

Suddenly, Kate wanted to talk to Martin Sheehy very badly. "Do you think I could find Martin at the historical society now?"

"On a *Sunday*?" Susan looked at her as if she'd lost her mind. "It's closed. Tell you the truth, the historical society doesn't really keep hours, per se. Anyone wants to visit, they just drop Martin a line through the website. I just call him, of course."

"Would you mind . . . ?" Kate left the thought unfinished.

Susan smiled at her, stripped off her gardening gloves, and laid down her hose. "I knew you'd want to speak to him," she said, wagging her finger at Kate as she turned back to the house. "All you brainy types always seem to get along. You go ahead and get going. I'll let Martin know you're coming. He'll be thrilled, believe me," she added, when Kate started to protest. "I'm telling you—the man will use any excuse to talk old *murders*."

And she winked.

NINETEEN

When Kate pulled up to the Berkshire historical society—a diminutive colonial that itself looked as if it should be part of an exhibit—an elderly man with a single tuft of gray hair and a belt cinched high on the swell of his gut was just unlocking the doors. Kate assumed this was Martin Sheehy.

"I hear you're an author, too," was the first thing that he said to her.

Kate shook his hand and had to resist the urge to wipe her palm on her jeans. "How do you know Susan?" she asked.

"Believe it or not, I took her to prom. That was back in '73, mind you. But I guess she had an okay time. We've been friends ever since."

"Susan tells me that you're an expert on the Gray Lady," Kate said.

"Oh, well. Folk stories are a hobby of mine. We've got plenty of legends in this part of the world. Have you heard of Hoosac Tunnel? Or the Barrington Bigfoot?" When Kate shook her head, Martin grinned. He gestured for her to enter the building ahead of him. "I'm not surprised. The Gray Lady's got legs. She gets most of the press."

Inside, Kate was overwhelmed by the smell of mildewing paper, carried on a punch of heat. Martin went around turning on lights, and Kate had the telescoping impression of a room narrowing around a profusion of boxes, display cases, and bookshelves, which ran in rivulets toward a disorderly heap in the back.

"Sorry about the swelter," Martin said. He navigated the clutter expertly, giving Kate the impression of a manic pinball, before punching on the air conditioner mounted high on one wall. "We get our whole budget from a handful of donations. Can't keep the air running as much as we should. But it should take just a few minutes to cool down. Now," he said, turning back to Kate, "as far as the Gray Lady is concerned, the first reference to the legend in print comes from an article from the *Berkshire Weekly* . . ."

Martin wrestled out an enormous scrapbook and opened it on one of the display cases. He gestured Kate over. "From 1923. The Blue Pine Resort had just opened its doors, right on the same property the camp took over in the '60s. It was a popular retreat for middle-class families from New York, who couldn't afford the higher-end Adirondacks resorts. A woman named Georgia Darling was vacationing with her children when both girls went missing. She claimed to have seen a woman dressed in a wedding gown playing with the children by the lake. Of course it wasn't true. The girls' bodies turned up eventually in a shallow grave a mile from where the mother had been staying. It turned out the girls' father was an alcoholic and a gambler, had ruined the whole family with debt. Both parents were eventually convicted of plotting to dispose of their children. But by then, the legend of the Gray Lady had taken hold."

Kate carefully paged through century-old newspaper headlines announcing the legend into existence. Phantom Lady Makes Away with Two Children. Were the Darling Girls the Victim of a Curse? She recalled that at the time, a wave of spiritualism had swept across America and Europe. Séances were in fashion. Psychics were all the rage. Psychology, such as it was, was still in its infancy. Freud, its most celebrated figure, was primarily concerned with hysterics, and treating specters of his own. The Gray Lady had burst into imaginative life on the force of the zeitgeist.

"Of course, you could say our Gray Lady is just a riff on an even older archetype. Mythology about a phantom woman dressed in white, usually a harbinger of death or misfortune, appears around the world. The White Lady dates back to medieval legends, but there are versions of the story all the way from Brazil to Japan."

Kate knew, dimly, about the legend of the Lady in White. She recalled seeing a movie by that title in her childhood. Funnily enough, it had never occurred to her that all the stories of the Gray Lady were just the old myth, given local coloration—possibly because the Gray Lady had been grounded, literally, in the mysterious abandoned cemetery in the middle of the lake.

"What about Fair Isle?" Kate asked. "Do you know anything about its history?"

Martin made a chuffing sound, a laugh that reminded Kate of the wheeze of an old book spine. "As much as anyone," he said. "Which is to say, not much." Now he pivoted, rebounding toward yet another cardboard box. "We know the graves on Fair Isle have been there at least since the early 1800s. Archaeologists at the University of Massachusetts dated the stone back in the '80s. We can assume that the major settlement dates from the same time." He pulled out a leather-bound book, held together tenuously with duct tape. "The 1870s county register lists a residence on 'Faher Island'—Faher, presumably, was the name of the owner—which might have given rise to the modern spelling. And sometime in the 1890s, a Dr. Willard applied for a permit to conduct medical treatments at 'Faher House,' although the address listed was for a post office box in Stockbridge—what they called 'lockboxes' at the time. No telling if he was actually living on the island."

Kate bent over the pages of the old register. They were brown and crumbly with age, covered by a faint spiderweb scrawl. She imagined for a moment what it would be like to follow the ink down into the lull of forgotten history, to lose herself asking questions that no one needed answered anymore.

"Even when I was a kid, the mystery of Fair Isle had gotten mixed up with the legend of the Gray Lady. I wrote about it in my second book, actually, *The Gray Lady of Lake Sauquamet* . . . ?" He trailed off hopefully.

"I'll look it up," Kate said. Martin seemed to swell almost visibly. "What about the case of the Twin Falls John Doe? I've seen his death attributed to the Gray Lady. Do you know anything about that?"

"I know *everything* about it," Martin said. "At least, I know as much as there is to know. You could say the Twin Falls John Doe marked the beginning of the modern legends of the Gray Lady. His death sparked the first conversations about the 'Berkshires Triangle.' Wait here."

Martin vanished up a set of stairs almost entirely occluded by stacks. It was amazing that he seemed to know where everything was. To Kate, the whole place seemed to exist in Byzantine disorder. But he was soon back, puffing and blowing around a third container, this one made of plastic and actually labeled.

"Here you are," he said. "Twenty-six years of dead ends, and at least three separate investigations." He set down the plastic bin with a *whomp*.

Inside, Kate was stunned to see everything from police reports, neatly clipped into a binder and meticulously dated, to what appeared to be crime scene photographs. She stared at Martin in wonderment.

"How did you get all of these?" Kate asked.

"It took a lot of wheedling," he said. "Fortunately, I can be a big pain in the ass when I want to be. It doesn't hurt that Matt Bishop used to play basketball with my son."

There was that name again: Matt Bishop. Supposedly, he had reopened the investigation into Becca's disappearance. It occurred to her that if Matt Bishop interviewed Jenny Lin, she might mention that Kate had come digging around for information. That was if Mariana didn't simply cave and go to the police herself.

If she told the truth, would the police believe it? Would they believe that an otherwise-healthy fourteen-year-old girl had died suddenly, in the span of thirty minutes, for no known reason? And that her friends had panicked, thinking in their confusion it was proof of a supernatural curse they'd brought down? Didn't it make more sense that the girls who had disposed of Becca's body had done so out of guilt, and a desire to hide their involvement?

Kate saw only one solution: She would have to bring the police answers before the police could start asking questions.

"I'd be careful, if you're at all squeamish," Martin said as Kate flipped to the next photograph. She immediately saw why: The image was a close-up of the boy's face, partially gnawed away by an animal. Kate felt her stomach rise to touch her throat. She forced herself to look at the image clinically, without attachment, as if she were looking at a puzzle. She noted the marbled blue skin, the almost violet lips, the mouth pulled away from the teeth, as if the boy had died screaming.

Just like Becca.

"Not everyone thinks historical crime is worth preserving. I say, history is history, even if it's ugly."

"Historical *crime*," Kate repeated, latching on to the word. "You think the Twin Falls John Doe was murdered?"

Martin grinned at her. "You don't miss much, do you?" Then he sighed. "I wish I could take credit for the theory. But plenty of people think the first investigation was mishandled. There was evidence that the boy had company before he died. Someone looted the campsite, for one thing. The kid showed no signs of long-term exposure to cold. That means he must have had a jacket, probably a hat, gloves. But all of it was gone."

"Anyone could have come along and robbed the body afterward," Kate pointed out, even though earlier she'd had the same thought.

"Sure," Martin said. "But add two different kinds of cigarettes, with two sets of DNA . . ."

He flipped through several photographs of the campsite, partly surrounded by bored-looking officers marking the perimeter, and stopped on a close-up of a firepit. About a dozen cigarettes had been stubbed out in the ashes—Camels and Marlboros, from the look of them.

"And the police never had a suspect?" Kate asked.

"If they did, I never heard about it." Martin gave that same chuffing laugh. "I don't blame the department for letting the case go cold. It's difficult to claim murder when there's no motive, and no known method. It's almost impossible to find motive without knowing who John Doe was. And without assuming a murder, it's easy to overlook possible methods. Half the boy's face was missing by the time he was found. Who knows what evidence went with it. That's what makes it a perfect crime, you know, for the legend. Lonely teenager in the woods, struck down by some unknown force . . . plenty of time for rumors to start flying."

The final photographs contained all the personal items recovered from the campsite. A camper stove. A plastic lighter. A toothbrush. Kate almost skipped over them, until she spotted a bottle of Fireball whisky laid out next to an assortment of soup cans and packaged jerky. Seeing it sparked a memory of Becca, leaning forward in the canoe, trying to press the bottle into Kate's hand. Come on. *Just one sip won't kill you.*

"Fireball," she said out loud.

Martin gave that same chuffing laugh. "Wouldn't be my first choice," he said. "But I guess at that age, you're just happy to get your hands on a bottle."

Kate frowned. She'd been shocked when Becca had produced the whisky that night—shocked, but not totally surprised. Becca had tried to con a passerby into purchasing beer on one memorable field trip to Saratoga Springs. *Hey mister*, she called it. As in *hey, mister, wanna buy me a beer?* And Mari had nearly coughed up a lung behind the boathouse when Becca had assembled her friends to share a purloined cigarette. She'd stolen it from Ferdinand's pack when he was busy hosing down the docks. But Becca had refused to say where she'd gotten the alcohol.

Kate wondered if it could be significant. Two teenagers, mysteriously dead fifteen months and less than a mile apart, with the same brand of whisky in their possession. Was it possible, she wondered, that the alcohol had been contaminated? A few years ago, an epidemic of bootleg liquor had sickened tourists in a Dominican Republic resort. Two of them had even died. She could imagine Becca getting her hands on a bottle from some stranger she'd met on one of their field trips; in Saratoga she'd dragged them into head shops that reeked of patchouli to admire massive glass bongs shaped like frogs, swirling with threads of colors, and tried to charm the guy behind the counter into admitting that he sold weed. It was strange to imagine, after all this time, that Becca's death might have been accidental. A tragedy of timing, circumstance, and stupid decisions.

But she was getting ahead of herself. She had seized on a connection between the deaths that might be only incidental. Fireball was a popular whisky, especially with teenagers.

Before taking her leave of Martin Sheehy, she made a point to admire the books on display near the window, many of them published by Martin himself. She purchased two: one titled *The Berkshires Triangle: Unsolved Mysteries* and one called *Haunted: On the Trail of Massachusetts' Ghosts.* Martin told her, as he was fumbling around to find the cashbox, that he'd spent his first year in retirement visiting all of Massachusetts' most notorious paranormal hot spots—sometimes alone, sometimes with ghost-hunting groups that had proliferated in recent years.

"So you really believe in all of this stuff, then?" Kate blurted out. "Ghosts and cryptids, *haunted* houses, that kind of thing."

When Martin smiled, his eyes narrowed into folds of wrinkles. "Oh, it all depends. I believe in the power of our beliefs, certainly." Kate remembered saying something similar to Emily Haskell at their first meeting. It felt like a lifetime ago. "And what does it mean to be haunted, anyway? It means that certain stories, certain facts, certain questions won't leave us alone. They consume us—no matter how hard we try to forget."

Kate squeezed her hands into fists, until she could feel the bite of her nails in her palms. She understood what Martin meant. Too well.

"I'll give you an example," Martin said. "One of the places I toured is called the Belchertown State School. You ever heard of it?" When Kate shook her head, he went on, "It used to be called the Belchertown School for the Feeble-Minded. It shut down for good forty years ago. There'd been decades of reported abuses—kids tied to beds for days at a time, forced into solitary confinement, left to drink from toilets. People have tried to burn the place down. They say it's evil. Police patrol there every night. I had to get special permission to take a tour.

"In one room, I found a bed with a pair of restraints still lashed to the headboard. In another, old metal bathtubs, stained with filth. But the thing that really got me was the children's toys—a heap of them, abandoned in the basement. Looking at them, it's like I could see the children—abandoned, forgotten, abused, moldering there while the rest of the world went on with its business. I could feel them. It felt like drowning in that place. I'll never forget it. I even dream about it, sometimes."

For a second, standing there in the quiet, Kate could feel it, too: a quiet pressure, as if invisible mourners were gathering around them.

Martin cleared his throat. "I don't know if you'd call that seeing a ghost. But it's a haunting, sure enough."

Outside, the sky was just deepening into a dusky blue, thinly lined with pink at the edges, like something sliced up and bleeding. Kate thought then of something she'd heard in the first—and last—Alcoholics Anonymous meeting she'd attended: *Nothing in God's world happens by mistake.* She didn't see how anyone could believe that.

She had several missed calls from Emily Haskell, as well as a handful of texts.

Are you there?
Henley had an incident.
Can you come over?
Please.
We need to talk.

A razor-thin moon was floating out of the deepening blue above the trees, smiling sideways at the stars, when Kate pulled up the Haskells' driveway. A wind shook up some of the heat, stirring it around without actually cooling anything. The insects sang their nightly dominance.

She wondered how they could stand to keep it up so long, what they could possibly have to say.

She found Henley inside, already dressed in her pajamas, sitting on the sofa with a picture book and looking sulky. She didn't respond when Kate greeted her, just stood up and flounced off into the dining room.

"Henley's mad because I took away her iPad," Emily explained. "She was very bad today."

"What happened?" Kate asked. Emily, she thought, looked rattled. The spiderweb creases at the corners of her eyes were more visible than usual. Kate wondered if she'd been crying.

"Henley had a playdate today," Emily said, gesturing for Kate to follow her up the stairs. "One of her friends, Ava, came over this afternoon. It was too hot to be outside, so I sent them up to Henley's room. A little while later, I heard Ava screaming."

She flipped on the lights in Henley's room. Dolls, toys, LEGOs, and puzzle pieces were strewn across the floor—evidence of an afternoon of rambunctious, chaotic play. Kate didn't see anything alarming.

"What am I looking at?" Kate asked.

Emily crossed over to the closet. "This."

Cold seized Kate by the neck as Emily swung open the closet door. The entanglement of scarves and sweatshirts that belonged on a hanging peg inside had been removed, balled into the closet in a jumble, leaving the inside of the closet door bare. Kate saw that Henley had covered it instead with dozens of *eyes*—some inked huge, with pupils swirling with red ink, others tiny, the size of a dime, clustered together like buds on a branch. Immediately, she thought of the markings on the stones that she, Mariana, and Lennie had found in the woods all those years earlier.

"When did Henley do this?" Kate asked.

"I have no idea." Emily threw up her hands in frustration. "I took away all her markers and coloring things today, after I found Ava in the closet."

"In the closet?" Kate repeated.

"Henley had locked her inside," Emily said. "Apparently, they'd been having an argument—something silly, about what to play next. I guess Henley got angry. She told Ava there was a surprise in the closet. Then she shoved her inside, and stood against the door. Ava was hysterical." Emily's mouth tightened with anger. "And do you know what Henley said when I found her like that? She said, 'It wasn't my idea, Mommy. She made me do it.'"

"She," Kate repeated. "She meant Ava?"

Emily shook her head. "The Gray Lady," she said. Kate recalled that when Henley had shown her the doll house, and the closet door taped off in one of the bedrooms, she had mentioned that the bad lady lived there. Kate realized that she was reenacting that night, playing out the trauma, this time as the aggressor—a not-uncommon response when children had experienced violence or abuse.

But that suggested that Henley really had *experienced* it. The memories were in her body, webbing a remnant terror into her cells.

"What do I say to *her*?" Emily asked. "I know how to talk to Henley. But how do I talk to her? To Becca," she clarified, when Kate stared. "This is all her shit, isn't it?"

Kate didn't answer. How could she? What had started as a routine trip to disentangle fact from fiction had plunged her instead into a morass of old stories, legends, fears. She could feel her heart beating behind her ribs, frantic, like a caged animal. She had a sudden image of plunging a hand straight into Henley, finding the part of Becca that was still alive, still tormented, and throttling it.

"There's something else," Emily said. She took a deep breath, as if steadying herself for some physical exertion. Then she said, "I got a phone call today from a local newspaper."

Kate stared at her uncomprehendingly.

"A reporter named Jack Johnson. He asked if I was Henley's mother. I said yes. I was so confused; I thought he might be calling about the Butterfly Pageant. That's a dance recital. Henley's performing this year."

The cold feeling settled in Kate's stomach. "But he wasn't."

Emily shook her head. "He asked if he could interview Henley," she said. "He'd heard that she was claiming to be the reincarnation of Becca McGuire. He *knew*. How did he know?"

In a flash, Kate understood: Mariana. She'd told Mariana about Henley, the day they visited Camp Sauquamet together. Fucking Mari. Kate should have known that she would never keep her mouth shut.

The cold was gone, replaced by a rising anger. She struggled to keep her voice neutral. "What did you tell him?"

Emily gave Kate a look of open hostility. "I told him to fuck off. Henley is a six-year-old child. She's not a sideshow, or a news story."

"I'm sorry." Kate knew that Emily's anger must be masking a deeper fear: She didn't know how to help Henley reconcile both of her identities. She must have felt, on some level, that she was suddenly parenting a stranger. "I mentioned Henley to Mariana Edwards, one of Becca's old friends. She still lives in the area, teaching music. I thought she might be the one who'd put the idea in Henley's head."

"That's why you asked me for the list of names," Emily said dully. Kate nodded. "You think she told somebody at *The Journal*?"

"She may have," Kate said, although she was certain of it. "Mariana's always been . . . spiritual." *Obsessive* was closer to the truth—Kate thought of the home full of a mishmash of Buddhist and Hindu artifacts, self-help books, and faux-esoteric quotations, even on her coffee mugs. "She may have thought she was helping."

"Helping what? Helping *who*?" Emily fired back. When Kate didn't answer, she rubbed her eyes. "This was a mistake. I should never have reached out to Dr. Rushkin. I thought I was doing the right thing for Henley . . ."

"Let me talk to her," Kate said. "Something must have happened today. Ava may have said something that triggered her." When Emily hesitated, she added, "That's why you called me, isn't it?"

"I don't know why I called you." Emily made every word sound like a sigh. "I didn't know *who* to call." But finally, she tipped her head into a nod. "Make it quick. It's almost bedtime."

Downstairs, Henley was engulfed in a big armchair, pretending to read. Her eyes tracked Kate across the room, and then ticked back to the page. For a moment, Kate stood there in silence, letting Henley get used to her again.

"Hi, Henley," she said. Henley barely murmured a response. "I heard what happened today," Kate said. "I heard that your friend Ava was pretty upset."

"It was her fault," Henley said. "She was being mean."

"Mean how?" Kate said.

Henley lashed out with her feet, but didn't answer right away. "She wouldn't listen," she said. "Nobody ever listens to me."

"I listen to you," Kate said. Henley kept kicking, her mouth furrowed in a little scowl. Kate squatted beside Henley's chair. "I went to visit Natalie Horace today. Remember? You told me that she was there on the night that you got hurt. You were right. She followed us out to the island. She wanted to play a trick on us."

"I know," Henley said simply. Kate got that creeping feeling along her spine again.

"Can we talk a little more about that night?" Kate said gently. "Can you remember anything else about what happened?"

"I couldn't breathe," Henley said. "I got scared. I couldn't move my arms and legs. I was all blue. I didn't like how I looked."

"How you looked," Kate repeated. Her mind flashed to the research that Dr. Rushkin had provided her: 20 percent of children who claimed to recall a past life also reported memories of the time *between*. "Does that mean you could actually see yourself?"

Henley nodded. "I could see everything. I saw you in the woods with Natalie. Then I went through the tunnel."

"What tunnel?"

Henley shrugged. "I don't know. It was dark inside. I was scared at first. But then I wasn't anymore."

"Do you remember anything else?" Kate asked. "Do you remember what happened after you went through the tunnel?"

Henley frowned. She thought about it, drawing a small fingernail along the armrest. Eventually she shook her head. "Just that I had to be a baby again," she said. "I had to go back in mommy's stomach."

"And did that make you happy?" Kate's thighs were burning, but she stayed where she was, watching Henley's face change around a complex series of emotions.

"I love my mommy," Henley said, almost fiercely, as if Kate had suggested otherwise. She scrubbed a little harder with her fingernail. "But I liked being bigger. Then I could do whatever I wanted, and everyone listened to me."

"What kind of things?" Kate asked. Henley wiggled around a bit, looking at Kate under her lashes. Sly. "What kind of things did you get to do when you were bigger?"

Henley leaned forward, cupped her hand to her mouth, and pressed it to Kate's ear. "I had boyfriends," she whispered. Then she leaned back, kicking her feet, electrified by the disclosure.

Kate opened her mouth in mock surprise. "You did?" she said, keeping her voice light. Henley nodded vigorously. "Do you remember any of their names?"

Henley gave her that sly look again. "I'm not allowed to tell you."

"How come?" Kate asked.

"Because it's a secret," Henley said. "I'll get in trouble."

"How about if I guess?" Kate said. She heard Emily moving in the dining room. Listening, undoubtedly. "Was your boyfriend's name . . . Benjamin?" Henley shook her head. "Was it . . . Harold? Or . . . Wilson?" Henley squealed with laughter. "Was it . . . Cameron?"

Almost immediately, Henley's smile evaporated. She wiggled in her chair. "No," she said. "That's not his name." Abruptly, she stood up and darted out of the room. Kate heard her footsteps running up the stairs.

To Kate, it was confirmation.

Jenny Lin was right. Something had happened between Cameron and Becca that summer. All of Becca's teasing—the way she'd joked about Cameron's old-man skin, and outed Kate's crush to the whole bunk—it was all just misdirection, a cover for her own feelings.

But what did it mean? Did it mean anything? Cameron was eighteen—old enough to get in trouble for dating Becca if someone reported him. He would have lost his job at the camp, certainly, if Harriet had known he was hooking up with one of the female campers. But mostly, it would have been Kate who felt betrayed. Was that why Henley was reluctant to tell the truth?

Was she bound to keep Becca's secrets, even now?

Her knees protested as she angled to her feet, leaning heavily on the chair for leverage. God, she was getting old.

She turned around and startled. Emily had entered the room behind her. She had a grim expression on her face.

"What did Henley say?" Emily asked. "Did she explain why she locked her best friend in the closet?"

Kate realized, with a needling sense of guilt, that they had barely discussed it. "She was frustrated," Kate said evasively. "She misses the freedoms that came with being older."

Emily turned away, letting half her face get carved into darkness. "I don't believe this," she muttered.

"I think that Becca was dating one of the counselors," Kate said. "It's possible he was the one who lent her the keys to the boathouse—"

"Becca." The word came out like an explosion. Emily turned back to her, eyes sparking. "I don't care about Becca. I care about Henley, my child, my baby."

"But to Henley, they're the same thing," Kate said. "She can remember what it was like to be Becca." As soon as she spoke the words out loud, she was hit with the weight of them, swinging back like a pendulum to knock the air out of her chest. Henley could *remember* what it was like to be Becca. It was true.

"Well, she'll have to forget," Emily said sharply. Then she sighed. "I heard from Dr. Rushkin this morning. He wants Henley to be included in a new study. I told him no."

Kate felt a spark of panic. "This is important, Emily," she said. "What this means about consciousness—what it means for the field—"

"I don't care about that," Emily said. "What it means for my daughter is she'll stop obsessing about the life of some girl who died twenty-six years ago."

"Are you sure about that?" Kate asked.

Emily gave her a mutinous look. "I appreciate all your help," she said stiffly, leaning on the last word a bit, giving it the bite of sarcasm. "But I don't want you to see Henley anymore."

Kate had had parents pull the plug on sessions before—plenty of times, and usually right when she was making progress—and she'd learned not to take it personally, to swallow her fear and concern for the small lives she saw trailing out of her office for the last time, shooting her backward glances. But this was different. She *needed* Henley.

If she was ever going to figure out what happened to Becca, she needed the girl who remembered.

"Emily, please—" she started.

But Emily cut her off. "I'm sorry," she said. "I've made my decision. And here." She pivoted out of the room briefly and returned with the camp yearbook. "Take this. I don't want it in the house anymore."

Kate could tell that there was no point in arguing. She felt suddenly awkward, aware that she was now an uninvited guest, taking up space that wasn't hers.

"Please tell Henley I said goodbye," she said after Emily had edged her, not so subtly, toward the door. "And you have my number. If you ever need me . . ."

"We won't," Emily said. She closed and locked the storm door behind her—the first time Kate had ever seen her do so.

Kate felt the distance to her car exaggeratedly in every step she took along the driveway. The trees were radiating whispers, shaking loose conversations that had been stilled by a stifling, airless day. When she reached her car, she glanced back at the house.

She saw a movement in the upstairs windows, a dark flitting. Then she recognized Henley, standing in her mother's bedroom, peering out into the dark, backlit by the room behind her.

Kate lifted a hand to wave. After a second, Henley lifted a hand, and placed it against the glass. A strange, intimate gesture. Just the way Kate used to do with Becca, when the bus arrived to carry her back to New York City, and from there to her real life.

And for a second, standing there, she allowed her imagination to resculpt the dark figure she saw with her hand on the window, to contour the silhouette into the shape of a different girl—the first girl she'd ever really loved.

"Goodbye, Becca," she said out loud.

Becca was still there, and still watching her, when the house dropped from the rear view into dark.

THEN

The woods rebounded the sound of Becca's name. Kate could hear the distant shouting, the staccato syllables, BEC-CA, through the infirmary windows. To her, it sounded like gunshots, firing off into the air, like a warning and a threat.

The counselors had organized the older kids into a search party, to walk the trails shouting for Becca, just in case she'd gotten lost in the woods. Kate knew that it was just a distraction, a way of killing time. Harriet was gone—sequestered all day with the police. Two squad cars were still marooned in the upper parking lot. Just looking at them reminded Kate: They were trapped.

The police had already located the drifting canoe, with one of Becca's earrings lodged beneath a bench seat. Every time someone glanced in her direction—a counselor, another camper—her face burned. She had the sense that everyone knew. *She had fantasies of drowning, of simply sinking down into the lake until the mantle of quiet and darkness overcame her.*

She wished she had been the one to die.

She'd spent most of the day in the infirmary—rocked with stomach pains, and roiling nausea that never produced any vomit and thus gave her no relief. Already, rumors were whipping around the camp—Harriet would get in trouble. The counselors would be fired. Everyone would be sent home early.

Camp Sauquamet, as they knew it, was over.

Kate looked up at a soft knock on the door. It was Cameron—wearing his favorite hat, as usual, and a girdle of woven bracelets on his wrist.

"I heard you didn't feel well." Despite everything, Cameron's voice filled her with a kind of warmth, and she sat up, regretting all the hours she'd spent crying. She must look like a toad. "Care for some company?"

Kate nodded. She could hardly draw enough breath to speak; all day, she'd felt as if her lungs were being squeezed, gripped by an iron fist.

Cameron took a seat on the empty cot next to her. Up close, Kate could see the faint lines at the corners of his eyes—sunshine lines, she liked to think, which looked like miniature rays. He leaned forward, elbows on his knees, and looked at her. Kate's heart began to climb into her throat. For a second, she thought wildly of kissing him.

Then he said, "Becca will come back, you know."

Kate looked away, fighting the urge to cry, to confess to everything they'd done. Instead, she scraped out in a whisper, "What if she doesn't?"

"She will," Cameron insisted. "You know Becca. This is probably her idea of a joke. Ten bucks says she snuck off for the night just to cause a panic. She'll be back," he repeated. "You'll see."

It was no use. Tears stung Kate's eyes again, blurring her vision. Soon, she was sobbing again—heaving huge amounts of grief and guilt onto shuddering breaths that sounded like animal cries.

"Hey." Cameron moved next to her, and put one arm around her. Kate buried her head in his fleece. He rocked her against him. He spoke into her hair. "Hey. It's okay. It's not your fault, okay? It's not your fault."

TWENTY

Kate was too amped to return to her Airbnb. The thought of packing up, of going back to Virginia, now seemed intolerable. She had been nudging closer to understanding what had really happened that night on Fair Isle, teetering on the edge of the truth. She could feel it.

And Mari had gone and spoiled it all.

She found her way to Mari's house for the third time, this time from memory. The house, brilliantly lit against the night, reminded Kate of a ship moored in the darkness. Through the windows, she could see Mari moving around the living room, unconscious that she was being watched. She flitted in and out of sight, like something caught on the wind.

But at the touch of Kate's headlights, Mari came to the front door. Kate saw her face, narrowed in concentration as she peered out into the night.

She was opening the door as Kate came up the steps. "I've been calling," Kate said. As she stepped onto the porch, she thought she saw Mari's face seize around a look of fear. Or possibly guilt.

"Sorry," Mari said simply. She stood, blocking the doorway for another beat, and only belatedly inched the door a little wider, indicating that Kate could come in. But she didn't look happy about it. "I thought you were going back to Virginia."

"Change of plans," Kate said, following her into the living room. Mari had rearranged the furniture, she noticed, clearing space for a wooden console cluttered with burning candles, picture frames, and tchotchkes. The room smelled overpoweringly of vanilla. "Here. Here's your book back."

Mari barely glanced at the camp yearbook. Her mouth tugged at an expression of disdain as she shucked it quickly on a side table, as if to minimize physical contact with something distasteful. "I'm sorry I haven't called," she said, turning away from Kate, and moving to the console, where her fingers fretted over the various objects on display—adjusting them by millimeters, angling the photographs in their cheap frames toward the candlelight. "I was in shock, I think. After what you told me . . ." She shook her head, her ringlets of gray shaking against her shoulders. "Well, I honestly didn't believe you at first."

"And now?" Kate asked.

Mari turned to glance at her. For a second, she didn't answer. Then she said, "Becca always frightened me." As if that answered the question. "I sometimes prayed for something bad to happen to her. I sometimes prayed that God would punish her. I wanted her to suffer. Sometimes she made me feel so—so bad about myself, I wanted her to pay."

A pull of sympathy relaxed some of Kate's anger. "It wasn't your fault, Mari," she said. "It was an accident. None of us meant for Becca to get hurt."

"Didn't we?" Mari said in a curious voice. She reached for one of the photographs on display between two candles, dislodging a lighter that had been propped against it and sending it skittering to the floor. Kate bent down to retrieve it and froze.

It was silver, ornate, with a single blue stone embedded in the metal. Maybe an opal. She felt a sudden pain in her shoulder, as if only now she'd been touched by the hot metal, marked by Becca in the ceremony to brand loyalty into their skin forever.

Flipping over the lighter, she saw that it was engraved with initials: *C.D.* Becca must have stolen it from their counselor. Either that, or it had been a gift.

"Where did you get this?" she said. Her voice sounded hollow in her ears.

"It was Becca's," she said, and made a motion with the photograph in her hands so the candlelight slid off the glass. For the first time, Kate registered the person inside the frame: a grainy picture of Becca, sitting on the porch railing outside their bunk, flashing the peace sign. Now, suddenly, one by one, the items on the console took on meaning, as if slotting into place in her awareness: the hand-labeled CD, the small ceramic puppy dog, the lighter, the letters, the beaded friendship bracelets. They were all from Becca—either gifts to Mari, or discarded belongings—nestled among the candles like some kind of shrine. She felt a sudden pull of fear, looking at Mari with those big eyes, sparking with reflected candlelight, her face glowing with the devotion of a true believer.

"What is all this stuff?" Her voice broke on the question. "What are you doing with it?"

Mari returned the photograph to its position next to the others, all of them photos of Becca alone. "I've been praying for Becca's forgiveness," she said. "I've been asking for her soul to find rest."

It occurred to Kate that Mari was, after all, a little unstable.

"You called someone at the newspaper about Henley Haskell," Kate said. "Why?"

Mari blinked at Kate, as if she could hardly understand the question. "It's extraordinary," she said, in the breathy voice of someone who'd just been running.

"Becca's still here. She's still with us. We have the chance to make things right."

"Henley isn't Becca, Mari. She's a six-year-old girl with bad nightmares. She's confused and frightened. She's not a phenomenon."

"No?" Mari looked faintly puzzled. "Then why did you come? And why have you stayed?" She smiled, then, in a way that turned Kate's stomach. Like someone caught inside of a rapture, a fantasy of unknown voices. "There's a reason for all of it, Kate. Becca needed you. She wanted you to come back here. Don't you see?"

"Well, she's going to be disappointed. I'm going home tomorrow." Kate deposited the lighter back on Mari's console, suddenly eager to be rid of it, to get out of there, to drop Mari and her creepy shrine back down the well of the past.

"But you can't go home," Mari protested. She still had that serene, almost beatific smile, and Kate was reminded, suddenly, of the time early in her career when she'd been called in by the FBI to perform a psychological evaluation of a fourteen-year-old girl who'd stabbed both of her baby sisters to death, after journeying with them all the way to frigid Northern Michigan with the promise that they were going to see Santa Claus. "Not really. Not anymore. Becca's made sure of it. So long as Henley is alive . . . so long as she remembers—"

"Becca is dead. She was murdered. That's what Henley remembers."

As soon as she said the word out loud—*murdered*—she felt the truth of it. Hadn't that been, after all, what she had carried with her all these years? Concealed and embedded inside of the terror of what they'd seen in the woods, interlaced with the guilt and shame because of how they'd treated her body—hadn't she always known, deep down, that someone had killed Becca? For years, she had felt that in some way they had been to blame. She had thought that their resentment of Becca, the undercurrent of hatred they'd carried for her, had somehow taken on physical shape on that island, invaded the mausoleum and snatched Becca's life away. They had brought the curse down on them, by looking for the Gray Lady, by invading her final resting place; and Becca had paid the price for it.

But all of these were just stories, fantasies wrapped around the mystery of that sliver of time between Becca, alive and dead. She didn't believe it was an accident. She'd never believed that it could be.

That was what Henley was trying to tell her. That was why she had nightmares, why she defaced the door in her dollhouse to keep the spectral figure of the Gray Lady locked in her imagination. Someone—a monster—really had hurt her.

Kate was eager to get away from Mari, away from the overstuffed house, and her creepy shrine, and the cloying smell of vanilla. As soon as she was out on the porch, she felt better.

"Did you know about Becca and Cameron?" she asked at the last moment. If anyone had known, it would be Mari; she had always trailed after Becca, worshipped her as much as she'd feared her. "Did you know there was something between them that summer?"

Mari's face was in shadow. She turned, and an arc of light just traced her profile. "I saw them once," she said. "In the boathouse. They were arguing." Mari shook her head, letting the trace of light bounce off her. "I asked her about it afterward. Becca was furious. She made me swear not to tell. She said that if anyone found out, she would conjure the Gray Lady to suffocate me while I was sleeping." Mari rasped a laugh. "It sounds stupid now. But I really believed she could do it, at the time. I thought Becca could do anything."

"We all did," Kate said. "But somehow, Becca was the one who wound up dead." She started for her car.

"She was scared, I think." Mari lifted her voice a bit, to catch Kate where she was standing.

"Of what? Of the Gray Lady?"

"No. No, I don't think so. Of someone else. I think—I honestly think Becca thought that the Gray Lady could protect her."

"Protect her from what?" Kate asked.

"Maybe you should ask the girl," Mari said. "Ask Henley. You know how Becca was about secrets."

She withdrew into the house. Kate was suddenly aware of the invasion of darkness all around her. She saw Mari drifting back to her candles, her lips moving over some prayer or incantation. Quickly, she got into her car.

But on the short drive back to her Airbnb, she remembered how Henley had looked at her sideways, her eyes suddenly narrowed around a shrewdness too old for her, when Kate had asked her about all the things she had been allowed to do when she was bigger, and who she had been doing them with. *I'm not allowed to tell.*

And she couldn't stop thinking about what Mari had said: *You know how Becca was about secrets.*

She couldn't shake the unease that trailed her back from Mari's house, a clinging waft of bad feeling, like the smell of something awful. She was reassured to see that the lights of the main house were still burning; the guest house was dark, and she hurried down the gravel path as quickly as possible.

As soon as she was inside, she locked the door, took her computer, and began a search for Cameron Dunbar. If he and Becca had really been dating in secret, she might have told him about the plan to go to Fair Isle. He might conceivably have been the one who'd given her the Fireball whisky; Cameron had only been eighteen, but according to Jenny Lin the counselors had had no great trouble chasing down alcohol. And after that summer he had simply melted away—perhaps just across the New York border.

Becca had been a collector of other people's secrets. It was time to find out what Cameron's had been.

Kate turned up plenty of Cameron Dunbars in her search, including a handful from Vermont, but none of them were the right age. At the bottom of the page of results, she stumbled across an article from the *Phoenix Herald* about a Cameron Dunbar who'd gone missing twenty-seven years ago at the age of seventeen. Jenny Lin had mentioned the case; according to her, it was the wrong Cameron. Still, she clicked on the link, wondering whether Jenny might have been wrong. The ages synced up. And Cameron might have lied about where he was from. Maybe he'd been a runaway; Jenny had said that Camp Sauquamet often took on counselors from troubled backgrounds. She scrolled down until she found a picture of the missing boy.

And her heart stopped.

She knew him. She knew that face.

But not as Cameron Dunbar.

Quickly, she jumped across the tabs still open to articles about the Berkshires Triangle and the various local tragedies that over the years had been attributed to the Gray Lady. There it was: the police reconstruction of the Twin Falls John Doe, released several years after his body had been discovered. Her pulse came roaring back, flushing blood into her face. It was unmistakable: the narrow nose, the high forehead, the eyes, spaced slightly too far apart.

After twenty-seven years, the Twin Falls John Doe had a name: Cameron Dunbar, from Austin, Texas.

Now her thoughts were running up against each other, shuddered by the enormity of the coincidence. Twenty-seven years ago, the body of a missing boy had turned up in the state park, just across the lake from where another boy—the same age, and with the same name—would turn up for his job as a camp counselor two months later. The boy's cause of death was unknown. Just like Becca's would have been, undoubtedly, if Kate and her friends hadn't panicked, and sunk her body into the lake.

Could it be a coincidence? Cameron Dunbar wasn't a very common name. That meant two dead teenagers, both connected—one by name, and one by secret relationship to the counselor that had been Kate's first serious crush, the boy who'd taught her to stretch her hands on the guitar neck to strum her first G, the boy who'd once touched her face and told her she had pretty eyes.

The boy who had, it seemed, vanished into thin air after the summer was over.

THEN

Mari rode back in the canoe between Kate and Lennie, gripping her knees to her chest. With every stroke, Kate half expected to feel a hand seize the oar, lurching them into the water. She couldn't believe that any of it was real, that Becca was gone. Even as she'd helped tip Becca's body into the water, she'd felt only as if she were watching the scene from above: Becca's hair, dispersing for a minute on the surface before the weight of the stones in her pocket pulled her down; Becca's skin, that marbled blue color, reflecting the moonlight even as she descended; the way her arms drifted upward, as if she were reaching for them one last time. She imagined that Becca would be waiting for them when they got back to the dock, gloating about the vicious joke she'd played on all of them. Or maybe she'd be angry—they had failed one of her tests.

But there was no one on the beach. Kate kept squinting through the mist, imagining she saw forms materializing in the shadows—police, possibly, or one of the counselors. Then the clouds shifted and the moon fell down on the slumbering camp, paralyzed by sameness, exactly as they'd left it. No calamity had hit. No wind had arrived to tumble the cabins from the hill, to rip the flagpole from its cement, to whisk away the sleeping campers. Kate could hardly believe it. It was just after one o'clock; they'd snuck out a little before eleven.

But by morning call, she knew, everyone would find out: One of the girls was missing.

What, she wondered, would happen to them then?

They pulled up the canoe and carried it between them to the boathouse. The tension of the silence was so great, Kate almost had the urge to scream, to shatter it with a confession. Surely someone knew. Surely, they would never get away with it.

Still, no one came. They returned the canoe to the boathouse. Lennie replaced the padlock. Click.

It was done.

"Remember. We don't know anything," Lennie said. It was the first time they had spoken since leaving Fair Isle. They had communicated, coordinated, in spellbound silence—almost automatically, as if the same instructions had been whispered to all of them at once. Load Becca into a canoe. Paddle her out into the water. Release her. Bring her down to me. *"We never left our bunk. We don't know what happened to Becca. This was all just a dream. Swear it."*

"I swear." Kate could hardly speak the words past the pressure in her throat. She glanced at Mari. Mari's face was bloated from crying, and her hair was a mess—whipped out of her ponytail, plastered to her skin. She had the same distant look in her eyes as Becca, when they'd found her lying in the mausoleum. As if her vision had withdrawn, turned inward. Gone somewhere else.

But Mari whispered, "It was all a dream."

Kate was shivering so hard by the time they made it back to their bunk, she was sure that Cheryl would hear her teeth rattling in her skull, feel the tremor of her body under her blankets. She didn't expect to sleep. She thought she might never sleep again.

It was all a dream, *she kept repeating to herself.* We don't know anything. We didn't do anything. *She imagined Becca, stirring in the bunk beneath hers. She imagined Becca, still in the grips of sleep, walking out into the lake until the water closed above her head.*

A dream, a dream, a dream, *Kate thought. And at some point her mind let go. She stopped holding on to the idea of Becca, lost in her own dream, swallowed by the water.*

She slept.

TWENTY-ONE

The Berkshire County Sheriff's Office was located in a redbrick building, washed a tawny orange in the morning sun. Kate had reluctantly packed up her Airbnb, after her texts to Emily Haskell went unanswered. She knew, from the little time she'd spent with the Haskells, that Emily was just that kind of woman; she had told Kate that they were done speaking, and she meant it.

At the last minute, Kate considered simply forgetting about the police, forgetting about Matt Bishop and the Haskells, forgetting about Becca—as she had tried, with varying degrees of success, to do for twenty-six years. She would drive back to Virginia, letting the narrow Berkshire roads spit her out into the funnel of highways that would sweep her home. There, she would be swept up in the middle-of-August frenzy before her coursework began this fall. There would be schedules to approve; tasks to assign; the usual tensions between rival academics to navigate at department meetings. She would need to sign off on the work of the graduate students in her lab. And there was her agent, angling for yet another book, this time about the so-called "sleeping sickness" that had afflicted those migrant children in Switzerland.

But instead, she turned north, toward the investigation that was waiting.

Deputy Sheriff Matt Bishop didn't seem entirely surprised to see her.

"Kate Willis," he said. "So you really *are* following me." He gestured for her to sit. In his office, surrounded by the typical architecture of paperwork and electronics, he seemed to have absorbed a kind of brisk formality. Kate couldn't believe that only a few nights ago, she'd been contemplating what it would be like to kiss him.

"I guess so," Kate said as she took a seat across from him, feeling suddenly self-conscious, overly aware of her hands, as if they'd only just been attached. She wondered whether Matt Bishop had, from the beginning, recognized her name, known it right away from his information about Becca.

"What can I do for you?" He leaned back a bit in his chair, swiveling it slightly. He was smiling, but Kate caught the glimpse of something else in his expression. Wariness, she thought. Or just simple curiosity.

Kate took a deep breath. "About twenty-seven years ago, some hikers came across a dead body in the state park. They call him the Twin Falls John Doe." Bishop gave a minute nod. "I think I know who he is."

Bishop leaned forward as Kate opened her laptop, toggling between two tabs—one that showed the police reconstruction of the victim, minus the evidence of animal activity that had removed a chunk of his face; one the twenty-seven-year-old poster circulated after seventeen-year-old Cameron Dunbar went missing. She had expected—what?—some kind of reaction, possibly amazement, possibly distrust. But Bishop just kept looking at the screen, his eyes barely moving, as Kate plunged into an explanation of how she'd googled an old camp counselor and turned up a photograph she recognized.

"Recognized," Bishop repeated. "You'd been following the case of the Twin Falls John Doe, then?"

"Not following it, no," Kate said. "To be honest, I hadn't heard of it until a few days ago. I was researching the Berkshires Triangle," she added, when Bishop gave her a quizzical look.

Bishop crooked a smile. "Don't believe everything you hear on the internet," he said. His eyes clicked back to her computer screen. For a moment, absorbed in thought, his fingers drummed on the desk. Finally he roused himself. "So you think this camp counselor—Cameron Dunbar—wound up dead in the state park?"

"No. Cameron started as a counselor two months *after* the John Doe was found dead. He was there the following summer, too."

"So we're talking about two Cameron Dunbars," Bishop said. "One of them dead. The other one this counselor that you haven't been able to track down." Kate nodded. Bishop grunted. "That's quite a coincidence."

"I thought so," Kate said.

Bishop looked at her thoughtfully. "This old camp counselor. You said you were looking for him. It's been quite a few years, hasn't it? Any reason in particular you wanted to track him down?"

Though he kept his voice light, Kate felt the question like a knife blade, whittling her life down to a choice: to tell the truth, finally, or not.

"Yes," she answered. "I wanted to ask him about Becca McGuire."

Bishop froze, just for a second. Kate watched his hand move, as if on its own, to a notepad and pen on the desk. "And why is that?"

Kate took another deep breath. "Because he knew Becca. They were apparently . . . close before she disappeared. Very close. I never knew. Not until I started asking questions."

"You were one of Becca's bunkmates, weren't you?" So he had recognized the name. Again, Kate nodded. "So why now? What made you come back here after all this time?"

Kate couldn't tell him about Henley; he would simply think she was insane. And she felt, suddenly, that she needed him to believe her. She needed someone to know what had happened to Becca. She needed someone else to wonder whether Cameron—her Cameron—had known something or somehow been involved.

"Because I've been lying for twenty-six years about that night," she said. The words came out like a gigantic exhale. "And I know it sounds crazy. But I think . . . I think that Becca needs me to tell the truth."

The whole story came out then: how they'd grown obsessed with the legend of the Gray Lady that summer; how they'd made a plan to take the trip out to Fair Isle; how Becca had been drinking, had opened the mausoleum and tried to push Mari inside. At that point, Bishop asked if he could record the conversation. Kate agreed, feeling a slight twinge of misgiving. But it was already too late to stop.

She skipped over the part where they'd thought they'd seen the Gray Lady in the woods—she didn't feel right dragging Natalie into it—and instead simply told Bishop about returning to the graveyard to find a deafening silence, as if Becca had been whisked away in their absence.

Then, the horrifying moment when they'd opened the door and found Becca lying, mouth deformed in a grimace, dead on the stone floor.

"Why didn't you go for help?" Bishop asked her.

"I don't know," Kate said. She couldn't ever explain the horror of the moment, the fever that had gripped them all, as if they'd fallen into a nightmare. "She was dead. We knew that no one could help her. And we were afraid . . ."

"Afraid that you'd be blamed?" Bishop said sharply.

Kate shook her head. "Afraid of the Gray Lady," Kate said. "We thought—we thought it was the curse. We panicked. We weren't thinking."

"Let me make sure I have this right," Bishop said. "You and your friends snuck out to Fair Isle. You were all angry at Becca. There was a fight. You pushed Becca inside the mausoleum. You locked the door. Then you ran away for thirty minutes. When you came back, Becca was dead."

Kate nodded. There was a knot in her throat that felt like it was strangling her. The room felt suddenly airless. Coming here had been a mistake.

"You don't call for help. You don't try and revive her. You don't bring her back to camp." Bishop let each sentence drop like a gavel. "Instead, you decide to fill up her pockets with stones, sink her in the lake, and hope that her body was never found."

To her horror, Kate realized she was on the verge of tears. She looked down, squeezing her hands in her lap, struggling to get control of herself. "It was so stupid. It was awful. But we were kids. We had no idea what to do."

"You were old enough to know what not to do, and you did it anyway." Bishop leaned forward. His face had transformed. Gone was the easygoing guy who'd been flirting with her at the bar. Now his face was hard, screwed up like a rivet to pin her in place. "You're asking me to believe that the same people capable of drowning their best friend's body and lying about it for twenty-six years didn't have anything to do with her death?"

"I didn't say we had nothing to do with it. We left her alone. We locked her up in that horrible place."

"But you locked her in alive, according to you," Bishop said. "And thirty minutes later, just like that, she was dead. How do you explain it?"

"I can't explain it." The words came out as an eruption. "That's why I'm here. That's why I'm telling you. I hoped *you* could explain it."

"All right." Bishop dropped his pen, shifted back in his chair, and stared at her. "I'll give it a shot. You and your friends go out to this island and have an argument with Becca. You shove her, or someone else does. She falls, she hits her head, you guys panic."

"No," Kate said. "No. She was alive when we left her."

"Look, it was an accident, right? No one meant for her to get hurt."

"No." For one wild second, Kate could imagine it: shoving Becca, hard, and seeing her head crack on the doorframe. She'd remembered—she could have sworn—that it was Mari who'd pushed her. But Henley had said it was Kate. Could her memories have twisted somehow, obscuring some deeper culpability?

But no. They'd left Becca alive. It was supposed to be a joke, a prank, a way of getting back at her. That was it.

"Look," Kate said. "I didn't have to come here. There's no reason for me to lie about what happened. It's been twenty-six years. But something happened to Becca in that half hour when we left her, just like something happened to Cameron Dunbar—the real Cameron Dunbar—on that campground."

"The real Cameron Dunbar," Bishop said sharply. "What do you mean by that?"

Kate hadn't meant to say it; the words had just slipped out. She thought of Cameron, patiently repositioning her hands on the guitar strings; dressed in a goofy wig in the camp talent show, performing a boy-band style dance with some of the boys from Bunk Three. She'd filled a whole journal that summer with an outpouring of emotion about him, detailing every minor interaction, wondering if he felt the connection she imagined they had.

"I don't know," Kate admitted. "One Cameron Dunbar dies in the woods, and goes unidentified for years. A second Cameron Dunbar shows up in the area at the same time, and then takes off again at the end of the summer. In the meantime, his girlfriend dies."

"Girlfriend? You mean Becca McGuire?"

Kate nodded. "Supposedly she and Cameron got . . . close that summer."

"He was older, wasn't he? If he was a counselor . . ."

"Eighteen," Kate confirmed. "But Becca was . . . mature in some ways. In other ways, she was still a child."

Bishop grunted. He spun his pen on his desk. "And you know for a fact they were involved in—what?—a sexual relationship?"

"I don't know for a fact," Kate said. "I only know that something was happening between them. Becca claimed to know a secret about Cameron. And Jenny Lin—the head counselor—spotted them alone in the boathouse together, twice."

"I know Jenny Lin," Bishop said. He lapsed into silence. But after a minute, he roused himself. "What was your goal coming here today, Ms. Willis?" Kate noted how quickly he'd slipped back into formality. "What did you hope to achieve?"

Kate forced herself to meet his gaze. "If my son had gone unidentified for twenty-seven years, I'd want to know," she said.

"So this wasn't about Becca? You don't feel bad about where *she's* been lying?"

"Of course I do." Kate was too tired to be angry. "I feel horrible about it. Becca was . . . troubled. But she was my friend. For several years, she was my *best* friend. I guess I'm hoping that Cameron—*my* Cameron, the one I knew—might have some answers." As soon as she said it, though, it occurred to Kate that she hadn't really known Cameron at all. She'd imagined him, cobbled together a fantasy version of him from a collection of minor interactions and observations, slivers of facts he let drop—like the fact that his older brother had been sick with cancer.

She wondered now how much of it was true.

"And this counselor, Cameron Dunbar . . . do you remember anything else about him? Where he was from? Where he went to high school?"

"He said he was from Vermont," Kate said. "I think that he was heading to Binghamton in the fall. He had an older brother. A half brother, Cameron told me. He'd died from leukemia. My mother had leukemia," Kate added, when Bishop looked at her strangely. "Maybe he only said it so that I wouldn't feel alone."

Bishop had been taking notes. Now he flipped the notebook closed, and had her repeat her name, phone number, and address into the tape recorder.

He stood up to walk her to the door. But the gesture didn't feel friendly.

"Oh, and, Ms. Willis, do me a favor," he said just as Kate was finally reaching for the door. She turned to see Bishop smiling at her narrowly. "Don't plan any international trips."

TWENTY-TWO

On the drive back to Virginia, Kate kept checking her rearview mirror, half expecting to see the whirl of police lights behind her. She wondered what Matt Bishop would do with the information she'd given him. Speak to Mariana, maybe. Kate wondered whether Mariana would deny it, stick to the story they'd given all those years ago.

Kate wondered whether Matt Bishop would believe her if she did.

She felt better as soon as she turned off the highway and funneled down into the Charlottesville streets. It hadn't even been a week, but she felt like someone returning from exile. She'd always loved the University of Virginia, with the burnish of its brick buildings, its stately quad, and the happy sprawl of faculty and graduate school housing running slowly into busy streets, cluttered with bars and pizzerias. But now, slowing to a crawl between the usual line of traffic on McCormick Road, she felt something close to joy.

She drove straight to Steve's condo. The dogs spent minutes agitating and whimpering when they saw her again, as if they, too, felt that she'd been gone for years.

"I was worried about you," Steve said. "You didn't call."

"Should I have?" Kate asked him, raising an eyebrow. Steve shrugged. Neither of them knew quite how to manage the friendship, and there was a part of Kate that knew, or suspected, that it couldn't last.

Steve poured them both iced tea, and they sat together on the sunny balcony. It was easy, friendly, and familiar—another aspect of home, Kate thought. She pretended not to have noticed the pair of earrings on the side table inside.

"So? What's the verdict?" he asked her once they had settled down at the table, next to a lone bromeliad striving hopelessly to bud.

"I can't explain it," Kate said. "I can't explain *her*." She looked away, so she wouldn't have to watch Steve smirk.

"Aha!" was all he said. "So, what now?"

"What do you mean, what now? The Haskells are done talking—to me, to the department, to anyone. I couldn't help her at all."

"But this changes everything, don't you see?" Steve leaned back in his chair, his hair mussed as always, his glasses somehow deepening the darkness of his eyes. "If Henley is telling the truth, think about what this means for your field. Think about what it means about identity, about consciousness, about personality, about nature and nurture."

"I'm mostly thinking about a long shower, and an early bedtime," Kate said. Steve was right, of course. But she was too tired to contemplate the big questions. Confessing to Matt Bishop, letting the secret go after all these years, should have brought her a sense of peace. Instead, she felt worse than ever. Now she had betrayed not only Becca, but Mari and Lennie as well.

"Something's bothering you," Steve said. "What is it?"

Kate gave him a look. "How much time do you have?"

"I'm serious," Steve said. "You're noodling something. I can tell. Your fingernails look like shit, and you've got that vein showing in your forehead."

Kate wondered what Steve would say if she told him that, as of six hours ago, she might very well be the prime suspect in a murder investigation. Instead, she blurted out, "Why would a teenager want a fake identity? Why would they need one?"

"You're the psychologist, not me."

"I'm serious," Kate said.

"Teenagers run away all the time."

"Sure. But they don't take on a fake name. Not unless they're trafficked, and someone forces them to do it. They just . . . disappear."

Steve shrugged. "Same reason anyone takes on a fake identity, I guess. They're afraid of being found."

"Or of being found out," Kate said slowly. Jenny Lin had mentioned that the camp director, Harriet, had made it a point to hire counselors from troubled backgrounds. But she wondered how far that lenience extended. If Cameron Dunbar—her Cameron Dunbar—had gotten into serious trouble under a different name, he might simply have found it easier to adopt the name of someone he'd met. Hypothetically, he might have stumbled on the boy's campsite and simply robbed it.

Except.

Except that it wouldn't explain why two teenagers, both connected to the boy she'd known as Cameron Dunbar, had died suddenly, seemingly without cause, within fifteen months of one another.

"What is this about?" Steve was watching her curiously, his head tilted, like a bird's. "Is this still about the girl, Henley?"

"I don't know," Kate admitted. "But I think it's about Becca."

For a moment, Steve said nothing. He craned his head back, angling it toward the sun. Now he looked like a plant. Finally, he sighed. "You never really let her go, did you?"

Kate thought of Becca's big blue eyes, and the smatter of freckles on her nose. How Becca could make her laugh until she snorted Diet Coke. How one time, when they were nine or ten, Jeremy Allen from Bunk Three had put a garter snake down Kate's shirt, and laughed when she started crying. And how afterward, Becca had spread a rumor that Jeremy still wet his bed, and gotten everyone in camp to believe her. Becca had been a tyrant—beautiful, and terrible, and unpredictable.

But Kate had loved her fiercely, in her own way.

Kate could only shake her head. Looking at her ex-husband, she felt an unaccountable urge to cry. He, too, was gone in a way—the man she'd loved, the man she loved still, transformed into a mystery whose dimensions she could only half appreciate, in remnant clues, like those earrings in his living room. It was strange how people got lost to each other. It was strange how they returned. The same, but somehow different.

"I couldn't," she said finally. "We made a pact."

TWENTY-THREE

August rollicked toward September.

Kate was soon engulfed in faculty meetings and research paper reviews. Her lab opened again, and was filled daily with the hum and chatter of graduate students conducting interviews, comparing notes, popping into Kate's office to ask for help structuring experiments or organizing their results.

She managed to put the Haskells, and her time in Massachusetts, out of mind—securing it again in the mental vault where it had moldered for twenty-six years.

She didn't pick up a drink. She thought about it all the time, though, an obsession that swallowed her, threw every liquor store and wine bar and tumbler into stark relief in her awareness, floodlighted by a desperate growing urge to *escape*. Sometimes she felt as if she were physically knuckling onto her sanity, onto the routines that kept her churning through the days without having to think too much. Sometimes, lying in bed, she experienced a sudden spike of panic, terror that descended on her from everywhere and nowhere, a sense that she was rocketing toward a fatal drop.

Something had changed. Something had come loose inside of her. She got a prescription for sleeping pills and for days agonized about whether or not to open the bottle. She knew, somehow, that once she did, she would be on the path to drink again.

But sleep came only in snatches, in disturbed fragments that left her feeling unclean, as if she'd somehow had the slick of Becca's hands on her in the night.

She was surprised when, a few days before the start of the semester, she saw an email from Courtney, introducing her to a Dr. Gulati, a specialist in respiratory disease. Kate had almost forgotten that she'd requested the introduction. Still, she dialed the number that Courtney had emailed her.

The conversation was short—she could tell from his voice that Dr. Gulati was busy, and eager to get off the phone—but decisive.

"Even acute asthma attacks are rarely fatal," Dr. Gulati told her, after she'd described, in a general way, the manner of Becca's death. "And they don't develop just like that. You'd expect to see a pretty lengthy progression of symptoms over the course of several weeks."

"What about other respiratory disorders?" Kate asked. "Do you know of any that might contribute to sudden asphyxia? Maybe under conditions of stress?"

"Sudden asphyxia," Dr. Gulati repeated. "How sudden are we talking?"

"Twenty minutes. Thirty minutes, maximum," Kate said.

Dr. Gulati stuttered his surprise. "Diseases don't work that fast, luckily," he said. "Unless we're talking a grand mal heart attack, I'd look to other causes."

"Like what?" Kate asked.

He paused again. "Asphyxia can occur under any number of conditions," he said. "Drowning, obviously. Carbon monoxide kills quickly. Manual strangulation . . ."

"The girl wasn't strangled," Kate said. "She was alone when she died."

"Then I suggest you speak to a toxicologist," Dr. Gulati said.

"A toxicologist?" Kate repeated. The idea had never occurred to her.

"Many poisons cause acute respiratory failure. I'm not sure how quickly, though. Like I said, I'm not an expert. But I can make an introduction, if you like . . . ?"

"That's okay," Kate said. "I actually know somebody."

After she hung up, she sat for a minute, letting her heartbeat romp in her chest. For the first time since returning to Virginia, her mind raced toward something other than the possibility of a drink. Whatever had killed Becca, it wasn't an asthma attack. Was it possible, was it even vaguely feasible, that Becca had been poisoned? Kate had a hard time believing it. Poison suggested premeditation, and planning. She had always assumed that whatever had happened to Becca had happened there, on the island, in the window of time when they'd left her alone. But if Becca really had been poisoned, it meant that her death had been predetermined well before they stepped foot on Fair Isle.

If Becca really had been poisoned, it was only a coincidence that she'd died after they'd locked her in the mausoleum to punish her.

It had been two years since she'd last seen Stephanie Morrow, a toxicologist with the NIH. But she knew that Stephanie would remember her. They'd spent weeks together, both investigating the same phenomenon: a sudden outbreak of hysterical symptoms at a girls' boarding school in upstate New York. That was at the end of Kate's drinking days. Every night, Stephanie would sit up with her at the bar, quietly sipping on her Diet Coke, while Kate made excuses for her third or fourth glass of pinot noir—knowing, all the while, that she had another bottle waiting for her in her room. And every morning, Stephanie would show up in the lobby with two coffees, and pretend not to notice Kate's crusted makeup, oversize sunglasses, and seeping ooze of alcohol.

They met for lunch at Union Market in DC, a cavernous hall of individual food stands bustling with the usual midday foot traffic. Stephanie hailed Kate from across the room like someone greeting the arrival of a lifeboat, and Kate soon found herself engulfed in a hug so warm it surprised her. Stephanie seemed almost overflowing with joy and energy as she shepherded Kate around the market, pointing out her favorite dishes. Had she always been so enthusiastic, so open, so light? Kate couldn't remember. She'd been so locked into her own addiction when they'd last met; she remembered little of Stephanie but the challenge to keep her from recognizing Kate's drinking.

Now, however, it was the first thing that Stephanie mentioned when they sat down.

"You look good," she said with a sharp look. "Clearer. Are you still drinking?"

"No." Kate looked away, instinctively tightening her fingers on the table. She didn't want to admit that she had, only minutes ago, let her gaze linger lovingly on every bottle of beer arrayed on the bar of a German sausage purveyor, let her mind reach out and taste a pilsner as it went down to cool the roil of discomfort inside. She didn't know what was wrong with her; she'd never even liked beer.

"Congratulations. How long?" She clarified when Kate looked at her, "How long have you been sober?"

"Nine months," Kate said, and stopped herself from adding, "And three days." She didn't want Stephanie to know that she'd felt every one of them keenly, that she'd actually mourned over her last drink as if over a loved one.

But Stephanie seemed to understand, because she laughed. "And you've been white-knuckling it ever since," she said. Kate stared at her. That was, in fact, exactly what Kate had been doing—exactly what it had felt like. "I get it," Stephanie went on. "Believe me, I do. I strung together a few months here and there before I got to A.A., and it was torture."

Kate hoped her surprise didn't show on her face. "You're—you were . . . ?" She trailed off. She didn't know exactly how to phrase the question without being offensive.

But Stephanie just laughed again, as if the whole thing was one big joke. "A drunk? An alcoholic? Oh yeah. Big time. I almost lost my job, you know. I had two DUIs in six months. Thank God, though. I clipped a biker the last time I drove drunk, and it finally pushed me to get help."

"Help," Kate repeated. *Help*. A funny word. Half promise, half plea. "What kind of help?"

"Oh, I'm a twelve-step girl through and through. It's amazing what A.A. did for me. I haven't touched a drink in more than six years. But I'm still a lunatic, you know, without the program. A.A. really saved my life. Still saves my life, one day at a time." Stephanie began maneuvering her chopsticks through a bowl of Dan Dan noodles and added, almost as an afterthought, "Have you been?"

"No," Kate said. "I mean, once. I couldn't handle all the higher power stuff. It's not really for me."

Stephanie smirked, as if Kate had made a joke. She angled her chopsticks in Kate's direction. "Ah. But that's the point, isn't it? That's what we struggle with. That's why we're all so fucked up."

"What is?"

"We can't handle the higher power stuff. We can't handle the fact that we're not in control, that we don't have all the answers, that there are things—powers, rules, patterns, some kind of overall intelligence—that we can't touch or understand or throttle to do our will. We can't handle the fact that we're only participants here, not directors. So we fantasize, and deny, and warp. And we drink." Stephanie shrugged. "You know what I'm talking about. You've seen it in your work."

Kate said nothing. She was hit, suddenly, by the simple realization that Stephanie was right. Human beings couldn't handle being out of control—she *knew* this. It was the reason for the ritualistic compulsions that went along with OCD, for the black-and-white thinking that characterized borderline personality disorder, for the fantasy life that so often swallowed the abused child. The ego, faced with the mystery of being alive in a world that was largely out of our control, began to build stopgaps, delusions, frantic attempts to seal off that awareness.

She, Kate, had been wounded by this mystery early on. Something had happened to her on Fair Isle—something terrible had happened to all of them—and she had been trying for her whole life to escape it, to investigate everything she couldn't understand, to bludgeon the world into a spreadsheet, into experimental data that would explain it all.

For the first time ever, it occurred to her that the task was impossible. She would fail.

For the first time ever, the idea felt like relief.

"You should come with me some time," Stephanie said. "I go to a great meeting downtown. Lots of happy nutcases. You'd like it. We can have dinner afterward."

"That sounds nice," Kate said before she could think about it. Something in her chest and stomach—that awful gnawing feeling—relaxed almost immediately. Perhaps she really had been headed toward some change, some pivot point in her life.

But perhaps letting go didn't always mean drowning.

Stephanie seemed to recognize that she'd said enough. She turned the conversation to the reason that Kate had reached out to her. Kate had barely described the circumstances of Becca's death when Stephanie cut in.

"There are plenty of poisons that kill almost immediately—depending on the dose, of course. Strychnine, for example. But typically you'd see contortions, diarrhea, vomit. It's a messy way to die."

"What about blue skin?" Kate asked.

Stephanie was busy picking out the scallions from her noodle bowl. "Blue? Or kind of purplish?"

"Purplish," Kate said slowly. "Like someone who'd been dead a long time."

"Cyanosis," Stephanie said immediately. "Caused by severe hypoxia."

"English?"

"Certain kinds of toxicity attack the neural system. Others paralyze the heart. And still others provoke severe respiratory failure of one kind or another. When the blood rapidly deoxygenates, it's called hypoxia. It means that there simply isn't enough oxygen in the circulatory system.

When that happens, you expect to find cyanosis—a distinctive purplish-blue color to the skin."

Kate felt a stirring of excitement. "So what causes hypoxia?"

"Acute cyanide poisoning, for one," Stephanie said. "Botulin. Tetrodotoxin poisoning. That's the toxin inside of blowfish. Fatal within thirty minutes of exposure. But it's heavily regulated. You won't find it outside of a lab in this country." Stephanie shook her head. "If you're thinking it *was* poison, I'd put my money on sodium nitrate."

"Sodium nitrate?" Kate stared at her. "Isn't that the stuff they put in bacon?"

Stephanie smiled. "Sure. And fertilizer, and gunpowder. Sodium nitrate and sodium nitrite are common ingredients in everything from food preservatives to adhesives. But they're toxic. A few hundred milligrams of sodium nitrate is enough to kill you. It's fairly soluble, and you wouldn't necessarily taste it. If anything, you'd just taste the salt."

Kate's mind flashed immediately to the bottle of Fireball whisky that Becca had brought with her to Fair Isle. "How fast?"

"Without medical intervention? An hour, tops. But high stress will hasten the process." She looked at Kate sideways. "What's this about, anyway?" she asked. "Research? Curiosity? Or something to do with a patient?"

"None of the above," Kate said. "Just some unfinished business."

"Don't tell me that Rushkin has you running around chasing after ghosts these days."

"These days, the ghosts are chasing after me," Kate said.

And maybe it was true, after all. After Kate said goodbye to Stephanie Morrow, she was startled to see a missed call from Emily Haskell. It had been almost two months since Emily abruptly put an end to their meetings—and now, on the same evening that Becca's ghost was still nudging her toward the truth, Emily had chosen to reach out.

A line from the single Alcoholics Anonymous meeting she'd attended came skating back to her, like a smoke trail on the sky of her mind.

Nothing in God's world happens by mistake.

"Is this a good time?" was the first thing that Emily asked. Kate could hear the strain in her voice.

"Sure." Kate was still sitting in her car in the parking lot behind Union Market. "How are you doing? How's Henley?"

Emily rapped a short, humorless laugh. "Henley's fine. I'm a mess." Then: "The police think I had something to do with Becca's disappearance."

"What?" The word came out as an explosion. "What are you talking about?"

"Apparently someone told them about Henley's . . . other life. They found out about all the memories she's been having. And of course they don't believe it. They think I must have fed her information. Meantime, the local news won't stop calling . . . they want to feature Henley on a segment. The county news ran a story about her on the home page. They didn't name her, specifically. I don't think they have the right, do they? But everybody knows. You said that our interviews would be confidential . . ." Now her voice turned accusatory.

"They were. They are." It was Mari. Had to be. Kate should never have disclosed her reason for being in Massachusetts; it had been a bad miscalculation. At the same time, she couldn't help but feel a stirring of relief. If Matt Bishop was chasing down Emily Haskell for a lead, it meant that they either didn't take Kate's story seriously, or that they believed that she really hadn't killed Becca on Fair Isle.

"So why do the *police* think that I'm involved?" Emily careened over her words, zigzagging across topics. "They came to my house. They asked me about my sister, whether she ever dated someone named Cameron Dunbar. I've never even *heard* of a Cameron Dunbar."

Kate decided to respond to Emily's first question with honesty. "Mariana Edwards must have told the police about Henley. She must have told them that Henley knows what happened on the night Becca died."

"On the night she died?" Emily responded sharply. "I thought you said that Becca disappeared, that the police thought she drowned."

"That *is* what they thought. That's what we told them," Kate said. She took a deep breath. "But we lied. Becca never made it off Fair Isle that night. Something killed her on that island. I'm pretty sure that she was poisoned."

There was a long silence. Kate felt all of Emily's disappointment, her anger, her panic, gathering like a pressure in the ensuing silence. But when she spoke again, she sounded calm.

"I need you to tell the police that I don't know anything. You can explain that you work with the University of Virginia. You can show them your notes. Tell them you believe that Henley is telling the truth about what she remembers. Tell them I had nothing to do with it." Then, more forcefully, "You're a famous psychologist. This is your job, isn't it? Tell them she isn't making it up. And tell them I didn't feed her the story."

"Okay," Kate said simply. She stopped herself from adding, *But I doubt they'll believe me*. She was the one who'd told Mari about Henley. She was the one who needed to fix it.

Emily didn't respond. For a moment, they hung again in pendulous silence. Kate held her breath; she could feel something else, some new and terrible thing, gathering in the seconds between them.

"There's something else," Emily said at last. "Henley got a . . . note. At least, I think it was for Henley."

The back of Kate's neck began to tingle, as if a phantom hand had brushed it. "What do you mean?" she said sharply. "What kind of note?"

"It was addressed to Becca," Emily said, and Kate's gut twisted forcefully, surging an acrid taste to her throat. "I found it in the mailbox. Someone must have dropped it off. There was no stamp, and no return address."

"What does it say?"

"Just one line. *Remember, we had an agreement.*"

"That's it?"

"That's it." Emily's voice cracked a bit. "What do you think it means?"

Kate's thoughts were spinning frantically, sweeping up an assemblage of unrelated memories: Becca leaning on her elbows, whispering that she had new *collateral*; Henley on the swing set, tracing an arc toward the sky. The boy in the woods, the teenage runaway, Cameron Dunbar, staring blindly at the sky.

"I don't know," Kate said. She felt a heaviness in her body, as if she'd been weighted suddenly by stones. As if she were sinking, sinking down into the dark. "But at least one person *does* believe Henley. At least one person thinks that she really does remember who killed Becca."

TWENTY-FOUR

In the two months since she'd last searched Cameron Dunbar's name, a flood of new results had hit the internet, all related to the identification, after twenty-seven years, of the boy formerly known as the Twin Falls John Doe.

Back home, ignoring the dogs nudging at her shins, Kate maneuvered her open laptop onto the kitchen counter and started reading. According to a press release issued by the Berkshire County Sheriff's Office, the police had used genealogical DNA to whittle down the John Doe's true identity from a vast list of relatives over the course of nine months. Matt Bishop was even quoted.

Kate felt a creeping sense of embarrassment, remembering how she'd behaved in Bishop's office, trumpeting a discovery he must, by then, have known already. It must have seemed doubly suspicious to him that she'd arrived at the same conclusion only a few weeks before the results were made public.

Still, Kate had only stumbled across the picture of the *real* Cameron Dunbar—and matched it to the police reconstruction of the Twin Falls John Doe—because she'd been searching for a trace of the counselor she'd once known. The police hadn't known about the *connection* before. Kate was increasingly sure it couldn't be arbitrary.

One Cameron Dunbar dead in the state park; another Cameron Dunbar surfaced across the lake. One name vanished, wiped off the internet. Another one recovered, assigned a face and a body.

She didn't like it.

Kate skimmed several articles in a row that gave nearly identical details to Cameron Dunbar's backstory. A bright, adventurous, and athletic teenager, Cameron had spent his weekends hiking the Bastrop State Park near the family home outside of Austin. He'd graduated high school a year early and announced his intention to take a year off before college to hike the Appalachian Trail. He had begun his trip in Tennessee in September; the last his family had heard from him was on Christmas, when he called from Pennsylvania. They'd had no idea he'd made it all the way to Massachusetts, nor that he'd left the trail to explore a local state park.

At least now the sheriff's department had agreed to reopen the investigation into Cameron Dunbar's cause of death. Kate should have felt relieved. But she felt nothing but a stubborn dread, a feeling that something awful was taking shape just beyond the field of her vision, something dangerous that she couldn't see. It reminded her of the feeling she'd once had standing with Becca in the woods on the way back from the campfire, dimly convinced of a silhouette watching them from the shadows.

Kate clicked on a three-week-old *Dateline* interview featuring members of Cameron Dunbar's extended family, all their voices twanged with a bit of Texas, and belabored with both grief and exhaustion. It had been twenty-seven years since they'd last heard from their son, or cousin, or older brother. Twenty-seven years of uncertainty. Of hope, and crushing disappointment.

Twenty-seven years of swirling questions, all narrowed now to one: What—or who—had killed Cameron Dunbar in the state park?

His parents insisted: There was no way that their son had simply frozen to death. He was an accomplished hiker and outdoorsman. He took the dangers of the wilderness seriously, and had rigorously prepared and planned out every detail of his trip.

Besides, there was his missing wallet. His missing jacket. And his prized possession: an engraved lighter, studded with a blue topaz, gifted to him by his beloved grandfather, never recovered from the campsite.

Reading the words, Kate felt a jolt, as if they'd touched off an explosion in her head.

She had seen that lighter before. She had held it only recently.

Mari had it displayed on her makeshift altar to Becca—the girl who'd used it, once, to burn their bond in place.

TWENTY-FIVE

The following morning, Kate was on an 8:00 a.m. flight to Albany from Richmond, Virginia, a small commuter plane that shuddered through the turbulent skies, rattling Kate's teeth and leaving her stomach lurching. Luckily, she didn't teach on Fridays; she'd sent a message to her graduate students explaining that a family emergency would keep her from the lab that afternoon.

Steve thought she was crazy for making a day trip to Massachusetts. But he'd greeted her without comment in the predawn morning, her wearing only sweatpants and some outrageous bedhead, to let the dogs in.

She had noticed a strange car in the driveway, parked cozily next to his. So. He was dating someone else.

What else did Kate expect?

It was raining by the time she retrieved her rental car, a steady October drizzle that seemed almost mechanical in repetition. Kate felt a heavy dread descend, enfolding her like a second skin. The leaves on the trees were a riot of colors, oranges and reds that seemed to smolder against the gray sky, like something burning. The whole landscape was slaked with mud and evidence of windstorms, giving it a battered, bruised look. The houses seemed to hunch furtively between the trees; small towns ran quickly into a slurry of gas stations and shuttered farmstands, and then vanished again.

Mari was home, luckily. Her Subaru was parked in the driveway, and Kate heard what sounded like the television as she approached the front door.

She was surprised when, instead of Mari, a boy answered the door. His face was pocked with acne, and he was almost comically tall. Still, Kate recognized Mari's mop of unruly blond curls; she'd forgotten that Mari had a son in college. She reached for a name for several seconds before remembering: Alex.

"Help you?" he asked, in a quintessential adolescent grunt.

Kate was almost itchy with impatience. She tried to see past him, hoping to spot the lighter still in place on Mari's bookshelf. But she couldn't get a view of the living room. "I'm here to see your mom. Is she here?"

Alex shook his head. "She went shopping. Do you have a lesson or something?"

"She said she'd be home," Kate lied, deliberately ducking the question. "I can wait for her . . . ?" She blinked up at him expectantly through the rain, waiting for him to take the hint and invite her inside.

He didn't budge. "What did you say your name was?"

"Kate. Kate Willis. I'm an old friend of Mari's. We went to camp together."

Instantly, Alex's face changed. The standard look of adolescent boredom fell cleanly away. "Oh yeah. I've heard about you." Then: "You're one of the ghost hunters."

Kate felt a twinge of electricity in her spine. "Excuse me?"

"Sorry," he said, not sounding sorry at all. "I know it's a big secret." He took a step backward and gestured her inside. "You can wait inside, if you want."

But Kate didn't move. "You know *what's* a big secret?"

"That time you went with mom and Aunt Lennie and your friend Becca to Fair Isle," he said, shrugging. "Aunt Lennie told me about it once. It was Christmas. She was kinda drunk." Then he added quickly, "My mom doesn't know I know."

Kate followed Alex inside. When Alex closed the door, she could still hear the rush of the rain, mirrored by the drumming in her brains. "What exactly did your Aunt Lennie tell you?"

"I think it's badass," Alex said quickly, as if that was Kate's primary concern. When she just glared at him, he squirmed, raking a hand through his hair until it went off in all directions, screaming. "Nothing much. Just that you took a canoe out to Fair Isle, and actually *found* the Gray Lady, like her grave and stuff. And how you locked up one of your friends inside her mausoleum."

Now all the blood had rushed to Kate's head. She felt suddenly dizzy. A picture was resolving, floating into clearer resolution, like a face from the fog. "And that's it?"

Alex gave her a crooked grin. "Why, was there something else? Did you guys murder someone or something?" Seeing Kate's face, his smile quickly dropped. "I was kidding. Yeah, that's all. The next morning she told me not to say anything to my mom. Aunt Lennie said my mom was still sensitive about it. She's sensitive about a lot of things . . ."

Kate remembered what Mari had told her when they'd met at Camp Sauquamet: She only knew Henley because her son had babysat her a few times. "When was this?" she asked.

Alex shrugged again. "Maybe three, four years ago. It was definitely before Aunt Lennie had her last recurrence. After that, she went downhill pretty quickly . . ." He squinted up at the ceiling, thinking about it. "Yeah. Definitely four years ago this Christmas. Why?"

Kate did the math in her head. Four years ago this Christmas would be right around the time that Henley had first started reporting memories about her "other life." It would have been around the time the nightmares started, too.

"You told Henley Haskell, didn't you?" she blurted out. "You told her the story of that night on Fair Isle."

Alex stared at her. "Henley? No. No way. She was a kid. But," he added, a little sheepishly, "she might have seen my book once or twice."

"Your . . . ?" Before Kate could complete the thought, Alex turned away and slipped down the hall into his bedroom. He returned seconds later with an iPad. Flipping it open, he swiped and tapped a few times and then pivoted the screen to Kate.

"I used to draw a lot," he said. "I was really into graphic novels . . ."

Kate's breath froze in her chest. Instantly, she felt as if she'd pitched forward into the black-and-white drawings on-screen: panels drawn with an almost gruesome ferocity, in bold sweeps of ink, showing two canoes on a pitch of black water, headed to an island that loomed on the horizon; four girls fighting their way through an entanglement of trees, reaching out to clutch at them with straggly arms. There was Becca's name, and Lennie's too; bubbled in dialogue, written into the action neatly narrated in block letters. Kate swiped to the next page, which showed a looming graveyard, and a mausoleum with its door gaping open, like a mouth.

"There's more," Alex said. He leaned over to tap through the file. Images leaped at Kate: a girl, presumably Becca, pounding at a locked door; a full-page illustration of the Gray Lady, face rotten like a corpse's, lunging with her arms outstretched. "I should probably finish it someday."

"You said that Henley might have seen these?" Kate said.

"We used to draw together," Alex said. "Her mom didn't want her watching too much TV, and Henley loved to color . . ."

Kate's mind was turning, grinding back over all her conversations with Henley. The fact that Henley had seen these drawings—actually sat and watched her babysitter bring the story to life—could explain her drawings of Fair Isle, how she knew about the Gray Lady, all her nightmares about being trapped and suffocating. Kate knew how sensitive children were at that age, how absorptive, as their own developing self-concept got twined around their experiences. She was convinced that she'd landed, finally, at a rational explanation, the truth about Henley's so-called "memories."

True, Henley had known details about Becca's childhood; she had reacted physically to Kate's name; she had drawn Becca's yellow house; she'd picked out Natalie Horace from the yearbook. And yet . . .

Suddenly it was as if a lens in Kate's mind had sharpened, or turned, showing all these interactions in a new light. What had Henley said about her "other" childhood, really? That she had had a dog named Sammie, and a baby sister, Noodle. It was Kate who'd suggested both names to Tammy McGuire, and then been persuaded when Tammy seemed to remember a doll—or possibly, a stuffed cat—named Spaghetti. And the yellow house . . . how many yellow houses with tree houses must there be in Massachusetts? Thousands, surely. That had been her first instinct: to accept the drawing of the yellow house as coincidence.

It was Kate who'd prompted Henley to keep going through the yearbook, looking for someone who'd followed them to the island. Henley hadn't even pointed to Natalie Horace directly. She'd slapped a whole hand on the page—it was *Kate* who'd decided she'd been pointing to Becca's archnemesis.

Was that because all along, some unconscious part of Kate knew who had followed them, had recognized her in the woods that night, underneath her costume?

All along, she had been looking for proof that Henley was suggestible, prone to false beliefs. But maybe Kate had been the suggestible one. Maybe, on some level, she had wanted to believe that Becca wasn't fully gone—that she still had the chance to make things right. She was the one who'd told Emily Haskell that Henley's memories were those of Becca McGuire's; and after that, she had shown Henley the old camp yearbook, reaffirmed the entanglement of memory and story in her head.

Kate had been persuaded that someone had been manipulating Henley, shaping her beliefs.

Now she understood: It had been *her.*

Kate heard the front door creak open behind her. Mari entered, braced between two overstuffed grocery bags, her hair flattened by the rain. She froze when she saw Kate. Quickly, she recovered, directing her first words to her son.

"There are some more bags in the trunk. I couldn't get that Gatorade you wanted, by the way."

Alex took the hint. Shoving his shoes on at the door, he ducked out into the rain.

Mari eased a bag of groceries into Kate's arms. "A little help?" she said with a brief, flitting smile. When they'd deposited the bags in the kitchen, she finally turned, swiping the hair from her eyes. "What are you doing here?"

"I came for a favor," Kate said. Mari's expression turned guarded. She obviously hadn't yet forgiven Kate for dredging up old memories. Kate wondered what she would say about the drawings her son had kept hidden for years, which had mutated the worst night of their lives into a comic book–style adventure. "Last time I was here, you had a shelf of Becca's stuff in your living room. Photos, a friendship bracelet, your old necklace. And a silver lighter."

Mari's eyes flickered. "Becca's lighter," she said.

"It wasn't Becca's lighter," Kate said. "It was Cameron's. It was engraved with his initials. Except it didn't belong to him, either."

Mari just stared at her blankly.

"I need it."

Mari didn't move. "Becca gave it to me," she said, and Kate heard the old childhood whine in her voice.

Kate didn't believe that. "No, she didn't," she said. "You took it. After she died, you went through her stuff. Didn't you?"

Mari looked away. "I just wanted something to remember her by. I wanted to remember her the way she was—alive. Happy." Mari turned back to Kate. Kate was surprised to see that her eyes had brightened with tears. "She was happy, wasn't she?"

Kate felt the old pull to protect Mari, to shield her from the truth. But she resisted it. Mari was almost forty now. She'd been living in a fantasy long enough. "I don't know," Kate said. "I don't think so. I think she was in trouble."

"In trouble?" Mari repeated. "What do you mean?"

"Where's the lighter, Mari?" Kate said.

Mari stared at her for another long beat. Then, caving, she turned and disappeared from the kitchen. Kate heard a drawer scrape and the floor creak her return. Then she was back, slotting the lighter into Kate's hand. The metal was warm, as if she'd been gripping it. Kate felt a thrill when she saw the blue stones and the faint etching of those initials, CD, in the silver. It was proof. Proof that, at the very least, the boy she'd known as Cameron Dunbar had been the one to rob the Twin Falls John Doe. And if he'd taken the lighter, it made sense that he'd taken the boy's identity, too.

The only question was: Had he killed for it also?

And if so, why? And how did Becca fit in?

"What are you going to do with it?" Mari asked.

Kate carefully pocketed the lighter, reassured by its heft in her jacket. "Take it to the police."

Now a look of fear skated across Mari's face. "The police?" She reached out a hand to grip one of the kitchen chairs. Her eyes sharpened with suspicion. "What's going on, Kate? What is this about? First you come back here and tell me horrible stories—tell me that Becca didn't drown the night we all saw . . . *what* we saw—"

Kate cut in. "It was Natalie Horace. She followed us out to the island dressed up as the Gray Lady, hoping to scare us."

Mari stared again. Then she lowered herself heavily into a chair. Kate saw her shoulders tremble and, for a second, thought Mari was crying.

Then a ribbon of laughter reached her. Mari was laughing, shoulders shaking.

"My God," she said. "All these years . . ." She rubbed her eyes. "I've been stupid about things, haven't I?"

Kate took a seat next to Mari at the table. She reached for her hand, and for a second the years dissolved between them, and she saw Mari as she used to be: eager and credulous, vulnerable and loyal.

"We've all been stupid," Kate said. She thought of what Martin Sheehy had said about *hauntings*, about the way the mind stalled out in certain dark pits of memory. They'd all been haunted, too. "Now it's time to set things right."

Mari exhaled—a slow, shuddering breath. "Matt Bishop called me in, you know," she said. "He wanted me to admit that we killed Becca. You, me, and Lennie. He insisted that we'd killed her and then gotten rid of the body. I told them they were wrong. I said that we had proof—that they could speak to someone who remembered, and she would tell them that we left her alive."

"You told them about Henley Haskell," Kate said.

Mari gave her a quick sideways look. "I *had* to. It was the only way to prove we didn't kill her." She began worrying one of the place mats on the table. "Of course, they didn't believe me. They thought I was crazy, talking about reincarnation . . ." She looked at Kate a little desperately. "But I'm right, aren't I? Becca *did* come back."

Kate thought about telling Mari what she now knew—that Henley had been exposed to stories about Becca, vivid images of her last night on Fair Isle, right around the time she started reporting memories. That she—Kate—had been unconsciously guiding and shaping Henley's words and actions to mean that Becca had returned. Maybe she had needed to believe it, on some level. Maybe she'd needed to believe there was still time to undo what they'd done.

But she just said, "No, Mari. No, I don't think so. Becca's never coming back."

Mari let the statement fall without comment. Marooned at the kitchen table, surrounded by water-spotted grocery bags, hair frizzing from the rain, she looked like someone who'd washed up on solid land after a disaster.

Kate heard the front door bang open. Alex was back, passing wordlessly into the kitchen to deposit more grocery bags on the counter. Kate stood up to go. But as soon as Alex was out of earshot again, Mari said, "Kate? What's so special about the lighter? What did you mean that it didn't belong to Cameron, either?"

Kate pivoted back to her. Mari's glasses picked up the kitchen lights, winking at her like firelight. "The year before Becca died, a teenage boy turned up dead in the state park, not far from the lake. For decades, they couldn't identify him. But they did, only this year. His name was Cameron Dunbar."

Mari's face bunched up around her confusion. "Like our counselor?"

"Exactly like him. Same name, same age. Just a different backstory." Kate shook her head. "I think the Cameron we knew was responsible for killing him."

"*Killing* him?" Mari's voice jumped octaves. "You're not serious."

"I think he might have killed Becca, too," Kate said. It was the first time she'd spoken the words out loud, and they felt almost dizzyingly absurd in the open air.

"How?" Mari said. "There was nobody with her. You told me yourself—we locked her inside the mausoleum alone."

"That was a coincidence," Kate said. "I think there was something in the whisky she was drinking. None of the rest of us would drink, remember? And she wouldn't tell us where she'd gotten it. My guess is that she was so freaked out when we left her, she just kept drinking. Otherwise it might have killed her slowly. Made her sick over a period of weeks." She got a quick flash of Cameron showing off on water skis, carving a big fluid arc on the lake. Cameron, strumming his guitar behind a scrim of campfire smoke, smiling at Kate across the pit. The rings he wore on those long fingers. It was impossible to imagine that he'd deliberately poisoned two people, siphoning sodium nitrate into bottles of cheap alcohol. And Kate feared there would be no way to prove it.

But the lighter proved, at least, that he had known the camper in the woods. And that was a start.

"But why?" Mari was staring at Kate as if she'd suggested that the Gray Lady was not only real but also waiting outside to talk with them. "What possible reason could Cameron Dunbar have for wanting Becca dead?"

"Because he wasn't the real Cameron Dunbar," Kate said. "And somehow, Becca found out."

For a long minute, there was silence, except for the hard sputter of rain against the windows. Finally, Mari sighed.

"Becca used to warn you that Cameron wasn't who you thought he was. Don't you remember?" Kate shook her head. "After I saw them together, I thought she was just trying to keep you away from him. But maybe she meant it literally."

It was true: Becca had teased her relentlessly about her crush on Cameron. *You don't even know him,* she always said. *You think he's, like, some god with a guitar. He could be anyone. He could be a serial killer.* Kate had resented the way that Becca spoke as if she were decades, not months, older. At the same time, Becca by then spoke knowledgeably about blow jobs, hinting occasionally that she'd lost her virginity over the winter.

I'm just trying to protect you, KittyCat, she would say whenever Kate replied that maybe she was the one who didn't know Cameron, didn't understand him the way that Kate did. The way she thought she did. *You'll understand someday when you're older.*

Kate hated that. They'd been equals for so many years. But somehow, mysteriously, Becca had crossed a gulf, moving with a knowledge and secrecy that Kate could only dimly make out.

Maybe, Kate thought, one of those secrets had killed her.

She stood up. It was time to face Matt Bishop again. She only hoped he would believe her about the lighter and where it had come from. *Who* it had come from.

Mari walked Kate to the door, where another pile of grocery bags was pooling rain onto the hardwood. Her son had disappeared. Kate heard the muffled cadence of a video game, the occasional punctuation mark of an ejaculated remark.

"Wait a second," she said just as Kate was about to leave. She looked smaller, older, shrunk into an oversize fleece, her damp hair standing up in strange curlicues and question marks. "If Cameron Dunbar—the one we knew—wasn't the real Cameron Dunbar, then who was he? Where did he come from?"

"I don't know," she said. As she turned into the rain, her mind flashed to the message shoved inside the Haskells' mailbox.

And where, she thought, *is he now?*

TWENTY-SIX

Matt Bishop didn't exactly look happy to see her again. Kate was half expecting him to steer her straight into one of the department's two interrogation rooms—each the same bleakly lit box furnished with a single metal table—and was unexpectedly relieved when instead he gestured her into his office.

"Kate Willis," he said. This time, he didn't wait before nudging the recorder on his desk. "Your colleagues say nice things about you. They told me you're an author."

So he had been following up on her. Kate met his stare evenly. "I'm a researcher," she said.

"Yeah? And have you *researched* any more cold cases for us?" His words were faintly inflected with irony.

"No. Just the same ones we spoke about." She took the lighter from her pocket and slid it across the desk. He barely caught it before it could skid over the edge. But she saw his face change when he clocked the engraved initials and the dull-blue stones against the silver.

"Where did you get this?" he asked sharply.

"Becca," Kate said. There was no reason to drag Mari back into it. "And she got it from Cameron, our counselor. Maybe he gave it to her, or maybe she just took it. She had a habit of taking things that weren't hers." When Bishop didn't say anything, she added, "It belongs to your old John Doe, doesn't it? It belonged to the real Cameron Dunbar."

Bishop flicked open the lighter and struck his thumb against the spark wheel, as if expecting to see flame. Then he closed it.

"You know that story you told me last time you were in here—that story about you and your friends, and what happened on Fair Isle?" He shook his head. "Problem is, I can't seem to find anyone who'll confirm it. Lenora's gone." Kate blanched, hearing Lennie's full name; nobody ever called her that. "And your friend Mari tried to sell me on a real head-scratcher. She called a *six-year-old* child her alibi."

Kate looked away, debating how much she should disclose. But there was no point in dancing around the facts now. "Henley Haskell believes she can recall memories of a past life," Kate said.

"A *what*?" Bishop's eyebrows practically jumped through his skull.

"It's more common than you think," Kate said defensively. "The University of Virginia has collected interviews with thousands of children all over the world—"

Bishop raised a hand. "I'll take your word for it," he said dryly. She wasn't surprised. Most people had the same reaction to the phenomenon that the Division of Perceptual Studies investigated.

Now anger flared in Kate's chest. "Henley has nothing to do with Becca's death," she said.

"But *you* do," Bishop said. His voice scraped into sharpness. "You were there when Becca went missing—or turned up dead, according to you. You were there when her body went into the lake. So how do I know you got this lighter from Becca? How do I know you didn't pluck it off the body yourself?"

"Because I was thirteen years old, and living in Virginia, when the real Cameron Dunbar died in the state park," Kate snapped. "If you're so sure I murdered Becca, then why haven't you arrested me?"

Bishop looked surprised, even amused, by the outburst. For a second he sat there, looking at her as if he was considering it. Then he opened his desk drawer and deposited the lighter inside. "I don't think you murdered her," he said bluntly. "I don't even know she was murdered. That's *your* theory. We're still investigating."

After a moment's hesitation, he stood up and crossed over to close the office door, muffling the periodic shrill of the telephone and the hum of conversation. Then he settled down across from her again with a small sigh.

"Let me ask you a question: Does the name Gregory Owens ring a bell?"

"Should it?"

"Maybe." He drummed his fingers on the desk. "Becca never spoke about him?"

"She might have," Kate conceded. "My memory's good. But it's not that good." *And Becca had plenty to say when it came to boys,* she almost added. "But why? Who's Gregory Owens?"

Bishop produced a manila folder from his desk. He hesitated before sliding it over to Kate. "Thirty years ago, a fifteen-year-old boy named Gregory Owens enrolled for his sophomore year at a high school in New Jersey. It was a real sad story. His parents were both dead. Older brother, too. He was living on the street before Jersey PD picked him up. Ultimately, he landed with a great foster family, seemed to be doing well. He tried out for the basketball team. Got a sweet girlfriend in his class. Was making straight A's." Then: "It's all in the file."

Bewildered, Kate flipped open the folder. She found a high school enrollment form, followed by a series of photocopied articles about the New Jersey Devils' record-setting varsity basketball season back in the late '90s. More confused than ever, she kept flipping.

"Maybe Gregory was a bit *too* lucky—perfect grades, perfect girlfriend, spot on the junior homecoming court—because the kids started whispering that something wasn't right about him. But nobody ever dug too hard into the kid's background. He was sweet, shy, good natured. Sure, there were strange things about him. He never took his hat off, for one—he even slept with the thing on. When his foster parents took him to the dentist, everyone was surprised to find he'd already had his wisdom teeth removed.

That doesn't usually happen until people are in their late teens, early twenties.

"The trouble started when the basketball team won the state championship, thanks to a last-minute assist from Gregory. Gregory was sixteen at the time. The local newspaper did a profile about Gregory's tragic upbringing in Vermont and his brand-new start in New Jersey. The problem is, the story got picked up by media outlets all over the tristate area and beyond. Human interest, feel-good, happy-ending kind of stuff. That's it," he said, seeing that Kate had landed on the photocopied article titled Gregory Owens's Second Life. The title reminded her, uncomfortably, of Becca and Henley. Only this had been a different kind of resurrection.

Then her eyes dropped to the photograph of Gregory Owens, pictured beaming next to his foster parents, and the floor fell away underneath her.

"That's him," Kate croaked out. "That's the boy I knew as Cameron Dunbar."

Bishop nodded, as if he'd expected that. "Gregory Owens, it turned out, wasn't Gregory Owens at all. And he wasn't sixteen. He was at least twenty-five—and he'd been busted in Pennsylvania for pulling the same act two years earlier."

A shape-shifter. The word—absurd, mystical, frightening—leaped to Kate's mind. She imagined a man sloughing off one face for another. This Gregory Owens, the boy holding a basketball proudly under one arm, would two years later become Cameron Dunbar with a guitar.

She felt a sudden pull of nausea, remembering the time that Cameron had thumbed a tear from her cheek on the beach. How old had he been then?

"I don't understand," Kate said. "How did you find out about Gregory Owens?"

"I ran your old counselor's prints," Bishop said. Before Kate could ask where he'd gotten them, he added, "There's an old cement wall at Camp Sauquamet where the counselors put their handprints, the same summer that Becca went missing." Kate felt a thrill. Of course. She remembered the day they'd poured the concrete, and Becca had angled to add her initials to it. "I used to wonder whether one of those *hands* had something to do with what happened to her. It was just a passing idea, you know, like a hunch. But after you came to see me about your old counselor, I decided to take the prints and run them. When we did, it pinged an old arrest in New Jersey, when Gregory Owens was booked for statutory under his alias."

Kate's mind was careening through the decades—between names and identities, between Gregory and Cameron, Becca and Henley. Ghosts, all of them. Phantom ideas, assigned new identities in time. She took a deep breath, struggling to focus. "And you have no idea who he is really?"

Bishop shook his head. "He refused to say, even after his arrest. He kept insisting that his name was Gregory Owens, that he really was sixteen years old."

"Maybe he really believed it," Kate said. She knew of isolated cases where grown adults had successfully passed themselves off as teenagers, sometimes for years at a time. There was a famous case in France of a serial impostor, Frédéric Bourdin, known in the press as "The Chameleon." Over the course of his life, he'd taken on more than five hundred different identities, many of them teenage boys. It was an extreme example of age regression—the natural tendency of all humans to revert to certain childhood beliefs and attitudes, especially when frightened or overwhelmed—and seemed in these pathological cases to share traits with dissociative identity disorder as well. Bourdin himself had said that he craved the love and care he had missed as a child; passing himself off as an adolescent gave him the chance to try again.

Except that the hole, Kate knew, could never be filled. And she had never heard of anyone killing to protect the delusion.

"Becca must have known," Kate said. She shut the folder that Bishop had given her and practically shoved it back across the desk. She couldn't stand to look at Cameron's—Greg's, whoever's—face any longer. "She must have found out that Cameron Dunbar wasn't who he was pretending to be."

"Any idea how?"

Kate shook her head. "Becca liked secrets. She liked collecting them. I think it gave her a feeling of power." She even wondered now whether Jenny Lin had mistaken the interactions between Becca and Cameron in the boathouse. Maybe Becca was blackmailing Cameron, like she'd tried to blackmail the two girls who'd been caught in bed together. Memories returned to her: Becca teasing Cameron for having *old-man nipples*, suggesting that the reason he always kept his hat on was because he had an enormous bald spot. Kate had always figured that Becca just didn't like Cameron very much, was maybe even jealous that he liked Kate better. But Becca was taunting him, deliberately dangling his true identity. Laughing at him. Reminding him that she was in control.

But Becca wasn't in control. She was a child.

And Kate felt sure that by the time he showed up at Camp Sauquamet, Cameron—or Greg—had already killed once for his secret.

"Well, if you think of anything that can help us track this guy down, you've got my number." Bishop slotted out a business card from a tray on his desk and passed it to Kate.

"That's it? That's all you've got?" Kate felt a lashing sense of panic that seemed to strike out blindly, touching all her memories at once. Uneasily, she thought of the way Henley had responded when Kate had asked her, straight up, whether she'd ever had a boyfriend named Cameron in her other life. Henley's face had knotted up, darkening her eyes with an expression Kate couldn't identify.

She'd said, *That's not his name.*

Coincidence, probably. Now Kate knew where Henley had gotten her stories about Fair Isle. And she suspected that she herself had been subtly influencing Henley, unconsciously directing her toward an outcome that—for all her skepticism—she desperately wanted deep down. After all, if some part of Becca had returned, it meant that Kate still had a chance to make things right.

It was the only logical explanation.

And at the same time . . . Kate couldn't shake a heavy premonition, a feeling that Henley and Becca had become entangled somehow, like one of those quantum particles that communicated across distance and time. Becca had known that Cameron Dunbar wasn't who he was pretending to be. She had cautioned Kate about it, subtly, whenever Kate had mentioned her crush on the new counselor. She had known that Cameron Dunbar *wasn't his name.*

Kate wondered what, ultimately, Henley had been trying to tell her that day—whether she was again reading meaning where there was none, or whether Henley had an instinct, an *intuition*, that extended all the way back to Becca's death.

Bishop's expression softened. For a second, Kate thought she detected sympathy. "Look, that story you told me about the night you kids went out to Fair Isle . . . what happened to your friend Becca out there . . ." He shook his head. "It's an awful thing. And if this guy—this counselor posing as Cameron Dunbar—had something to do with it, then we'll find him. It may take some time, but we will."

Kate thought of the note that had been dropped in the Haskells' mailbox. *Remember, we had an agreement.* Matt Bishop clearly didn't believe that Henley could recall details of Becca's life—and her death. *Kate* hadn't believed it at first.

But there was obviously someone who *did* believe.

It occurred to her suddenly: It would take time to find out who the boy pretending to be first Gregory Owens, then Cameron Dunbar, really was. It would take more time to find him.

And she couldn't help but feel that, after twenty-six years, *time* was running out.

TWENTY-SEVEN

How had Becca known?

Kate's flight back to Virginia was due to depart in three hours. But after sitting in her car, motionless, for twenty minutes, she still hadn't put the keys in the ignition. Something was rooting her to the spot, some premonition of dread, a desperate idea that she had missed something critical, and obvious.

How had Becca known?

Her mind lurched back through that final summer, bumping against old memories, shaking them into a portrait she had misunderstood all these years. *You don't even know Cameron. He could be a serial killer. He has old-man nipples, you know.* Hints, breadcrumbs that Becca had scattered over the surface of the conversation, all of them pointing to a deeper truth.

She'd known that Cameron Dunbar was not really Cameron Dunbar.

Was any of what Cameron had told her true? Had he really had an older brother who died of leukemia? Somehow, Kate doubted it. It was a sob story, a confession poured out to Kate when she was vulnerable, an attempt to earn her trust and sympathy. What else did she know about him? That he played guitar and worshipped Johnny Cash; that he was from Vermont, not far from a haunted bridge that had spawned its own legends.

Suddenly inspired, Kate pulled out her phone and typed in the lyrics she could recall from the song he had played them occasionally, the one about the jilted woman who'd supposedly roamed the covered bridge.

She felt a thrill when the results loaded: both the song and the "Wailing Lady Bridge" were real. The song dated back to the 1920s. The bridge, twenty years before that.

And it was located not in Vermont, but a few miles west of Portland, Maine.

With a shock, she remembered something that Tammy McGuire had told her on their first phone call about Becca's early childhood. She dug out the McGuires' phone number and dialed with shaking fingers, holding her breath until, once again, Tammy herself rasped a hello.

Kate reintroduced herself.

"Right, yeah. I remember. Becca's friend from camp," Tammy said. "Are you the reason we got newspapers calling us up out of the blue?" Before Kate could respond, she went on, "Someone from the paper told me there's a local girl claiming she knows what happened to Becca. Bullshit, I said. She's just doing it for attention. That's what Becca would have done. Girl couldn't open her mouth without lying. Wish I could say she'd learned it from someone else . . ."

Kate wasn't in the mood for Tammy's guilt. She got right to the point. "Last time we spoke, you mentioned that Becca only lived with you until she was five. After that, she went to live with your parents."

"It was that or lose her to the state," Tammy said.

"You told me that Becca went *down* to New York, while you stayed in Maine," Kate said. She had dimly registered this at the time. But there it was, written in her notebook, along with other scattershot phrases that she'd picked up during their call. Force of habit, from years of clinical work. "Can I ask where you were living at the time?"

"Portland," Tammy said promptly. "I followed Becca's dad up there just after high school. You want to talk about a liar . . ."

Kate's heart stuttered. Fumbling, feeling her way along an instinct, she said, "When you were living there, did Becca ever talk about the Wailing Lady Bridge?"

"She might have. Like I said, I was using a lot back then. When I wasn't working, I was drunk. I used to leave Becca most nights in the motel room where we were living. I'm not proud of it. We had some neighbors who would check in on her, make sure the creeps in the place didn't get too interested."

Kate was still reaching—desperate, certain there must be a connection. "What about Gregory Owens? Does that name ring a bell?"

"Greg Owens?" Tammy sounded surprised. "Sure. I heard about him. Everybody did. Terrible story."

Kate froze. "Heard about what, exactly?"

"You're talking about the Greg Owens who died in that house fire, right? The whole family burned up. There were three of them—Greg, his father, and his stepmother. Just awful. The night of the fire, we could see the flames from the bar I was working at, on Fore Street. Only one who wasn't home was Greg's stepbrother, Richie. Now *that* was a crazy story . . ."

Kate hadn't moved. But she felt instinctively as if she had reached the edge of the mystery, the place where all familiar ground gave way. She gripped the steering wheel hard, as if to keep herself from falling. "Richie?"

"He was older. Twenty-one, maybe twenty-two. He lived at the motel for a little while. Nice guy, I always thought. He used to check in on Becca. Played his guitar for her when she couldn't sleep."

"Tammy." Kate could barely keep her voice steady. "Do you have any pictures of Richie?"

"Me? I doubt it. After me and Alan broke up, I got out of there quick. Dropped Becca with my parents and wound up dead-ass broke and sleeping in my car in South Beach. But I bet you could find him online. Richie Novak was his name. His mom was Polish."

Kate scribbled the name in her notebook. "Do you think Becca might have remembered him? I mean years later, if she saw him, do you think she might have recognized who he was?"

"Maybe." Tammy sounded uncertain. "She was pretty young, but she liked him. His room was right next to ours, and he spent a lot of time looking after her. We all felt sorry for him," she added, slightly defensively. "Whole family wiped out overnight. It wasn't until after he left that we knew."

Kate closed her eyes. She was falling, dropping toward the truth, a hard reality that reached up to punch her. "Knew what, Tammy?"

"That police were looking into him," Tammy said. "They think he was the one who lit the fire."

TWENTY-EIGHT

Kate ricocheted out of the car, driven by an invisible pressure that catapulted her across the parking lot. Richie Novak. She had a name; she was sure that this was the man who had pretended to be first his stepbrother, Gregory Owens—and later, Cameron Dunbar.

She was sure that Richie Novak had killed Becca, to keep her from revealing his secret.

The rain was coming down harder now, in flinty jabs that slicked her hair and numbed her fingers. Inside the police station again, she looked around wildly for Matt Bishop and instead landed on Emily Haskell, huddled in a plastic chair next to the watercooler, her hand around her stomach and one knee agitating. Kate was shocked; she hadn't noticed Emily pull in.

Emily looked up and saw her at the same time. Kate was surprised when Emily practically flew out of her chair and pulled Kate into a hug.

"You came." Even after she pulled away, Emily kept a tight grip on Kate's shoulders. "How did you get here so fast?"

With a sinking feeling, Kate realized that her instinct—or premonition—had been correct. Something terrible had happened. They were too late. "I flew in to meet with Matt Bishop," she said. "What is it? What's wrong?"

"I called you. I left you a message. Henley's gone." Emily's words came out in a single shuddering breath.

Instantly, Kate's whole body went cold. "What do you mean, gone?"

"I mean gone. She never made it home from school today." A shudder moved visibly through Emily's body as she raised her voice to a desperate pitch. "My daughter's missing, and nobody's doing anything."

Several deputies at their desks swiveled their heads in Emily's direction, meeting the accusation with a low murmur, and the continued shuffling of paper. At the same time, Kate saw Bishop beating his way from the back office, flanked by two other detectives.

His blue eyes barely flicked to Kate. "Ms. Haskell, this is Detective Ruiz. She's going to ask you some questions."

"I've already told you. I don't know anything." She turned beseechingly to Detective Ruiz, whose eyes were softened with sympathy. "You should be looking for her. You should be out finding my daughter."

"There's a deputy on the way to Henley's school," Ruiz said. "We're trying to reach her bus driver now."

"But she never made it *onto* the bus," Emily burst out.

Bishop's gaze sharpened. "What do you mean?"

Emily closed her eyes, drew a breath, and said, a little more evenly, "Henley's the last drop-off. I was waiting for her at the end of the driveway, like I usually do. I waited and waited, but the bus never came. Finally, I called the school. And they called Henley's bus driver. He said Henley never got on the bus. He figured she'd left school early . . ."

"She probably went home with a friend," Ruiz said soothingly. "My daughter did that plenty of times when she was in middle school. Used to drive me up the wall."

"Henley's not in middle school. She's six." Emily's voice broke. Kate had never seen her look so fragile—eyes raw, no makeup, her hair frizzing from the rain. She looked like a child herself. "Besides, I've spoken to Henley's friends. I called around to all their parents. She's not with any of them."

Emily's voice was peaking toward a shout. Bishop cut in. "All right, how about you have a seat, take a few breaths. Detective Ruiz will get you some tea. You like tea?" When Emily didn't answer, he gave

Detective Ruiz a nod, and she peeled off. "I'll take a trip over to the school, have a chat with Henley's teachers. As far as we know, Henley could have gone home with a new friend, someone you wouldn't think to call. There's no reason to assume the worst. Kids are funny. She could be hiding out in a bathroom, for all we know."

Emily nodded. But Kate could tell she didn't believe it. And Kate didn't believe it, either. It was too coincidental—first the note in Henley's mailbox, addressed not to Henley, but to the girl she claimed to be before; and then, just days later, her sudden disappearance. She was sure—she knew instinctively—that Cameron Dunbar, or Richie Novak, or whatever name he was using now—had gotten to Henley.

Bishop must have noticed the look on Kate's face, because he turned to her abruptly.

"You," he said. "Come with me."

Once they were alone in his office, he rounded on her. "All right, what do you know?" he said. When Kate hesitated, unsure of where to begin, he snapped. "Go on. Spit it out. I can tell you've got something to say."

"I think I know why Cameron Dunbar—my Cameron, the one I knew from camp—killed Becca," she blurted out. "I think Becca recognized him. She knew his real identity."

Bishop stared at her for a beat. Then, swallowing a sigh, he sat down on the edge of his desk. "Go on," he said. Kate thought he sounded tired.

"I just spoke with Tammy McGuire, Becca's mother. Before Becca moved to Hillsdale, she lived with her mother in Maine. Becca's mom remembers a Gregory Owens. He was the victim of a house fire, along with his father and stepmother." Bishop swiveled off the desk as Kate was talking, opened his laptop, and began typing—presumably to look up old reports of the fire. "The only survivor was his stepbrother, a guy in his mid-twenties named Richie Novak. He lived for a while at the same motel as Becca's mom. He used to *babysit* for Becca. And police think he was the one to start the fire. But by the time they went to arrest him, he'd disappeared."

Bishop was still, his attention fixed on something on his screen. "And you think . . . ?"

"I think Richie took his younger brother's identity and turned up with a new backstory," Kate said. "He tried it out in Pennsylvania, and then in Jersey. Whenever people began questioning his identity, he vanished again. This time, he crossed paths with Cameron Dunbar—a seventeen-year-old thousands of miles from home. An easy target."

"You figured all of this out from a phone call?" Bishop said incredulously.

Kate ignored that. "Richie has been pretending to be someone else his whole life. Staying young. Reborn as a teenager, or a college student, someone tragic, who might need help, money, employment. Someone that other people would be inclined to care for." Kate knew that this was a feature of adults who reverted back to adolescent identities: the pressures of adulthood were too overwhelming, or they felt that something had gone wrong in their lives that could only be corrected by a do-over. "When you go looking for him, you should be looking for *that*."

"Half the people in this county need money, help, or employment," Bishop said. "Besides, we've got no reason to think he's still in the area. He could be halfway across the country, feeding someone in Arizona or Kalamazoo his latest sob story."

"I don't think so," Kate said. She told Bishop about the note that had turned up in the Haskells' mailbox, the one addressed to Becca. "If it *was* Richie who put it there, he must have seen local news coverage linking Henley and Becca. That means he *must* be in the area. And he believes Henley's telling the truth about what she remembers."

"Reincarnation?" Bishop shook his head. "Come on."

"It doesn't matter if you believe it or not. It doesn't even matter if it's true," Kate argued. "What matters is that *Richie* believes it."

Bishop absorbed that. Kate saw him sucking on the inside of his cheeks—in, out—and thought of a fish. "You think this note has something to do with the fact that Henley never came home from school?" he finally asked, in a low voice.

Kate could only nod. Suddenly, she'd lost her breath. This was all her fault. Emily Haskell was right; her interviews with Henley had only placed her in harm's way.

Bishop's eyes slid, just for a second, into a look of sympathy. "Why don't you go and keep Ms. Haskell company," he said. "Take her home. Try not to worry too much. My bet is that Henley just went off with a new friend and doesn't even have a clue that her mother's worried sick."

"And what if you're wrong?" Kate fired back. "What if Henley's in trouble?"

"I'll tell you what," Bishop said. "Getting all worked up isn't going to help anybody. We'll get to work on locating Henley. All right? I appreciate all your help," he added when Kate started to protest. "But you have to let us do our job."

That was it; Kate was dismissed.

In the waiting area, Emily Haskell's tea was sitting on a chair, untouched, unraveling steam into the air. Emily was pacing, looking just as agitated as when she'd come in. Once again, she seized Kate's hand when she appeared. Together they watched Detective Ruiz and Bishop shunting on their jackets, conferring for a moment at the door. Then Detective Ruiz turned back to them.

"You should go home," she said to Emily, and Kate could tell from her tone that it wasn't the first time she'd made the suggestion. "What if Henley comes back?"

"I can't just . . . sit there," Emily protested, arcing the words into a plea.

Bishop simply said, "You'll be the first to know when we hear anything."

"They're right," Kate said to Emily, after Bishop and Ruiz had departed. "There's no point in hanging around here. At least you'll be more comfortable at home."

"I *won't*." Emily's face caved in at the center. "Henley should be there."

Kate couldn't stop thinking about the note in the Haskells' mailbox. What if Bishop and Ruiz were wrong? What if Henley hadn't merely wandered off with a new friend? Every minute might make a difference; who knew how long it would take them to check with Henley's teachers and friends, to establish a timeline.

"Could someone else have picked Henley up?" she asked. "Would Henley *go* with anyone else?"

"I'm not sure. Pickup can be chaotic, especially when it's raining. All the kids wait for the buses in the gym." Emily shook her head. It was amazing how worry had carved up her face, aging it by a dozen years in an afternoon. "But Henley knows not to go anywhere with a stranger."

Kate seized on that word—*stranger*. She thought of the list that Emily had written out for her of everyone who'd had regular contact with Henley over the past few years. She'd been looking for familiar names, people associated with Camp Sauquamet. But suddenly it occurred to her that whatever name Richie Novak was going by now, it likely wasn't Cameron Dunbar. Cameron Dunbar, too, had aged; Richie's compulsion for staying young, staying dependent, undoubtedly meant that he'd found or fabricated a new identity for himself.

So what if he *wasn't* a stranger to Henley? What if she *knew* him from somewhere?

Kate's heartbeat picked up. She could feel it drumming in her ears. "I'm going to describe someone to you," she told Emily. "Tell me if it sounds like anyone you know, okay?" Emily said nothing. But she nodded. "This person is probably posing as someone in his twenties. But he likely looks significantly older. He's undoubtedly mentioned some tragedy in his history, something that makes him very sympathetic—something terrible, for example, that happened to his family. Maybe an accident, maybe an illness. In any case, he's an orphan. He might work odd jobs. Possibly, he lives off someone else—someone who looks after him, someone who felt bad about his history and was moved to help. And"—she flashed back to those evenings by the campfire—"he plays guitar."

Emily had been frowning. Now her face cleared. "That sounds like Annie Winters' tenant . . ." she said slowly. Then: "Annie Winters lives over in Chatham. That's on the New York side. She's the one who gives Henley swim lessons. She has a tenant—Ethan, I think? Something happened to his family. I know he was homeless, before she rented him the guest house. He does work around the property. I think he's in college, too." She shrugged. "He always seemed nice enough to me." Now her face gathered into a look of fear. "Why? What's Ethan got to do with it? Do you think he's the one who took Henley?"

"We don't know that anyone took her," Kate reminded her. But even as she said the words, she didn't believe them. She felt a rising panic; Henley had been missing for nearly two hours. They were running out of time. If Richie *had* taken Henley, it was for only one reason: to silence her. Then he would disappear again, dissolving into a new life and a new backstory, popping up somewhere to claim a new youth, to start over again, to cycle forever through young adulthoods.

She thought, wildly, of tracking him herself. But it was impossible. Massachusetts was nothing but rangy forest and abandoned outbuildings; there must have been hundreds of old barns, thousands and thousands of untended acres in the county alone.

Richie could have taken Henley anywhere.

And then it hit her—an electric bit of inspiration, a sudden clarity, like the answer had been whispered in her ear.

Richie could have taken *Henley* anywhere.

But she was sure—she was positive—that he would bring Becca only one place.

She was sure that he would take Becca back where she belonged.

TWENTY-NINE

The rain was a steady drum by now, slashing leaves from their branches, darkening the evening prematurely. It was five o'clock. In an hour or so the sun would set altogether, and Henley would be alone, absorbed into the dark. They would never find her then.

Kate's tires skidded around curves. There were hardly any other cars on the road. Dimly she was aware of her phone pinging—text messages from Steve, probably wondering whether she'd caught her flight, whether she would be home to collect the dogs. She didn't answer. She couldn't focus on anything but the road in front of her, the long distance of pavement that separated her from her destination. She didn't know what she would do if Henley wasn't at Camp Sauquamet. She didn't know what she would do if Richie was. She had told Emily Haskell to go home and wait for the police to be in touch, not wishing to alarm her. Now she wondered whether that had been a wise idea; maybe she should have waited for the police.

Still, she kept driving, pulled toward Lake Sauquamet as if by gravity, by the weight of what had happened there all those years ago—and what she herself had done. She knew, somehow, that the past really had come to life again. But this time she wouldn't abandon Becca on her own—afraid, imprisoned, in need of help. This time she would fix it, stop it.

Finally, she reached the turnoff, and the "No Trespassing" signs lurched into her headlights. The dirt road was soupy with mud and riddled with tire tracks collecting the rain. This gave Kate hope. Some of them, she thought, must belong to Richie.

Some of them, she was sure, must point the way to Henley.

But she was disappointed when she arrived. There were no other vehicles in the upper lot; when she jerked her car to a stop next to the old administrative cabin, she saw no evidence of activity, no sign that Richie and Henley had been there. Still, she rocketed out of the car, remembering belatedly to grab her phone for the flashlight. The sound of the rain was white noise, shushing out her ability to think. Wildly, she scanned the cabins, looking for movement, color, something that didn't belong. She heard nothing—no screaming, no sounds of protest.

Nothing but the rain, drumming the lake.

The lake.

Kate sprinted down the hill toward the dock, panic spiking her whole body, heartbeat thrumming in her ears. The rain slurred the sky and water together, dimming the view into a sludge of gray. Fair Isle in the distance was nothing but a shapeless mass—the ruins indistinguishable from the trees at this distance.

For one wild second, she didn't see him.

Then, scanning again, she snagged on a canoe barely visible on the water, just edging into view around the tip of the island. She might have missed it but for the bright-red windbreaker of whoever was working the oar, burning like a small flame among the deepening gray. It occurred to her all at once that Richie—Cameron—*Ethan* must have pushed off from the side of the state park.

"Ethan! Ethan!" She cupped her hands to her mouth to shout. She couldn't tell whether he heard her; he was so far away, just nosing around the north side of the island. But she was sure it had to be him. Who else would be on the water in a thunderstorm in October? She pictured Henley huddled miserably in the boat—cold, soaking, afraid.

Or, perhaps, already dead.

She pushed the thought away as soon as it stumbled, zombielike, into her consciousness. Henley couldn't be dead.

Not this time.

She turned instinctively for the boathouse before remembering that the boathouse was closed, shuttered, empty. Then she remembered that she'd seen a rowboat, overturned in the woods next to the beach, the first time she'd visited.

She ran for the beach, timing the same words to every step—*come on, come on, come on.*

The rowboat was still there, thank God. When Kate righted it, she found a pair of oars, skeined with spiderwebs, stashed beneath it. Grabbing them, she heaved the rowboat down to the water, praying that there were no leaks in the hull. She didn't have to go far.

But she had to go fast.

It had been years since she'd paddled a boat. She pushed off from the beach, where the surface was clotted with a heavy scrum of fallen leaves. The oars were much heavier than she remembered, harder to manipulate. A swirl of water collected at her feet as she maneuvered, struggling to find her rhythm. Her mind was spitting out random feedback, memories of the last time she'd been in a rowboat. That had been . . . what? Seven? Eight years ago, now? A picnic with Steve. She'd had white wine stashed in a water bottle, and kept setting down the oars to check her phone.

She thought, belatedly, stupidly, to let someone know where she was. A single bar of service was winking in and out by the time she fished her phone from her pocket. She noted four new voicemails—Steve, maybe, or Emily Haskell. Her fingers were bloated with cold, her phone screen slick with rain, and slow to respond.

She managed at last to type out a text to Emily: At lake. Need help. She prayed that it would actually make it to its destination, and picked up her oars again.

The evening descended, bit by bit, like a lowering veil. The sky belched thunder and sent lightning skittering across the underbelly of clouds. Kate imagined, for one wild second, a bolt might descend to strike Richie out of his boat. If there was a God, a higher consciousness, shouldn't It be watching?

Kate pivoted in her seat, tracking Richie to the center of the lake. Kate had assumed at first that he was heading for the island, but instead he'd paddled out to where the lake was deepest. She still saw no sign of Henley. She flashed again to an image of Henley's body crooked at his feet, still and small and pale. Like Becca's had been, when they'd taken her out to sink her in the water.

It was all happening again. *Punishment*, Kate thought. *Punishment, for what we did then.*

Her arms were burning, her breath coming in short gasps. She would never make it in time. Every few strokes, she turned around, willing away the distance between them.

By now, Richie had stopped paddling. She was close enough to make out the details of Richie's jacket, and the baseball cap hooding his face. From a distance, he looked just like any other college student, and Kate again had the sense of time doubling, folding back on itself, spitting her back twenty-six years.

"Ethan!" she shouted again. She was sure that Richie could see her—but if so, he didn't appear concerned, and instead seemed lost in the mechanics of some private ritual occurring on the water. She saw him pitch something into the water and for a terrible, electrifying second, imagined it was Henley. Then her vision sharpened around the colorful shape before it sank.

Not Henley. Henley's school bag.

Panic spiked through her. Where was Henley?

"Ethan, can you hear me?" She was torn between the impulse to keep rowing and to keep her eyes on Richie. He had his back to Kate, fumbling with something she couldn't see. "My name is Kate Willis. We met a long time ago, at Camp Sauquamet." She had to be careful what she said. People in delusion—people with severe dissociative traits—hated to be confronted with their lies. It confused them. It would only make Richie decompensate, consumed by terror and the desperate urge to fix it. "I'm a psychologist now. I'm here to help you. Can we talk for a minute?"

No answer. Another rip of lightning broke an unexpected brilliance across the sky, and in that second, as Richie turned, Kate could make out the form of something—small and limp and huddled in his arms.

"Richie, no!" Her scream spiked across the water, and this time Richie froze and turned to look at her. She wondered how many years it had been since he'd heard his real name; she wondered whether he recognized it, whether he even identified with it anymore. Maybe he was too far gone, lost in a lifetime of delusions, of years that could be sloughed away, identities that could be worn and discarded like clothing.

"Stop, Ethan," Kate said, quickly reverting to Richie's assumed name. Kate found herself reaching out a hand—stretching uselessly, as if she could tether Henley to her through the air. Henley wasn't moving. Kate could see her little legs, sloped over Richie's arms. Her sneakers. White. Small. "Let her go. It's over."

Minute by minute, the light was dwindling, bleeding out on the rain. Richie's face was nothing but a blur, a softening shadow; Kate had the impression that soon, he would simply dissolve away, melt into the water, and take form somewhere else.

"Sorry," he said. She thought that was what he said, anyway.

Then, almost without moving, he rolled Henley's body out of his arms and let it drop.

THIRTY

Kate didn't think. She stripped off her coat and dove into the October lake. The cold was so great it punched away her breath and paralyzed her thinking. Her sweater seemed to drag her backward, like an anchor. She fought to the surface, cloth slurping at her arms and legs, and stroked hard for Henley. Already, she was gone—descending somewhere in the black water.

"Henley!" Kate screamed. "Henley!" She surfaced every few strokes to shout. Suddenly she couldn't be sure she'd even swum in the right direction.

"Henley!"

Her clothes clung to her skin. She should have taken off her shoes. Her arms ached, and her heartbeat felt raw in her throat. The cold iced her breathing, made every gasp hurt. How long could she stay in frigid water before she, too, succumbed? Still, she kept paddling, certain that she had seen Henley vanish somewhere close. But in the water, distances spread in waves, turned fluid and tricky. Richie was long gone. Only a bare squeeze of light remained, eking out of the clouds.

"Henley, where are you?" Her voice fizzled out into the answering rain. "Henley!"

Finally, she heard something—a splash, a roil of something moving in the water. She turned, and briefly saw a hand, surfacing to claw the air in desperation. Then it was gone. Of course. Emily had said that Henley hadn't yet learned to swim.

"Henley, hold on!" She propelled herself forward, her clothes suctioning her arms and legs, making every stroke burn. She kept her eyes on the little tumult of water where Henley—awake, alive, still alive—was fighting to reach the surface, occasionally breaking through with a hand or heel.

Kate was three feet away when the thrashing stopped, and the water went still, trembling beneath the pummel of rain. Two more strokes, and miraculously, Kate had her arms around Henley.

"I've got you, I've got you, I'm here."

Henley was limp in Kate's arms, slick and freezing. Kate rolled onto her back, hooking Henley beneath the arms, as she'd been taught to do years ago when she'd lifeguarded at the local YMCA. Kate was shaking, exhausted—the rowboat, barely visible, seemed hopelessly far away.

With a sinking feeling, it occurred to her: She would never make it.

Still, she started swimming—not toward the rowboat, but toward Fair Isle, scalloped against the sky. Close. Every kick was an agony. Her shoulders burned. Her lungs felt like they would explode. Henley was still, motionless against her chest, her head lolling against the crook of Kate's arm.

"Hang on," Kate gasped—to herself, to Henley. Finally, her shoes scraped rock, and then the silt of the lake's bottom. The island arced its trees overhead, close enough to drive off some of the rain, and Kate staggered to her feet, dragging Henley now up the bank, and onto solid ground. Kate was shivering uncontrollably now, aware that soon she would begin to lose her head to hypothermia.

Where were the police? Why hadn't anybody come? She'd left her phone in her jacket on the boat. Idiot. She couldn't even call for help.

Henley looked hopelessly small, lying on her back, in the middle of an entanglement of muddy weeds. Her chest and rib cage seemed too fragile to take Kate's fists as she began CPR. She counted out compressions, tipped Henley's head backward, breathed into her small, wet mouth.

"Come on." Kate had started to cry without realizing it. As a child, she had felt a presence on Fair Isle—something dark and watchful.

Suspicious. But now, she felt hopelessly alone, stranded on the edge of the world with nothing but the indifferent rush of rain. "Come on, Henley. Come back to me."

And then a shudder rocked Henley's whole body, a tremor that rolled her over while she vomited lake water. Kate leaned back on her heels, her desperation suddenly breaking into a wave of relief. Then Henley was clinging to her, clawing at Kate's neck, sobbing into her shoulder.

"He said that he was friends with Becca. He said he would take me to the graveyard, that he would show me the place where I died." Henley was babbling, as if the words, too, were coming out like a vomit.

"It's okay. It's okay, Henley." Kate's mind was already racing, turning up solutions, ways they could stay warm until someone thought to look for them. They would have to go to the ruins. Kate would have to swim for the boat once the storm passed.

"He gave me a soda to drink," Henley said, and Kate felt a black hatred rise into her chest, grip her throat. Richie must have drugged her—or poisoned her. Thank God the water was so cold. It must have shocked her awake, at least for a minute. And the vomiting would help. Regardless, Henley might still be in danger.

"We need to move," Kate said. "We need to get dry. Can you walk?"

"I want to go home," Henley wailed. "I want my mommy."

"We're going to get you home," Kate said, taking Henley's shoulders. "But first, we have to get warm. Can you stay strong for a little bit longer? Can you be brave?"

Henley's expression was barely visible in the dark. But her breath shuddered into silence, and she nodded. Kate felt a surge of love for her that reached all the way back to Becca, the girl she had failed to save.

She needed to keep Henley safe. She needed to get help.

Somehow, this was penance. She understood now—this was what Becca had wanted all along.

She took Henley's hand, pulling her along the slippery bank, dodging thick gnarls of wet and bald tree branches. She didn't want to risk heading deeper into the island; they might spend hours fumbling in the dark, blind and turning circles, and by then they would both have hypothermia. Thankfully, the old camp was now fitted with floodlights—likely to deter trespassers—and the brightness reflecting off the lake edged the perimeter, making it just possible to see. Still, it was slow going. The banks tumbled into the lake in heaps of rock or simply vanished abruptly, exposing giant fans of tree roots to the water. Kate couldn't see the ruins, could only estimate their progress by the view across the lake as they drew parallel to the camp. She strained for the sound of sirens, for the promise of help arriving. But all she could hear was the steady flush of rain in the woods.

By then, Kate wasn't even cold anymore. She felt a buoyant warmth, almost an exuberance.

Not good. They needed to get out of their clothes.

They had reached the south side of the island. The ruins must be on their left. Bishop had mentioned they were fenced off to keep out intruders. But if they could find their way to shelter, to an overhang—even to the old mausoleum—they could at least dry off. Kate wondered whether they might even find the detritus of old gatherings still scattered among the ruins. Maybe a sweatshirt, or an old blanket.

Henley had stopped crying. She'd stopped shaking, too. She walked in almost terrifying silence—robotically following Kate as she carved left into the forest, groping through the trees. At least with the leaves down, it was easier to spot the old trails, although the farther they got from the lake, the denser the darkness. Quickly, Kate realized that it was hopeless. The ruins could have been five feet away or five miles. She would never find them.

Then, through the slurry of rain in her eyes, she thought she saw a light—an earthbound star, winking at her through the trees. For a second she thought, wildly, of the Gray Lady—she imagined they were being summoned, lured deeper into the forest.

She reminded herself that the Gray Lady wasn't real. That they were all alone on the island.

Why had no one come?

"This way, Henley. Almost there now." She spoke the words without meaning them. Her thinking had turned sludgy, dull with cold. Approaching the light, she found the tattered remains of a campsite. A battery-powered lantern cast an eerie light on an old tent and a plastic tarp slickened with rain. Kate's heart leaped at the sight of the sagging chain-link fence behind it, studded with "No Trespassing" signs. She seized hold of the lantern, swinging the light upward, beyond the fence, where several old headstones were tipping into view. They'd reached the old graveyard. The stone angel, and the mausoleum, must be just beyond the trees.

For the first time in half an hour, Henley made a whimpering sound. Kate saw that she had gone rigid with terror.

As if she knew the place.

As if she really did remember.

"Please," Henley said in a whimper. "I want my mommy. I want to go home."

Before Kate could respond, she heard a sharp crack, the rustle of a footstep behind them.

Turning, she came face-to-face with Ethan. In the glow of the lantern, his skin was pasty white and unnaturally smooth, as if he'd barely moved his face in years. Gone was the easy smile she remembered from her counselor. Gone, too, was the hemp necklace, the baseball cap, the wing of hair fanning out from underneath it.

"You shouldn't have come back here," he said. Only his voice was the same; Kate was shocked by its sudden familiarity. So he *did* remember her. He hadn't entirely escaped the centrifugal pull of his old identities.

"I came for Henley," Kate said.

"I didn't mean you. I meant her. Your friend. Becca." Ethan's eyes were fixed on Henley, sparking back twin points of light, as if consumed by inner fire. Kate saw the shape of a gun in Richie's hand.

"She isn't Becca," Kate said. "And your name isn't Ethan, is it? It's Richie Novak."

"My name is Ethan," he practically snarled. He took a step closer with the gun. Kate would have to tread carefully. Ethan was committed to his new identity. He would do anything to protect it.

And yet—she knew that he remembered her. Maybe, just maybe, he remembered that they had once been friends.

"I knew you as Cameron Dunbar. Remember? You taught me how to play guitar. I had such a big crush on you." The admission made Kate nauseous now. But she had to find a way to bring Ethan—*Richie*—out of delusion. Carefully, though—very carefully. "You knew Becca from even earlier, didn't you? You used to babysit Becca, when you lived in Portland. When you were Richie Novak." She held her breath.

For a moment, Ethan—*Richie*—said nothing. He palmed rain from his eyes. He appeared to be struggling, wavering between memories and identities. In the silence, Kate heard something—the sharp cant of sirens, pitching their wail across the distance. How far were they? Half a mile? More? How long would it take for them to reach the island?

"She promised to keep it a secret. She said if I just gave her money, she wouldn't tell anybody." He jabbed the gun a little closer. "You lied," he said, this time to Henley again. "You were always a liar."

"I didn't lie," Henley said in a broken sob. "I didn't do anything."

"She's not Becca." Kate's voice almost broke into a shout. She took a deep breath. Richie was sick. He'd lived most of his life in one pretense or another. "Becca's dead. You put sodium nitrate in her bottle of whisky. Remember?"

"Then how come she knows? How come she remembers?"

"I don't remember anything." Henley was growing hysterical now. "I made it up. Tell him. Tell him I made everything up."

"You're lying." Richie lunged toward them, and Henley screamed, ducking behind Kate as she stepped between them, her chest now level with the gun.

The sirens were getting louder. The police must have been approaching the turnoff. Still, they would have to find a way to reach Fair Isle. And how would they know where to look? In the darkness, they might miss the rowboat entirely. And it would take them half an hour at least to sweep the cabins. Richie had plenty of time to kill them both, get back to the state park, and disappear. Kate imagined him sloughing off this ugly section of his life, transforming as he dove into a brand-new personality, with a new name, a new backstory, new fabricated memories of a life that had never been his. Resurrected.

She had to keep him calm. She had to keep him grounded here, in the moment, in reality.

"It's cold, Richie," she said. "Your hands are shaking."

"Don't call me that," he spat. Kate had made an error. "I told you, my name is Ethan Moore. I live in Austerlitz." He spoke the words mechanically, as if in recitation of an old prayer. Kate wondered briefly whether there was a missing Ethan Moore somewhere, decomposing in a gravel pit or a forest. But changing identities was easier now than it had been when Richie had killed Cameron Dunbar for his name. She hoped that—in this way, at least—Richie had evolved.

"Okay, Ethan. I'm sorry. Let's talk about it, okay? Let's talk about it *together*." Kate used her best clinical voice: soothing, supportive. "Do you hear those sirens in the distance? The police will be here any minute. You still have time to let us go. You still have time to fix this. I know you don't really want to hurt us."

"Shut up." Richie's voice cracked. He was losing control now—breaking apart where his fantasy and reality collided. That was bad. That was dangerous. But at least his attention was off Henley. "Shut up. I need to think."

"Henley and I are very cold," Kate said. "We were both in the water. We need to get somewhere dry."

"I said *shut up*." Suddenly, he'd closed the gap between them, and Kate felt the hard bite of the gun underneath her chin as he spun her around, pinning her back to his chest. She dropped the lantern, which rolled to Henley's feet, illuminating her face in pools and recesses. She wanted to scream for Henley to run, but she couldn't. The gun was strangling her vocal cords, paralyzing the words in her throat.

Henley looked as if she'd gone into a trance. Her eyes were fuzzy, fixed somewhere on the distance behind them.

Then she said, in a strange voice, "Hello."

"What's she doing?" Richie's breath was sour on Kate's cheek. Musty smelling. *Old.* "Who's she talking to?"

Another rip of lightning tore across the sky, rolling a belch of thunder with it. Henley still had her eyes fixed in the distance. In the angled light of the lantern, she looked strange, even ghostly. Her lips dark blue from cold. Her eyes deep hollows. Strangely enough, she looked as if she was smiling.

"You don't see her?" Henley said, still in that same serene voice. As if whatever she was looking at had suddenly reassured her.

"See who?" Richie shouted. He aimed the gun briefly at Henley, then drove it back into Kate's throat. "See *who*?"

"The lady," Henley said. "She's pointing at you."

Richie was shaking—in rage or anger, Kate couldn't tell. With a strangled cry, he spun around, shoving Kate away from him and swinging his gun wildly to the dark.

"Leave me alone!" he screamed. "Do you hear me? Stay where you are."

He took two steps toward the ragged edge of darkness, where their small circle of light was absorbed.

"I said leave me—"

Crack. It happened quickly. He slipped, or fell, or was pushed—Kate couldn't remember afterward if she'd tried to tackle him or just thought about it. He went down at the same time the gun in his hand went off, and Henley screamed—a high, piercing wail that seemed to carry on forever, that seemed to stretch out endlessly in every direction—as Richie lay suddenly still, one eye turned to the sky, jawbone exposed in the torn-up blast of his cheek, a black slick of blood pooling out onto the leaves from the hole where his face was missing.

THIRTY-ONE

Kate was mortified to find Steve ambling around the hospital lobby, trailing a gigantic balloon, by the time she was cleared to leave. Bishop had insisted that Kate be admitted alongside Henley, to receive emergency treatment for hypothermia and monitor for symptoms of shock. Kate was mostly annoyed—insistent that she was just fine, and worried about Henley. Finally, Bishop had threatened to book her for trespassing on private property unless she consented to an overnight stay. She'd woken in the morning to find him back at her bedside, with an offering of cider doughnuts and hot coffee—no doubt to brace her for the interrogative process that would follow.

How did she know where Richie would bring Henley? Why hadn't she alerted anyone at the station where she was going? How did Richie end up with half his face blown off? Who had been holding the gun?

Kate answered as best she could, nimbly dodging the elements that Bishop would have difficulty swallowing, like the moment when Henley, seemingly in the grips of some hallucination, began speaking to a phantom woman in the woods.

Imagined or not, Kate was certain: The Gray Lady had saved their lives.

In the lobby, the October sun streamed through the hospital windows, striping the linoleum with wide, fat grins. Steve swallowed her in a bear hug, and for a moment, smelling him, Kate ached to return to a lost past, a past that had never existed: a time that ended in a different future, without the drinking and the distance, without the space between them that had widened into a gulf.

But that was impossible. The past, she thought, never exactly died. But when it returned, it was always in a new form. Always wearing an unexpected face.

"Who's watching the dogs?" was the first thing Kate asked.

"George. It was the only way I could stop them from buying a plane ticket up here," he said. "I thought the whole lab might threaten to come with me."

Kate fought the urge to reach out and neaten his hair, which was sticking up at all angles, like it, too, had had a sleepless night. "How did you know I was here?"

Steve quirked a smile. "I'm still your emergency contact," he said. When Kate blushed, he added, "Don't worry. You're still mine."

Kate jerked her chin toward the balloon, bobbling with oblivious cheer at the end of its string. "You know I hate balloons."

"It's not for you. It's for *Henley*."

Immediately, Kate felt a spike of alarm. "Is she okay? Have you seen her? Where's Emily?"

"She's fine," Steve said, and Kate exhaled. "I've been talking to Emily all morning. She's up with Henley now. She said to come up whenever you were ready." He handed her the balloon. "Here. You can even say it's from you."

Kate couldn't help but smile. Steve had never met a gift shop he didn't love. It had once driven her crazy, the way he'd putter around, marveling at obscenely priced souvenirs and trinkets, collecting T-shirts and tacky figurines from every trip they took, every hotel they visited, every roadside museum they found. But Steve had spent much of his life studying the incredible, the impossible to believe, the extra normal. Now she knew—she understood, deeply—that in some way, Steve saw the extraordinary everywhere.

For the first time ever, she found herself admiring his way of looking at the world.

"You didn't have to come," she said.

"Yes," he said simply. "I did."

Kate gave him a last squeeze and went to find the girl who'd saved her life.

~

Henley's room was easy to find. The nurses, obviously fussing over her, were sticking close to the open door. Inside, Kate found Henley sitting upright, focused intently on coloring while Emily stroked her hair.

Emily stood up when she saw Kate and crossed the room in three strides. Then she had drawn Kate into a hug so tight that Kate felt it in her ribs.

"Thank you," was all she said. When she pulled away, Kate saw that her eyes were bright with tears. Kate turned away, pretending not to notice.

"Hi, Henley." Kate went a little closer to the bed. "How are you feeling?"

"Good," Henley said simply—her voice clear, unencumbered, free from any knowledge of the inherent contradiction of this statement. She looked up, and her eyes traveled immediately up the string in Kate's hand to the balloon knocking its head on the ceiling. Her eyes widened. "Is that my balloon?"

"It is your balloon," Kate said, laughing as Henley immediately set aside her drawing materials and tried to move onto her hands and knees to grab it.

"Careful, Henley," Emily said as a variety of monitors and drips made noises of protest. "They had to flush her system out," she explained. "She tested positive for codeine. They're still running her blood for other toxins. But so far, she's not showing symptoms, thank God."

"Can I wear the balloon?" Henley asked, extending out a wrist encircled by a hospital bracelet.

"Of course," Kate said. Stepping next to the bed, she noticed for the first time what Henley had been drawing: a moonfaced woman with long blond hair and a sloppy smile, surrounded by colorful flowers, holding hands with a little girl.

She knotted the balloon carefully around Henley's wrist and then helped settle her back against the pillows, returning Henley's drawing pad to her lap. Casually, she said, "That's a pretty lady. Who is it?"

Henley reached for a light-blue crayon and began meticulously coloring in the woman's dress. "That's the lady who helped last night. The nice one. She said not to be scared of the bad man."

"She said that?" Kate asked, and Henley shrugged, as though saying, *You were there.* "And what about her?" Kate indicated the child standing next to the blond woman in the picture. "Is that you?"

"It's not me," Henley said reproachfully. "It's *her.*"

"Who?"

"The girl in the lake. The one you were looking for. Becca."

The one you were looking for. Kate's heart squeezed in her chest. It was true. All these years that Kate had been running from the past, from what had happened to Becca, what she had really needed was to turn around. To face it. She sat down carefully on the foot of Henley's hospital bed.

"Henley, last night you said you'd made everything up." She heard a whistling sound as, behind her, Emily sucked in a quick breath. "You told the bad man you'd only been pretending to be Becca."

Henley's crayon faltered on the page. She looked up at Kate with her clear, bright eyes—so like Becca's—filled with sudden uncertainty. "I—I don't remember."

"You don't remember telling him that?"

"I don't remember anything," Henley said, this time insistently. Kate let it go. In all likelihood, she would never know for certain the truth about Henley and what she had claimed to remember.

She gave Henley a hug. She promised to come and visit her again.

When Henley looked up at her, her face was like a moon, and her eyes two lakes inside of it. "So we can still be friends?" she asked shyly.

Kate smiled. "We'll always be friends," she said.

"Do you *pinkie* swear?" Henley said.

Kate laughed, hooking her pinkie into Henley's. At the same time, she had the sense of the scene doubling, occurring both in the present and at some time in the distant past, some time she could barely remember . . . "I pinkie swear."

Henley gave her finger a squeeze. She said, in a different voice, "You shouldn't laugh, you know. Forever is a long time."

Kate nearly lost her breath. She remembered, then, that day on the lawn with Becca—the slow drift of clouds above them, the wet entanglement of their hair, the way Becca had squeezed her pinkie until it hurt. *Forever is a long time.*

She remembered, too, what Dr. Rushkin had told her. Some mysteries were too great, too big, to be untangled.

Besides, she thought, what did the truth matter? Henley had indeed been the key to unlocking the truth about what had happened to her friend all those years ago.

Poor Becca. She had only been trying, desperately, to take power back over a world she couldn't control.

Kate hoped that wherever she was—*if* she was anywhere—Becca had learned, at long last, to let go.

EPILOGUE

In Virginia, October was just beginning to ripen into color. Returning there, Kate felt as if the short time she'd been in Massachusetts had blown open a door in her mind, allowing her to appreciate everything she saw as if for the first time: the university, all russet brick and emerald quads, burnished by the afternoon sun; the happy packs of students, bounding like puppies between coffee shops and classrooms; her sweet little town house, on a dozy, quiet street not ten minutes from her office.

She said goodbye to Steve, dropped off her bags, and strolled over to the lab to meet George Turner and retrieve her dogs. The air was crisp, just edged with a cool wind, but warm enough that Kate quickly shed her jacket. On the corner of Washington Avenue, the Episcopal Church had its doors open, floating out the sound of choir rehearsal. Kate wondered if the church ever hosted A.A. meetings. She would look it up. Maybe she would go.

Kate's research lab was housed in a converted outer wing of the Health and Human Sciences Center. Kate loved the lab, with its scrubbed wood and glass and long stripes of sunlight. But that day it struck her as especially beautiful.

She wasn't surprised to find five of her most devoted graduate students assembled there to meet her on a Saturday. They swarmed her with rapid-fire questions as her dogs, confined to a first-floor conference room, scratched and whined piteously at the doors.

"What happened? Steve said you were in the hospital. Are you okay?" That was George, their curly hair in disarray, wearing a voluminous sweater covered in dog hair.

"Dr. Rushkin left, like, seven messages. He wants you to call him immediately. He said he's been trying your cell." That was Henry Janczyk, a punctilious fourth-year with the hands of a pianist.

"Someone from the Associated Press called. She said something about a kidnapping?" Marcie Hayes, a postgrad with a cherubic face and an intuitive understanding of other people.

"That lawyer called again. The one from Richmond. He begged me for your cell." Lucas Frommer, another postdoc, who'd recently collaborated with the biology department to produce a paper on the interactivity of oxytocin receptors and dissociative states.

Kate arched an eyebrow. "Don't tell me you all came in on a Saturday just to gossip," she said. "Don't you have work to do?" She couldn't help but smile at their crestfallen faces. "Don't worry," she conceded. "I'll tell you everything soon."

They brightened again, and Kate felt a warm pull of affection for all of them—these bright, devoted students, who believed they could peel back every mystery of the human mind, expose its every shadow to the light, map its every corner. Of course they believed it; that was what Kate had been telling them for years.

And Kate *still* believed it, to a large extent. The human brain *was* organized; the mind *was* rational, however disorganized it appeared, if you only understood the conditions under which it was operating.

But perhaps it was true that there was something larger and deeper than both at work in the universe.

While her students scattered, either back to their work or to feigning it, Kate rescued her dogs from the conference room and turned them out into the small enclosed courtyard, bounded on four sides by university offices. She knew she should open her email and try powering on her cell phone again—retrieved by the police from the abandoned rowboat in the early hours of Saturday morning, when Kate was still asleep in her hospital bed, and now hopelessly, perhaps fatally, waterlogged—but for the moment Kate was content just to sit there. The clouds scudded across an electric-blue sky. Shadows chased one another across the lawn, turning the grass from light to dark and back again. Moving, always moving.

Kate sat perfectly still.

From inside, she heard the muffled shrill of her office phone. Inwardly, she groaned. It better not be a reporter.

"Can one of you get that?" she shouted. She stood up to toss a stick to Moshi, who was on his feet, wagging his tail, looking at her piteously. A second later, the ringing stopped.

Then Marcie emerged, poking her head out of the sliding glass doors. "It's the lawyer. The one who's been calling all week."

"Tell him I'm in Costa Rica," Kate said.

Marcie didn't blink. "He says Dr. Agerwal gave him your number."

Kate swallowed a sigh. Priya Agerwal, a celebrated forensic psychologist, had been her favorite professor in graduate school, and they'd stayed close over the years. She stood up and returned inside, leaving Moshi happily stripping his stick of bark and Bo lolling around on his back in the sun.

"Dr. Willis? This is Benjamin Connolly." Connolly didn't waste any time. "I'm a defense attorney in Allegany County. I'm sorry I've been badgering you, but I'm working a special case—a very special case—and I'd love to get your opinion on it."

Kate was instantly skeptical. She'd fielded phone calls like this before, typically from lawyers representing one side or another in a vicious custody battle, looking to assign blame for a child's diagnosis on their former partner. Still, she had no idea why a defense attorney would be involved. Typically, that kind of case went through the family courts.

"I'm sorry," Kate said. "I'm pretty underwater this semester—"

Connolly barged on as if she hadn't spoken. "Last month, a teenage Jane Doe was discovered bludgeoned to death inside a vacant Pennsylvania property. My client was arrested. He's twelve years old."

Kate's blood instantly went cold. Child murderers were exceptionally rare, and usually came from only the most abusive homes.

"His parents, David and Lydia Robinson, brought me on to serve as his defense. I've known them for years. They're good people. They're both in shock." Kate could almost hear Connolly shaking his head. "Frankly, I'm out of my depth here. Their son needs a full evaluation."

"Do you think he's innocent?" Kate asked.

Connolly paused. "Not exactly," Connolly said. "All the evidence points to him. And he hasn't denied it." But Kate heard something in his voice, some unease skirting around the edge of the conversation.

"You think he had some kind of psychotic episode?" she said. Her mind was already racing, spinning toward possible explanations.

"Maybe. He says he doesn't remember any of it." Now Connolly sounded almost apologetic. "The thing is . . ." He trailed off, and once again Kate could feel that unspoken thing, pulling at Connolly's attention.

"What?" Kate said. "What is it?"

Connolly cleared his throat. "The thing is, he says he was asleep," Connolly said. "He says that when it happened—when he murdered the girl—it was because he was having a *nightmare*."

ABOUT THE AUTHOR

Photo © 2024 Elke Rosthal Photography

Lauren Oliver is a screenwriter, media entrepreneur, and author of multiple *New York Times* bestsellers, including *Delirium*, *Pandemonium*, and *Requiem* in the Delirium trilogy; *Before I Fall*, which was adapted into a feature film; *Panic*, which was adapted into an Amazon Prime series for which Lauren wrote every episode and served as executive producer; and the Replica duology. Lauren founded the IP company StoryGiants, helping to package and edit nearly one hundred other novels. She also cofounded Incantor AI, devoted to ethical treatment of IP in artificial intelligence technologies for media and entertainment. Raised in Westchester, New York, Lauren attended the University of Chicago and got her MFA from NYU. She now divides her time between Maryland and Los Angeles. For more information, visit www.laurenoliverbooks.com.